Thursday's Child

A NOVEL

Richard James Haigh

PEANUT BUTTER PUBLISHING
Seattle, Washington
Portland, Oregon
Denver, Colorado
Vancouver, B.C.

Canadian Cataloguing in Publication Data
Haigh, Richard James
Thursday's Child : A Novel

ISBN 0-89716-661-2
I. Title.
PS8565.A382T58 1996 C813'.54 C96-910654-8
PR9199.3.H295T58 1996

Editor: Dr. Eugene Smith
Production: Fiona Raven
Cover Design: David Marty

First printing October 1996

PEANUT BUTTER PUBLISHING
Suite 230 - 1333 Johnston Street • Pier 32, Granville Island
• Vancouver, B.C. V6H 3R9 • 604-688-0320 •
226 2nd Avenue West • Seattle, WA 98119 • 206-281-5965
e mail: pnutpub@aol.com
Internet: http://www.pbpublishing.com

Printed in Canada

For Phyl

ONE

Moving Out

It was a late Thursday afternoon in early June. And as usual on Thursdays at this time of day, the pay station had quickly filled with forty to fifty men, a few young, more older. Patiently they stood or leaned, chatting quietly, waiting for the wicket to open and grant them their pittance for another week's labour. Despite the warm weather, many still wore flat caps, their badge of honour in a working class town. Most had walked to the pay station, some from four miles away, in order to save the tuppeny bus fare. Part of the dreary building was used to store barricade materials. They were piled in an untidy jumble, up into the dark recesses of the wooden roof. Outside, a couple of motorbikes stood propped up against the pay station door. One or two labourers owned motorized bicycles, which were nothing more than tiny engines built into the rear wheel. They spluttered along at a respectable thirty miles an hour and got well over a hundred miles to the gallon. Behind the building, in a separate compound, stood two large gasometers. A familiar sight in Britain's industrial regions, these ugly monstrosities stored the nation's coal-gas supply. Both, judging from their extended height, were nearly full.

The men lining up for their pay envelopes were civic workers, largely unskilled, who toiled in the muck and grime of the town's undertakings.

"Name?" demanded a sullen female from behind the narrow wicket.

"Michaels. Six-two-eight-five," replied the clean cut young man who wasn't wearing a cap. Stooping to see who was handing out the pay envelopes that day, he already knew it couldn't be the pretty young girl with the dark blonde hair whom he'd been eyeing for the past couple of months. He would have recognized her voice. The workers were paid in cash. The envelope, heavy with coins, jangled as the young man stuffed it into his back pocket.

"So tha really thinks tha'd like ter do this fer the rest o' thi' days, eh?" asked an older man standing behind him. He was tall and gaunt, thin-lipped with a face tanned from years of working outside, and lined from an equal number trying to raise a family on his sadly inadequate income. In contrast to his heavy boots and baggy trousers, the shirt he wore was clean, and finished off with a tartan tie, tightly knotted. Only his eyes, dark brown and with a hint of twinkle in them, compromised the outward austerity.

The young man turned to his older counterpart, shrugged, smiled, and moved aside. He could have ridden down on his bicycle but had decided instead to walk with his friend from the municipal park where they both worked and take advantage of the fine weather.

Moving towards the wicket, the older man called out his name. "Haywood. One-six-three-two." The clerk pushed out a pay packet only slightly fatter than the young man's.

"Time's a temptress, Harry," the older man continued in his broad Yorkshire dialect as they left the public-works yard. "She allus lets on there's more. But tha knows, time, an' what tha can do wi' it, are two different things." He added ruefully, "Thee be ruled by me, lad. Ah know. Believe me, ah know."

This was northern England in 1961. The two men, like all the others gathered in the pay station that day, worked for the County Borough of Barnsley, a Yorkshire coal mining town twelve miles north of Sheffield. And both, in their own unique fashion, represented the living product of a half-century dominated by two world wars. Bert bore the scars of the first; Harry was a victim of the second. Bert was only marginally skilled, a gardener for practically all of his working life and more recently a part-time chauffeur for the man who owned the cottage he rented. Like many of his contemporaries, he was glad to have a job in an economy starting to demand more brains than brawn. The same could be said for Harry, except that his limited horizons had as much to do with a lack of opportunity as a lack of brains.

In 1961, sea changes were beginning to sweep the country, but only a few visionaries had the wisdom to notice that the Industrial Revolution was marching off to other shores. Obsolete manufacturing plants continued to produce inferior products heavily subsidized by the government and hamstrung by truculent unions. Taxation weighed ever more oppressively upon all but a small, privileged elite. Although unemployment was well below two percent nationally, many British males could look forward to pay packets of less than sixteen pounds a week. The migratory hemorrhaging of the 1950's, when thousands responded to Britain's post-war impotence by fleeing the country for America and 'the colonies', had shrunk to politically acceptable proportions.

In Germany the Berlin Wall was up. Throughout the West, people had begun learning to live with something called the Cold War. Americans were still trying to convince themselves that hiding under school desks and kitchen tables represented effective protection against nuclear fallout. Independently minded, the British preferred to keep their Anderson shelters. After all, what was good enough for Winston Churchill was good enough for everyone else. Communism had become public enemy Number One. But while Britain might have found itself hard-pressed to smell a communist under every bed, spy scandals were erupting onto the national scene with embarrassing frequency. In March of 1961, Gordon Lonsdale and company were convicted of spying on the underwater-detection establishment for the Evil Empire. To many weary Britons, it seemed that war and pestilence were now as unavoidable as death and taxes.

But to Robin Harold Michaels, along with most young men of his age, these evolutionary tremors had little relevance beyond their impact upon his limited job chances and the pay packet he took home. Other events were more germane. From across the Atlantic, Elvis Presley was turning popular music upside down, and to the delight of the younger generation, offending most of those old enough to remember Queen Victoria. Those of a gentler persuasion were humming along to the innovative arrangements of America's new orchestra leaders.

At home the farthing disappeared in 1961, and the Sunday Telegraph published its first issue on the fifth of February. Architecturally, all things Victorian were being covered by hardboard. Although hopelessly outgunned by American designs, British Ford and Vauxhall were creating a mini sensation with some surprisingly enlightened new car designs. Television, after starting life as a government monopoly, was now being opened up by one or two commercial companies. Like old chewing gum, American influence had begun to lose its war-time flavor, but it still set the pace in a country growing tired of a social caste system masquerading as tradition.

Bert Haywood's chance remark at the pay station had struck a chord with his young friend. And so, three months later on a golden September morning, armed with little more than the blissful ignorance of youth, Robin Harold Michaels found himself marching into the Derbyshire County Offices for a job interview. Before that, for the first time in his life, Harry had spent a couple of soul-searching weeks pondering his future. It was uncharacteristic, sending his mother into a fit of concern for his health. He was only twenty-two, but savvy enough to conclude during the course of that fateful period of navel-gazing that if he didn't act, and soon, he would indeed spend the rest of his days in boots and baggy trousers. The parks department where he worked was a comfortable niche for a young man with no responsibilities. He'd spent two years there doing his practicum before attending the Yorkshire Farm Institute. After graduating with a certificate in horticulture, he returned, settling into a nascent career as a junior gardener. But he didn't need a crystal ball to see that the carefree years of youth could quickly turn into a Sisyphean hell. Time was indeed a temptress. Twenty-two, he figured, would quickly become thirty. And thirty soon coasted into forty. And so on. Despite his youthfulness, Harry was a homebody. He wanted a place of his own, not some cold-water flat, and with enough money left over to enjoy life.

On the way home from work, he began picking up *The Times*. Cautiousness came as a byword to Harry's family; only government jobs enjoyed stability and prestige. And while he didn't wholeheartedly buy into that credo, he had inherited just enough of his father's genes to adopt it as a yardstick in the search for employment. The staid and respectable *Times* published government postings nationally. In a country top-heavy with government, there seemed to be plenty of them, even though most beckoned beyond his grasp. A better job, he had decided, was only part of the quest. Just as much, he wanted to live somewhere else. Preferably far away from the grime of the Yorkshire coal fields and the suffocating complacency of his family.

An advertisement in the fifth newspaper he picked up looked promising. It was a sort of omnibus advertisement and it took up nearly a quarter of a page. The Derbyshire County Architect's Department required several draughtsmen for an assortment of duties among various echelons in that large bureaucracy. Harry liked Derbyshire. Several times in the past he had gone there with his mother on day trips in the car. It was a surprisingly rural county bordering

Yorkshire's southern boundary. Not that far away, but 'away' nonetheless. Despite a dubious distinction of being part of the locus of Britain's Industrial Revolution, much of the county had escaped the blight. To the west ranged the sparsely inhabited Peak District, over five-hundred square miles of limestone crags and grassy slopes. The northern peaks, stretching north of an invisible line between Buxton and Chesterfield, comprised the largest portion of the country's first national park. South of that line, slightly more populated and less hostile but still within the park boundaries, lay the low peaks, To the east of the county stretched a long coal seam corridor of mixed industry extending from the Sheffield suburbs down to the Staffordshire potteries, and interspersed throughout with pretty market towns built from limestone or grit. Derbyshire was home to Chatsworth House and a dozen other country estates, and a host of mineral spas that had lured wealthy Victorians by their thousands a century before.

One particular position, in the Landscape and Playing Fields Section, caught his eye. It required, for the most part, training in ornamental horticulture, with some experience in draughting and surveying. Harry's accomplishments in surveying had, to date, been limited to the opposite sex, and even that with a conspicuous lack of aptitude or success. The pay, starting at seven-hundred and eighty pounds a year, seemed positively bourgeois by comparison with what he had earned to date. Still, he told himself, nothing ventured, nothing gained, and the cost was only a postage stamp. So he wrote up a resume, richly embellished with half-truths and outright lies, and tossed it in the post box.

Three weeks later, much to his astonishment, a letter from the County Architect's Department arrived in the mail, requesting his appearance for an interview in ten days' time. The writer instructed him to meet someone by the name of Robert Dickie, head of the Landscape and Playing Fields Section. Harry congratulated himself on another piece of creative literary licence. He couldn't do math, didn't know algebra from trigonometry, but he'd always been able to write, or more specifically, to craft with words. This baffled his mother, whose late accountant-husband routinely blinded his government colleagues with fancy figures while struggling vainly to express himself on paper. She also worried that her son's exaggerated claims on his resumes would one fine day catch up with him and cause them all acute embarrassment. She agonized over the possibility that perjuring one's resume might even be a criminal offence. Young Harry could wind up in jail and the family would be socially ruined. In any case, she argued, how much job experience is a twenty-two-year-old expected to have? He assured her, as he always did, that everybody put a little extra bloom on their talent claims and most employers accepted this fact. Still, the thought crossed his mind that in this particular job the proof of the pudding could be in the eating. What if he actually had to go out and do some surveying? He couldn't book off sick on those occasions indefinitely. He shrugged off the thought with a familiar rationale: it was a problem for another day which, with a bit of luck, might never come.

Harry didn't know it at the time, but he was to become involved with a county council in transition. Three years earlier, they had packed their bags and moved. And not just down the street. The story of Derbyshire's acquisition of new office space had become something of a legend in bureaucratic circles. Prior to this propitious move, all major departments had been located in Derby, scattered through that venerable city in mostly old, overcrowded buildings. Despite years of ad-hoc alterations and additions, the overcrowding and chronically bad telephone service provided by the General Post Office monopoly were dragging the county bureaucracy into an even lower state of efficiency than normal. Politicians and senior government mandarins all agreed, and numerous studies confirmed, that something had to be done to reduce, as academic geographers would say, 'the frictions of distance'. They had to find some way of housing all the civil servants under one roof, or at least considerably fewer roofs than the number at present. A feasible solution eluded everyone until 1958 when, to the surprise of many and the dismay of some, the County purchased a fortress-like building locally known as Smedley's Hydro for the magnificent sum of £128,200. Then they spent almost twice as much to fix it up.

A major bone of contention centered on the fact that this building wasn't located in Derby, but some eighteen miles north in a small town called Matlock. Even by the time Harry had been called for his interview, three years after the purchase, more than half the staff were still being bused every day from their homes in and around Derby. No one, it seemed, wanted to live in Matlock. So at 6.30 every morning, Monday through Friday, a long caravan rumbled up the A-6 to deposit several hundred disgruntled civil servants at their place of work. At five PM the same convoy headed south, clogging Matlock's narrow roads with a column of aging charabancs that stretched for half a mile.

Until the middle of the nineteenth century, Matlock was a sleepy hamlet, cut off from the rest of the shire by a pile of rock called Scarthin Nick. Had it not been for a reinvented fad, Matlock might have stayed a sleepy hamlet for much longer. The Industrial Revolution spurred many technological advances, including medical science. During Queen Victoria's reign, the medical profession rediscovered the healing properties of mineral waters. Spewing from the limestone rock, these natural springs occur in many areas of Derbyshire, particularly in the Peak District. Local people had used them for centuries. The springs all contain high levels of carbonic acid and very little else. No matter. Once they had received the establishment seal of approval, anything was possible. And besides, it might be argued, simply taking a bath could be considered therapeutic for some people. The enterprising Victorians gilded the lily, so to speak, by packaging these bubbling cash cows into elegant resorts called hydropathic establishments. This made all the difference in the world for the style conscious. Suddenly, 'taking the waters' was all the rage among Britain's aristocracy, the nouveau riche, and anyone else who could afford the price. After a road was blasted through Scarthin Nick in 1818, two railway lines appeared on the scene, and commercial spas began to sprout across Matlock. Although Buxton later gained preeminence as a spa town, by the end of the nineteenth century over thirty were in operation in Matlock. However, Matlock Bath, a hamlet to the south of Matlock, preempted Matlock proper as the earliest commercialized locale in the vicinity for taking the waters, and eventually built up an impressive clientele. All this came to an end as the Industrial Revolution spawned a new class with fewer social graces but substantially more discretionary income. The hordes descended upon Matlock Bath, forcing the aristocratic elite to look for new venues. Several blossomed in Matlock, but in terms of sheer size and elegance none matched Smedley's Hydro.

From the start, Smedley's Hydropathic Establishment set out to take up the slack from Matlock Bath's declining fortunes. It did much more, becoming Matlock's definitive statement that it had joined the spa industry. Begun in 1853 by John Smedley, the enterprising son of a Derbyshire hosier, the imposing structure enjoyed immense popularity during its heyday. Smedley built his colossus halfway up Matlock Bank, a steep incline which overlooked the town below. History records that, following hydropathic treatment for his own problems, he decided to develop a programme for the benefit of his own mill workers. This bit of munificence started with the purchase of a small house on the site of an area containing several mineral springs, reportedly one of the richest in the region. Soon afterwards the building bug set in, and new plans were drawn up. The building eventually straddled both sides of Smedley Street, linked by an enclosed footbridge. Smedley proved to be an astute judge of the Victorian psyche. During the ensuing decades several additions were made, including a sumptuous winter garden. By the end of the century Matlock had become one of the most fashionable spa towns in Britain, rubbing shoulders with its arch rival Buxton and other watering holes like Harrogate in Yorkshire.

For a while, the steep haul up Bank Road presented a serious obstacle to clientele accustomed to being carried around. So local entrepreneurs planned a tramway from Crown Square at the foot of Bank Road up to the hydro. The project languished for years because the road was too narrow. However, after a wealthy publisher by the name of George Newnes rode into the fray in 1892, some buildings were cleared from one side and the tramway opened for business on 28 March, 1893. It charged 2d for the ride up, and one penny to come down, the cheaper fare presumably being subsidized by gravity. For over sixty years, thousands rode or struggled on foot up Bank Road to the imposing limestone edifice, prepared to pay almost any price to drink and soak their arthritic limbs in the hot water, and receive counselling on such personal matters as diet and English etiquette. Sadly the proud little tram suffered the same fate as the hydro, finally closing in 1929 because of declining profits. The tramcars were sold and the shelter at the foot of Crown square moved to its final resting place in Hall Leys Garden.

In a curious lapse of savvy, John Smedley later decided to build a mock fortified residence on a barren hill some miles away overlooking Matlock Bath, from which to admire his empire. Rumour has it that water supply problems hobbled the project from the outset. Why he didn't take the trouble to look into this rather important utility beforehand isn't certain. But Smedley died there twelve years later in 1874. For a while the lonely place became a prep school. The new owners may have experienced the same problems because it was once again abandoned in 1929, remaining empty until the onset of the Second World War, when the buildings were temporarily used as a food-storage depot. That was its final mission, gradually crumbling afterwards into a roofless ruin dubbed 'Smedley's Folly' by the locals, and supposedly complete with a platoon of poltergeist, which on occasion would hurl the loosened stones about the place. In Harry's day, Smedley's Folly was no more than a forgotten piece of history, surrounded by windswept moorland. More recently it has become known as Riber Castle, home of an immensely popular fauna reserve. Harry came to know this place well, although not once did the ghosts ever hurl any rocks at him.

The hydro also finally fell upon hard times, hastened by the onset of the Great Depression. Much of Smedley's clientele was financially ruined; the remainder were in no humour to pay outrageous prices to sit in hot water and be underfed. By the outbreak of the Second World War the building had been abandoned, but it enjoyed a brief reprieve when the government turned it into a school for military intelligence. When workmen moved in to upgrade the ancient plumbing they discovered Smedley's best-kept secret. It is difficult to understand how he managed to hide the fact that no hot springs bubbled from the Derbyshire hillside, just a cellar full of boilers, vats, and chemical silos. Legend has it that staff in the know were sworn to silence. By war's end the old building was a sad patchwork of false walls, boarded-up doors and bricked-in windows. Many of its opulent fittings had disappeared, no one knew where, and much of the structure was in disrepair. It finally closed its doors in 1955, remaining silent and empty for nearly three years. A few purists decried the County-Council purchase, claiming that it was nothing short of heresy to turn such a grand monument into an office building. But the fact was that, unless a buyer had been found, it would probably have been demolished.

In some ways it was the best buy the County had ever made, except that the hydro's much-altered floorspace had become a virtual labyrinth, in which unwary visitors could be lost for hours. The quantity surveyors firmly entrenched their reputation as the chosen few by being assigned the ballroom, with its exquisitely sprung dance floor still intact. Surrounded by huge cantilever windows and a glass-domed ceiling, they basked in sunshine amid a garden of palms and aspidistras. A small orchestra would have nicely completed the picture. It was, the surveyors concluded, well worth the jealous scorn of other departments which found themselves crammed into far less lavish quarters. Overall, the county's quest for centralization turned out to be a hollow victory. The huge, rambling structure, with its retrofits and add-ons, defied the planners' attempts to keep departments together. Many wound up with their dismembered sub-components scattered through a maze of narrow corridors, wings and stairs. It was in this curious piece of local history that Harry was about to begin his career.

Upon the appointed day he walked through the building's imposing front entrance, past the half-glazed vestibule doors with their still carefully polished brass handles. It was dark inside and the foyer smelled of linoleum. Brown linoleum, as it turned out. To his right a small, high, three-sided counter stuck out from a wooden wall topped with glass. It reminded him of a church pulpit. Behind the wall female voices chattered amid the clack of switchboard pins being pushed and pulled. He could see a peaked cap bobbing behind the pulpit monstrosity, and, assuming it must be the reception area, walked over. As he approached, the hat, and then the face under it, rose like a jack-in-the-box. A pair of eyes, slightly above the counter top, blinked suspiciously in the poor light. Leaning over, Harry found to his surprise that the man had been standing all the time. The extra height was provided by a shallow wooden box which he clambered on to greet visitors. He was a very short, thin, elderly man, and clearly much less interested in receiving visitors than reading the newspaper which spread before him on a small desk. As he eyed Harry, one hand slowly stirred a gigantic mug of tea.

"I have an appointment with Mr. Dickie of the County Architect's Department," Harry announced in his most business-like voice.

The porter's lined face twitched only slightly. "Wot time?"

Harry looked at his watch. "Just past eleven o'clock. But it's a bit fast."

"Ah mean," replied the face under the cap, "wot time's yer appointment?"

"Oh, eleven o'clock." Harry pulled the letter from his jacket pocket to make sure.

"Dangerously close ter lunch time," said the porter. "Dangerously close ter lunch time fer Mr. Dickie."

Dickie's lunchtime schedule appeared to be something of an in-joke, for a cackle of laughter wafted from behind the high wall. The porter's thin lips parted into a sly smile and, while never taking his eyes off Harry, he cocked his head towards the voices. "Doris, ring up to Radical Bob's, there's a darlin'. We don't want the young lad 'ere to walk another 'arf mile for nowt."

There was a pregnant silence as the woman rattled her cables. Some muffled conversation and a giggle followed. "'E's in," said the voice.

"'E's in? Well, well! Your lucky day. Better get up there afore Mr. Dickie **goes** fer lunch, 'cause when Mr. Dickie **goes** fer lunch, 'oo knows when 'e'll be back!"

Another cackle rose from behind the wall.

Harry found the exchange between the porter and the switchboard crew puzzling. They all seemed to know his prospective boss surprisingly well, considering the man was only a fairly small cog in a complex of much larger bureaucratic cogs. And there was also an air of insolent familiarity in their tone, which suggested that Dickie's personal habits might be a frequent topic of discussion. He was partly correct; as he found later, Dickie was nothing short of a legend.

The porter's right arm rose as though he might be bringing an orchestra to order, gesturing vaguely at the same time into the shadows beyond the switchboard. "Walk up them main stairs to the third floor, then turn left an' then left agin'... an' then right."

A cackle once again wafted from behind the wall.

"...An' then right agin. Go down as far as sum double doors, but yer don't go through 'em..."

"Yer turn right again!" yelled the hidden chorus. Another cackle of laughter.

"Right, yes. Yer turn right again. Silly buggers," continued the porter. "An' then left, down some steps, through a glass door, and there y'are."

"An' there yer are. Lost!" added a woman's voice.

"There's actually a short cut," the porter added. "But ah won't trouble yer wi' it t'day."

Why not? Harry groaned inwardly. It couldn't possibly be any worse than the nonsense he'd just listened to.

"'Cause y'ave ter go ahtside, and it's only a short cut if yer already ahtside, if yer see wot ah' mean." The thin lips let out a short hiss.

Harry didn't see what he meant, but judging from the building's exterior, anything could be possible, including getting lost for several days.

After an unscheduled visit to three of the building's numerous lavatories and a brief chat with a couple of girls in an as-yet unidentified typing pool, he finally blundered through the aforementioned single glass door and into a large office filled with draughting tables. Poring over the one nearest Harry's entrance was a tall young man dressed in a stylish cableknit sweater with the sleeves pushed up almost to his elbows. Three other people were in the room. On the far side an older man sat hunched at a draughting table in front of a row of large windows. He appeared to be asleep for his bowed head twitched slightly each time he let out a breath. Everyone else seemed to be ignoring the fact that he had gone to sleep with a lighted cigarette in his mouth. On the same side of the room was another man, possibly in his mid-forties, leaning over the top of some filing cabinets flanking a door marked 'Fire Exit'. He looked a bit like an emaciated buzzard, draped in a navy-blue blazer that literally hung off his thin frame. With his chin resting on clenched fists and his face a picture of utter fatigue, he gazed gloomily towards the same set of windows. A slightly younger man sitting at one of a pair of draughting tables in the centre of the room gave Harry no more than a cursory glance. At least two tables were empty and, judging from the dust, looked as though they had not been in use for a while.

The young man in the cableknit sweater glanced up at the intruder and scowled slightly. "Methinks you will be another recruit," he said quietly before turning his eyes back to the table.

Harry looked at the speaker more closely. He appeared to be in his early twenties, roughly his own height, with a sallow complexion and eyes that seemed to match his light-brown hair. There was no mistaking the Welsh accent, and Harry's spirits sank a little as he recalled his mother's old saw about a

Yorkshireman and a Welshman never getting along. Still, no good pre-judging somebody.

The Welshman had an unusually flat face, barely relieved by an equally flat nose. When he spoke his thin mouth moved more sideways than vertically, revealing a set of very small, shark-like teeth.

"Is this the Landscape and Playing Field Section?" Harry asked brightly.

"It is indeed," replied the Welshman in a very soft voice. "And are you, as I assume, our newest candidate?"

Harry nodded, then shook his head. "I'm just here for an interview with a Mr. Dickie."

The Welshman smiled faintly. "Our noble chief." He turned toward the sleeping man over by the windows and raised his voice slightly. "Bill! Your tie's on fire!"

The man jerked bolt upright and, to the chuckles of the two other seated men, began flapping wildly about himself with some papers. Then, hearing the laughter, he turned towards Harry and the Welshman and shook his head.

"Has to see Radical Bob," said the Welshman.

Sliding off his high stool, the older man ambled over. "You must be Robin Michaels," he said with a gentle smile. "I recall Bob talking about you the other day. Come with me, I think the Old Man's in."

Harry nearly corrected him on his name, as he frequently found himself doing with strangers. True, his first name was Robin but he'd been ragged unmercifully at boarding school on account of it being bi-gender. So, early in life, he dropped Robin in favour of his middle name, Harold, which abbreviated handily to Harry. Did he look like a Harry? Probably not. But as far as he was concerned Harry sounded a lot better than Robin.

The man's pale blue eyes twinkled. "I should explain out that the boss is referred to as 'Radical' by our younger upstarts because his initials are R.A.D. Naturally, the more seasoned members of our august company show a little more respect."

"My arse," said the Welshman without looking up.

Listening to the dialogue, Harry suddenly realized that both men were Welsh. Both had the same lilting musical voices, but the older man's accent was much more muted.

"I'm Bill Lewis, the senior draughtsman... in more ways than one," he said as he ushered Harry towards the door marked 'Fire Exit'. Jerking a thumb back at his younger colleague he added, "And that there is Terry Jones, in case he didn't introduce himself."

Terry nodded a curt acknowledgment and turned to his draughting table again.

"Takes himself very seriously does our Terry!" Bill whispered, just loudly enough for Terry to hear. Chuckling to himself, he led Harry past the man leaning over the file cabinet, who smiled weakly but said nothing. No introductions were made. Through the door they came to another short corridor; beyond it a flight of stairs disappeared into the building's bowels. But to their immediate left they confronted yet another door, unusually small and half glazed with frosted glass. A faded wooden label with the words 'Fire Buckets' stenciled in red paint had at some time in the distant past been screwed to the lower panel. Bill rapped quickly on the glass, poked his head into the room and announced Harry's arrival. "Bob, we have a Mr. Michaels here."

Fleetingly, Harry pondered the door's label— more specifically, why no one had taken the trouble to remove it. His musings were cut short by the sight of a man crouched behind a very large and very abused metal desk, feverishly stuffing something that clinked like glassware into one of the side drawers. In terms of both space and style the room admirably suited the storage of fire buckets but much less so its conversion to an office. An equally battered filing cabinet, which had also been squeezed in, left so little space that anyone sitting behind the desk would practically have to open a window in order to lean back in his chair.

"Ah, so here's our new recruit!" said Dickie, rising, flushed. He rolled unsteadily around the desk with outstretched hand, a cigarette bobbing from his lower lip. The man looked to be in his late fifties, short and overweight, with a florid complexion and thick, Brylcreamed, greying hair brushed straight back from his round face. A pair of ill-fitting reading glasses perched on the end of a narrow nose. Despite a lingering fog of cigarette smoke, Harry could smell alcohol. Bill smiled at them both and quietly departed, leaving the door ajar.

"What d'you know then?" Dickie asked, retreating to his chair without removing the cigarette from his mouth. In a sitting position he reminded Harry of Humpty Dumpty.

Know about what? Harry silently asked himself, in his nervousness forgetting that some people used this as a rhetorical question in the same way that they might ask "How are you?" Dickie scrutinized him for a moment and then grinned through a thin, purple mouth. It was a deceptive grin Harry would later come to know very well.

After a short pause he began again. "Well, Robin..."

"Harry. Everyone calls me Harry," Harry blurted out, then proceeded to trot out the accompanying explanation in a voice reminiscent of an airline flight attendant intoning the seat-belt instructions prior to take-off.

Dickie didn't seem to mind being interrupted. He nodded approvingly. "Pukka show, Harry. Sounds okay to me." The flabby hand jerked again. "Sit down why don't you, and take the weight off your mind. I'll acquaint you with the workings of this blighted bureaucracy."

Since Harry had already helped himself to the only other chair, he simply nudged his bottom farther towards the backrest. There was a short silence while the two eyed each other.

"We need new blood in this department," Dickie continued. "And I mean badly. Most of the blokes out there are over the hill. Take Bill Lewis, for example. He's a harmless old fart but he's useless. Got some sort of problem. Can hardly hold a pencil anymore and he's forever setting his tie, or his flippin' shirt, on fire. One of these days the silly sod's going to burn us all to a crisp. Thank God he'll be retiring in a year or two, then perhaps we can put the fire extinguishers away."

Another pause ensued as Dickie, deep in thought, tapped on his desk with a pencil.

"Then there's Morley Singleton. Did you meet him? Tall skinny chap who droops?" Without waiting for an answer, he added, "I suspect Morley died years ago but he's too miserable to tell anyone."

From the unflattering description, Harry assumed Dickie must be referring to the man who had been leaning over the file cabinet.

"New blood. That's what we need," Dickie repeated, putting down his pencil and slapping the desk to emphasize his point. "And we've made a start. God! I had a hell of a fight with the brass over it, I can tell you. We've been in a hiring freeze since the last ice age, so it's taken two goddamn years, but I got 'em in the end, the bastards. We hired young Terry Jones at the beginning of January. Met **him** yet? You probably walked past him on the way in."

Harry nodded and said yes.

"Capable fellow. Bit full of himself although I'll grant he knows his stuff. Went to technical college in Swansea. Should be around for a while. The lad's engaged to be married, y'know. Nice girl, Marion. Sort of prissy, but nice. Probably wears her knickers in bed... You know the type. Welsh, too. Nothing like a wife and kids to settle a chap down."

The bit about a wife and kids seemed to have prompted some deep seated angst, for no no sooner had those last words left his mouth than his face clouded over and he fell silent again. However, after staring at Harry for a few more seconds, he resumed his original theme. "At present there are six of us. Old Bill Lewis, Lol Dobson who's our mainstay; Morley Singleton, if he ever gets up enough energy to do any work; Angus McGregor, Terry Jones and myself. You, or whoever, will make seven. Out of that lot, would you believe only Terry is under forty-five? Bloody ridiculous! Angus is about as much use as my weeny. Spends most of his time sick. Christ! I don't know what to make of that man. D'you know, his nose runs constantly. Don't ever have a meal with him; it's disgusting to watch. Wish we could get him another job somewhere, perhaps back in Aberdeen where everybody's nose drips."

Dickie conveniently omitted to mention that it was he who had hired Angus in the first place, an omission that very much characterized his lifelong philosophy of ignoring one's own mistakes and taking credit for other people's successes.

Harry, who up to that day had been blissfully unaware that everybody's nose dripped in Aberdeen, sat mesmerized by these candid revelations. It was all interesting stuff to be sure, but even if it hadn't been, sitting on a chair which felt like the tip of a ball-point pen pretty well ensured Harry's attention. The motley crew in the adjoining room clearly fell below their boss's expectations, and this had obviously become a source of aggravation. Nevertheless, the coarse language and unbridled criticism of Lewis, Singleton and McGregor had caught young Harry somewhat off guard. Granted, he had very little workplace experience but this kind of behavior from someone in a position of authority seemed unusual to say the least. He would later discover that whatever virtues Dickie might possess, neither gentility nor diplomacy were among them.

The tiny office fell silent once again. Harry shifted uncomfortably while his interviewer continued to rap on the desk with a pencil. And all the while those small ferret eyes never left him.

"We here in the Landscape and Playing Fields Section look after, well, all the bloody landscaping and playing fields," Dickie suddenly continued. "Anytime the County builds a new school or an old-folks home, we clean up the mess the builders leave behind. Lol looks after most of our big playing-fields jobs, but young Terry has indicated an interest in taking on some of it, so Lol's taken him under his wing. Playing fields demand pretty keen design because the gradients and the drainage have to be just right, as you probably know, otherwise the grass sinks and the politicians get pissed off at us. Bill Lewis used to do a lot of that work, but..." Dickie grimaced, then repeated what he had said just moments before, "he keeps falling off his chair and he can't hold a pencil anymore. Damned shame, damn shame."

Having just encountered Bill Lewis, fast asleep at his desk in the middle of the day, Harry could see that there might be some cause for concern, but at the same time he doubted whether Dickie's claims were completely true. Clearly there seemed to be something about Bill Lewis that especially rankled Dickie, for this was the second time within minutes that he had returned to the subject of his senior draughtsman's deficiencies. He was like a dog gnawing at a bone.

Dickie's purple lips parted into another grin. "We do the designs, we draw up the specs, and then we fire it all off to the Fred-Astaire studio downstairs." He lit a new cigarette with the butt of the old one, and inhaled deeply. "I'm referring of course to the quantity surveyors. D'you know those buggers are holed up in the bloody ballroom? The bloody ballroom for chrissakes! Pampered lot. Anyhow, enough about our side. How about you? I see you've graduated with a diploma in horticulture, and that's fine as far as it goes. We certainly need more chaps who can tell a lilac from a wallflower." He again nodded towards the wall dividing his office from the draughting room. "Which, except for Angus, is more than can be said for that bunch next door. But gardening isn't really what we're all about. In fact, landscape design is a chore that the architects dumped on us a few years ago. Hoyty-toyty sods couldn't be bothered with it. And since we're in the County Architect's Department and the head honcho is the County Architect, we do as we're bloody well told. Before, we were simply known as the '**Playing Fields** Section', which was a hell of a sight easier to pronounce than the silly handle we've got now. The essence of our business is engineering and surveying. What do you know about surveying?" He thumbed through Harry's single-page résumé. "You don't mention much about that here. Did they teach it at the farm-school place you attended?"

Harry searched for a suitably nebulous response to the question he knew he was going to have to answer sooner or later. He vaguely recollected on one occasion his class had messed about with some pegs, some thin twine and an oversized T-square but he couldn't remember for the life of him if it had to do with surveying or whether it was another of their groundskeeper's harebrained schemes for keeping birds off newly seeded grass. He did recall that it amounted to an unutterably boring exercise.

"Very little **practical** experience, I'm afraid," he replied carefully. "Mostly theoretical and not too much of that either, although I'm sure I can pick it up as I go along."

"Pick it up as you go along? Pick it up as you go along?" The cigarette bobbed frantically on Dickie's lower lip. "My dear chap, surveying is **not** a skill one picks up as one goes along. Surveying is a science, and an exact one at that. Mind you, these days they're a lot sloppier than when I was in the field...as it were. Dirty equipment. Idiots standing around picking their noses. Saw some clod in the surveyor's department a while ago propping open the boot lid of his car with his theodolyte. Can you imagine, for Chrissakes? They get away with murder these days, some of 'em. Bit more spit and polish in my time, I can tell you."

A *faux pas* of some significance had just been committed, Harry knew that. He racked his brain for a half intelligent rejoinder that might help redeem the situation. As usual, nothing presented itself, so he simply coughed apologetically and shuffled his bony bottom for a second time.

"Anyhow, my young friend," Dickie said, looking at his wristwatch and slapping his hands once again on the desk top, "it's nearly twelve noon and time for a sandwich and liquid refreshment. You and I will adjourn to the *Hanging Gate,* where I will interrogate you further. Lunch is on me. Remember it well. I do this only once."

With this he stood, hitched up his baggy trousers, flicked the cigarette ash off his tie and rolled around the desk, scooping up Harry with outstetched arm as they swept out of the office, down the back stairs and out into the street. Instantly, Harry realized that this must be the 'short cut' the porter had mentioned. And later he found that, yes indeed, as the porter had also noted, one would have had to leave the building to take it since there proved to be no internal access to the staircase except from their office.

He glanced at his own watch. It wasn't even eleven-forty, but Dickie hurried up the narrow street like a man with a mission, his short legs in comic contrast to Harry's long sticks. Dickie waddled; Harry strode, as he always did, with effortless speed, slowing down several times to allow his out-of-breath host to catch up. Neither spoke. Harry was itching to ask a few oblique questions that might give some indication of whether or not he had a chance at this job, if only he could think of some. It sounded like he did. People in the office had referred to him as 'the new recruit,' hadn't they? Nothing explicit had been said though.

He wanted the job, no doubt about that. For starters, it was away from his mother. Try as he might, Harry couldn't live at home for more than a couple of days without getting into a fight with her. It was sad because he knew deep down that Mother thought the sun shone out of his backside. When Harry was nine and his sister six, their father had died suddenly of polio, so it was inevitable that the family should view Harry as the male heir-apparent. Trouble was, he didn't see himself in that role. In fact, the seeds of Harry's anarchy had been sown when, six months after his father's death, he found himself in a starchy Hertfordshire boarding school. Mother, while undoubtedly hoping for a renaissance Einstein, was in truth motivated more by desperation. As she saw it, a private school education, even a second rate one, offered salvation from the inevitable delinquency that proxied for growing up in a coal mining town. It probably did, but Harry fell far short of genius. He couldn't remember ever being so utterly miserable. And the misery expressed itself in a headlong slide from a respectable entrance berth in the 'A' form, to dead last in the 'D's by the time the school finally threw him out at the age of sixteen. Mother was not amused. The relatives were not amused. And the experience left a psychological scar which would stay with Harry for the rest of his life. After a while, psychologists tell us, loneliness and despair will build a resilient shell around the innermost self, where no one can reach. For some it functions as an effective defence mechanism; it can occasionally separate those who survive from those who put an end to themselves. Harry built a very resilient shell. Throughout all the bullying, the beatings, and years of being told he was chronically stupid, the tough little alter ego which directed his inner self promised him invincibility by a simple strategy of self-reliance. Instead of dancing to the tune of the world outside, Harry custom-created his own world. It worked exceedingly well. By the time he was sixteen he had developed a Walt-Disney imagination and an independence that bordered on narcissism. Harry had become a survivor, still caring in a largely uncaring world, but fundamentally selfish.

Since age nine, he had spent just under two years at home, and even that brief period had seemed like a lifetime. In Harry's day, agricultural colleges required a year's practical training prior to admission. Out of sheer necessity he lived with his mother during his apprenticeship in the local parks department. For the most part it had been a disaster, and Harry found himself praying for his first term to start. Mother would have liked him to come home each day but happily for Harry it was much too far for a daily commute and, besides, the college had live-in facilities. After graduation and back in the parks department, he lived once again at his mother's house. Within easy cycling distance of work, it proved to be very handy. But the arrangement was still a disaster. Harry wanted to go places. Anywhere. The youthful free spirit clashed with his mother's fiscally dictated caution. They always seemed to be arguing about something. He loved his mother dearly, but the situation had become dysfunctional. This job, miles away from Barnsley, would give him the freedom he yearned.

They turned off into an even narrower lane where Harry spotted a low slate roof partly hidden by a clump of trees. A white-painted wooden post with a small gate hanging from its crosspiece discretely announced that they were at the right spot. At first Harry thought the squat limestone building had only one floor, but then he noticed a curtained window in the gable end facing the lane. Underneath it an algae-covered stone trough also caught his eye. Judging from several iron rings set into the wall above, horses must have been tethered there in the days before combustion engines.

The *Hanging Gate*, like Smedley's Hydro, faced southwest, out across a shallow valley which cradled the town centre of Matlock. In front, a small forecourt sported half a dozen trestle tables and an assortment of wooden benches and garden chairs. Behind, the lane continued on, curving gently into a slight incline and coming to a dead end capped by a low stone wall. Below, the hillside fell sharply into some allotments. Dickie knew this lane and its discrete shadows; it was a handy spot to park his car on evenings when the beer flowed too freely.

With the arrival of the County-Offices, the pub quickly became a popular haven for staff. Already it bustled with the lunch time crowd, some of whom were sitting outside at the trestle tables. Others sat on the pub's low window sills. A couple of young women, deep in earnest conversation, had opted for the shade of an adjacent elm. Harry could see that Dickie was familiar not only with the place but also with its patrons. He waddled towards the door.

"Hi'yer, Bob," a voice called out from one of the trestles. Dickie looked over, grunted back at the voice, and barged inside.

"Used to be a free house but the chap who owns it... ex policeman type... has gone and sold it to the bloody brewery," he growled over his shoulder as they stumbled through the tables. "He's staying on as manager. No doubt they'll do it up nicely; God only knows, the place needs a face-lift. But they'll ruin the bloody beer...How do, Arthur!"

The recipient of Dickie's greeting was a tall, sturdily built man in his mid-fifties who stood behind the bar with an air of someone accustomed to being firmly in charge. A pretty woman, roughly ten years younger, was at his side, busily serving up sandwiches and pickled eggs. Harry hungrily eyed the huge glass jar and those delicious eggs steeped in vinegar and herbs. He assumed the woman to be Arthur's wife. She had a cheery disposition and a tinkling laugh, which carried easily above the chatter. The man returned Dickie's greeting and for the third time that day Harry could detect a strong Welsh accent. Was everyone around here Welsh?

He looked around. The *Hanging Gate* had joined the ranks of a dying breed. Dating back to 1823, many years before John Smedley built his spa down the road, it had remained virtually unaltered since. The small front door, overhung with wisteria, opened into a long, narrow lounge with the bar in the corner of one end and a monstrous stone inglenook fireplace at the other. Smoke stains from the mantle piece and up the chimney breast gave clear evidence of extensive service during the chilly days of winter. This warm September day required no fire, and the hearth was swept and clean. In front of it Arthur's wife, Kath, the pretty woman with the tinkling laugh, had set a fat brass jug filled with sprays of michaelmas daisies and garden chrysanthemums.

A small opening adjacent to the bar led into a tiny, uncomfortable-looking room lined with high-backed wooden benches and inappropriately named the snug. Patrons would bellow their orders through a hatch that one had to bend almost double to see through. Behind the back wall lurked the pub's tap room, every bit as barren as the snug, roughly three feet below the floor of the lounge and running half its length. Patrons were obliged to enter through a door that led to the outside lavatories. But the tap room came by its name honestly, since the space also accommodated the beer barrels. They would be rolled out from an adjacent cellar on to a wooden rack with their spigots facing a rectangular hole in the wall adjoining the bar. After allowing the beer to settle for a day or two the publican would fill his glasses straight from the barrels. A narrow shelf above the rack enabled tap room customers to be served through the same hole in the wall. In today's labour-conscious society the arrangement would be regarded as absurdly inefficient, but the beer which flowed from those barrels ran clear, dank, and delicious, with no gas bubbles to spoil the taste.

The *Hanging Gate* not only pre-dated John Smedley, but also the age of interior designers. At best, the decor could be described as 'spartan'. Her walls were half-wainscoted in oak darkened from nearly a century and a half of soot. Rising damp revealed itself in pustules of loosened distemper and size crystals that erupted from the surface like ugly boils. In many places the plaster had separated from the stones behind, creating saggy bulges laced with cracks. Nor had the pub taken kindly to electricity. Wiring clung awkwardly to walls and ceilings. Switches, plugs and light fixtures had remained, for the most part, unchanged from the first installation. The switches reminded Harry of those at his grandparents' house: big brass things that looked like a bell mounted on a wooden base.

But despite its uninspired decor, Arthur's pub glowed. The woodwork, including the ingrained soot, was freshly polished. Everywhere, brasswork shone with a deep lustre from years of loving attention. Besides the inevitable horse brasses, Arthur had acquired a magnificent ship's clock which chimed the eight bells of the watch instead of regular time. It took pride of place by the front door and received regular polishing along with everything else. A barometer underneath completed the set. Typical barroom smells mingled happily with furniture polish and Brasso.

"Two pints, two plates of sandwiches, Kath," Dickie called out as they hustled through to the snug, feet clacking on the stone-flagged floor. Completely out of breath from his walk, he slumped onto one of the benches and swiped a fleshy fist across his perspiring brow. "As I was saying," he panted, beckoning Harry to sit, "the brewery's going to turn the place upside down. Won't be the same." After lighting a cigarette he drew deeply and swallowed the smoke. "Don't understand why Arthur can't leave well enough alone. First thing they'll do is install pumps. I loathe bloody pumped beer. Leaves you so full of gas you spend the entire evening farting like a damp squib. We won't even have to go outside for a piss anymore," he added, as though this assault on tradition had just occurred to him.

Harry correctly surmised from the last remark that, like many old pubs in Britain, the *Hanging Gate*'s lavatories were somewhere in the back yard. In summer they customarily stank and attracted millions of flies, while in winter going outside to relieve one's self could occasionally set an Olympic speed record.

"What's in the sandwiches, Kath?" Dickie yelled towards the hatch.

"Caviar!" came the reply.

"In other words, ham and cheese, I suppose?"

"The same!"

"That makes a real change!" he said sarcastically, at the same time winking at Harry.

Arthur's wife stuck her head around the corner. "You can always go to the *Duke*, Robert," she said in mock seriousness.

This remark was greeted with a chuckle from a few of the other people in the snug, including a little man with rosy cheeks who sat in the corner, legs crossed, next to the serving hatch. Harry noticed that he had what appeared to be his own tankard. Made of very heavy pewter with a glass base, it sat solidly on three claw-shaped feet. Along with everything else, it had been well polished. The old man sipped his beer, wiped his mouth with the back of his hand, placed the tankard back on the table, and resumed his scrutiny of everyone from beneath a large cloth cap. He had deep blue piercing eyes which seemed to dart in all directions as he spoke. Harry figured him to be in his late sixties. This part of the pub appeared to be his regular spot, for people made a point of ducking in to say hello.

Dickie briefly looked in the old man's direction. "Well, young Frank, what'you know?"

Frank broke into a grin. "Aw, nowt much, Bob. Finished digging spuds and had to come wet me whistle. It's a thirsty job. As y'know, Missus used to handle them things 'cause ah'm an ornamentals man, mi'self. But she's 'ad a bad back lately, an I'm not as young as ah used ter be. None of us are, ah reckon. Mind, ah dig 'em better'n she does. Ah don't skewer as many of 'em!"

Dickie took the 'thirsty job' remark as a cue. "Arthur!" he shouted, "get Frank here another pint. How are you for cigs, Frank?"

Frank laughed again, visibly pleased by the attention he was receiving but also giving a strong impression of being thoroughly accustomed to it. He spoke with a heavy Derbyshire dialect that contrasted sharply with the broad Yorkshire Harry was accustomed to hearing in his home town. Derbyshire folk, he found, spoke with a slight twang, with more emphasis on 'e's' than 'a's.'

"Cigs 'is 'oldin' out very nicely, thanks!" he replied.

Kath came in with the sandwiches, Arthur following with the beer and assiduously removing Frank's tankard for a refill. Harry took another look around, at the relaxed smiling faces, the warm autumn glow coming through the windows, and the piled up sandwiches, and decided he was going to like it here, provided he had the job. Keeping his foot out of his mouth for the next hour or so would help enormously.

Dickie patted Kath on the bottom while she placed the food on the table. "Kathleen, this here's Robin Michaels, properly known as Harry. We're interviewing him for a job with our illustrious department, poor bugger. Harry, meet Kath. She runs this establishment."

Harry started to stand up to say hello, as he had been taught in boarding school. Kath patted him on the shoulder, gently pushing him back into his seat. "Bob's the one who should be getting up, he needs the exercise!" she replied, flashing a smile. "I'm very happy to meet you, Harry. Enjoy your lunch." Then, nodding again in Dickie's direction, she added, "And don't let him bully you too much!"

"Never did ask you whether you were a beer man," Dickie said, grabbing a sandwich, "but then, I haven't met a Yorkshireman who didn't drink beer. Arthur sells Watney's Red Barrel and Worthington's. Hope either of those suit your fancy."

Harry nodded approval. Hardly a beer connoisseur, he'd nevertheless had the pleasure of getting plastered on Worthington bitter several times. It was undeniably good beer. Of course, had he been alive, his father would have protested that neither could match Barnsley Bitter. And he might have been right. But Barnsley Bitter could be enjoyed only in and around Barnsley, while Worthington's and Watney's had almost a nation-wide distribution. And Watney's happened to be the brewery buying Arthur's pub.

"I drink beer," Harry reassured him.

"See Frank over there?" Dickie said in a loud whisper. "Guess how old he is. Just guess."

Harry studied the man more closely. He had the ruddy complexion of someone who has worked outdoors most of his life, and the large, callused hands, which were out of proportion to his small frame, confirmed it. As Frank chatted and laughed with the people who stopped by, Harry couldn't help noticing that one of his front upper teeth was cracked. Moreover, dentures which had been fitted long ago to a much younger man, were now too big for his face. When he spoke, the upper and lower plates clicked noisily together.

"I would say around sixty-eight."

"Ha!" Dickie chortled, slamming his hand onto the table, as he usually did to make a point. "The old bugger's going to be eighty-seven in a couple of weeks' time. And his wife's a year older than him. We bought him that pint pot for his eighty-fifth. If I were in half that shape I'd be hiring myself out for stud services." Catching Harry's look of surprise, he looked pensively at Frank for a moment. "That's what happens when you spend your life doing something you like. Frank was a gravedigger. A bloody gravedigger, if you please! But he says he loved it. His dad was a gravedigger, too. Taught his son well. Frank told me once how many graves he dug in his life but I've forgotten." He leaned over. "Frank! How many graves d'you dig?"

Frank had been asked that question many times. "Seventeen-thousand, eight-hundred and sixty-two," he quickly shot back.

"Can you imagine, nearly eighteen-thousand bloody graves! He dug them for fifty-five years. Great life, doing a job other folks were dying to get into!" Dickie chuckled at his own joke. "Out in the fresh air. Nobody to push you around. If anybody gets on your back, just tell 'em to drop dead. Ha, ha, ha! Great life I'd say. Certainly didn't do him any harm, although he apparently came down with polio just before the First World War. Couldn't join up because of it. He must have had only a very mild case, otherwise he'd be dead. Still walks with a slight limp. He told me digging graves was the best therapy he could have asked for. Personally, I'd rather had polio."

By then Dickie had finished his pint and was prying another Player's from a silver case he had slid out of his jacket pocket. In an entirely mechanical gesture he tapped the end on the lid before lighting up. Once lit, the filterless cigarettes sat on his lower lip until they had come within a hair's breadth of setting fire to his face. Harry studied Dickie's flushed complexion, the nicotine-stained mouth, and the traces of cigarette paper that marked the spot, and wondered how he could possibly enjoy making such a mess of himself.

"I think we'll have another pint," Dickie said. "Job interviews deserve a long lunch hour." He poked at Harry's glass. "Finish that up. I don't want to look like a damned lush drinking on my own." This remark, it seemed to Harry, displayed a rather hollow ring. He was beginning to get the impression that Robert Dickie was intimately acquainted with long, liquid lunches. The second pints came and the lopsided consumption continued. They chatted about the world in general, with an occasional diversion when Dickie paused to bellow at someone else. Another round was ordered, with Harry mildly protesting that he really couldn't handle another. After three pints Dickie began to relax, but at the same time his speech had taken on a noticeable slur.

"Got a girlfriend?" Dickie asked bluntly.

Harry shook his head. No such luck. Even worse, he was still a virgin, an issue which rankled him considerably. He cursed his dismal skills with the opposite sex.. Some of his friends had the gift of the gab with girls and he watched them ply their charms with envy and admiration. They could open their mouths, out would pour this seemingly mindless babblespeak, and the girls would lap it up. Or so it appeared. Finally, he'd come to the conclusion that his conversational style was far too serious for many females. Most were looking for a good time, not for some geek who talked earnestly about gardening and long walks in the rain. But Harry wasn't good at mindless babble; when he tried to imitate his peers, the result had been farcical. Painful memories of a party the year before still lingered, during which a girl he was chatting up had set her former boyfriend on him because she thought Harry was taking a rise out of her. He spent weeks picking tiny bits of glass out of his forehead.

"We'll have to change that," Dickie said from behind his beer glass. "And I have someone in mind. She's cute, if you like short women."

Harry almost laughed. Considering the luck he'd had so far, height seemed rather irrelevant.

"My better half's taller than me," Dickie continued, lighting up another cigarette from the stub of the last one.

Harry didn't see how that would be too difficult.

"A good two inches taller, in fact. But y'know," he leered at Harry, jabbing him with his elbow, "they're all the same height lying down!"

Harry gurgled into his beer. A woman sitting a few feet away on Dickie's side and listening intently to the conversation, giggled. Her male companion, a man in his forties with a moustache and dressy suit, glared at the two of them.

Dickie rambled on, unaware that his voice had risen appreciably during the past hour and oblivious to the attention he was beginning to attract. To those who knew him, it was a familiar process, and good entertainment value for the customers. No one knew this better than Arthur Bassett.

"During the War we had more women than we knew what to do with. Christ, didn't matter whether they were married or not. If you had a uniform on it was like a licence to fuck. Of course, being married, I just looked. Well, most of the time anyway."

"You were in the armed forces?" Harry asked. A politically correct question, no doubt, but not without some genuine interest. Dickie's face lit up.

"Yes, my friend. Royal Engineers. Bomb disposal. We defused things that went crump in the night. Or the day. Or whenever. You'd be surprised at the number of bombs Jerry dropped that didn't go off. So much for German dependability, eh! Towards the end of the war, when they'd lost their air superiority, our fighters would give them such a rough time they'd often turn tail and run before reaching their target. Then they'd dump their bombs without arming them. Actually, those bombs, we called them duds, were easy to deal with because they normally didn't go off without warning. It was the ones which **had** been armed, and which didn't go off, that could ruin your day. And sometimes Jerry would booby trap the bombs. The bastards. They were the shits to deal with. Lost two of my best friends on those fucking things. One thing about it, if the buggers went off while you were working on them, you didn't need to waste money on a coffin. Just a shovel. Just a fuckin' little shovel."

Dickie paused for a few more seconds of reflection, as though the flood of memories had created a bottleneck. He looked down at his beer. Harry noticed small beads of perspiration on the man's forehead. He also noticed that no one in the room was listening anymore. Maybe it was because the war had been over for fifteen years and everyone wanted to forget it. Or maybe they'd heard it all before. Harry suspected the latter. Even Frank, whose ears and eyes seemed to be in all directions at once, was half-turned away, talking to Arthur through the hatch. Dickie used the lull to excuse himself.

A few minutes later he could be heard talking loudly to someone in the lounge as he shambled back. "Problem was, defusing bombs didn't give a chap any chance to fight," he continued, flopping into his seat and addressing no one in particular. "Used to think I'd do anything for a chance to dish it out for a change. You know, get up in a Hurricane and blow some arsehole out of the sky or shoot some bugger's backside off. We got a lot of flack from people who thought we spent all our time riding around in cars! But Christ, some of the jobs were messy. And I'm telling you, we had help. But when you got assigned to a bomb, nobody got a free ride. We once had to disarm a five hundred pounder that came down in the Salford sewage works. Right in the bloody settling ponds. Took us three days. I stank of shit for a month! But at least I **lived** to stink of shit, which is more than some poor buggers did. Best one I remember was in '42...no, it was '43. October, '43 I think it was. A bomb went off as a friend of mine approached it. Vibration caused by the sappers when they cleared an access could be just enough to trigger some fuses. This damned thing had buried itself under the floor of a house that had already been hit. The blast blew a crater thirty feet across and fifteen feet deep, and it threw Geoff over a fence into a neighbor's cabbage patch. When he got up, he didn't have a scratch on him but the fella who owned the vegetable garden gave him hell for wrecking his cabbages!"

Dickie talked on. These were anecdotes he had trotted out hundreds of times before. What he didn't mention was the incident that nearly cost him his stripes. When Germany began bombing Britain in 1940, the disposal of unexploded bombs was initially the responsibility of the Home Office. Local police forces dealt with them as best they could. This wasn't a very satisfactory arrangement. By the end of 1940 there were nearly four-thousand unexploded bombs lying around. So the War Office asked the Royal Engineers to do the job. Later, as the war dragged on, the Royal Air Force and voluntary organizations joined in. Dickie became one of a rather celebrated elite, even though there was little doubt they earned their perks. Bomb-disposal companies were identified as much by their cavalier style as by the beetle-shaped insignias on their uniforms. Early defusing strategies were crude, to say the least. Usually the officer tried to pry off the fuse timer with a chisel. Often, as Dickie had noted, the vibration was enough to explode the bomb. Eventually, enough parts were salvaged to enable the bomb squads to figure out their design and permit systematic dismantling. But enough were also booby-trapped to ensure that bomb disposal remained a precarious occupation.

Then, just when the Army thought they had the situation in hand, the Germans started indiscriminately dropping powerful magnetic mines, normally destined for shipping lanes and harbours, onto land targets. As Dickie always liked to tell everyone, these mines were not bombs; they were dropped by parachute. Instead of an impact fuse, they were triggered by barometric pressure, usually before they hit the ground. All were unpredictable and deadly.

The task of clearing oceanic mines had always been the domain of the Royal Navy. And despite the fact that these mines were falling onto houses and factories, it was decided that the Royal Navy should deal with them, too. It made sense only in a bureaucratic context, since a large number were simply blown up rather than dismantled. His Majesty's Royal Engineers had strict instructions to do no more than secure and clear the area once an unexploded mine had been reported. Then they were to turn things over to the Navy. A few bomb-disposal officers resented this directive, especially since neutralizing mines was viewed by some as a more glamorous way of committing suicide than de-fusing bombs.

Manchester became the recipient of many parachute mines. Dickie's team was in Salford after a heavy raid, and they responded to a mine that had come down in some row houses, burying its nose in a front parlour floor. Dickie immediately knew it was a mine from the huge green parachute that had draped itself across the roof. The chute flapped aimlessly in an early-morning breeze. Ignoring standing orders, he proceeded to defuse the one-ton behemoth. Fortunately for him it wasn't booby trapped. Later at the disciplinary hearing, a recalcitrant Dickie had insisted that the mine was familiar, the job routine, a piece of cake. But in fact he had been very lucky. Even luckier, the mine wasn't a photocell model, Navy succinctly pointed out; otherwise he probably would have annihilated himself, his team, and the neighborhood. Even the briefest exposure of the cell to light would have detonated it. Later, Dickie privately admitted that luck had indeed been on his side that day. As he put it, that's how it was with any kind of bomb disposal. No matter how careful you might be, if luck wasn't on your side, you died. So what was the difference? Since the moral high ground had been soundly captured by the navy, the brass were forced to concede that there was indeed a difference. Dickie was handed a stern reprimand.

Luck stayed with him for the rest of the war. But the work took a terrible psychological toll nonetheless. After nearly five years of staring death in the face, the endless, sweating fear of each new assignment and following all-too-brief rush of success became a nightmare that peacetime couldn't erase. Following demobilization, Dickie's wartime lifestyle insidiously transformed itself into a debilitating cycle of escalating pressure regularly releasing itself, like the fault lines of an earthquake zone, in an explosive outburst of self-recrimination. Alcohol dulled the raw edges, just as it had during the war, but it was never enough. Back in civvy street, his uneven behavior and ongoing battle with the bottle quickly lost him jobs with two private firms. Local government represented the final, tenuous option. This job was his last chance and he knew it.

More pints came and went. Harry stared despairingly at his untouched mugs, lined up one after the other, and then at the growing mound of cigarette butts in the ash tray. Dickie was fast becoming inebriated, his flushed face getting redder and redder. Laughing furiously at the memories, he teased yet another cigarette from his silver case, made to tap it on the lid as usual, missed, and the cigarette fell on the floor. Harry, feeling light-headed himself, stooped to pick it up for him. Dickie ignored the gesture and instead lumbered to his feet, announcing to the room at large that he was going for another piss. He weaved unsteadily past Frank, who gave him a knowing grin, and disappeared, leaving Harry fumbling awkwardly with his beer glass in one hand and Dickie's cigarette in the other.

Arthur had suddenly appeared from nowhere and was sitting quietly by Harry's side. "I reckon you'll be working for Bob then?" he said, more as a statement than a question.

Harry shrugged, smiling self-consciously. "Hope so, but this is just my interview. I think there'll be others applying for the job as well."

The publican seemed to think that was funny. "Some interview, eh! Well, I should warn you that this is a little wrinkle you'll have to get used to. Captain Bob's one of the nicest chaps I know. But four years sitting on unexploded bombs did something up here." He tapped the side of his head. "He's got quite a temper, especially after a skinfull. Most of the other chaps in your office won't go for lunch with him anymore because he winds up either falling down in the street or getting into a punch-up with someone. Last year he got into a row with some Scots fellow and damned if they didn't start duking it out right here in my pub. Had to throw them both out and call the constable. Bit of a shame 'cause it was Bob who started it all. Kept picking on the other fellow, like he was trying to make him mad, you know. And then he poured a whole pint of beer down the poor chap's trousers. Well, I mean, nobody's going to stand for that. Real shame. Haven't seen the other chap since, which is perhaps not surprising. Anyhow, I'll keep an eye on Bob. It's about time he packed it in for the day." Then Arthur sidled back to the bar as quietly as he had come.

He must have been talking about Angus McGregor, Harry thought. No other person with a Scottish name had been mentioned by Dickie. Angus didn't look the type to duke it out with anybody, although, as they say, even a worm can turn. He looked at his watch. They had been at the *Hanging Gate* for two and a half hours. Dickie had consumed five pints and, he counted them carefully, twelve cigarettes. He appreciated Arthur's concern but at the same time he couldn't fathom out why a pub would continue to serve beer to someone who could hardly stand up. Later he would learn that the Landscape and Playing Field Section's fearless leader was at his nastiest when only half-drunk. After a few more pints he could usually be shepherded down the street and up the back stairs to his office with comparatively little fuss. Arthur Bassett had learned a few things as a policeman, and a few more tending his regulars.

Dickie staggered in from the lavatories, babbling and excusing himself with every piece of furniture he ran into. No one seemed particularly offended at his behavior; one young man seated with two others by the fireplace pulled a chair out of the way with his foot while another called a cheery greeting. Arthur executed a smooth interception, gently diverting his inebriated patron to one side with a brawny arm before he reached the snug. Some heated conversation followed, with Dickie listening, head slightly bowed and the ever-present cigarette dangling sadly from its usual position on his lower lip.

Arthur beckoned Harry to join them. "I telephoned your office a short while ago," he said. "And Bill Lewis... you met him? Good. He'll be along to walk Mr. Dickie back. So if you please, Bob, I think we'll call it a day. Your young friend here..." Arthur fumbled for the name.

"Harry."

"Harry? Yes. Right. Harry will stay with you until Bill gets here."

Dickie glared balefully about him. "I don't need a bloody nursemaid, Bassett," he proclaimed, without much conviction. "I'm standing, aren't I? What do you think this is?" He pushed himself away from Arthur and was standing with his arms out like a penguin as Bill Lewis ambled through the door. It was Harry's second look at Dickie's senior draughtsman. He saw a frail man, close to retirement age, losing his hair. A few wispy strands on top, carefully slicked back, and some more thin wisps falling untidily over his ears. The shapeless tweed jacket he'd thrown on at the office had worn practically threadbare at the elbows. An assortment of pens and mechanical pencils tumbled from a breast pocket. What Harry first took to be a sun tan now seemed closer to jaundice. Bill Lewis was clearly not a healthy man, and unquestionably underweight for his build. Yet, despite all this there was a certain spryness and quiet self assuredness in his manner. Given a staff and a white robe, Harry could easily picture him parting the Red Sea.

Eyelids half-lowered, Dickie watched the man approach and growled, "Jesus, here's Mary Poppins."

"Hullo, Boss," Bill said with the easy familiarity of one who had done this many times before. Even so, a very slight smile flickered in his face, as though he enjoyed the odd chance to catch his boss in a compromising situation. "Shall we adjourn?"

"Shall we adjourn? Shall we adjourn?" Dickie mimicked sarcastically as he struggled to maintain his balance. "Yes, alright, we shall adjourn. But lay a finger on me, Lewis, and I'll kick your arse."

Harry couldn't imagine Bill being that reckless. And he wasn't. Completely unfazed by Dickie's rudeness, he chatted amiably while guiding Dickie out of the pub, down the lane and into Smedley street, and without once making physical contact with him. Harry was greatly impressed. They walked casually back to the office in the late-afternoon sunshine with Dickie still babbling about his war-time experiences. Then Bill sent Terry down to the cafeteria for coffee. The kitchen had closed for the day, but one of the short-order cooks, a kindly lady who knew Dickie well, in particular his penchant for liquid lunches, brewed some fresh and brought it up herself. With the boss safely parked behind his desk, Bill took the time to introduce himself, and the other two who were still in the office, more fully. This time the room seemed much bigger, with six draughting tables arranged in pairs facing each other, and another a couple, separated by map drawers, which sat beneath a row of large cantilever windows. Leaning forward a little, Harry could see that the windows faced onto the street they had just come down.

By this time Morley Singleton had unraveled himself from the filing cabinet and was now drooped across his table. But despite the sallow face and sad eyes, Harry found him surprisingly congenial and concluded that he must simply be shy. Which he was. Painfully shy.

"You met the boss, I gather?" Morley said to Harry with a sly smile.

"The lad did indeed," Lewis interjected in his lilting Welsh dialect. "Our Radical Bob was in fine form." He lit a Woodbine cigarette and let out a long plume of smoke as if to emphasize the point. Then he turned to Harry. "Morley here does most of our heavy spec writing, and when he's not doing that he restores old cars. Since he's a confirmed bachelor he's got the money to do things like that. Must be nice. My car's an antique, but that's only because I can't afford a new one. I keep trying to get Morley to restore it!"

Morley ignored Bill's gentle bantering, studied Harry for a few seconds, then smiled again. "Got a place to live?" he asked.

"Well, actually, I'm only here for an interview," Harry replied apologetically. "I don't know if I've actually got the job yet."

This statement had amused Arthur Bassett, and it amused these two men just as much, for they both smiled knowingly at each other. Morley leaned back on the draughting chair, thin legs stretched out in front of him, and sucked on his mechanical pencil. Harry couldn't help notice that his socks were mismatched.

"Don't think Bob would take you for lunch if you didn't have the job, but I could be wrong," he said, adding with another sly smile, "I suppose he told you he does that only once?"

Harry nodded, and the two men laughed. Evidently, handling Bob Dickie amounted very much to a team effort in which everybody played a role, depending upon their position in the office hierarchy. Bill had told him earlier that he was the senior draughtsman, but he said it in such a self-deprecating manner that Harry wasn't sure whether or not he was joking. Senior or not, he definitely exercised some influence over his boss, in spite of the contempt that Dickie showed for him. Collectively it presented a picture of a long-time association.

"Well, if you do get the job and you need some digs, let me know."

Harry thanked him for the offer.

Bill grinned. "Morley here knows digs. As far as I know, he's sampled just about every boarding house in Matlock. And Derby before that. Unlike us masochists, he moved to Matlock when the County bought Smedley's. Couldn't stand our company on the Smedley caravan, could you, Morley!"

"Ever been in digs before?" Morley asked, again ignoring his colleague.

Harry shook his head.

"Y'have to get a place that feeds you. Any old place can provide a bed, but if they can't put on a decent meal, they're useless as far as I'm concerned."

Eyeing Morley's gangling frame and sallow features, Harry couldn't see much of an advertisement for his own digs. On the other hand, he was a wiry type, and wiry types had a reputation for being tougher than they look, even though Dickie evidently saw Morley as an exception to this rule.

Bill ushered him over to the other remaining person in the office. Harry instantly recognized him from Dickie's unflattering description earlier in the day. He had a cold. One hand clutched a soiled handkerchief, with which he frequently dabbed his damp and reddened nose. He looked to be in his mid-forties, about the same height as Lewis and stoutly built with a fresh, round face crowned by curly, reddish hair. A pair of horn rimmed glasses had been pushed back above his forehead while he attended to his dripping appendage. No doubt about it, this had to be Angus, the very same who had duked it out with his boss at the *Hanging Gate*.

Flicking the man's glasses back onto his nose, Bill made the introductions. "Harry, this is Angus McGregor, and he's married although Lord only knows why anyone would want to put up with him. Very unhealthy is our Angus!"

Angus nodded from behind the handkerchief and held out his free hand, which turned out to be his left, and Harry shook it.

"When he's well, which isn't often, Angus is our landscaping expert," Bill continued with tongue-in-cheek. "Did his training at Kew Gardens, didn't you, Angus?"

Angus nodded again from behind the handkerchief. Harry wondered if he would ever hear Angus speak.

"But he doesn't let that go to his head. In fact the only thing that goes to Angus' head is colds. Isn't that right Angus?"

The unhappy man blew a resonant note into his sodden handkerchief. "Aye, Goddamit," he mumbled. "Ah think sometimes ah should stick a tap on it. At least then I could turn it off once in a wee while. Pleased t' meet ye, Harry. Don't mind me."

Angus, it turned out, was a bit of a conundrum. As Dickie had implied earlier, the Scot had indeed been raised in Aberdeen, the son of North Sea fisher folk. A month premature, he'd nearly died of pneumonia at the age of six months. After that, to the astonishment of all concerned, he took on new vigour and became a strapping young lad, despite his short height. But susceptibility to infections continued to plague him. As a juvenile he'd been nicknamed 'Black Angus' by his peers, in an oblique reference to the black death epidemic which ravaged England long ago. His wife Mary, a Scottish lass herself and also from Aberdeen, couldn't have been less like her husband. A hale-and-hearty woman of slender build, she appeared to have never come down with a cold in her life. Or at least, none that she would admit to. Between them they raised two equally hale-and—hearty girls, now in their mid-teens. So Black Angus was left to suffer his miseries alone. The thing that rattled Dickie wasn't particularly the man's perpetual drip, but the fact that he was smart. Not only did he possess a thorough grasp of plant nomenclature and a flair for design, but also an encyclopedic memory for his boss's numerous indiscretions. Naturally it was the latter talent that irritated Dickie most. Angus had a habit of mentioning these little incidents, in his blunt Scottish manner, on the worst possible occasions.

"Well, there you are then," Bill said. "That's everybody but Lol accounted for. He's a tricky one to catch. Always on site, or so he says. Bit of a lady's man is our Lol. Nothing serious mind you. He's married. But I've never met anyone with the gift of the gab like our Lol, have you, Angus?"

Angus obviously hadn't, for he shook his head.

Bill was about to launch into some Lol-Dobson anecdotes when Harry noticed that it was nearly four-thirty. The last train for Sheffield left Matlock at five o'clock, and from there he had to catch another train to Barnsley. So he made his farewells, thanked Bill for his kindness, and departed. Before leaving the building, he ducked into Dickie's office but it was empty. A coffee Thermos sat uncapped on the desk blotter, the ash tray full of cigarette butts. After closing the door, he made his way back to Matlock's tiny railway station, wondering what to make of the day's adventure. Dickie had disappeared without a word, which Harry found unsettling. It would have been nice to know if he was still in the running for the job. Had he said something to offend Dickie perhaps? Mulling over the course of events, he couldn't think of anything. What if Dickie perceived him as a bit of a wimp for failing to drink all the beer Arthur had served up? How ironic; given enough time he could have done justice to all that beer and more, but then both of them would have wound up plastered, and that didn't seem such a good idea on a job interview.

The job sounded ideal— white-collar job, more money, and a chance to travel around a bit. Dickie was something else. It didn't take a rocket scientist to see that this man had a serious problem. In fact he had a lot of problems. Everyone has their demons, and Dickie seemed to have more than his fair share. But despite his crudeness, and an obvious weakness for alcohol, Harry couldn't help feeling a twinge of sympathy for this troubled, little man. If the other people in the office were able to handle him, he probably could too. One thing was certain: life would never be boring in that little bureaucratic backwater. As the oversprung diesel train swayed gently up to Sheffield, he chuckled to himself at the thought of Dickie's bizarre performance, and the oddballs he had met in the draughting room. No doubt about it, with very little coaching, Radical Bob and the boys would make wonderful material for a television sitcom.

TWO

Settling In

During the second week of October, roughly three-and-a-half weeks after Harry's interview in Matlock, he received a letter from the County Architect, offering him the position of 'Landscape Draftsman, Level One,' commencing November 1st. While Level One was the lowest level on the totem pole, it didn't matter. It was a real job, the first solid step towards a career, and it certainly paid better than Barnsley Parks Department. Harry could hardly believe his good fortune, especially since the interview had turned into a bit of a farce. Obviously, Dickie's alcoholic binge hadn't completely obliterated it, and Harry must have done something right. Of course, there was also the possibility that Dickie had been so embarrassed by the affair that he was offering Harry the job to assuage his guilt. It didn't make much difference. What mattered was that he **had** the job, his ticket out of coal-mining country and into self sufficiency.

Harry swiftly wrote back, accepting the position. Accommodation had to be found. He remembered Morley Singleton's offer to help in this matter, although Dickie also had mentioned some possibilities. However, Morley seemed to have the benefit of experience. A place had to be found close to work, since he didn't have a car, and a short walk would be nicer than having to catch a bus every day. Harry's mother responded to the imminent move by buying him enough underwear to last the siege of Leningrad, and a large suitcase, which the underwear practically filled.

He had never been more than marginally interested in clothes— another legacy of his boarding school years. That school had left an indelible impression on young Harry's dress ethic. For several years afterwards he found it difficult to buy clothing that didn't look like the school's sombre, and uncomfortable, regulation attire. The first time he purchased a pair of non-black shoes without laces, he remembered feeling like a vacuum-cleaner salesman.

He telephoned Dickie, intending first of all to thank him for the job offer, and then to ask for assistance in finding digs. Dickie was not around. The operator had no idea where he could be found, which, judging from what he had heard, was not unusual. After making three phone calls and getting the same answer, Harry decided to ask the switchboard for the Section's draughting office. The vaunted Lol Dobson answered it and, after extending a breezy welcome, passed him on to Morley Singleton.

"I suspect Bob would have recommended Slater's," Morley said. "That's where Terry here is staying. They run a petrol station just down the road. I used to stay there when we first relocated to Matlock. **He's** okay but Flossie drinks like a fish and she can't cook. The reason Bob likes them is because they go boozing together, and, when he drives his car into a lamp post or something,

George gets it fixed cheap. They should stick to selling petrol; running a boarding house isn't one of their strong points. I think you'd be in better hands with Battleship Bertha, metaphorically speaking, of course."

Harry could hear Morley and someone else in the office laughing. They're just having another joke at my expense, he thought. However, Morley assured him that Battleship Bertha, otherwise known as Miss Bertha Twigg, was no joke. She was very real. A spinster in her early sixties, she ran a boarding house near the town centre, about fifteen minutes' walk away, cooked up a storm, and offered very reasonable rates. Problem was, she had been thinking of retiring, and Morley wasn't sure if she would be prepared to take on any new boarders. They were good friends, he said, although he never explained how that came to be. He had never stayed with her, but the relocation of the county offices had been a windfall for boarding houses in Matlock, and Morley had sent a fair bit of business her way in the past. A recommendation from him would carry weight.

Still, Harry's spirits were a bit dashed.

"Don't worry, I'll ring her," Morley said. "And then I'll call you."

Harry had to tell him that they didn't have a phone at home; he was using the one at the fire-and-ambulance department, where his mother worked as a payroll clerk. Morley took the Department's number, told him to stay where was, and said he'd call back within fifteen minutes. Twenty minutes later the phone rang.

"I gather Bertha has no lodgers at the moment, except a couple of teenage girls belonging to her younger sister," Morley informed him. "She tells me the parents are in the middle of a scrappy divorce. The home environment wasn't too good...the husband apparently beats them up on a regular basis... so she agreed to take them until things settle down. Anyhow, she says that while she's looking after them she might as well look after you! So there you are. I think she just likes having young chaps around. Two pounds ten a week and that includes breakfast and an evening meal. Sounds okay to me. What shall I tell her?"

Harry said to tell her that would be great. He would like to move down and settle in a couple of days before starting work. This being 1961, November 1st fell on a Wednesday. If he arrived in Matlock on the Sunday before, that would give him two full days to find his way around. Morley said he didn't think Miss Twigg would charge him for the extra days. He would advise her to expect him on the 29th.

"Her address is *Derwent House*, Knowlsdon Place, and her phone number is Matlock 3636. Easy to remember. She's not far from the railway station. You can easily walk from there. And you can't miss the house. Bloody great place, and ugly as my backside. Used to be her parents'. Backs on to the river, hence the name *Derwent House*, I reckon. Just one little tip. She gets really pissed off if you're late for meals. So be sure you let her know if you're going to be late or not around. Okay?"

"Okay," replied an elated Harry.

What Morley omitted to mention was that it might be an easy walk to Miss Twigg's from the railway station, provided it wasn't raining. By the time Harry had reached Sheffield, what had started out as a pleasant, late-October day had turned into an ugly downpour, whipped by a brisk northwesterly wind. After getting off the train from Barnsley, he had to trek half a mile to another station for the trip to Matlock. Manhandling the large suitcase and its generous cargo of underwear through twenty minutes of wet streets and flooded pavements, he cursed the miserable state of local train service.

The train to Matlock was late. Harry sat for several minutes on one of the hard, graffiti covered benches in the waiting room, before his trousers began to feel wet. Too late, he realized that the back of his soaked raincoat was even wetter than the front and that was the bit he'd been sitting on. For the better part of an hour, as the antiquated train rattled through northern Derbyshire, he huddled, cold and miserable, moving occasionally in the hope that the seats would soak up some of the moisture. They didn't.

It was still pouring when he reached Matlock. The mid-afternoon sky had become so dark that the railway station's gas lamps had been turned on. Hissing faintly, their greenish glow reminded Harry of the tiny freight-station at Notton, where his late grandfather had once been stationmaster. Like Matlock station, it was built during the golden days of steam when Britain's early rail-transportation system was little more than a patchwork of privately owned fiefdoms. And also like Matlock, it had enjoyed few improvements since, despite or possibly because of nationalization. Many British railway stations remained illuminated by gas lamps well into the 1960's, especially those in rural districts. They were hopelessly obsolete, and the declining profitability of passenger service for the most part guaranteed they would stay that way.

As he sat in the station waiting room for the rain to abate, he smiled privately at the childhood memories of being hoisted up onto footplates of sturdy little tank engines as they shunted wagons up and down the Notton yards. They seemed to have a voracious appetite for coal, most of which, judging from the enormous clouds of black smoke, went straight up their tall chimneys. Just as vividly he remembered the wonderful herbaceous-flower border that ran along the back of the station's single platform. Grandfather had been a devoted gardener. During the summer months that border, and those flanking the station house where he and Grandmother lived, were a riot of oriental poppies, cranesbill, Russell lupins, pinks and lavender. Harry credited his interest in horticulture to his grandfather. His grandfather in turn had decided his grandson's talent for growing things must be divinely ordained when, at the age of fifteen, the young lad had quietly relocated all his prize roses from the back garden to the front, in the middle of August. Not one died.

The rain continued to dash against the waiting-room windows. Great swirls of dirty water, mixed with fallen leaves and rubbish, washed noisily into the gutters. With little to lose, since he couldn't get much wetter than he was already, Harry finally decided to make a run for it. Pulling up the collar of his raincoat, he grabbed the suitcase and pitched into the street towards Knowlsdon Place. Morley's 'easy walk' proved to be slightly more than twenty minutes. The road wound past an untidy park, a tearoom, and some shops before passing *Derwent House*. Flapping up the narrow walk with water oozing out of his shoes, he lunged at the doorbell. Nothing happened. Faint noises emanated from the bowels of the house but no one seemed interested in answering the door. After pressing the button again, Harry stepped back from the shallow porch to see if there were any signs of life in the windows. Morley was dead right on both counts. It was a very big house, typically Georgian with the ornate, white front door in the centre flanked on both sides and above by symmetrically placed sash windows. On this grey day the weathered Derbyshire limestone walls only added to the gloom. And it was ugly. Very ugly. A huge elm to his left spread out its craggy branches like arthritic fingers high over the roof, moaning as the wind and rain thrashed through its yellowed leaves. The weed-riddled, postage stamp-sized lawn looked as though it hadn't been cut for months.

Leaning forward to attack the doorbell one more time, he was interrupted by the sound of someone scurrying up the path behind him. The small chubby figure, half-buried beneath an enormous black umbrella, was muttering something. It pulled up short a few paces away, the umbrella tilted back, and the round, pink face of a young girl emerged. "Auntie Bertha doesn't use the front door. It's just fer boarders. Yer 'ave to go round back," she announced in a thick Derbyshire accent.

With that, the umbrella dropped down once more and she disappeared around the corner. Harry shrugged, scooped up his suitcase and followed the girl's bobbing backside down a narrow, stone-flagged path, through a heavy wooden door and into a small courtyard paved with bricks. The place had a bad odor which Harry couldn't precisely identify, but cat dung mixed with decaying leaves would have come close to it. In one corner an outbuilding spilled coal from its rotting door. Rain swirled down cracked drain pipes, creating puddles among the sunken bricks.

The girl quickly folded her umbrella at the back door, beckoning Harry to enter. A warm, delicious smell of cooking wafted out into the rain. As he struggled to shed his raincoat, a woman lumbered into view, drying her hands on a soiled apron. She was tall for a female, and very large. The apron, punctuated by three massive bulges representing her chest and stomach, strained at its ties. Her features testified to a life of hard physical work, but the fat, rosy face creased into a frown of concern at Harry's bedraggled state. She directed the girl towards something on the largest kitchen table Harry had ever seen. Feeling a little like Oliver Twist, he gazed at the jumble of pots and pans, vegetables, meats and pastries, all vying for space on its scrubbed surface. Amid the clutter sat a large ginger cat, seemingly unaware of the gastronomic opportunities surrounding it. A monstrous green painted cupboard, laden with crockery, sat at the far end of the kitchen. The girl, her task at the table now completed, had plunked herself down in a rocking chair beside the coal-fired stove and was scrutinizing Harry with very round, closely set eyes.

He was conscious of several puddles his wet clothing and suitcase were making. To make matters worse, the water, following the law of gravity, had begun to form a small stream. It slowly made its way along the uneven floor towards an oval mat in the centre of the kitchen.

"I'll take this," the woman said, whipping away Harry's raincoat and flapping it several times outside the door. Returning, she peered at him over her reading glasses. "You'll be our Mr. Michaels. I'm Bertha Twigg. Morley Singleton told me you'd be arriving today about this time. That's good." She smiled. "No doubt he told you about my passion for punctuality."

Harry nodded, and was about to speak but she interrupted him. "Well, it seems to me the first thing you need to do is get out of those wet clothes. What a trial, this wet weather. What a trial. Morley told you my rates, did he?" Again, without pausing for an answer, she continued, "Good, good. Well, we have a few house rules. I don't like my boarders to smoke in their rooms. No electric fires and no cooking in your room; the electricity bills would have me bankrupt in a month! I expect you to make your own bed, keep your room tidy. We change the towels and bed linen once a week and I'll do a load of washing for you once a week, too, but I won't iron suits or anything like that. If you need to press your trousers, you can borrow my ironing board. Breakfast is at seven-thirty, except for Sundays, when it's an hour later. Dinner's at six o'clock sharp every day of the week. Oh, and no visitors of the opposite sex are allowed upstairs." She added some emphasis to the last point.

Harry glanced behind Miss Twigg at the girl. She was grinning broadly.

Miss Twigg caught the glance and turned. "Oh, yes, and this here is my niece, Sarah," she said, pursing her lips when she spoke, as though she might be blowing smoke rings. "Her parents have some difficulties at the moment so she and her sister, Darlene, are helping me around the house. Lord only knows I have enough to do in this place. Like me, it's not so young as it used to be. Did Morley tell you I'm retired?"

"Er, yes. He ..."

"It's hard to retire in a house this size. But I'm too old to leave. I was born here. And both Mum and Dad died upstairs. Mum died first, and then Dad passed away a few months later. I think he died of a broken heart." She paused, then corrected herself. "Well, actually he died of a broken neck. Fell down the stairs. Would have gone all three flights if he hadn't put his head through the rails. Mind you, that was a while ago and we had the banister repaired so you don't have to worry about falling through yourself."

What a relief! Let's see, when did he last put his head through some banister rails? A couple of weeks ago? Three, perhaps? And it was so thoughtful of her to inform him that Mum and Dad had both died upstairs. He contemplated the gloomy prospect of being assigned to one of her parents' rooms, and spending night after night in a cold sweat as their ghosts danced around his bed.

Still, mustn't be cynical; for now he just hoped that the rest of the house, was as cosy as this kitchen.

The sight of Harry's shivering frame cut short Miss Twigg's reminiscing. "Are you wet all the way through?" she asked with genuine concern. "You are, aren't you?"

He tugged at his sodden shirt. "I'm afraid so."

"Of course, you must be. Sarah, take Mr. Michaels... Or is it Harry? Yes, alright. Take Mr. Harry to his room. Then bring his wet things down and I'll wash and dry them." Her flabby arms gave an expansive flourish towards the heavens. "I'm putting you over the kitchen. It's a bit warmer during the winter months."

The girl made a face and affected an exaggerated cough at her aunt's statement.

Looking through the kitchen window at the driving rain, Harry had no choice but to accept Miss Twigg's assurance at face value. That it held truth only in a relative sense would become painfully apparent later. He followed Sarah into a narrow passageway, shivering again as the warmth from the kitchen fire quickly faded.

Putting a chubby foot on the bottom step the girl swung on the banister rail to face him. "Are yer married, or anythin'?"

Harry shook his head, thinking this an odd question. Why would he be taking board and room if he were married?

Her round face broke into another grin. "Are yer goin' ter be married?"

"No. At least, not right now."

"D'y'ave a girlfriend?"

Bad question. Searching for a straw to grasp, he fleetingly thought of his sister's buxom pal, Heather, to whom he'd made an unsuccessful pass on a couple of occasions. Overall, not much to brag about. "Er... Well, sort of... No. Not at the moment," he finally confessed, putting on as brave a front as possible.

Sarah let out a satisfied sigh and proceeded up the stairs with Harry and his suitcase-full of underwear in tow. "Yer should see me sister, Darlene," she said as they reached the landing. "She's seventeen, an' she's got a job. Mind, there's a fella at the moment but she don't like 'im. I don't like 'im, and Auntie Bertha don't like 'im either. Won't let 'im in the 'ouse."

Harry's curiosity was aroused. Why would Sarah's sister persist in going out with somebody whom everyone, including Darlene, couldn't stand, for goodness sakes? But then, this seemed to be a common scenario in the mating game, he told himself. He'd found that female siblings often had rather strange relationships among themselves, entering into little conspiracies, with one acting as bagman, apologist and publicist for the other. He'd known one or two pairs of sisters during his teens who fit this description to a tee. Nothing could happen to one without the other knowing about it. They coexisted in a sort of love-hate-dependency with some hapless male rounding out the triangle.

"Why doesn't your sister like him?" he ventured to ask.

"'Cause 'e smells and 'e talks dirty all the time, and 'e's always asking 'er fer money."

"Oh," replied Harry, nodding indulgently.

They had reached the second floor when Sarah again stopped abruptly. Turning, she gave him another cheeky grin. "But 'e lends me magazines. Y'know. The ones that show yer 'ow ter do it!"

She allowed him to digest this bit of information by lapsing into another short silence. In the semi darkness, Harry could feel water running down his back. They walked down a narrow corridor, towards the open door of a lavatory. From its cistern high on the wall a long flush chain swung gently to the tune of some hidden draught. Just before reaching it, they turned right into a small vestibule punctured by three half-glazed doors. Originally, this had all been one large bedroom; during Miss Twigg's boarding house heyday, it had been converted into three. Sarah flung wide the door on the left. As she did so, a tiny piece of frosted glass from the bottom corner of a cracked pane fell out. Barely stopping, she picked it up and casually stuffed the piece back into place.

"I've done it, yer know," she said, so quietly that Harry almost missed the remark. They were both standing in front of a large, solid brass, double bed. The type for which antique hounds these days would cheerfully lay down a year's salary. Sensing trouble, he ignored the conspiratorial look on Sarah's pimply face, heaved his suitcase onto the heavy quilt, and then, realizing how wet it was, put it back on the floor.

But Sarah was not going to be robbed of her chance to make a titillating confession. "Did it wi' Len." she added.

"Who's Len?" he asked, hating himself for letting morbid curiosity get the upper hand of discretion.

She plumped herself down on the edge of the bed, legs dangling. "Darlene's fella, the one who lends me the magazines. But it 'urt, so ah wouldn't let 'im do it again." Her eyes narrowed. "It's not supposed ter 'urt, is it?"

Harry contemplated the girl for a moment. He'd never been much good at guessing a female's age, but Sarah looked to be around fourteen or fifteen and obviously a latecomer into puberty. She still had a lot of puppy fat. Shivering in his wet clothes, he was not really in any frame of mind at that moment to be offering sexual advice to under-age teenagers. In any case, like the local priest offering advice on raising children, even if he was, he would hardly be speaking from first-hand experience.

"I er... think it often does the first time," he offered, reluctantly.

Sarah's eyebrows lifted. "'Ow come?"

Red with embarrassment, he tried to remember what Doctor Waglund had offered on the topic during his annual sex education lectures at school. It might have been less of a challenge if the fellow hadn't insisted on making the process sound like painting-by-numbers.

"Skin, I think. Yes, er, I think there's a piece of skin inside... inside... Well, you know... That, er, gets broken when you do it for the first time. At least, I'm pretty sure that's what happens."

This was obviously encouraging news to the girl. "So it don't 'urt after that?"

"It's not supposed to."

She breathed a long sigh of relief while idly stroking the rumpled quilt.

"Look," Harry said abruptly, "I have to unpack and get out of these wet clothes before I catch pneumonia."

"I'll 'ang on while yer take 'em off."

"No, you won't! You go and help your aunt. I'll bring them down myself shortly."

Sarah scowled, breathed another heavy sigh, and slowly got to her feet. "'Oller if yer need another towel," she said as she left the room, adding as the door closed, "bathroom's over yonder, next ter the lav."

Dumping his suitcase on a chair in the corner, he looked around his new home. It was a far cry from the cosiness of Miss Twigg's kitchen. Once painted a light green, the walls had darkened with age to a colour reminiscent of army vehicles. Behind the door he found a cavernous wardrobe with mirrored doors facing the bed. One of the doors refused to close properly, choosing instead to creak open unexpectedly at the most inconvenient times. On the opposite side of the room was a window, which, he discovered, overlooked the courtyard through which he'd earlier entered the kitchen. On the same wall to the right of the window, a small washbasin echoed faintly to the steady drip of a leaking tap. Above it was an even smaller mirror, discoloured by years of unrelenting damp. One token picture, a stained lithograph of Scarborough's seafront, hung forlornly on the wall opposite the foot of the bed.

After a quick glance to see if Sarah had somehow slipped back in, Harry stripped off his clothes, dumped them into a pile, and shivered again. The worn linoleum floor felt ice- cold to his feet. Despite Miss Twigg's kindly gesture, little heat appeared to be finding its way up from the kitchen below. If this was the warmest bedroom in her house, he hated to think how chilly the others must be.

Fumbling in his suitcase for some fresh underwear, he was startled by a sound in the direction of the bedroom door. It remained closed but in the poor light his eye caught something that moved quickly behind the frosted panes. He yanked the door open. Although the hallway was deserted, he detected a slight warmth in the cold air, as if someone had been standing there moments before. Glancing down he spotted the tiny piece of glass that, a few minutes before, Sarah had stuffed back into place.

His wristwatch showed nearly six o'clock. Miss Twigg hadn't said anything about serving him an evening meal that day. In fact, neither Miss Twigg nor Sarah had even shown him the dining room. But feeling cold and hungry, he considered it worth a try. Pulling on a thick sweater his mother had knitted, he made his way downstairs. The dining room loomed large and sombre off the hallway to the right. And in keeping with the rest of the house, it had all the old-world charm of a dentist's waiting room. A solitary light fixture hung over the massive table, behind which stood an equally monstrous sideboard. No one was in the room. Harry sat self-consciously at one end and waited. Then he remembered his wet clothes were still upstairs. Should he sit quietly for a while and see what transpired, or go and retrieve the clothing? He could take it into the kitchen as an excuse to find out if there might be any food coming his way.

His deliberations were abruptly terminated by a crash as the doors of a small serving hatch on the opposite wall flung wide. Miss Twigg stuck her head through. "Ha! You're there," she said, and disappeared again.

Feeling like the captive audience of a Punch-and-Judy show, Harry silently watched the scurrying activity through the hatch opening. Shadows danced, accompanied by the clanking of pans. Shortly, two fat arms appeared, cradling a steaming plate. "Come and get it," commanded the headless torso. The plate was plunked unceremoniously onto the hatch shelf, and the doors slammed shut. Miss Twigg was not a woman of many words.

Harry quickly picked up the plate and had turned back towards the table when the hatch doors crashed open again.

"Tea or coffee?"

"Coffee, please," Harry replied. He'd never been much of a tea drinker, especially after dinner.

"Where's the wet things?" the voice asked.

"Sorry, I forgot them. I'll go and fetch them in a minute."

There was a grunt and the hatch doors slammed shut again.

The meal came and went: roast beef and Yorkshire pudding, gallons of dark gravy, and some rice pudding for dessert. It was good, and there was plenty of it. Miss Twigg belonged to the old school. No frills, just honest-to-goodness cooking. He poured himself another cup of coffee from the large jug she had pushed through the hatch, noting that it had been made the same way as his mother did it, by pouring boiling water over the grounds and then letting them settle to the bottom. He'd oftentimes wondered whether the British had borrowed that idea from America's frontier cowboys, or whether the innovation had diffused westward.

Sitting in solitary silence, Harry lit a cigarette, reminded himself once again that he was supposed to be quitting, and cast his eyes around at the uncomfortable room. It had once been wallpapered. Heavy stuff, like many pre-war wallpapers, with an embossed and ornate pattern. Whatever the pattern might have been, it had long ago faded into an amorphous brown haze. Miss Twigg's reluctance to renovate obviously extended to the structure. A picture rail separating the wallpaper and frieze ran along all four walls. From it, several heavy pictures hung on long cords, dusty glass reflecting dim light from the ceiling lamp. There was even an aspidistra balanced, almost self-consciously, on a dark, wooden pedestal in the window. Gracie Fields would have heartily approved. Beneath his feet, Harry could feel the softness of a scatter rug. But apart from this little oasis the room was bare to the floorboards. Once stained and polished, now they were almost black from successive coats of dark brown paint.

Indeed, it appeared that Miss Twigg had resisted the temptation to do anything much with the old house. Unfettered by sloppy makeovers, it was gradually crumbling away.

Sarah appeared in the doorway, standing, as always, with her arms hanging limply. "Ah forgot to tell yer," she said. "Mi bedroom's next t'yours."

A month later and heading into the Christmas season, Harry had settled into his new job. Dickie, sensing his latest recruit's bewilderment when it came to surveying principles, had teamed him up with Bill Lewis. Together they were designing landscape layouts for a couple of old-age homes. At least, that was the way it was supposed to work. However, Harry found that, likeable though Bill might be, he was bone idle. So Harry did the work while Bill chain-smoked and created a constant distraction with juicy office anecdotes.

He'd been assigned the desk opposite Terry Jones, just inside the main door to the office. From his vantage point he could see the stairs which connected with the corridor half a floor above. Every day, almost without fail, Dickie fell down these steps. For the life of him, Harry couldn't figure out how the man did it and, more importantly, how he avoided killing himself. But after a few months of watching his boss attempt to get through life in a sitting position, he eventually concluded that these pratfalls weren't such a bad thing after all, since they amounted to the man's only exercise, short of lifting a beer glass. Moreover, the crashing and swearing served as a sort of early-warning system, giving everyone in the office sufficient time to get back to work. Unfortunately, Dickie used the door to the back stairs much more often, and he would come barging through that one with no warning whatsoever.

Angus McGregor still had a cold. Or an an allergy. It wasn't that the rest of the office resented Angus's ailments; they had simply become so chronic that nobody took any notice anymore. So Angus dripped and wheezed every day in splendid isolation in his corner by the window. The mysterious Lol Dobson also finally appeared in the flesh, and Harry was introduced to the Living Legend by a very diffident Terry. Notwithstanding a certain cockiness, he turned out to be a very pleasant fellow. And he did indeed have a way with the opposite sex , just as Bill Lewis had claimed. Harry eventually learned a few things about interpersonal attraction from Lol, chiefly, that looks weren't everything. Lol should know. Born in east London, he was a tall man in his late forties, with balding, sandy hair, large protruding teeth, and eyes of the palest blue. Chronically shortsighted, he always wore a pair of tortoise-shell glasses, which constantly slipped down his nose. Harry never saw Lol wearing a suit that fit him. He slouched about with baggy trousers topped off by an equally shapeless jacket. Someone must have mentioned that colorful ties were trendy because he had a collection of the most tasteless things anyone could imagine, and nearly all spattered with an assortment of food stains. All in all, Harry had never witnessed a more ungainly, mismatched person in his life.

But Lawrence held one major ace in the hole: he could charm the paint off a car. No one had ever caught him at a loss for words. And even though the words were often utterly meaningless, he spoke them with such panache that women would find themselves lapping up the drivel like thirsty dogs. Especially noteworthy were Lol's telephone skills. During an age when office switchboards were mammoth contraptions of wires and plugs, often manually operated, 'getting a line out' on busy days could be as rewarding as winning the football pools. Lol never failed. He simply picked up the phone and verbally stroked the switchboard operator in his east-London accent. There was Doris, Val, Mabel and someone he always referred to as 'Babs'. It didn't matter; they all fell for his charms. Trying to pick up some pointers, Harry often eavesdropped on the conversations but seldom found anything particularly special in what Lol said. **How** he said it made the difference. It came as no surprise to Harry that Terry had adopted this odd-looking man as his role model. Even though they were as different as chalk and cheese in appearance, the two had similar egos. Unlike Lol, Terry was blessed with rakish good looks. Unfortunately he knew it, and Harry found his smooth, contrived patter with women smugly conceited. Lol wasn't conceited, just very self confident in an unassuming sort of way. Harry found it curious that both personalities achieved much the same results.

During Harry's job interview the previous month, Dickie had mentioned his intention to add a total of two new recruits to the Landscape-and-Playing-Fields staff, bringing the draughting room compliment up to seven. As it turned out, Harry was the first addition. The second arrived three weeks after Harry started work and his name was Clement Walker. Clem was something of an enigma from the beginning. Apparently Dickie had never mentioned his name in hiring discussions with senior-staff members, and there were some raised eyebrows when he quietly showed up that fateful Monday morning. While not an unfriendly individual, Clem said very little, preferring instead to observe everyone from time to time with dark brown eyes that never seemed to blink. When he did speak, it was so softly that one almost had to watch his lips. Harry put him at about twenty-five years old, although the rounded shoulders and slightly bent frame made him look older. With some exercise he could have had an acceptable build. But the weight had instead gone into an unhealthy looking flabbiness, which his pallid complexion only exacerbated. When very young, Clem's hair might have been a reddish brown. Now it was a similar colour to Lol's.

Clem seldom took a lunch break. Promptly at five o'clock, after neatly storing his draughting equipment, he would disappear into the early-winter darkness. It was months before he mentioned where he was staying. Morley of course knew the place and expressed shock and dismay. While Harry saw his new colleague as harmless enough, there was nevertheless an aura about him which hinted at some personal tragedy, as though someone, or something, had wronged him so deeply that it had scarred his very soul. From the day he arrived, Clem seemed oddly out of sorts with the environment in which he now found himself. Nearly everyone in the office interpreted this unease as snobbishness, and, without bothering to look closer, began to ignore him. But Harry saw in Clem a little of himself, particularly the lingering need for inner sanctuary, and after a few weeks the two struck up a loose friendship. It became frustratingly one-sided. During the entire time that Clem was with the department he revealed virtually nothing about himself except, perhaps, his age, and even that surfaced only as an implied remark during conversation. It was sufficient to make Harry suspect that his original estimate was off the mark by quite a few years. Finally Dickie, in one of his frenzied moments, revealed that Clem was thirty, and unmarried. Did Harry's boss know anything else about Clem? If he did, he remained uncharacteristically tight-lipped. But for those who took enough trouble to observe, there were signs, such as the uneasy familiarity between the two men, which suggested that Dickie knew far more about Clem than he was letting on. Harry noticed the signs, and they ultimately proved him correct.

THREE

Emma

Trailing cigarette ash and alcohol fumes, Dickie came bumbling into the draughting room one Friday afternoon at the beginning of December, and called Harry to join him at Bill Lewis's window. "Just take a gander at this, Harry my boy," he said, pointing down to some object on the street below.

Harry put down his pencil and walked over.

"What d'you make of that? Nice, eh?" Dickie's ferret eyes danced with conspiracy.

Standing outside Madison's chemist shop at the corner of Smedley Street and Bank Road were two women in white uniforms, austensibly engrossed in some recently completed window dressing. One of the women was tall, with greying hair and large hips. Harry could tell that the other was younger, much shorter and slimmer, with reddish hair. She stood, feet slightly straddled, with her hands clasped behind her back.

"Nice, eh?" Dickie said again.

Harry studied the pair for a moment, groping for the politically correct response. "Which one?"

"Which one?" Dickie spluttered incredulously. "Whad'ya mean, which one? The short one with the tight arse, for Chrissakes." He added emphasis by carving a shape with his stubby fingers.

Bill, peering over his reading glasses and a smoldering cigarette, joined in on the scrutinizing. Terry, who missed little, and even less connected with the opposite sex, also quickly joined the assembly and was followed by Angus, trying hard to see while rummaging for something in the map drawer.

"They both have tight arses," Bill said.

"How the hell would you know, Lewis?"

"Sorry, Boss. I keep forgetting."

Dickie pulled Harry closer and poked his finger downwards. "I'm talking about the little one on the right. Name's Emma somebody or other. The horsey old baggage on the left is our merry widow, Mrs. Johnson. She's the manager, in more ways than one. Since she put her husband six feet under the sod eleven years ago, she's managed to screw half the bloody males in this building. Horny old witch. For all I know, she might have even screwed Lewis here. She can't see a damn thing without her glasses."

Lewis, true to type, ignored the remark and impassively blew a smoke ring.

There was a short silence as the gathering contemplated the scene below. Harry wished that the girl would turn around. He had to agree with his boss; she did have a nice figure, at least from the back. And presumably the front would be equally acceptable.

"Well?" Dickie demanded again.

Well what? Harry asked himself. Dickie was a tactless clod with a knack for making subordinates feel thoroughly uncomfortable.

"Too short," Lewis said.

"They always look tight in those uniforms," Angus sniffed, before sauntering back to his desk. Over his shoulder he added, "Can't be very good for their circulation, ye know."

"Circulation?" Dickie sneered. "Who the hell cares about their circulation?"

"Very nice," Harry offered weakly.

"'Course she is, 'course she is. Just right, I'd say."

"What if she's married? Or if she's going steady with somebody?"

"No, dear boy. She's not married," Dickie assured him in measured tones, as though he might be talking to a half-wit. "And she's not going steady with anybody, believe me. She lives on a farm, for Chrissakes. They go to bed at nine o'clock on farms. No time for fooling around. I've done my bloody homework. I happen to know Mrs. J. down there and she told me all we need to know. So there y'are. Get to it."

"Er, yes. Right ho," said a blushing Harry, wondering what he was supposed to do next. Dash downstairs, race across the street and sweep her into his arms? She probably had a boyfriend, who would hear about this and beat him into dog food. And he doubted Dickie's assertion that farm people went to bed at nine o'clock about as much as the claim that everyone's nose dripped in Aberdeen. Unfortunately, trying to argue with the boss was about as futile as staring down a blast furnace. Radical Bob would always be right, and that was that. The four men stood silently while the air turned thick with cigarette smoke.

After a couple more minutes the two women appeared to have completed their appraisal of the window design. Mrs. Johnson headed for the shop door. Following behind her, Emma turned slightly towards the office window before disappearing from view. It was so quick that Harry couldn't see her face. But it struck him as odd that she would flash a glance at their particular window. While he couldn't be sure, he had a sneaking feeling that she knew they were watching her.

The exercise completed, Dickie lit another cigarette and grinned with satisfaction at the others in the group. Harry found himself mesmerized by this man's smoking habits, the most intriguing aspect being his ability to keep the cigarette ash attached, regardless of what he might be doing. They were invariably nonfiltered varieties which, as any smoker will attest, have a tendency to stick to one's lips. They always stuck to Dickie's lower lip, with the result that the cigarette bobbed vigorously when he spoke. Yet, despite this jiggling, the ash would grow to a phenomenal length before falling off. During the past five minutes Harry had watched it, wondering at what point the ash would break off and tumble onto Dickie's tie. On this occasion he reckoned it had grown to at least two inches.

"Well, there you are, Harry my boy," Dickie said, dusting himself off. "I've done my bit. The rest is up to you. We'll be expecting great things. Big things, of course, not little things, if you get my meaning. Ha, ha, ha.!"

"Hm," said Lewis, settling back onto his stool again.

"Hm," said Harry, initially failing to grasp his boss's meaning, and then when he did, sensing the redness surging again up his neck as everyone in the room grinned knowingly.

For the remainder of the afternoon he stewed silently. Each time he looked up from his work, there was Terry leering across the draughting tables at him. While Dickie's bullying style rankled, Harry's testosterone told him that a girl friend would be very good medicine. Emma certainly had a nice figure. But what if the rest looked like the back end of a bus? He wouldn't know that until he had a chance to see her more closely. The time had come to plot some strategy. Matlock had a cinema, and there was another one in Matlock Bath. He'd been to both, alone, several times since arriving in Matlock. Maybe she would go with him to a show. What was currently playing? He couldn't think. But then, Dickie had said she lived on a farm. What if it was miles away in the middle of nowhere and she couldn't stay in Matlock after work? Bus service to the outlying villages was poor, to say the least. He'd found that out first hand when Lewis sent him on a site inspection to Belper a couple of weeks previously. The bus ride took so long he thought he was going to have to stay overnight.

There was no doubt in Harry's mind that he'd been set up for this, but why? He remembered Dickie talking about introducing him to someone during his interview. Was this the same girl? Dickie wouldn't get involved in this unless he thought the introduction would amount to something. He'd more or less said as much, hadn't he? But what if this hadn't been a set-up after all? What if Dickie had merely happened to notice the two women standing down there in front of the shop and thought he'd mention it? Then there would be a very big risk of being rejected, or worse. While he'd been rejected so many times in the past, they didn't get any easier. Silly trivialities such as these swirled around in his head for the rest of the afternoon.

Having finally put aside his doubts and insecurities, Harry devised a game plan. After work he would go down to the shop on the pretext of buying some aspirins. If she wasn't wearing an engagement ring, and if she greeted him warmly, and if she wasn't terribly ugly, he would take a gamble. Otherwise, he would just buy the aspirins and beat a hasty retreat. A tooth cavity had been nagging lately, so the aspirins wouldn't be a total waste of money. He would ask her to go with him to the pictures tomorrow, it being a Saturday. Perhaps they could go for a drink afterwards if time permitted.

Five o'clock came with Harry still fretting. Terry gave him a parting grin as they donned their raincoats and left the office. He crossed his fingers and hoped that Dickie wouldn't come in for a parting shot at him. As luck would have it his door was closed and the lights turned off.

It was spitting rain as he walked across the darkened street to the brightly lit shop. He could see now that what the two women had been inspecting in the front window was a Christmas theme. All cotton wool, baby dolls and talcum powder, it was a skillful blend of seasonal spirit and commercialism. They had done a good job. Through the shop door he could see a woman customer inside, and his heart sank. He couldn't possibly ask this girl for a date with other people around. Mercifully, as he fumbled with the doorknob, the woman came bustling out, giving him a condescending smile when he stepped aside for her.

Then in an instant he was alone, and surprised to find no one behind the counter. Peering around self consciously for the aspirins, just in case, his eye caught someone who had started to appear from behind a stack of shelves. Whoever it was, he thought it must be Mrs. Johnson, ducked back again. A moment later Emma walked in from the same direction. Immediately, he could see that a hasty retreat wouldn't be necessary on account of looks. Emma was a very attractive girl, and certainly nothing like the stereotypical farmer's daughter. He estimated her height to be just over five feet, even shorter than she had appeared from his office window. Her hair, which earlier had looked to be red, now revealed itself as auburn and it curled attractively. Grey-green eyes complimented the kind of smile which suggested she knew more about you than you knew about yourself.

"Hello, Harry," she said with a delicious smile framing perfect teeth. She came around the counter and stood in front of him, hands thrust into her uniform pockets.

So he had been set up. Dickie **had** done his homework, just like he said.

"I, er, um," replied Harry. Not a good start. Someone out of view snickered. Mrs. Johnson in all likelihood. Damn her anyway.

"You're Emma," he spluttered. What a bloody silly thing to say. Of course she was.

Emma's smile broke into an extremely fetching grin. Typical female, he fumed inwardly, getting their jollies out of letting a fellow make a total ass out of himself. But what the hell, he thought, taking a deep breath, he might as well go for broke.

"I was wondering if you'd like to go to the pictures tomorrow night? I'm not sure what's playing but I can find out. Of course, I know you live out of Matlock, so that might not be convenient. So if it isn't...er... Might be too late... If you have to catch a bus or something... er, perhaps we could do something else... Go for a drunk... I mean, drink..." Harry helplessly babbled on, feeling the colour once again rising up his neck.

At this point Emma decided to put him out of his misery. "I'd love to," she said pleasantly, and with only just a trace of a Derbyshire dialect in her voice. "I have to work tomorrow but I'm off at five-thirty. I can meet you there if you like." The grey-green eyes flashed again. "If you're an Elvis fan, 'G.I. Blues' is playing at the Ritz!"

Harry was not an Elvis Presley fan. However, at this point in time he would gladly have sat through a town-council meeting if it produced a date.

"That would be great," he said, hardly believing his good fortune. "But I'll come and pick **you** up at five-thirty."

The two stood in silence facing each other for a moment, with Harry gawking as though he had just encountered an alien from outer space. Yes, he silently reaffirmed, she was indeed a extremely attractive girl. Unlike many short females who try to make themselves look taller with the highest heels they can find, Emma wore a pair of plain white, medium-heeled court shoes. The white uniform fit like a glove, with no evidence of it affecting her circulation. She used very little makeup; just a touch of eye shadow and some lipstick.

Maybe Dickie wasn't such an empty blowhard after all.

"The only problem is," she said, "I live in Elton and the last bus leaves Crown Square at nine-thirty, so I'll have to go after the picture ends. Unless you have a car."

"I wish," Harry replied.

Mrs. Johnson sidled into full view this time, flashing him a toothy smile as she checked him out. Harry returned the smile. She looked to be in her mid-fifties, a large woman who had obviously determined she wasn't going to age gracefully. Dickie's choice of the term 'baggage', while perhaps a little crude, didn't seem too far off the mark. She had squeezed herself into a uniform that was at least a size too small; everything inside was staying in place more by virtue of some sturdy corsetry than by the grace of God. Her hair, long since grey, had been dyed a rather brassy brown and permed into a mass of tight curls. Lower down, a pair of highly ornate spectacles hung off her ample bosom like two tiny Siamese ducks about to dive for fish. Completing the picture was more cosmetic jewelry than he'd ever seen in one place. Her left wrist sported an oversized watch while the other arm was covered almost up to the elbow by a pile of bangles and bracelets that jangled violently every time she moved. Too much make-up. Too much of everything. All in all, Mrs. Johnson looked like she'd been around. And around again. Harry smiled back at her as she made a contrived attempt to busy herself behind the counter.

Emma, her head cocked slightly to one side, waited patiently for him to continue. He knew this was a time for some small talk, but as usual the words had taken flight.

"Mum has a car," he said, gazing beyond Emma to the back wall of the shop.

"That's nice."

"But she lives up in Barnsley, so that's not much use to us here."

"I suppose not."

Oh, God, if only his brain would connect with his mouth once in a while.

"I hear you live on a farm?" he prattled on, clawing desperately for something intelligent to say.

"Yes, I do."

"So I suppose you go to bed pretty early?"

Emma evidently considered that a very funny remark. "Only when we run short of candles!" she replied with a laugh and a toss of her head. Mrs. Johnson added a snicker from behind the counter.

"Sorry," he stammered, "I thought that, er, well, you know, up early, milking and all that..."

After a reasonably good start, the conversation seemed to be suddenly taking a nosedive. Clearly, Dickie had screwed up on the bit of trivia about early-to-bed farming types.

"Well," Harry began again, "I'd better go. Don't want to get you into trouble."

At this, Mrs. Johnson's snickering broke into an earthy giggle. Emma, barely able to restrain herself either, looked over her shoulder and wagged her finger.

It was time to leave. With red face and sweaty brow, he pulled up the collar of his raincoat and made for the shop door.

"The picture starts at seven," Emma said, still smiling.

Damn! That should have been his line. He nodded. "I, er, us... we, should have something to eat before its time... I mean, we should have time to get something to eat before it starts."

"Lovely. So, see you tomorrow at five-thirty?"

"Er, yes. Bye."

Grabbing the doorknob, he lurched into the rainy street, casting a quick glance back into the shop as he did so. The look that the pair were exchanging couldn't be mistaken. Most certainly he had been set up. Both women had triumphant smiles from ear to ear. But where had Emma seen him before? For his part, this was the first time he'd set eyes on her. Why didn't an attractive girl like her already have a boyfriend? With those looks she could have half the young males in Matlock at her beck and call. Why him? Racing back to Miss Twigg's with these questions unanswered, he couldn't decide whether his ineptitude on this occasion had been a blessing or a curse. Not that it really mattered; she had said yes, and besides, a matter of almost greater urgency loomed at that instant: he was late for dinner.

Saturday morning dragged itself at a snail's pace into Saturday afternoon. The day would have gone a little faster if he could have slept in. But then he would have missed breakfast, his favorite meal. Initially he found Miss Twigg unyielding with meal times, as she had promised. That had come home with some force a couple of weeks before when he'd overslept after a heavy evening at the *Hanging Gate* with Terry and a couple of his harem from the teacher's-training college. The following morning had been Sunday, with breakfast at a leisurely eight-thirty but he'd missed it by a country mile. He found the dining room hatch shut tight and the kitchen silent. Not having the courage to go and grovel, the only other option was dining out. There was a fish-and-chip shop down Snitterton Lane, one of several in Matlock, which opened at noon and served very good food, all hot and steamy and wrapped in newspaper. Harry loved fish and chips, even though they were a poor substitute for his beloved bacon and eggs, so he wound up there. As time went by, this little shop, with its wooden carving of a monstrous fish perched on the roof, became a familiar grazing ground on Sundays and late nights, since they stayed open until eleven.

The day of Harry's first date was a cold one. Cold enough to snow, as they say. He hoped not. Sliding on his backside down Bank Road would only compound the fool he'd made of himself twenty-four hours earlier. And stuff like that could leave a lasting impression. By mid-afternoon a watery sun had poked sullenly through the clouds. He took it as a good omen.

To pass the time, he'd gone to the public library. Ever since his school days Harry had been fascinated with exotic and far-off places, places he hadn't a hope of seeing in his lifetime. Libraries provided fodder for the imagination, and an armchair ticket to escapism. The farther off those exotic places happened to be, the more fascinating he found them. The Matlock library was a pleasant spot, with a cosy reading room, and he'd found himself spending a good part of the weekends curled up in a warm corner next to a radiator. If Miss Twigg had ever put a fire in her dining room he would have been glad to take his books home. But she never did; the only fire in that entire house resided in the kitchen, and his ice box of a bedroom barely passed for tolerable at night, let alone during the waking hours.

Small islands held a particular appeal for Harry. Perhaps it was because they captured the essence of a lifestyle that he found decidedly wanting in England. A lifestyle of ineluctably sunny days, warm evenings, and a work ethic dictated by whim, rather than by time. Among the library's meagre travel offerings he had come across a book written by Ida Wench, entitled *Mission to Melanesia*. The author, who happened to be a nun, had spent several years in Western Samoa as a medical assistant, and she probably would have been highly flattered had she known the kind of impression her book made on Harry. Some day, he vowed, he would leave these cold and windy shores and go to live in a place like that. Apart from contracting some sort of embarrassing rash from sleeping on a beach, the experience hadn't done Miss Wench any harm.

Eventually the gathering darkness outside the library window offered a reminder that Emma would soon be off work. He pondered again what he might serve up for casual conversation. If he were Terry, the girl would be eating out of his hand by the time they reached the bottom of Bank Road. Alas, he wasn't. She obviously liked Elvis Presley, but he didn't and had no stock of Elvis-Presley trivia with which to impress her. For that matter, he couldn't see that he had much of anything to offer. Was she a soccer fan? It wouldn't matter if she was because he didn't follow sports either. And he certainly wasn't into pharmaceutical shoptalk. Since she lived on a farm, perhaps she knew about farming? But he would feel a bit silly asking a girl on their first date how the old tractor was running, or what the industry had come up with in trendy new milking machines.

Harry struggled mentally and physically up Bank Road, cursing all the while for being such a conversational cripple, and vividly recalling the last social disaster that passed for a date. In fact, it had been the one resulting in a missed breakfast. Within minutes of entering the pub, Terry, conveniently forgetting his fiancee back in Swansea, had one of the neophyte teachers eating out of his hand. Harry attempted to make conversation with the other while trying to catch the small talk pouring from his friend's lips. All in vain. Within just as many minutes she excused herself to visit the bathroom. And a while later he looked across the bar to find her thoroughly engrossed with some other fellow she'd picked up. After a couple of hours Terry and his smitten one disappeared and Harry walked home alone. In bed, with the rain beating a winter tattoo against his window for company, Harry conducted the usual post-disaster autopsy. But try as he might, he couldn't recall anything particularly profound in his colleague's chatter. So, perhaps therein lay the key. Forget the gardening and photography; concentrate instead on such stuff as lavatory-wall grafitti, Hollywood scandals, and female anatomy. And sprinkle in a few off-colour jokes for good measure. It worked for Terry and Lol. If only it could work for him.

Harry arrived at the shop with his life's dilemma unresolved as usual. Emma was waiting outside the door. Inside, Mrs. Johnson flapped about with a feather duster. She gave Harry an exaggerated wave from behind the counter.

"Mrs. J. said I could finish a bit early," Emma said as she hopped down the front steps to meet him. "We weren't busy, anyway."

Together they scurried down the steep road, Emma struggling to keep up with Harry's loping stride. After a couple of minutes, she gently tugged on his sleeve and he slowed down. It was to become a familiar routine. While trudging up the hill to meet her, he had also been stewing about where to go for something to eat before the show. There wasn't much choice aside from the fish-and-chip shops. While most served good food, they couldn't be described as *haute cuisine.* In those days Matlock had no Wimpey bars, and McDonald's hadn't even thought about crossing the Atlantic. But there was a small cafe on Dale Road called the *Blue Bird,* which stayed open until the scandalous hour of 9 PM. Although Harry had never eaten there, he'd passed by many times and he liked the name. It wouldn't have looked out of place on the waterfront of a small tropical island. The kind of tropical island he'd like to escape to some day. Humphrey Bogart and Lauren Bacall might have hung out at the *Blue Bird*, with its chintz tablecloths and small, white candles stuck into Chianti bottles. They probably didn't. But they could have. As he had told himself before, first impressions were important. They would dine at the *Blue Bird.*

"So you like Elvis Presley?" Harry asked, begging the obvious.

"Love him," Emma said happily. "He's so good-looking, don't you think? I'd just die if I ever met him. I've seen every picture he's been in. We saw *Loving You* four times!"

"Who's 'we'?"

"Me and my sister Anne."

"Oh." There was another silence as Harry strove to keep the momentum going. He was conscious of their shoes clacking sharply on the weathered paving stones, creating multiple echoes that ricocheted around the almost empty street.

Emma smiled at him. "You've probably talked to her without knowing it."

"Who?"

"Anne."

"How's that?"

"At work, when you make long-distance telephone calls. She's an operator at the Matlock Exchange. Next time, ask for Anne Callingwood. Maybe she'll sneek you a free call!"

It suddenly occurred to him that up until then he hadn't known her last name. "So you're Emma Callingwood!"

Laughing softly at Harry's latest redundancy, Emma slid her arm through his. "My, you're fast!" she replied.

After that they walked the rest of the way to the *Blue Bird* in silence. But this time it was different. This time it didn't generate the same awkwardness that he'd felt with other girls. Somehow he knew Emma wasn't expecting him to make idle conversation just for the sake of creating noise. And that put him at ease. He liked the way her teal-coloured raincoat rustled with the quick, short steps she took. It was a brisk, self-assured walk, characteristic of someone who has a well-defined place in the world, and knows it. He also became aware of a perfume that touched his subliminal senses more than his nose. It reminded him of trips to Stairfoot as a child to see his great Aunt Laura, and the Pears semi-transparent soap which she always used. Like Emma's perfume, it lingered delicately, all through the house, in the bed linen and through the huge, fluffy towels piled high in the bathroom closet— even down to the scrubbed and whitewashed cellars. He wanted to ask what the perfume was called, but decided to save the question for later.

The cafe must have known they were coming, for it was no more than half-full, and they got a table away from the drafty door. Harry helped Emma with her coat. She sat and contemplated Harry for a moment, that same secretive little smile he'd seen yesterday flickering across her face.

"You don't always go to your office by the same route, do you?" she said.

Harry looked puzzled. "No. I sometimes go up through the old winter garden. It's sort of a shortcut, except that you have to go through the quantity-surveyors' department and they don't like people using their office as a corridor."

"Ah, that's when we don't see you. You must have gone that way yesterday."

"Er, yes. As a matter of fact, I did."

Her lips broke into a cheeky grin. "Mrs. J. and I watch out for you every morning. She thinks you're cute! We place bets on which way you'll come to the office!"

So that was it. She **had** seen him before. All these past weeks the two of them must have been quietly observing him from the shadows of their shop counter. While he couldn't help feeling a little flattered by all this, there was something slightly unnerving about being systematically spied on. What kind of notes were they exchanging? Had they noticed when his trousers weren't pressed or his shoes freshly shined? What if he'd forgotten to zip up his fly? He found himself trying to remember what he'd been wearing to work for the past few weeks. It wasn't especially difficult, since he wore practically the same clothes every day.

What had been Dickie's role in this? He must know Mrs. Johnson quite well, otherwise he wouldn't be privy to their clandestine activities.

"Does Mrs. Johnson think Bob Dickie's cute?"

She gave out a short laugh. "So, you've guessed the connection, then! Probably not anymore. I think they were having an affair at one time. But his wife found out about it and came to the shop and made an awful scene. This was before my time. Mr. Jeffries... he owns the shop... told me about it soon after I started work there. Mr. Jeffries is old man Madison's son-in-law. Mr. Madison sold the shop to him fifteen years ago. He's dead now...Mr. Madison, I mean. Anyhow, Mrs. J. nearly died of embarrassment since apparently there were some customers in the shop at the time. Mr. Jeffries threatened to sack her. She was furious with Mr. Dickie for having a loose tongue. Mind you, she's hardly one to talk; she's got an even bigger tongue than him. I've seen it in action quite a few times! She still sees him now and again, I'm pretty certain. I'm sure they were in the storeroom together a few months ago. I don't usually leave the shop for lunch, but on that day I had to pick something up for Mum. When I got back, the storeroom door was locked and I'm sure I heard them in there. There was a lot of grunting and shuffling about. He probably slipped out of the deliveries door. Later, Mrs. J. came around to the front of the shop to make me think she'd been out. But she was all red and flustered, and her uniform was partly unbuttoned. So I'm pretty certain about what was going on. They still go drinking together once in a while."

The connection had finally become clear. What a hypocrite Dickie was, calling Mrs. Johnson all those wretched names, and all as though he hardly knew her. It must have been she who asked him to arrange an introduction. Mrs. J. looked like one of those people who like to generate conspiracies for the sake of being in the middle of them. Harry's Aunt Phyllis was typical in that regard, and Mrs. J. reminded him of her. Always meddling, on the pretext of doing it in everybody else's interest. But was it entirely Mrs. J's idea, or had Emma made the request? There could be little doubt of Emma's involvement, since she was obviously expecting him when he came over to the shop. And from the way she behaved it was also obvious she wasn't being dragged into this bit of intrigue against her will. That some girl, and an attractive one to boot, would go to this trouble for him was decidedly a first in Harry's scant experience with the mating game, and one he found a trifle unnerving.

He scrutinized her as casually as he could while they waited for the menu. She had very fine features which entirely complemented her petite build: a small nose which turned up ever so slightly, and a small but very full mouth with lipstick applied to perfection. Her hair looked as though it had been freshly cut and set. Was all this for his benefit, he wondered, or merely something to be expected of people in her kind of job?

"How long have you worked at the shop?" he asked.

Emma hesitated for a moment. "About three years. At least, three years this last time. Actually I went to work there after I left school." She paused. "But I'd only been there a couple of months when Dad died. So I left to help my brother and Mum on the farm for a while." The smile flickered again. "I hated it. And I don't get along too well with Brian— my brother. Brian's twelve years older than me. He's always considered the farm **his** business since Dad died, so he wasn't very pleased with Mum when she asked me to help them. We had a lot of fights. I decided it was best if I got out of the way. So after a year I went back to work for Mr. Jeffries. My sister Anne had more sense. She's never had anything to do with the farm, and she says she never will. I don't think Mum blames her. Mind you, our Anne doesn't like getting her hands dirty!"

"What was the matter with your dad?"

"Oh, he had a lot of problems," she said slowly. "He got pneumonia." She appeared reluctant to talk much about her father. And it was only after they had been going out together for several months that he found that father and daughter had not been very close.

John Callingwood had entered the merchant marine at the outbreak of the Second World War and spent three wretched years on the Atlantic convoys, sailing vessels which today wouldn't even be allowed to leave port. Harry learned that this frail man had not only survived the sinking of his first ship less than a year after entering the service, but had also managed to survive when his second ship was torpedoed six months later. In both cases he had wound up in the water. On the second occasion flaming bunker oil left him with burns to his arms and shoulders, which never completely healed. Harry couldn't help but admire the man's courage in taking on an occupation which must only have aggravated his injuries. After discharge from hospital and a year's convalescence, he purchased the smallholding in Elton and developed it into a dairy operation. In July, 1956, six years after Harry's own father had died of polio, John Callingwood contracted the double pneumonia that killed him.

As they ate, and Emma poured tea for them both, Harry found himself doing some mathematical deductions to determine her age. She had the sort of features which change very little over time, and he had a sneaking suspicion that she might be older than he. Either his mental processes were utterly transparent or Emma was clairvoyant, because she saved him further trouble.

"You can relax., Harry," she said with a grin. "You're five months older than me! Mrs. J. found out."

"You were born in 1939?"

"Yes, but only just. And on one of the most important days of the year, too."

Harry couldn't think of any day that had any particular importance over the others, for him at least. "What day would that be?"

"Christmas day, of course! Yours is in July, isn't it?"

"July twelfth. On a Thursday, and in the middle of a thunderstorm, so I'm told. You know what they say about Thursday's child?"

"No, what?"

"Thursday's child has far to go. At least that's what the little rhyme says on the side of a biscuit tin my mother has."

"Is that a fact!"

"Yes. Well, I don't know it as a fact, just what it says on the biscuit tin."

"Bet you don't know the rest of the rhyme."

"I'll bet I do!"

"Prove it."

"Alright, then, I will." Harry cleared his throat and self-consciously recited the entire rhyme, word for word:

Monday's child is fair of face,
Tuesday's child is full of grace,
Wednesday's child is full of woe,
Thursday's child has far to go,
Friday's child is loving and giving,
Saturday's child works hard for its living.
And the child who is born on the Sabbath day, is bonnie and blythe and good and gay.

"I'm very impressed!" Emma said approvingly. "**Have** you gone very far as a Thursday's child?"

Harry smiled shyly. "Not yet. Unless moving from Yorkshire to Derbyshire could be considered far, which it probably wouldn't."

"Mrs. Johnson mentioned that you're from Yorkshire. Whereabouts?"

"Barnsley, about halfway between Sheffield and Leeds. Sometimes known as 'mucky Barnsley.'"

"Mucky Barnsley! Why's that?"

"Coal mining. Barnsley's a coal mining town. It's nearly all coal mining in that part of Yorkshire. Everything comes with a layer of soot on it."

"Your dad's not a coal miner though?"

"Good lord, no! He was a chartered accountant, and he died of polio when I was nine. I never really knew him. That nursery rhyme was right on the mark for my mother, by the way. She's a Saturday's child. Since Dad died she's worked her backside off trying to keep a roof over our heads."

"I'm sorry," Emma said, giving him another long look while she toyed with her fork. He was a good-looking fellow, on the lanky side to the point of being skinny. Grey-blue eyes, a quiet voice, and a shy smile that would have looked quite at home on the wrapper of some food product. What intrigued her most was the way he addressed life with a sort of choirboy innocence that could instantly fire the mothering instinct in any woman with eyes to see and ears to listen. But she wondered if the tongue-tied, foot-in-mouth routine was real, or artfully cultivated. While his antics seemed almost too slapstick to be genuine, they clearly frustrated him, and she could tell that he perceived his awkwardness as a serious obstacle to success. Yet, in spite of all this she detected a tough resilience beneath Harry's self-effacing persona. He didn't have to tell her he had once been very unhappy; she could see it in his face.

"That's okay," he replied. "It was a long time ago."

"Mrs. J. also told me you went to a posh public school. Was it really as stuffy as they say in the novels?"

Harry briefly pondered this question. He'd never looked upon his dismal boarding-school years as being stuffy. Plenty of other adjectives would have made a more fitting description. But stuffy? No. Definitely not stuffy.

"Not really. I suppose boarding schools are okay if you're athletic and you happen to be liked by everyone. I wasn't, and my dad had just died. When I think back, I can see that those who did really well were fellows who had got the system figured out. They did everything by the book, joined the right teams, the right clubs, did extra prep, etcetera. So even if they weren't too bright, the masters would look the other way. I've never been a team player and I certainly never got the system figured out, so I wound up just closing in on myself. It wasn't a very good experience, for them or for me! Mum felt she was doing the best thing, getting me a decent education, and it took a lot of her savings. Pity, because she really wasted her money."

"You mean the teachers would alter exam scores and things like that for their favourites?"

"Oh, certainly they did. I saw it happen several times. But it was really more the overall environment. You know what they say, nothing breeds success better than success. Once those chaps had been accepted into the system it just swept them along, and their parents made sure it all happened. Mum wasn't much good at that sort of thing."

Emma's brow furrowed. "**What** sort of thing?"

"School politics. Marching down there and reading the riot act to them. That sort of thing."

"Oh. Did you get any 'A' levels?"

Harry burst out laughing. "They threw me out when I was fifteen. Well, actually, it was just before my sixteenth birthday. For a while I had this idea of joining the Shell Oil tanker fleet and training to be a navigation officer. But I couldn't do math to save my life. Perhaps it was a good thing. Being at sea all the time must be hard. I should know. I seem to have been at sea most of my life, and I've never set foot on a boat!"

"What did you do then?" Emma asked, relieved to find that she didn't have a precocious young Einstein on her hands. In her circumscribed world of windswept villages and marginal farming, high-blown aspirations were topics of scorn; people who stuck out their necks too far were likely to get them chopped off.

"I liked gardening at school. The masters noticed it, and decided it might be something a useless clod like me could get into without too much brainpower. I went along with the idea, largely because I thought they might leave me alone if I did. At least it didn't require tons of math and the work would be mostly outdoors. Or so I imagined!" He smiled wryly at the thought of his new job, and the contractors who smirked behind his back when he came on site looking like a shoe salesman. How many times had he been tempted to say "I can do that physical work just as well as you people. In fact, I wouldn't mind trading places." And the mathematics he thought he would never need? Well, did he ever get that wrong. Nothing, it seemed, had worked out the way he had planned.

"Did you go to college? I mean, you must have learned to draw before you got this job."

Harry laughed again. "Would you believe, draughting was the one thing I didn't have a scrap of training for! But, yes, I did go to college. At least, to a farm institute. When I applied they told me I would need two years' practical experience first. So I went to work as an apprentice in our town parks department. Turns out, those were two of the best years I've ever had."

Emma wrinkled her nose. "What, getting all filthy every day? That's one of the things I didn't like about our farm. I didn't mind the work; it was the smell I couldn't stand. It seems to soak through your clothes. Even after a bath I could still smell cow poop."

"Oh, not me," Harry replied. "I enjoyed it. Three pounds ten a week and no worries... except having to live at home." Then the smile faded. This was something that still bothered him. While he'd been happy to live at home to save money, the best part of this new job had been getting away. After all, he was an adult and surely could choose his place of residence. But while he knew he hadn't done anything wrong, the thought of leaving his mother alone nagged constantly. Like a piece of dirty toilet paper stuck to one's shoe, it refused to go away.

"Our parks department had an old quarry which had been turned into a flower garden," he continued, brushing his guilt under the rug. "A path went through the middle and in spring each side was planted up with thousands of flowers. For some reason the outside staff did one side, and the inside staff—that was the crew I was with— did the other. I'm not sure why because we normally just took care of the greenhouses. Anyhow, this thing had developed into an annual contest, to see who could plant their side the fastest. Problem was, the local delinquents used to hide up in the rocks and shoot at us with air rifles. What puzzled me was that they only shot at certain people, such as our foreman, for example. He got a pellet up his backside nearly every spring. Of course, as soon as the shooting started, there would be mass chaos. Some of the kids usually got caught and they'd get dragged behind the rocks and given a good pounding. Then the police would come down and there'd be another big brawl. It was hilarious."

Emma clearly failed to see much humour in having an air-rifle pellet pried out of one's bottom. Her eyes widened with concern. "Did they ever shoot at you?"

Harry shook his head. "No, they never bothered with the younger staff. It was the older ones who got it all the time. The delinquents probably thought the old gardeners wouldn't be able to catch them. But one or two could whip up those rocks pretty fast when they got mad enough. The worst part about it all was that half the bedding plants got wrecked. I don't suppose anything like that happens in Elton."

"Well, no one's shot anybody. But a pig got loose a couple of years ago."

"A pig?"

"A very big pig called Luvvy. She belonged to a farm down the road. They left the gate open one weekend and Luvvy went for a walk. But when they tried to catch her she got all upset and started charging after people. Then she ran into Mayhew's vegetable garden and started eating everything in sight. Mr. Mayhew was so mad he went to get his shotgun. Fortunately Luvvy took off before he got it loaded. By teatime just about everybody in the village had got into the act. It was sort of sad in a way, because the following week she went to the abattoir. We all decided that it had been a final fling."

Emma obviously enjoyed listening to anecdotes; she had listened to the entire story without yawning or excusing herself. Harry was on a roll. He decided to toss out the one about the cockroaches.

"In the autumn I had to wash thousands of pots with nothing more than a worn out scrubbing brush and cold water," he said, tucking into his dessert. "Afterwards we put them in rows on the greenhouse heating pipes to dry. The worst part was when we had to fetch them out again."

"Why?"

That was exactly what she was supposed to say.

"Because cockroaches used to nest in them. We'd pull them off the pipes in long stacks and carry them over to the potting shed on our shoulders, and they would crawl out and down our necks!"

Emma's nose wrinkled again. "That's disgusting!"

"Do you know, Mac, our foreman, put me in charge of a greenhouse when I was seventeen."

"Oh," she replied with her mouth full.

Pride welled up in Harry's voice. "I was the youngest person on the inside staff to have ever been put in charge of one of the main greenhouses."

Since the finer points of operating a municipal parks department were, as might be expected, totally beyond Emma, she simply nodded as she ate. But Harry couldn't let his favorite topic go without a bit more elaboration. "I had to do all the watering and routine care of the plants," he continued. "We had eight thousand geraniums in that greenhouse each autumn, all taken from cuttings.

Mac must have had some faith in me because I could easily have killed them with too much or too little water. And once the geranium stock plants had been pulled out of the flower beds in October, we couldn't get any more cuttings to replace those which died. So there was a fair amount of responsibility." Harry sniffed happily at the memory. "Boy! On sunny days those geraniums smelled absolutely glorious. 'Course, that was another good part about being in charge of a greenhouse: I could find lots of excuses to stay inside when the weather turned cold!"

All through the meal Emma listened patiently. And as they were about to leave for the cinema it occurred to Harry that he had never been so relaxed with a girl before. He would come to know that listening comprised one of Emma's greatest virtues, and one which would be sorely tested in the months ahead. People who read a lot tend to be good listeners; Emma had an insatiable appetite for books. Mostly novels, to be sure, but a surprisingly wide array of topics interested her. Unlike Harry, who yearned to experience what his reading unearthed, Emma, in her typically pragmatic fashion, had come to terms with her lot in life. She would never do much beyond working in a shop, and she knew it. So she read about the world around her, and that was good enough.

They could tell from the gaggle of people lined up outside the cinema that it would be crowded. After just squeezing in they wound up seated behind a post in the stalls. Not that it mattered to Emma, who clearly wasn't the only Elvis Presley fan in town. The building reverberated to the squeals of delight from several hundred captivated females. Elvis's hips were in fine form, his carefully coiffured hair fresh from an oil change, the Technicolor superb. The Matlock Ritz was one of a dying breed of British cinemas still operating a theatre organ. Before the show, and during intermissions, this pride of the Wurlitzer company would rise dramatically from the depths of what was once an orchestra pit, swathed in neon light, the organist's foot clamped firmly on the swell pedal. Harry loved its soaring, expansive sound. Nothing, in his estimation, could beat a theatre organ for rolling an entire orchestra into one instrument.

Afterwards they ducked in to a quaint little pub off Causeway Lane called the *The Laughing Dog* for a quick drink before Emma's bus left. A huge fire roared in the pub's stone fireplace and for a change on a Saturday night they found somewhere to sit. Emma could never be described as a drinker, but she was very partial to shandies which, like any other pint, take a while to finish. She sipped; Harry had a second pint. And while the fire crackled and the background chatter waxed and waned, they talked about everything and nothing. He knew she was going to miss her bus. But as he sat, watching the time inching closer to nine-thirty, his alter ego was telling him to stay put. He didn't really want her to go, did he? So why be such a hypocrite? Let her miss the damned bus. Then she wouldn't have any choice.

When Emma finally looked at her watch and gave out a little shriek, the crisis became very tangible.

"Oh, my God," she groaned. "Have you seen the time?"

It was twenty minutes to ten. Harry's alter ego, ever the Judas, had been quick enough to set him up, and now it just as quickly deserted him. To that point their date had gone perfectly. Why did he have to go and blow it at the end, especially after initially making such a good impression? From knight in shining armour to irresponsible clod in four hours. And who knows what her mother would think. It was so typical; he never knew when enough was enough.

While a very distraught Emma flailed with her coat, Harry jumped to his feet. Grabbing her hand they raced down to the bus stop. But even before they left the pub he knew it would be a lost cause. There wasn't a soul within half a mile.

"Are there usually other people waiting for this bus?" he asked, scanning the empty street.

Emma nodded. "Especially on a Saturday night." Biting anxiously on her lower lip, she peered into the blackness beyond the bus-stop sign and added, "I've missed the blessed thing, I know it."

Harry fidgetted with his coat belt. "Are you sure that's the last bus?" It was a silly question. She had been using it five nights a week for the past six years.

"I **know** it's the last bus, Harry. It leaves at nine-thirty, all year round. Mum goes nuts when I don't show up."

Time to start grasping for straws. "Is there anyone in Matlock you can stay with overnight?" he ventured. "Then we could give your mum a ring and let her know where you are."

She shook her head. "No, except Mrs. J. And she's probably in bed with some bloke already. And I can't ring Mum because we don't have a telephone."

Things did not look promising. Pulling up his collar, Harry glanced upwards. It was cool, with a few stars dotting the night sky. A watery half-moon bathed the pavement in its green glow. He could see Emma starting to shiver and again he cursed his stupidity. Then, as panic began to set in, a light bulb, albeit a **small** light bulb, flashed somewhere in Harry's brain.

"How far did you say it was to Elton? "

"About five miles."

Harry took a deep breath. "We could walk. I'll walk there with you and then walk back."

Emma turned and studied his face for a few seconds without saying anything.

"It's a clear night and there's a moon out, so we can see where we're going," he continued, warming to his brilliant idea. "And it's Sunday tomorrow so neither of us have to go to work."

"I said it's five miles, love. Have you ever walked five miles?"

"Lots of times," Harry said, truthfully. "Haven't you ever walked home before?"

She laughed. "No, Harry, I haven't." Then she looked down at her feet, and then at his. "There's another small problem. You're wearing a pair of solid shoes. I'm wearing heels."

Undeterred, he grabbed her hand again. "They're not **very** high heels, and we can walk slowly. Let's go."

"Harry..." she began. Then words seemed to fail her.

So they walked. Although little did she know it at the time, this would be the first of many long walks together. They set off briskly in the December moonlight, over Matlock bridge into Snitterton Lane and up the winding little road to the B5057. Looking over the bridge he could see the River Derwent, black as Indian ink, churning its timeless course through the town centre. A few hundred yards farther on the road rose into another slight hump as it spanned the deserted railway line from Buxton. Harry quickly got into his stride and it wasn't long before a hand tugged gently at his sleeve. He slowed down.

Emma knew this territory like the back of her hand. Houses and shops were soon replaced by a patchwork of fields contained by the familiar low stone walls. As they continued climbing, the air became cooler. Inside their raincoats, they both felt more than warm enough. Her low-heeled shoes were holding up well. Water gurgled through the grassy ditches, on its downward journey to the river. Out in the dew-drenched fields only a few impoverished hawthorns broke the skyline.

"Anne lives at home with us, but she spends a lot of time with her boyfriend," Emma said, making conversation as she puffed along at his side. "According to Anne, he's a mechanic." She sniffed. "He's a bit of a twerp, actually. And I don't think he's much of a mechanic. The last time he fixed our tractor Brian had to take it somewhere else afterwards, so it ended up costing him twice as much to get it done right. Bit of a twerp is Bruce, I think."

"Where does he live?" Harry asked, wondering if, twerp or not, Bruce might be close enough to offer some transportation.

"Winster. We go through Winster before we get to Elton. He lives in this dumpy little place his mum and dad made for him out of an old tractor shed. Anne took me there once. It smelled awful." Emma shook her head. "I don't know about our Anne. She does the dumbest things. She's always done dumb things."

"Is Anne younger than you?" He had to confess to a mild curiosity about her sister. Earlier he'd got the impression that Anne was a bit of a loose cannon. Someone, probably his mother, had once said that the youngest siblings tend to cause the most trouble in a family, especially if a large number of children are involved. It sounded like something Mother would have read in *Woman's Weekly*.

"No, she's two years older than me."

"Do you have any other brothers or sisters?" Harry persisted.

"No, just Brian. He and Anne are more than enough as far as I'm concerned."

So much for *Woman's Weekly*.

It was around that point that his luck ran out, too. With silence finally gaining on conversation, the moon abruptly disappeared and Harry felt the first spatters of rain. Pulling his raincoat collar more tightly about him, he let out an audible groan. With at least another hour of walking ahead of them this was the last thing they needed. The rain would be bad enough, but without the moon they could hardly see their feet, let alone where they were going. Walls and trees and barns quickly dissolved into a fuzzy blackness. Emma said nothing. She plodded on with singular purpose as the raindrops became more persistent.

"When do we sight human settlements again?" he asked, pulling his left foot out of the ditch.

"Wensley. It's about three miles from here, on the main road."

By 'main road,' he assumed she was referring to the B5057, which couldn't be much more than a paved lane. And three miles sounded a long way.

"Perhaps someone will give us a lift."

Emma snorted. "How many cars have passed us so far?"

He contemplated the empty road. "Good point. But there's always a chance."

She snorted again. "Harry, this isn't Piccadilly Circus, this is the middle of the Derbyshire moors. There are more cows up here than people, especially at this time of day."

"Yes, of course. I'm sure there would be," replied a chastened Harry.

"This lane's used mostly by farmers around here to get into their fields, so we're not likely to see many cars. On the other hand, we're not likely to get run down by one, either!"

Even before the one-street village of Wensley hove into view, it was pouring heavily. They could make out the usual jumble of houses, low-roofed, darkened, and uninviting, sending a chill through his cold limbs. Emma made for the covered gate of Wensley church in the forlorn hope that the torrent might be just a shower. But Mother Nature had other plans. A cold wind began to pick up, driving the rain into their increasingly wet clothing. In the light of a solitary street lamp he could see the water gathering into gigantic puddles.

Hunched over, he studied the rain as it swept across his line of vision. "Have you noticed that it's raining horizontally?" he asked, trying his best to be upbeat about their predicament.

Emma ignored him. "I suppose when we get to Winster I could see if Anne's at her boyfriend's. Bruce has a van. If it's working, and that's a big 'if', maybe he could run us home. He's got one of those vans that don't have any windows in the sides. Apparently you don't pay as much tax on them. It's like riding in a sardine can and it smells worse than his house. On second thought, I think I'd rather be wet."

Harry peered out from under the shelter. "It might stop soon. You never know. Why don't we hang on for a few more minutes?"

"No, I think we should get going again. We're just getting chilled to the bone standing here."

He could tell from the tone of her voice that it would be pointless to argue, so they set off, only to find they were now walking into the wind. Moaning like a wounded animal, it hurled the rain at them, icy drops stinging their eyes as they squinted into the blackness. His raincoat, once snug and warm, had long since given up any pretense at keeping out the water. He could feel his skin reacting to a cold damp seeping through into his tweed jacket. Emma must have been just as wet, but she never complained as she led them both along the narrow road. Glancing across at her frozen face, he wished the ground would swallow him up. What a disaster. Only a few short hours earlier they had been blissfully admiring Elvis's suntan. Now they were in the middle of a black hell, trying their best to catch pneumonia.

On each side broken-down stone walls stretched endlessly ahead. And still not a single vehicle had passed them in either direction.

"This road doesn't go anywhere important," she patiently explained after Harry had made this observation for the second time. "None of them go anywhere important around here."

"I don't suppose there is a faster way?" Harry asked, tactfully. He could hear Emma's teeth starting to chatter.

"Actually, we could have taken a different route. You go down Dale Road... that's just past Miss Twigg's... then onto a lane that eventually joins up with the B5056. But it's even quieter. This way at least there's some hope of a car or a lorry picking us up; the other way there's none at all. The other way's nice in summer, though."

"Oh, I see." Harry couldn't find much encouragement in this information, nor relevance either, for that matter. The moors might indeed be a veritable lotusland in summer, but this was eleven o'clock on a very wet December night.

They slogged through Winster, not quite as small but just as deserted as Wensley except for a solitary dog which briefly raced out from around the back of the *Miner's Standard*, yapping excitedly. After dancing about their feet for a few seconds it disappeared in the same direction it had come. The pub was closed, the gloomy shops that lined the road, were closed. The entire village was closed. Through the darkness he could make out a jumble of stone cottages scrambling up the hillside on the left-hand side of the main street. Only one had a light in the window. They paused under the old market hall to catch their breath, Harry stamping on the stone-flagged floor in a vain attempt to warm his feet. The stones gave out a sound similar to a tuning fork, suggesting cellars underneath.

By now they were both becoming tired. It would have been an easier walk had the terrain been reasonably flat. But this was low-peak country, miles of shallow limestone hills and rocky scree, nearly all of it exposed to the full force of the weather.

A fork in the road loomed up, which Emma proclaimed to be the more often travelled B5056. Sure enough, a couple of minutes later a car approached, going in the opposite direction. Harry cursed under his breath, telling himself that it would probably been the only vehicle they saw that night. It was. Ten minutes later, however, Emma suddenly veered to the left and down another narrow lane, even darker than the roads they had been on earlier. Eventually a light appeared ahead. Harry's soggy spirits rose a little. Since it didn't appear to be moving, he assumed the source had to be either a house or a street lamp. As they drew closer he could see that it was indeed a solitary street lamp, standing vigil over a narrow intersection bordered by high stone walls.

"We're just about there," she whispered, squeezing his arm. Then, pulling closer to the glow of the lamp, she looked at her watch and began to laugh.

"What's the matter?" Harry asked.

"You won't believe this but it's taken us about fifteen minutes longer than the bus! And in the pouring rain, too!"

"My God, it must be an awfully slow bus."

"Well, actually the bus goes at a good clip, but it doesn't go the same way we've just come. After leaving Matlock it goes up the A6 and turns onto the B5057, goes through Darley Bridge and Wensley and Winster, and then up the B5056 to the A6 again. We call it the 'scenic tour'. There's one place where I swear I could get off, hop through a couple of fields, and be sitting waiting when it comes past half an hour later! I meet it at the end of the lane we just came up."

Harry only half listened to her lengthy explanation. After another several hundred more yards of darkness they turned in to a large farmyard. Assuming it to be where Emma lived, his stomach tightened with apprehension. How was he going to explain all this to her mother? The house, long and low, with a chimney stack at each end, crouched beneath a massive, sagging roof. A light burned in one of the curtained windows. Stumbling a little on the uneven stone flags, he noticed for the first time how much noise his waterlogged shoes were making.

Seconds later they both stood in the kitchen, looking like a couple of drowned rats. Harry's saturated raincoat and trousers were stuck together as though they might have been glued. Emma hadn't fared any better. Even a recent perm was no match for the soaking it had received. Her hair hung in bedraggled strips, the water joining up with other little rivulets that dripped steadily into a widening pool at their feet. Harry also noticed what women have always known: mascara is not entirely waterproof. Emma's had smudged badly and was now beginning to congeal into thin streaks beneath her eyes. A casual observer would have been forgiven for thinking she'd been on the losing end of a pub brawl.

"That was fun, love," she said, blowing a large water droplet off the end of her nose. "Let's do it again!" Then she looked down at her shoes and let out a low moan. "Christ, I only bought these a couple of months ago. Look at them. They're ruined."

The shoes certainly looked to be in a sorry state, but so were his, and nothing he could say was likely to make the situation any better. As he stood, watching the puddle spread, he couldn't help thinking that this scenario was eerily reminiscent of his first day at Miss Twigg's.

A reluctant kitchen fire burned against the far wall. From where they were standing it might as well have been ten miles away. He wished he could get a little closer without looking too selfish, even though the improvement would have been minimal; in keeping with Britain's fondness for inefficiency, the fireplace was sending most of its heat, and there was precious little to begin with, up the chimney.

Upon hearing all the noise, Emma's mother cautiously appeared at the top of the stairs. In the shadowy light, Harry could see her peering over the banister rail at them. For a moment he considered putting on a brave face and offering a cheery 'good evening,' but decided instead to let Emma do all the talking. She knew her mother much better than he did.

"My goodness, you two," Mrs. Callingwood exclaimed, "Did you fall in the pond?"

"No, I doubt we'd be this wet if we had," Emma replied with icy sarcasm.

Reaching the bottom of the stairs, Mrs Callingwood let out a gasp. Suddenly there were hands everywhere, removing clothing and ushering the bodies underneath to a warmer spot. Some towels materialized and were divided equally.

"Mum, this is Harry." Emma said from under one of them.

"I gathered that," Mrs. Callingwood replied coldly. "You missed the bus, didn't you?"

The head under the towel nodded.

"So you walked home?"

The towel nodded again.

"That's a long walk, even on a summer's day. Whose bright idea was it?"

Emma proceeded to offer some convoluted explanation of events but her mother had already decided for herself. She gave Harry the type of look reserved for children who have just gone and played in the mud in their best clothes. Thoroughly uncomfortable, Harry flapped about with one of the towels, uncertain whether he should take off any more clothes or just continue dripping onto the kitchen floor.

Emma's mother was a stern-looking woman, with coarse features that reflected a lifetime of hard work, eking a living from a few milk cows. Tall and ungainly, with large limbs and calloused hands, she looked much older than her fifty-six years. She also had a very large nose; but for all its size she breathed mostly through her mouth, which always seemed to be open. Harry could see no physical resemblance between her and Emma.

Whether caused by chronic worry, or by her ill-fitting glasses, or both, Mrs. Callingwood's face had been squeezed into a perpetual frown. And she frowned a lot tonight. She frowned at Emma, and she frowned much more at Harry.

"Well, obviously your friend can't go back to Matlock tonight," she said. "He'll catch his death of cold."

Harry let out a silent sigh of relief.

"You can put him in Brian's old room. And he can borrow your father's dressing gown. I had it dry-cleaned after he passed away and it hasn't been used since. I think it's in Brian's wardrobe. In case either of you want a hot bath, I'll turn on the immersion heater."

Once again the towel nodded vigorously, so her mother went and flicked a switch by the sink and a large red light above it flashed on. Harry watched this with a certain amount of interest since his grandparents had a similar contraption. It was devices such as these, clumsy and hopelessly inefficient, which helped to explain why British industry was losing ground to foreign competition, he had decided. Early immersion heaters had no thermostat, so the red light was supposed to remind the user that it was turned on. In fact the heater itself gave a much more forceful reminder. As the water inside the tank began to boil, it would commence a loud banging which could easily be heard next door. Occasionally the tanks would explode, showering their hapless owners with shrapnel and scalding hot water.

The mopping up more or less completed, Mrs. Callingwood headed towards the stairs, then paused for an afterthought on the top step.

"Brian's bed hasn't been aired for a while so you might want to use the warming pan, Emma. Mind you don't use coals that are too hot, otherwise you'll scorch the sheets."

Then, with all the instructions completed, she went back to bed.

"Mum doesn't mean to be unfriendly." Emma explained after emerging from the towels. "It's just that she has to get up at 4.30 in the morning to see to the milking."

That might be so, Harry thought, but it was patently obvious that her mother had been less than overjoyed to see him. He wondered if there might be more to her displeasure than his ill-advised decision to walk her home. Emma assured him there wasn't.

"Mum's always like that," she whispered. "At least, she's been like that since Dad died. I think she worries a lot about the farm. Brian thinks he knows everything there is to know about farming. He spends money on stuff we can't afford. Dad always paid the bills on time, but Brian keeps people waiting and Mum doesn't like that. Some of them are people we've known for a long time. This past spring Brian went out and bought a new milk cooler on time and I think he's behind in his payments. I don't know why Mum doesn't put her foot down with him because the farm went to her when Dad died and it's still in her name."

"Where **is** your brother?" he asked cautiously. Obviously Brian wasn't around; otherwise Harry wouldn't be using his bedroom for the night.

"Oh, he got married a year ago." Emma lowered her voice another notch. "He had to. Got Beth in the family way. Poor Mum, she nearly died of embarrassment. It was a girl... the baby, I mean. But he's happy now and so is Beth, I think. They're renting a house just down the lane. We walked past it."

In that weather, Harry wouldn't have known if they had passed Buckingham Palace. Besides, right now he just wanted to get out of his wet clothes, have a hot bath, and go to bed. And wouldn't Emma make a wonderful substitute for the warming pan? He wondered fancifully how long it might take to persuade her to go to bed with him. Was she still a virgin? The thoughts flitted through his head as he warmed himself before the sulky fire, soon to be rendered even sulkier by the removal of half its hot coals for the warming pan.

The farmhouse didn't seem to have many lights. Wires running down the walls here and there indicated that, like the *Hanging Gate* pub and hundreds of other buildings in the area, electricity had arrived only recently. Emma led him upstairs to Brian's bedroom, drew the curtains and hauled out her father's dressing gown. There was no mistaking that it had been dry-cleaned; the smell of naphtha still lingered.

"Bathroom's downstairs, around the back of the stairs," Emma said. "Until five years ago we only had a privy outside and a tin tub in the kitchen. The privy was cute. Two seats and no waiting! But, wow, did it stink during the summer! Dad finally had the pantry under the stairs converted. It's small, really small. Still, it's better than the old tin tub. You go first, but try not to use too much water because the tank isn't very big and the heater takes a dog's age to warm up. I'm going to change and then I'll go and sit by the fire until you're done. Bring your wet things down with you. If we put them on the clothes horse they should be dry by tomorrow morning."

She disappeared into an adjacent room, leaving Harry to the sound of the winter fury outside. It was still raining heavily. Borne on wind that roared down from the peaks, it rattled with the staccato of a machine gun against the window panes. Periodically he could see the curtains fluttering as the gusts found their way through cracks and crevices. His bedroom was very small, and so cold that steam rose gently from his wet skin. The ceiling sloped off in every direction, forcing him to bend almost double to see out of the tiny sash windows. Not that there was much to see, except a small yard light, the rain, and a flock of dancing shadows. After stripping naked and towelling some warmth into himself, he pulled on the late John Callingwood's dressing gown, gathered up his wet clothes, and went downstairs. Emma was huddled a couple of feet from the fire, her tousled head poking above a very large terry-towel robe. The sight quickened his pulse. For some reason he had always found small women in large cuddly bathrobes particularly appealing. It worked well for movie stars, and Emma improved hers tremendously. He approached cautiously, still unsure whether she was angry with him over the long walk and the soaking.

"Emma, I'm terribly sorry about all this," he began lamely.

She laughed softly, reaching out and pulling him over to her side. "It wasn't your fault, Harry. Besides, the walk turned out to be good exercise and they say rainwater is good for your hair! Only problem is..." She looked down at her reddened feet. "I've got a blister on each heel the size of a half-crown! That means Elastoplasts for a few days. Ever tried wearing shoes with elastoplasts on your heels?"

Harry confessed that he hadn't. He started to apologize again.

"It's alright, honestly," she insisted. "What's done is done." Then, pointing to a small door on the far side of the kitchen, she said, "Bathroom's over there. I've put another towel inside if you need it. Remember, not too much water!"

With that she hung his clothes, along with some of hers, on the large wooden clotheshorse. He watched, slightly embarrassed, as his briefs and socks joined company with her underwear on the same rail. Then she pulled a very large brass warming pan off a hook on the wall and with a pair of heavy iron tongs began to fill it with burned coals from the fire. They glowed a dull red beneath their mantle of grey ash. She handled the pan with an easiness borne of practice.

"While you have your bath, I'll see if I can set your bed on fire," she said, snapping the pan lid shut.

Did her remark have a double meaning, he wondered? There was absolutely no doubt in his mind that she could set his bed on fire without the warming pan and was tempted to say so. But for a first date he had perhaps pushed his luck far enough, although probably not in the direction intended. So he took his hot bath, in about three inches of water, grateful for the extra towel. Emma wasn't exaggerating when she said it was a small bathroom. Half the space was taken up by an ugly copper hot water tank which sat on a crudely made platform at the end of the bathtub and rumbled ominously. But at least it kept the room warm; the kitchen seemed like an igloo by comparison.

He found Emma emptying the coals out of the warming pan when he re-emerged. That fluffy bathrobe fascinated him. Was she wearing anything underneath it? The pale-pink bra and panties hanging on the clothes horse suggested not. If only this were the right place and the right time, which it wasn't, it would have been worth a king's ransom to climb inside that bathrobe with her. Some day, if he could just refrain from making a fool out of himself every chance he got, perhaps he might.

"Your bed will stay warm for a while. The mattress and quilt are both downfilled," she said. "The immersion heater takes a while to heat up enough water for my bath so I've made some tea and there's some of Mum's biscuits in the tin. What do you take in your tea?"

Harry brightened at the prospect of something to eat. Biscuits weren't much, but better than nothing. "Milk and half a teaspoonful of sugar," he replied.

They sat by the fire and drank their tea. Harry had anticipated that, being a farmer's wife, Emma's mother would whip up delectable biscuits and pastries at the drop of a hat. At least, that's the impression one always got from the advertisements extolling the virtues of 'farm fresh', 'country goodness,' and so on. So he eagerly grabbed a couple. Unfortunately, Mrs. Callingwood had obviously never seen the advertisements. Her biscuits were as hard as cement and tasted much the same. He munched on one with great affectation and surreptitiously put the other back while Emma wasn't looking.

Half an hour later a faint rumbling in the bathroom indicated that the celebrated immersion heater had produced enough water for another bath. Emma put the tea things in the sink and took Harry by both hands, squeezing them gently.

"I think you should go on up to bed," she said. "If you wait for me, it will have gone cold and I don't feel like dragging out the warming pan again. Thanks for a wonderful evening. We probably could have done without the soaking, but even that was sort of fun in a way. And neither of us knew it would rain. It was very sweet of you to walk me home, you know." Then she looked up into his eyes, smiled that tantalizing smile, and kissed him.

Harry could swear both his feet left the ground at the same time. For a split second the self-doubt took over and he wondered if she was just being patronizing. But there was no mistaking the look on her face. This was nothing short of a miracle. She really had enjoyed herself, hadn't she? And she really must have forgiven him for ruining her hair and wrecking her shoes. There was no question about his feelings toward her. All in all, it hadn't turned out such a bad evening. In fact, in a perverse sort of way, he'd got to know far more about Emma during the past few hours than he would have on a normal date. Unfortunately, Emma's mother didn't appear to share her enthusiasm about him. Understandable, perhaps, considering the stupid stunt he'd just pulled. Was she, as Emma assured him, always like that, or did the hostility run deeper? According to his own mother, farming families tended to view urbanites with suspicion because they charged high prices, polluted the countryside with their cars, and treated rural people as country bumpkins. Surely, Mrs. Callingwood didn't regard him as a city slicker, did she? Admittedly, Barnsley was bigger than Elton, but not exactly a bustling metropolis. Perhaps relations with Emma's mother would improve tomorrow.

The bed was warm and snug. He slept soundly, bundled beneath a huge feather quilt. Sunlight streaming in through the low window aroused him at about eight-thirty the following morning. And a tentative nose pushed over the top of the quilt confirmed what everyone said about stone farmhouses: they were often colder inside than out. His breath steamed. A shiver ran through his stomach at the thought of having to get up. Minutes later, however, the delicious aroma of frying bacon provided a powerful incentive. As he lay speculating on the whereabouts of his clothes, the crisp sound of hobnailed boots rang out on the stone flags in the yard below. Curiosity got the better of the temperature, and he got out of bed to take a look. A man whom he presumed to be Brian was lugging some large cans into one of the outbuildings. Roughly Harry's height but more heavily built, he had a shock of unruly black hair that obviously hadn't seen a barber in a long time. His black duffle coat, much frayed about the cuffs and collar and tied about the middle with string, must have originally belonged to someone else, since it was at least couple of sizes too small. As Harry stared down, he also discovered why the bedroom had seemed so bright when he awoke. During the night, the sky had cleared and allowed the temperature to drop below freezing. Now, a light dusting of ground frost covered the roofs and paving stones.

Suddenly, the man looked up, scowled, looked again with eyebrows upturned, and went on his way. It was at then that he remembered he wasn't wearing any clothes. No wonder the man looked startled. Reaching for the borrowed dressing gown he was interrupted by a knock on the door and in walked Emma.

"Oops, sorry, love!" she said unconvincingly. "I thought you would still be in bed, you looked so tired last night. Anyway, here are your clothes. Just about everything dried overnight, including the raincoats. Your jacket's still a bit damp though. All that heavy tweed, I expect. So I wrapped it around the immersion heater. Should be alright after breakfast. I ironed your trousers and shirt." She grinned, "But I didn't iron your underwear!"

"Thanks," said Harry, preoccupied with the task of getting the dressing gown around his naked frame. One of the sleeves had pulled inside out, so he stood like a scarecrow, one arm stretched out and the other doubled over, with the gown hanging limply off his shoulders. Judging from the grin, Emma must have seen everything, although didn't seem to bother her. With a quick glance at his torso she took a step forward and pulled out the offending sleeve. Harry mumbled an embarrassed thanks. During his callow youth he used to fantasize about appearing naked in front of a woman. Well, it had happened. Why did he feel silly and awkward?

"Did you notice the frost?" she asked nonchalantly.

Harry nodded, red-faced.

"Mum won't be back for a while," she said. "I've made some bacon and eggs. Get down as soon as you can, otherwise they'll be cold. Things don't take long to get cold in this house, as you've probably noticed."

Yes, he had noticed. The clothes still contained some warmth from the ironing, his feet were stone cold, and he was hungry. After searching in vain for a bathroom upstairs and then remembering there wasn't one, he hurried down to the one off the kitchen. Sure enough, there was his jacket, wrapped around the immersion heater, just like she had said. He looked in the mirror. It would not be telling him he was the fairest of them all that morning. Six o'clock shadow had definitely set in and he had nothing to shave with. In a tumbler next to the bath were a couple of safety razors. He briefly thought about using one, but remembering the damage that those things usually did to his face, decided against it. Emma would have to put up with the rugged look.

Mrs. Callingwood had lit a fire in the kitchen hours ago. This time it was blazing and putting out some heat. Probably the fuel, Harry thought to himself with the experienced eye of someone who has grown up with coal. He'd noticed on the odd occasion he'd been in Miss Twigg's kitchen that the stuff she bought also tended to be variable in quality, with a fair amount of shale in it. His Uncle Clifford, who worked for the National Coal Board and knew everything there was to know about coal, once told him that this was a common problem with soft coal.

When he came out of the bathroom, Emma peered at him with narrowed eyes. "I think you need a shave," she said. "Why don't you use one of my safety razors? There's soap in the cabinet."

"I noticed, but I'm afraid they don't like me much."

"How come?"

"I get nicks and I break out in terrible rashes. I got tired of going around with bits of cotton wool stuck all over my face."

"Oh dear," she said, "I'm afraid I don't have an electric razor."

"Don't worry, I'll have a shave later." The sight and sound of an imminent meal seemed far more relevant at that moment.

"How did you sleep?" Emma asked as she manhandled one of the greasiest cast iron frying pans he'd ever seen. It sizzled, splashing tiny drops of fat over the rim. She had cooked the eggs, along with a couple of slices of thick, brown bread, in the fat of the bacon, Like Pavlov's dog, he could feel saliva building on his tongue.

"I slept very well, but I think I got frostbite in my nose!"

She made a face. "You ought to try sleeping in our house all winter. Actually, I should show you what's going on in the front room. It's so damp, nearly all the plaster fell off one wall in a huge lump and the stones behind are sopping wet. Years ago Dad tried to patch it but the plaster just came off again. Brian says it's because the builder filled up the space between the courses with rubble and it acts like a lamp or something."

"Er, a lamp wick," Harry corrected her, eager to air his second-hand knowledge on old houses. "They didn't have a very good grasp of insulation, apparently. They never realized that an air space between the inside and the outside walls makes better insulation than something solid. The rubble just sucked all the moisture out of the ground... like a lamp wick."

Emma grinned. "Our Anne used to hump her boyfriend in there, can you believe it? Sometimes I'd listen to them. She was really noisy! But the room got too miserable even for them. I remember once when we were small, it was so cold one winter that we all slept here in the kitchen. Dad kept the fire going all night. We had a terrific time."

Harry tucked into his breakfast. "Have you ever lived anywhere else?" he asked between mouthfuls.

Emma shook her head. "Nope. This is it." She paused, gazing silently at the window and the frost-coated farmyard beyond. "I don't think I'd **want** to live anywhere else. Maybe some day I might have to. But if I did, I'd probably get homesick. In fact, I **know** I'd be homesick."

He wolfed down the bacon and eggs, five slices of toast, and two cups of steaming tea. She watched the process with faint amusement. "You like toast, don't you?"

He nodded. "Probably force of habit. We ate a heck of a lot of it at school."

"Didn't they feed you anything else?"

He thought for a moment as he tried to remember the total range of dismal fare they had existed on for all those years.

"Oh, I suppose they did. But you know, the strongest recollection I have of that school is huge, long loaves of sliced bread! The house prefects were in charge of fetching the food from the serving hatches, and they'd come back with these bloody great loaves on big, metal trays. Everything else seemed pretty small by comparison. We never had butter. Always margarine, although we could bring our own into the dining hall if we had any. Big of them, eh! Mum used to send me little food parcels every few weeks. Parents could do that. Sometimes she'd put in a pound of white butter that my Aunt Mabel made. Sometimes we'd trade among ourselves. Most of the chaps didn't like white butter, so I didn't have much luck trading it. I still have my tuck box, and it still smells of butter and Marmite."

Emma wrinkled her nose again. "Marmite! You're kidding! How could you eat that stuff? Just the smell of it puts me off."

Harry laughed at her. "You've obviously never tried it on bread. Excellent stuff, Marmite. Bovril, too. Saved my life more than once, I can tell you. We didn't have any money to speak of because we weren't allowed outside the grounds without an exeat..."

"What's an exeat?"

"It's a pass, and you didn't get one unless you were in good standing with the head prefect, which I never was. Anyway, since we didn't get much of a chance to spend any money it wasn't much use. So we traded stuff like butter and Marmite and Bovril and Sunnyspread. One chap started a little bank, and instead of money he would buy and sell food things, can you believe!"

Pausing to sip his tea, it occurred to him that Emma's sister Anne had not yet put in an appearance.

"Anne? Oh, we don't often see her on weekends," she said casually. "Come to think of it, we don't see much of her during the week either. Not since her boyfriend moved into his new place. A few years ago it would have been a good thing because we only have three bedrooms, so Brian had his own while Anne and me had to share. Now Brian's married she uses his when she says overnight, which isn't often. Just think, you might have wound up sleeping with her!"

Wiithout the benefit of knowing Anne, his preference on that score lay firmly with Emma. And he would like it to be soon.

"When we're done, and if your jacket's dry, would you like to go for a walk to the lead mines?" she asked, changing the subject.

Harry nodded enthusiastically from behind a final slice of toast, wondering at the same time if Emma might have some reason for wanting him out of the house that early in the morning.

"Brian will probably be coming in pretty soon," she continued, answering his unspoken question. "I don't know why he has breakfast here instead of his house, except that Beth isn't much of a cook. There always seems to be something wrong with that woman. Either she's got a cold, or a headache, or a bad back, or something else. I think that's why he gets grouchy. Mind you, I don't think my brother's exactly a bundle of fun to live with either."

Recalling the slouching figure and scowling face out in the yard, Harry could see her point.

"I'd love to see the lead mines. I wasn't aware there *were* any mines around here."

Emma waved her spatula as she scraped the remaining fat out of the pan. "Oh, yes, we have lead mines. Mind you, ours is small compared to the Mill Close Mine over by Wensley. Mum says that one was the biggest around here. They're all shut down. The Wensley mine went out of business before the war and ours has been closed for a long time. There isn't much left of it. They sealed up the shafts and pulled all the buildings down. Mum says that lead mining was a really big industry in this part of Derbyshire hundreds of years ago."

"You seem to know quite a bit about local history."

"I think I got that from Mum and Dad... and from reading. Dad used to read a lot. Said he got into the habit when he was at sea during the war. He lost a lot of his books when he got torpedoed, but some of them are still in the front room, all full of mildew from the damp."

Breakfast finished, they washed and dried the dishes. While Harry helped her, he noticed that the Callingwood's used an electric stove. Somehow, he had expected something more 'rural'. Judging from the marks on the wall it looked as though the original oven, possibly one of those monstrous coal-fired, cast-iron combinations so common throughout northern England, had been torn out and replaced by a drab-looking tile fireplace.

Emma checked his jacket. It was very nearly dry, certainly dry enough to wear. She suggested he leave it on the immersion heater for a little longer, at least until they got back. But Harry decided to wear it anyway, arguing that body heat would dry it just as quickly. The real puzzle was his shoes. Although badly stained and stiff from their soaking the night before, they were now remarkably dry. He examined the still-warm leather.

"How did you get them dry this quickly? I've had wet shoes before and they've taken days to dry."

Emma grinned. "Mum put 'em in the oven!"

"Of course!" Her mother's little trick reminded him of an episode from his trainee days in the local parks department, when he attempted a similar favour for one of the gardeners. Had it not been for his forgetfulness, the gesture might have worked as well as Mrs. Callingwood's. Noticing the pair of boots sitting, early one morning, awash with mud outside the lunch room, Harry decided to dry them for an hour or two in the wall oven they used for warming up their 'snap'. Unfortunately he totally forgot about them. When lunch time rolled around, the owner arrived to put his food in the oven and discovered his boots, which by that time were reduced to a couple of charred cinders. Needless to say, he wasn't amused, and Harry had to fork out for a new pair.

It looked as though it might be a nice day for the beginning of December, with no trace of the icy rain that had drenched them the night before. The frost had already disappeared from spots which the wintry sun could reach. A few icicles melted at a leisurely pace from the farmhouse roof. Bundled up in their coats and with Emma wearing two pairs of socks and some rubber boots, they left the yard just as Brian reappeared. He looked at them and scowled again.

"Brian, this is Harry," she said, grabbing Harry by the arm.

Her brother paused, grunted a couple of unintelligible words, and continued on.

"Pleased to meet you, too," Harry said as a parting shot.

Emma looked back at Brian, made a face at him, and then turned to Harry. "Don't pay any attention," she said, steering him into the lane. "He's like that with everybody."

In daylight, Harry could see that the farmhouse was very old, and it looked as though what Emma referred to as the living room might have originally been an attached stable. A slight difference in the colour of the stones revealed where a set of double doors had been filled in and a window fitted. The house lay at right angles to the lane, with the kitchen end abutting it, and the back looking onto a small building that looked suspiciously like the celebrated privy. A low wall separated the lane from the farm property. Beyond the yard he could see a newer building, which he took to be the milking shed, and beyond that, a series of pastures enclosed by Derbyshire's ubiquitous dry stone walls.

There was a stark beauty to the little village. Few of the trees were much taller than large shrubs, with those in exposed locations bent almost double by the wind. The village houses, mostly former lead-miners' cottages dating back to the early eighteenth century, had been built for the climate: squat and unpretentious, with low soffitless roofs and tiny windows set deep into their sides. While the dominant building material was limestone, the quoins, lintels and door jambs of many of the houses were cut from gritstone.

"Brian and Beth live over there," Emma said, pointing to a row of three cottages on the other side of a large vegetable garden. "They're in the end one on the left. They wanted to buy it but the owner won't sell. He lives in Sheffield. It was left to him by his dad a long time ago and he's always said he might retire here. Well, he's now retired, so Brian says, and he hasn't shown any sign of moving in yet. I don't think he ever will." She pointed again. "Mr. and Mrs. Cooper live in the middle cottage, and Uncle Sid and Auntie Nell live in the one on the right. Actually, Auntie Nell died last year so Uncle Sid lives on his own now. It's a shame in a way. I liked her a lot better than him."

They walked up the street, past Elton Old Hall, in those days privately owned, more recently a youth hostel, then turned off onto another narrow lane, passing a small church and rectory and an off-licence, and finally coming to some ruined foundations. Behind, the land fell away sharply. All down the slope, piles of stones lay half-buried in the long grass.

"This was our original church," Emma said, pointing to the rubble. "Mum told me it was built around the end of the seventeenth century. She says a couple of hundred years ago some idiot started mining for lead in the cliff over there. One of his tunnels went off course and under the church, and when the tunnel roof eventually collapsed the ground above it also subsided and half the church fell down! So in 1812 they built a new one. I was baptized in it."

She took him by the hand and they stumbled down the escarpment to some more ruins. While little remained, he could tell that they had once been buildings. Two twisted lengths of rail and some rotting timbers told of a more recent system for moving the ore than the original buckets and barrows.

"Where are the mine shafts?" Harry asked, half-hoping there might be one still available for a guided tour. He had always been fascinated by tunnels.

"They're over there," Emma said, nodding towards an escarpment behind the ruins. "But they blew up the entrances a long time ago. People have been mining for lead around here for hundreds of years. Dad said that, when they first started the miners didn't have the machines to dig deep pits so they dug into the hillsides. It must have been an awful lot of work. According to Uncle Sid these rails are about a hundred-and-fifty-years old, but the mine itself is a lot older than that."

"Drift mines," said Harry, reciting a bit more of Uncle Clifford's wisdom.

Emma nodded, kicking idly at some of the stones. "I don't think they ever got much out of this one, but others did really well. Uncle Sid... he's a bit of an authority on stuff around here... once said that commercial farming only started here when the lead mines gave out. You should see the Mill Close Mine. There's lots more to look at. The owners left stuff all over the place. It looks like they just closed the gate and took off. Some day we'll go over there."

They wandered across the fields, hand in hand, to a shallow boulder-strewn stream that wound its tortuous path towards a farm in the distance. The water danced and sparkled in the early winter sunlight. In shady recesses, small patches of ice still lingered. Farther off, freshly milked cows were back in their pastures, happily sampling new grass which had sprung up after a long summer drought. Still marveling at his good fortune, he wondered if they were as happy as he was at that moment. A blue sky, a crisp December day, and this gorgeous girl who never made a pair of oversized gumboots look better. A short week ago he was being refused and abused by Terry's harem at the teacher's college. And now he had someone who actually wanted to be with him. Things had definitely picked up during the past twenty-four hours. Nevertheless, doubt nagged at him. What if all this were to end as suddenly as it had begun? What if she decided not to see him again? **Was** she expecting to see him again? Uncertainty was the only thing spoiling an otherwise beautiful day.

"This runs all the way down to the Derwent," she said. "If it was deeper you could get in a little boat and wind up at Miss Twigg's back door!"

Following the stream uphill, they came upon another road, flanked, as usual, by stone walls. While closing a pasture gate behind them Harry glanced at his watch. They had been out for two hours; it seemed like ten minutes. As they followed the road back to the village, he let Emma walk ahead, watching the sun weave light and shadow in her hair.

Slowing down, she pulled his hand into her coat pocket and squeezed it gently. "Don't take this the wrong way," she said, "but I'll have to put you on the bus when we get back. I always help Mum on Sundays. I think I made this problem for myself during the time I was working on the farm full-time. Mum got to depend on me for a lot of the things that Brian wouldn't do... and still doesn't do for that matter. He always tries to give the impression of being busy, but he's really quite lazy. Likes anything that he can do sitting on his bottom, like using the tractor. Other stuff, like cleaning the milking machines and the coolers, never gets touched. Mum and I usually wind up doing it. Hope you don't mind."

He was hardly in a position to protest. Considering what he'd just put her through, it was a miracle they were still on speaking terms.

"No, of course not," he replied bravely. "How often do the buses run?"

"Every two hours, at a quarter to the hour. It's hard to believe but the blessed thing takes an hour and a quarter to get to Matlock. Sorry, but that's the price you're going to pay for getting me wet last night!"

After returning to the house for another cup of tea, Emma walked him down to the lane end. Together they waited for the twelve-forty-five. It soon appeared, as do all things when they are least welcome, its faded-green roof rising like a humped-back whale, over a slight hill in the distance. Harry could hear the fearful grinding of gears amidst a lot of exhaust smoke, and the rest of the bus rumbled into view.

"It's okey dokey, luv," the conductress said as she descended from the bus steps to light up a cigarette, "we're running early. Take yer time." She went round to chat with the driver, tucked into his isolated little compartment at the front, while two passengers in the back sat snoozing.

"Can you drop by the shop next week?" Emma asked, still clinging to his hand.

Was she kidding? Of course he would like to drop by.

"Yes. er, fine...yes. We're busy in the office... but sure..." he found himself babbling.

"Well, if you're too busy, it's okay," she said, crestfallen.

And for the millionth time he cursed his shyness, and the despicable things it did to his mouth. Just say 'yes.' he told himself, then shut up and get on the damned bus.

"No, no, we're not that busy. Of course, I'd love to see you again. I'll pop over during lunch hour." He kissed her on the cheek, watched her face brighten considerably, then clambered onto the bus and went back to Matlock.

FOUR

Old Frank

It didn't take Dickie very long to learn that the great event had taken place; Mrs. J. must have been in touch with him. In keeping with long established habit, he avoided coming to the office on Mondays until after noon. But seconds after arriving he was in front of Harry's draughting table, his thin lips stretched into a silly grin punctured by the inevitable cigarette.

"Well?" he demanded, eyes watering from the smoke. As usual, he smelled strongly of alcohol.

"Ah," replied Harry, red with embarrassment. "You mean Saturday?"

"'Course I mean Saturday," Dickie persisted. "What else would I be talking about. How did it go? Get laid?"

Harry fumbled awkwardly with a pair of compasses. "Er, yes...I mean, no, of course not," he replied. It would have given him the greatest pleasure to punch his boss on the nose. Instead, he had to stand there looking like an idiot while Terry smirked at them both, savouring the spectacle.

"Some bloody stud you are," Dickie said, and laughed at his own joke.

After a short silence he must have noticed that no one else except Terry was paying any attention and worse, he might be making more of a fool of himself than his young assistant. He waited for Harry to say something. Harry didn't. So he mercifully backed off. "Better not put the lad in a tight spot this early in the game!" he said to the room in general before returning to his office. Then, turning to Harry, he added, "But we'll be expecting a progress report, you can be damned sure of that!"

Over my dead body, Harry swore to himself.

It was a long Monday, filled with self-doubt and uncertainty. For most fellows his age there wouldn't have been a problem, he told himself. Any other red-blooded male would have been over to the chemist shop the moment it opened. But not he. Only Harry would spend nearly two days agonizing over the possibility that Saturday's quirky success might be just a ghastly mistake.

Still, it had been Emma who had suggested he call her. But was she merely being polite? What if she had changed her mind? What if he went over and she just stood there behind the counter and laughed at him? That would be unbearable. Mrs. J. would probably laugh at him, too, and that would be even worse. Then there was the problem of Mrs. Callingwood, who, despite Emma's reassurances to the contrary, seemed to have decided he was a nitwit, and a rather dangerous one at that. Her brother obviously shared the same view. Harry hated suspense, even though deep down he realized that most of this particular dilemma was of his own making.

By late Sunday night he had made up his mind not to see her again. That way there would be no risk of being rejected. Then he spent Monday thinking about the auburn hair and those tantalizing grey-green eyes, and imagining what might be under that terry towel bathrobe. Saturday night's memories and Sunday night's resolution seesawed back and forth, each jockeying for supremacy. And Dickie hadn't helped matters either.

By Tuesday morning, after fretting for two days, Harry finally decided to put himself out of his misery. It was worth a gamble; he had nothing to lose. He would go over there at lunch time, his heart in his hands, and settle things once and for all.

"She's out doing a little errand for me, dear," Mrs. Johnson said in a very friendly tone. "If you'd like to wait she'll be back soon."

Crestfallen, he stood in the middle of the shop floor, feeling like a sailing ship that had just lost its wind. Mrs. J. made a clumsy attempt at coquettishness, her large mouth pursing into a smear of bright red lipstick. She reminded Harry of those tropical fish that posh restaurants love to have swimming around in big tanks near the reception desk.

"I know I'm a poor substitute," she twittered. "But I'd be happy to keep you company for a little while."

"Thanks," he said hastily. "Perhaps I can intercept her. Which way did she go?"

"She went down to the playhouse to pick up some tickets for me, dear." The jujube smile blossomed again. "I have a new beau, too, you know!"

"I'm very glad," Harry replied while backing towards the door. "Anyhow, I'll er, just, er, slip down the road. See you soon."

"Oh, I'm sure you will!" he could hear her say as the shop door closed.

As he stepped out into the street it began to rain again. Self-doubt once again leaped onto centre stage; this could be another omen. He wasn't sure, although one thing was certain, his raincoat was back in the office. Damn the rain. It was always raining in this part of the world. Turning up his jacket collar, he set off. Near the bottom of Bank Road he spotted a solitary figure trudging up the steep incline. Emma wasn't wearing a raincoat either, and she had her head down as if to protect her face. Stepping beneath a shop awning, he waited for her to come closer.

"Hello, remember me?" It wasn't a very original line, but better than nothing.

Emma looked up in surprise and her face broke into a smile.

"Mrs. J. said I might find you somewhere between here and the playhouse," he continued. "Thought I would meet you halfway."

"We have a habit of meeting in the rain, don't we?" she said, reaching out for his hand and turning him around so they were both facing uphill.

"Sorry again about the other evening," he found himself blurting out. "It was pretty stupid of me to suggest we walk all the way to Elton, especially with your sort of feet... I mean, shoes. I do silly things. A lot. I, er... well, I'd like to do some silly things again... No, actually, not silly things... I wondered if you... well, you and me actually... if you and me could go again with you... I mean, sort of go out again?"

Listening to Harry's incoherent babble, Emma tried to keep a straight face but finally broke into a giggle, clasping his hand even harder.

"Where were you yesterday?" she asked.

"Yesterday? At work. Why?"

"You said you were going to come over to the shop. I thought perhaps you'd changed your mind."

Changed his mind? The irony of that remark caused him to give out a short laugh. He was about to add something to the previous nonsense when she turned, the rain trickling down her face.

"Anyway, yes."

"Yes?"

"Yes. I would like to go out with you again. If that's what you were trying to ask!"

"So you don't think I'm a complete idiot?"

She smiled. "No, Harry, I don't think you're a complete idiot, although you do work hard at it. And you do seem to have a very contagious habit of getting wet!"

He almost deflated with relief. As they hurried back up Bank Road he wondered where he might take her. Until a few minutes ago there didn't seem much point in worrying about such things. She was bound to turn him down. So much for intuition. They could go to the pictures again, or he could take her for a drink, or both, again. Not the epitome of high romance but then, except for the pubs and one or two restaurants, Matlock pretty well shut down at six o'clock. Moreover, the options were further limited by his current financial situation. Having recently purchased a couple of Harris Tweed jackets and a pair of shoes for the office, most of his meagre savings had evaporated and payday was a week and light years away. England was a cash society then, with credit cards practically unheard of, and certainly beyond the reach of mere mortals like him. Simple pleasures had to suffice. At two bob a pint the average working stiff could enjoy a night out at the pub without spending a small fortune.

"Perhaps we could go for a drink tonight?"

"I think you said 'drunk' last time!" she replied, teasing him.

"Did I?" he lied. "I don't remember. You've probably noticed I put my foot in my mouth a lot."

"The other day you seemed to have more than your foot in it. More like both feet and your shoes as well!"

"I know it's not a weekend, but I just wanted to see you again. Have you ever been to the *Hanging Gate*?"

"That's Mr. and Mrs. Bassett's pub down Smedley Street, isn't it? No, I haven't. Actually, I don't go to pubs much. Mrs. J. says the *Hanging Gate* is where the County-Office crowd hangs out."

"Well, they do and they don't," he hastily assured her. "It's a popular spot for lunch but I haven't found too many office people in there in the evenings. Mr. Dickie says it's because quite a few of them still live in Derby. So when five o'clock rolls around they're on the buses."

"And Mr. Dickie would know, wouldn't he!"

"I think he might be right this time. Anyway, the Bassetts seem to be a very nice couple. Of course, if you don't like going to pubs that much we could do something else."

She laughed. "The reason I don't go to pubs isn't because I don't like them. It's because, well, it's because I haven't had anyone to go with. When you're a woman, going to a pub alone is like putting a piece of meat on a hook. You're a male. You wouldn't know about such things."

"No, I suppose I wouldn't," said Harry. "In fact I've usually had exactly the opposite problem!"

Emma squeezed his hand again. "But this time I wouldn't being going alone, would I? So, I'd love to go to the *Hanging Gate* for a drink, so long as I don't miss my bus again." As they reached Smedley Street, she asked, "Is that where you spend your lunch hour?"

"Hell, no. Bill Lewis was telling me that the boss doesn't like his staff drinking during the lunch hour."

His remark struck Emma as particularly funny. "He's a fine one to talk!" she chortled.

"Actually, I've had a couple of lunchtime sessions with the boss and one of the fellows in the office. But I certainly couldn't afford it every day. Not on my salary. It's funny, at my interview Mr. Dickie told me that he paid for other people's lunches only once. He obviously meant what he said because he's never paid for me since."

What Harry didn't know was that Emma had become quite familiar with Bob Dickie's escapades, even though she had never met the man. Dickie's drinking habits were legendary. He routinely got himself tossed out of pubs for unruly behavior and everyone knew about it. Emma received regular updates from someone who should have known Dickie as well as anyone: Mrs. Johnson. Considering her relationship with Dickie, it is likely that the information contained a certain slant, with Mrs. J. safely portraying herself in the most favourable light. She was as big a gossip as she was a man chaser. Every time Dickie got himself into another scrape, Mrs. J. would relay the details to Emma, and probably everyone else in the neighbourhood, with breathless enthusiasm. In the long run that had become Mrs. J's undoing; she couldn't keep her mouth shut.

"I don't think the *Hanging Gate* is Mr. Dickie's only watering hole in Matlock," Emma said, diplomatically. "By the sound of it he seems to get around quite a bit."

"You've heard of him?"

"Harry, love, everyone's heard of him!"

"Oh, dear," said Harry, wondering if he was going to be tarred by the same brush.

"Don't take it personally, I don't think he's your responsibility! Anyway, the *Hanging Gate* sounds like a nice idea. I'll finally get to meet Mr. Bassett. He's almost a legend himself. Mrs. J's often talked about him, and how he handles Mr. Dickie without getting into a fight. She told me he used to be a policeman. Did you know that?"

"Yes, the boss told me. You could almost tell from his build."

"I know **Mrs**. Bassett because she comes into the shop quite a bit. She seems like a very nice lady, and she likes you!"

"She does?" He shouldn't have been too surprised. Older women clearly found something in Harry's looks and demeanor that escaped the majority of their younger counterparts.

"Have you adopted the *Hanging Gate* as your local? Men always seem to have their favourite pubs."

He sensed that Emma might be fishing for information. "Not really. I go now and again in the evenings."

"With anyone in particular?" she asked casually.

So that was it. "No one in particular," he said. "A couple of the fellows in the office are single. Well, actually, Terry won't be very soon. I've gone with both of them a few times. And a few times I've just gone on my own, which wasn't much fun, as you obviously found."

By this time they had reached the chemist shop. Apparently satisfied with Harry's explanations, she squeezed his hand one final time and went into the shop.

"See you after work," he called as she closed the door behind her. Then he dashed across the rain-drenched street to his office. He would have to let Miss Twigg know he wouldn't be home for dinner. That created another problem. Where could they both get something to eat, cheap? Mrs. Bassett usually had some sandwiches and pickled eggs left over from lunch. And even if she didn't, fresh ones always seemed to materialize from somewhere in the back if he inquired. He knew Emma was right about her; she did like him.

It would be a pathetically short date. Just four hours. What could a chap do in four hours? Why did her bus have to leave so early? For that matter, why did she have to live on a farm up on the moors? Why couldn't she live in Matlock, like all the girls who refused to have anything to do with him?

Before entering the side door that led to the office back stairs, he glanced back at the shop. Mrs. J. and Emma were talking while looking in his direction. Emma waved and then disappeared behind the counter. Damn the weather. Perhaps it would clear up before five o'clock; otherwise he might once again be living up to his newly acquired reputation for spending half his social life soaked to the skin.

As luck would have it, the rain stopped just before five o'clock but it was a cold night. They walked up to the *Hanging Gate* in the gathering darkness, huddling against a sharp wind that gusted down Smedley Street and into Bank Road. The gutters smelled of sodden leaves pried loose from their summer moorings and left to rot where they lay. It was a nice smell, Harry thought. But then, he liked a lot of strange smells.

The pub was nearly empty, as might be expected for a Tuesday night. Kath had built a roaring fire in the lounge. It crackled and spat, sending hot embers against the wrought-iron fire guard. Arthur stood behind the bar, wiping glasses with that easy flourish which comes of many hours doing the same thing. He saw them as they came through the door and grinned broadly, raising a questioning eyebrow while looking at Harry and then at Emma.

"Can't stay away from us, eh?" he cried in his musical Welsh accent.

"Hello, Harry," said an unseen Kath from the tap room.

Harry returned their greetings. Several pairs of eyes turned to scrutinize them both. By now he had become accustomed to the once-over from the locals. They were a quiet, unassuming lot, many of them retirees, who kept to themselves. Yet, for all that, they could be generous and helpful when the need arose.

"Arthur, I'd like you to meet my friend, Emma," he said, pulling her in front of him.

Arthur nodded and winked. "You work at Madison's, don't you, young lady?"

Emma said yes. Arthur turned again to Harry and said mischievously, "So, then. Gave your other woman the bump, eh?"

Harry, always slow on the uptake, blushed scarlet, trying to think who Arthur might be referring to and concluded it must have been the girl from the teacher's college.

"Oh, er, that was Terry's friend." he waffled. "You know Terry. Always got several in hand."

"That's very true my boy, very true. Come to think of it, his friend got bored with you rather quickly!"

The heat continued to rise up Harry's neck. Emma looked at them both with a mixture of curiosity and amusement.

"I wasn't even trying... I mean, I was just chatting with her while Terry was talking to somebody else." He knew by now that Arthur was getting a rise out of him, but he could have picked a better time. He was still coming to terms with the fact that Emma was going out with him. The last thing he needed at the moment was someone sowing the seeds of suspicion in her. Finally, Arthur saw the discomfort on Harry's face and gave out a loud guffaw. "Couldn't resist a little dig!" he cried. "You young 'uns take life so seriously." Turning to Emma he said, "Mr. Harry was a model of gentlemanly conduct, my dear. You have nothing to worry about."

Emma frowned. "I don't know, Mr. Bassett. He tells me he's been living like a monk since he got here, but I'm not convinced."

"Oh, I wouldn't worry! Now, if he were his friend Terry, there might be cause for concern. That lad was doing a bit more than talking, I recall. Had his hand up the girl's skirt half the evening. Bit of a scamp is Terry, I think. Can't imagine why he'd be wanting to get married. He *is* the one who's going to be married isn't he?"

"Yes, he's the one," Harry replied. "And I can't imagine why he's getting married either."

Emma decided she wasn't going to be drawn any further into this bit of sport and started to walk over to a table.

"Pint of bitter and a shandy, Arthur." Harry said hurriedly.

Arthur nodded towards the snug. "Why don't you both go keep Frank company? I'll make it worth your while. He's melancholy tonight. Rheumatism's acting up again I think!"

"Who is Frank?" Emma whispered as they changed direction.

"He's an old chap who practically lives here. Got a good thing going, has Frank. And I don't think it costs him a penny 'cause every time his mug becomes empty somebody buys him another round."

"He doesn't **really** live here, does he? Hasn't he got a home?"

"Oh, yes. And a wife, too, although I've never seen her with him. She doesn't come here, as far as I know."

Frank was sitting alone in his usual corner, eyes half closed, nursing his beloved pint pot. Occasionally his face would twitch slightly as though he might be remembering something from the past. There was no one else in the room. Hearing them enter he sat bolt upright and peered in their direction. Arthur followed with the drinks.

"My my," Frank said with a smile that revealed his cracked tooth. "Yew lot must be somethin' special. 'E allus makes me fetch me own!" The ill fitting dentures clacked as he spoke.

"That's a bloody lie for a start, young Frank," said Arthur with another wink. "You get royal treatment here. As befits a regular customer, of course. But don't push it!"

Harry again pulled Emma in front of him. "Frank, I'd like you to meet my friend, Emma. She works at Madison's."

Frank looked her over and frowned. "Ooh, yer don't do yer? Ooh, dear. That's a pity. That's a pity an' all. Nuthin' agin you, though, Miss."

"Why's that, Frank?" Harry asked, afraid that Madison's might have inflicted some terrible indignity upon the old man.

"Ooh, they's too expensive, Mr. Harry. Too expensive. I can't afford their stuff on my little bit o' money. I allus go ter Woolworth's fer me med'cines."

"There isn't a Woolworth's in Matlock," Emma said.

"Oh, ah go ter Derby on the bus once in a while. Get everythin' there." He beckoned with a gnarled hand. "Any'ow, sit yer down an' rest yer bottoms."

Harry's quick arithmetic suggested that what it cost Frank to go to Derby would probably just about compensate for the higher prices at Madison's. But going to Derby was a day's outing and a change of scenery, and that was probably compensation enough. Perhaps his wife went with him.

Emma slid onto the bench that formed a right angle to the one Frank was sitting on. Harry slid in alongside. Frank gave them another once-over through the glass bottom of his beer mug.

"How's the Missus?" Harry asked as he took their own beer glasses from Arthur's tray.

Frank's face darkened into a frown and he tugged at his stained cloth cap. "Badly, lad. Very badly. Back's givin' 'er bloomin' ummer. She got some pills from the doctor but they don't seem ter do much fer 'er. It's a shame 'cause Alice allus liked ter get abaht. Now she's stuck indoors all't time."

None of this came as any surprise, except the name of Frank's wife. Harry couldn't recall him ever mentioning her name before. Or maybe he hadn't been listening. But each time Harry had spent an evening at the *Hanging Gate*, Frank had been there. And every time, Frank's reply had been the same: 'the Missus was badly.'

"Still," Frank continued, taking another swig of beer, "We 'ave ter go on, don't we?"

Harry and Emma nodded, lapsing into a short silence out of respect for Alice's bad back. From beneath his cap, Frank's blue eyes scrutinized Emma again. Harry watched him, noticing the wrinkled skin and farmer-style tan from a lifetime of working outside. He was so typical of a disappearing generation: hard working, staunchly independent and fiercely proud of his working-class roots.

"Well, young lady. Are yer goin' ter marry this lad?" Frank asked.

Emma blushed. Harry could again feel the redness spreading up from his lower back. What was this, some sort of *Hanging Gate* conspiracy to doom his first girlfriend?

"Oh, I don't know," she said with an embarrassed giggle and casting Harry a short glance. "I'm not sure he's the type for me!"

"Nor her for *me*! This is only the second time we've been out together," Harry added with a grin. It was pure bluster. At that moment he would have married her on the spot. She was still wearing her teal raincoat, collar turned up, and there was something about that raincoat, that collar. He felt a tremendous urge to sweep her up and carry her as fast as his skinny legs could go, down to Miss Twigg's and up to his room. Fat chance.

Frank leaned over, gently touching her hand. "It's a grand thing, lass," he said. "Don't let anyone tell yer different. Missus an' I 'ave been married sixty-two years, an' I don't regret a day of it. Not a day of it." He stared off into space, casting his mind back over those years. Then he laughed a short, snorting laugh. "We 'ad some good times. An' a few bad times. But that's life, eh?"

Harry felt Emma touch his thigh with her free hand. Reaching under the table he held on to it as though it might just as quickly vanish. Three other people had now come into the snug. All acknowledged Frank with a cheerful wave but none seemed to want to talk to him. And Frank obviously wanted to talk. So Harry decided to let him, as Arthur had requested. This appeared to be just fine with Emma, too. Nursing her shandy, she settled back in the seat, half leaning on Harry's shoulder.

"We'll talk about the teacher's college later!" she whispered in his ear.

"So, tell us, lad," Frank continued, "'Ow many blokes are there in that buildin' o' yours, now?"

Harry thought for a moment. He wasn't used to Frank asking questions. Frank enjoyed holding court, talking for hours about his own side of life, but he seldom asked questions. Perhaps his eighty-seven years had consumed all the questions he ever wanted to ask. But he had a lifetime of anecdotes, some of them sad, many of them funny. And he told his funny stories with a dry wit that could have his listeners convulsed in laughter.

"I think about seven hundred," Harry replied.

Frank whistled softly. "By gum. There's no wunder we 'ave taxes comin' out of ower ears. Things was a lot simpler when ah wus your age, that's fer certain. What do yer all do in there?"

"I'm not entirely sure. So far I've only seen about a tenth of the place!"

The old man tugged thoughtfully again on his cap; the blue eyes took on a faraway look. "Ah could tell yer a few things abaht that place," he said. "When ah wus a little 'un ower dad used to bring me up ter see all the rich fowk comin' up ter take the waters. In them days most of 'em came on the railway. 'Ad their own private carriages. Ah'm tellin' yer, there wus some pretty fancy carriages, an' all. Smedley's wus a regular beehive. Fowks comin' an' goin'. At night yer could 'ear the ballroom orchestra right across't valley. An' that ballroom wus quite a performance when they built it, ah can tell yer. They allus seemed ter be addin' sumthin' new. A lotta fowks don't know that Smedley put 'is first spa on't other side of Smedley Street. There wor nowt on't low side except a couple o' cottages. Ah can still remember 'em blasting rocks."

"Did you ride the tram up Bank Road?" Harry asked, lighting up his first cigarette in nearly a week. Although it tasted good, his resolution to quit reared its ugly head. He took several puffs, then stubbed it out. Emma looked on approvingly.

Frank shook his head. "Naw. It wus tuppence to go up and that wus a lot o' money in them days. Besides, they didn't want the likes o' us using the tram! Any'ow, it weren't built when ah wus a little 'un. Ah reckon ah'd be abaht twenty-two when they got it goin'. There wus a right kerfuffle fer a year or two 'cause 't road wasn't wide enough an' they wanted ter pull sum 'ouses down ter make room. One or two fowks didn't want ter move so's it took abaht five years an' sum o' old George Newnes' money ter get all that cleared up. George wor a publisher, ah think. Ah can remember goin' ter the openin' do. 1898, ah think it was, an' it must 'ave been early in the year 'cause ah can remember it wor bloody cold... February or March, seems to me. The thing 'ad a bloody big steam engine ter hoist the cars up. Ah can still see that steam engine. Used ter make a right racket an' all, clankin' an' rattlin' an' steam cummin' outa every which way! They made a fancy little shed fer it. Fowks told me it never made any money, but there allus seemed to be people on it. Naw, like ah said, we never rode it. When ah wus a little 'un Dad used ter 'oist me on 'is shoulders an' up th' Bank we'd go. He was a strong fella, wus my dad. An' a'll swear that road wus steeper in them days. Anybody could go in the gardens, y'know. Luvly gardens. We'd spend a Sunday afternoon walkin' around an' gawking at everybody! Sum of th' hoyty toyty fowks would give us th' evil eye. We didn't care! We never 'ad any money but we allus seemed ter 'ave enough ter manage on. Them's wus good times. Seems ter me everybody's got money these days but it don't make 'em very 'appy."

Harry nodded, wondering if he would ever be in that position.

"Did you ever work at the hydro?" Emma inquired.

"As a matter o' fact ah did fer a while, luv, shovellin' coal fer the 'ot water. That would be when ah wus abaht fifteen. Then ah went diggin' graves wi' me dad." He leaned forward with the conspiritorial air of someone imparting a state secret. "'Course, yer know there was no real spa water don't yer? Ah reckon everybody knows that now. They 'ad the tank rooms locked up like a bank vault. Only certin' fowks could go in an' they 'ad to swear an oath they wouldn't let on. But ah remember wagons deliverin' stuff in sacks, an' they told me it was fer t' go in the water."

"Are you sure about that, Frank, or are you making it up?" Emma laughed.

"It's true, luv. As God's mi' witness, it's true."

Harry could almost hear the clatter of drays and horses on stone cobbles, the hustle and bustle of men unloading heavy goods and the surreptitious glances of the house staff while the big deceit was being stashed away.

"Everyone around 'ere knew abaht it!" Frank continued. "It wor the worst kept secret o' Matlock." Then, almost as an afterthought, he added quietly, "Me sister, Ellen, worked there as well, as a chambermaid, until she got married."

Harry had never heard him talk about a sister before, although he had been told by Dickie that Frank had an older brother who was killed in the First World War.

"Is your sister still alive?" Harry asked.

The laugh vanished and Frank's face clouded. He paused for a moment, eyes lowered. "Naw, lad. She died givin' birth, two years after they wus married. Little 'un died, too. She wus such a 'appy lass, was our Ellen. She wor never very strong but she'd take nuthin' from nobody. By crikey, ah've seen 'er take on big strappin' lads that wor givin' me a bad time. Ah still miss 'er y'know. She's been gone sixty-five years. It really 'it me when Alice an' me got married, and she weren't there." He took a long drink from his beer mug and carefully placed it back on the table. "There wus just three of us, Ralph, Ellen an' me. Ralph wus killed in France in 1917. Ah wus the baby of the family, an' there's just me left!"

Listening, Harry found it hard to believe that the events Frank was recalling happened well over half a century ago. He spoke of them with such precision and clarity, they might have happened yesterday.

Noticing that the old man's beer mug was almost empty, Harry leaned into the doorway and signalled to Arthur for another round. Emma held up her hand to indicate she didn't want any more while silently mouthing f-o-o-d to him. Reminded that his stomach had begun to rumble on empty, too, he got up and went to find Kath. Alarm registered on Frank's face. He stopped in mid sentence.

"He's coming back," Emma reassured him. "At least, I hope he's coming back!"

Frank breathed out slowly. "Ee, ah thowt ah wus borin' everybody ter tears... an' ah've only just got started!"

Kath was in the tap room. She winked as Harry's head appeared through the hatch, nodding at his unspoken question. "So you're starving, are you, dear?" she said in her lilting Welsh dialect. Kath reminded him of an aunt in Harrogate, also named Kathleen, who according to Mother, came from Rhyl, in North Wales. A pleasant woman, by all accounts, with large breasts and a talent for making delicious pastries. There was some uncertainty over whether Uncle Norman and Aunt Kath were actually related to them. It didn't matter to Harry. He loved visiting because they had an abandoned nail factory on their property, with a small railway that connected the various buildings together. Uncle Norman, a delightful man with hardly a tooth in his head, would patiently push them up and down the tracks on a tiny flatcar while, high above, sparrows and starlings anxiously flapped about among the crumbling roofs. When that became a bore, they could go and play with the model railway that cousin Eric had built in the garden. Eric, every bit as eccentric as his father, had never married and never held a job in his life. But that railway was a paragon of craftsmanship, and Eric gladly ran it for them when they visited. Harry remembered being devastated when Uncle Norman died and Aunt Kath sold up and moved back to Wales. No one ever revealed what ailed Uncle Norman. Mother said he probably died of boredom, since, like his son, he'd never worked a day in his life either. It was, Mother declared, a classic case of old wealth falling into new hands. Norman's father had apparently made a fortune making nails. It was entirely possible Norman died of boredom, but it had crossed Harry's young mind at the time that the poor man might have actually starved to death since he couldn't possibly have been able to chew anything with so few teeth.

"Wondered if you might have anything left from lunch, Kath?" Harry said, unconsciously giving her the little smile that fired the maternal instinct in older women

Scrambling up the stone steps she patted him on the bottom. "You wouldn't want stale sandwiches, love, surely now! No, I'll knock another plateful together, enough for you both and more, since you might have to share a few with young Frank. For a man his age, Frank has a very healthy appetite. I think it's all the talking he does! How about ham and cheese, and a couple of pickled eggs?"

"That would be great!" Kath made marvelous pickled eggs. But he wasn't sure whether Emma would go for them. Not to worry, he would eat hers if she didn't like them.

"Go and sit down and I'll bring them round," she said, and disappeared into the back kitchen.

"Did your mother work, Frank? Outside the home, I mean," Harry asked, returning to his seat and mouthing to Emma that food-was-on-its-way.

Frank nodded. "Oh yes. Oh yes. When my muther wor a young lass she worked fer Nightingale's. Then Tom Smedley bought th' mill an' changed it to woosteds. Things wor very 'ard in them days. Nightingale's wor poor fowk ter work fer but it got a bit better when Smedley's took over. It wor Tom's son, John, 'oo did all the spa stuff. 'E wor a right goin' concern, wor that one. Lotta fowks didn't like 'im. Thowt 'e wor too pushy. Seemed right enough ter me, bit ah saw of 'im, which warn't much. Mum went back ter work when ah wus quite little but we lost 'er ter T.B. when ah wus ten. Ah suppose yer know they called it 'consumption' in them days. Ellen wus fourteen an' she stayed at 'ome and 'elped Dad look after us fer a few years, until she got married. She wor a grand cook wor our Ellen." He patted his stomach, "Yer'd never think ah wor a puny little bugger when ah wor young! But our Ellen filled me aht."

Harry had already told Emma a few snippets about Frank, including the fact that he'd spent most of his adult life digging graves. Emma wanted to know more.

"Didn't you find grave digging a bit spooky, Frank?" she asked him.

Frank chuckled at the thought. "Nah, lass, it wor th' same as digging fer taters, except deeper! Mind you' yer 'ad ter dig 'em proper, otherwise the coffin wouldn't drop in right. We 'ad some right times ah can tell yer, 'specially when th' pits would fill up wi' water after it rained real 'eavy. Ah've spent many an hour wi' a balin' can so's the undertakers could get 't coffin in next day."

Harry knew of one question Frank always loved. "What was your funniest experience, Frank?"

Frank lifted his cap and scratched his balding head. "Ee, ah don't know... Ah reckon the rummest was the woman 'oo buried 'erself wi' er 'usband."

"Buried herself?" Emma exclaimed. "How on earth did she manage that?"

He would be happy to tell them. This had turned out to be a banner evening, an audience willing to pay for his beer **and** actually asking for his conversation. Most just paid for his beer. Evenings like these were the best among a larger number which he cared to forget, those where no one came. Frank loved to talk, but in an age when everyone talked and nobody listened, he all too often lost out to the topics of popular culture and the noisy clamour of a younger generation. So he'd sit out the lonely evenings, hoping the next would be better.

"Oh, it must a' been abaht 1935, or '36," Frank said, savouring the memory. "This chap committed 'arry carry so they 'ad ter bury 'im in the municipal cemetery. Church wouldn't 'ave 'im. Any'ow, me an' me mate dug the grave an' they buried 'im. Well, I'm tellin' yer, 'is wife were beside 'erself, carryin' on at the burial, sobbin' 'er eyes aht an' sayin' she couldn't live wi'out 'im. Everybody wor lookin' at 'er. It wor very tragic, very tragic. Any'ow, smite me if the next mornin' we goes down there and somebody 'as dug the grave open. Coffin lid's off, and there's 'is wife lying on top of th' bloke, dead as a doornail! So we sent fer the coppers an' they came rushin' dahn', all in a dither. But there warn't much anybody could do. Friend o' mine 'oo worked at the 'ospital said she took poison."

"But how could she possibly have dug the grave open?" Emma asked, wide-eyed.

"It wor all a mystery ter me an' everybody else," Frank confessed. "Ah think somebody 'elped 'er. In fact, the coppers asked us if **we'd** dun it. Now, 'ow daft can yer get!" He grinned. "Well, ah might 'ave dun it if she'd paid me, but ah weren't abaht ter dig it aht agin fer nowt."

"Are you **sure** she didn't pay you to do it?" Harry teased him.

"Naw, honest! We never did find aht 'ow she got inside. They must 'ave dun it durin' th' night. Any road, it made sum extra work fer us 'cause we 'ad ter take 'im aht an' dig the grave deeper. A few days later they 'ad 'er buried on top of 'im." Ah think they must be still dahn there 'cause nobody ever dug 'em up agin as far as ah know!" Frank laughed uproarously, his dentures clacking along with the merriment. "Never found out fer certin 'ow she killed 'erself either, but like ah said, they thowt it wor poison."

The sandwiches arrived and Harry paid for them, first offering the plate to Frank as he did so.

"Ee, ah shouldn't be takin' yer snap, Mister Harry," he said, helping himself to a couple. Emma looked a little startled and firmly, but politely, commandeered the remainder. Then, munching on the sandwiches with his mouth open, Frank happily rambled on. The loose dentures didn't help, and Harry found himself having to look the other way to avoid laughing.

"Then there wor the grave where all th' flowers died," Frank continued. "Could still be, fer all ah know. That wor a rum un, fer sure. We buried a young lass. She must 'ave been in 'er early twenties... abaht the same age as ower Ellen when she wor taken. 'Orse trampled 'er. Any'ow, 'er mum and dad put sum flowers on 'er grave afterwards. Next mornin' they'd all shrivelled up. It warn't frost 'cause she wor buried around th' end o' May or beginnin' o' June. Any'ow, as usual, we got blamed fer it and we said we 'ad nowt ter do wi' it. So they put sum more there an' I'll be blowed if them didn't die an' all. Fer months the family kept comin' an' puttin' flowers in the little vase and they'd allus die. They kept tryin' fer nearly a year afore givin' up. Then they stuck in sum plastic ones. But fer years after, George an' me... George became me mate when Dad died... would now an' agin put a few real flowers there, yer know, just ter see. An' they allus died straight away. It wor weird. Grave's still there o' course, but she died ower thirty years ago so nobody's been fer a long time." He looked at Harry and Emma. "Ah've allus thowt graves are sad things when nobody comes anymore.

Course, these days lots o' fowk are bein' cremated. Took a big bite ahta' ower business, ah can tell yer!"

"How long have you been retired, Frank?" Harry asked.

Frank's chest puffed out slightly. "Ah worked regular until ah wor seventy-five. Then they pensioned me off, so ah went gardenin'. Still doin' it. Ah tak' care o' ower church grounds and a lady's place." He didn't elaborate on which lady. "Got ter keep workin'. Got no bloody choice on my pension. Mind, ah wouldn't be wantin' ter sit on me fanny all day long. We thowt abaht gettin' a telly but they's a bit pricey. Wunderful things, tho'. Ah can't figure aht 'ow they get the pictures through the air. It wor one thing ter get sounds, but pictures is another thing. Ah reckon we'll all be flyin' ter the moon sum day."

Frank chattered on and on. About shoes and ships and sealing wax, and cabbages and kings, as they say. Harry suddenly realized that he and Emma had hardly said a word to each other all evening. It didn't appear to bother Emma. She just sat close to him, her head cocked slightly to one side as it always did when she was listening to someone. The Chanel perfume she wore, fresh but subtle, lingered tantalizingly. And they were still holding hands beneath the table. The snug remained less than half full that evening, and even though most were people who knew Frank, they seemed very content to let him hold court with a newer audience. By now, after four pints of beer, one paid for by himself, one a gift from Arthur, one from Harry and the fourth by one of the regulars, Frank had taken on a rosy glow and was beginning to perspire very slightly. It amazed them both that through the course of the evening, Frank had headed for the lavatory only once. He must have a bladder like a camel's hump, Harry thought.

Finally, Emma began to surreptitiously look at her watch. Harry glanced at his; it showed just after nine o'clock. Where had the evening gone? Curse that bloody bus. Thanks to a silly schedule the evening had gone before it had barely got started. There had to be some sort of solution. He could think of one or two possibilities, all of which, at that stage, would probably get his face slapped.

"Sorry Frank, but we're going to have to take our leave. Emma's bus goes at nine-thirty and that's the last one for the night, unfortunately," Harry said, finishing his pint and placing some emphasis on the word 'unfortunately.'

"Where d'ye live, lass?" Frank inquired.

"Up at Elton. We farm."

"As everybody does around them parts! Wot sort o' farming? Milkin', like most fowks, ah imagine?"

Emma nodded.

"O' course, yer probably know that there used ter be a lot o' lead mines around Elton," he said. "A bit afore my time but it wor lead mines that put Elton on the map. That big 'ouse there wor built by a chap 'oo made a fortune from diggin' lead. Ah suppose yer know that. There weren't much ter do but farm after th' lead ran aht. A lot o' lads died o' lead poisoning in them pits. A tragic shame. Ah've got a few tales ter tell abaht them, too. But some other time ah reckon!"

"I'm afraid so," Emma said, touching his sleeve as they left. "It was nice to meet you, Frank. See you again soon,"

"Th' pleasure wor all mine, lass. Tak care, Mister Harry," he called after them.

Arthur leaned over the bar as they passed. "Much obliged to you, Mister Harry," he said quietly. "That'll be good for a pint next time you're in."

With another wink Kath waved good-by, and then they were out in the cold night air. Wrapping their coats about them, they scurried down to crown square and on to the bus stop.

"Sorry about that," Harry apologized, gripping Emma's hand as though she might suddenly drift off into space.

"Sorry about what?"

"Well, I asked you out and we spent the entire evening listening to old Frank. Couldn't have been very stimulating for you."

She nudged him gently. "I didn't mind at all, love. You've got to stop apologizing for everything! A lot of old people are very lonely. Some of them come into the shop and they just want somebody to talk to. Besides, Frank has lots of interesting stories. I'm sure he's told them a thousand times before, but I hadn't heard them, had you?"

"Mostly not. He talks about his grave digging career pretty regularly, and I think I once heard him telling some people the one about the woman who poisoned herself. I was with Terry from the office that night and our lovable Welshman always dominates the entire conversation, so I got to hear only about half of it. Of course, Frank likes to have an audience, too. But Frank's entertaining. Terry's a bloody bore."

There was a pause. Emma finally said, "So, Harry, tell me about the girls at the teacher's college."

He knew she wasn't really concerned, but he proceeded with an explanation anyway, if only to set the record straight.

"She was one of Terry's friends, honest! He seems to be on intimate terms with half the women up there."

"What was her name?"

"Who?"

"The one you were with, of course!"

"Vivian, I think. I didn't go out with her, though. We met her and her two friends at the pub. Besides, like Arthur said, she dumped me after about ten minutes and took up with some chap with a ring in his ear. I don't think I was her type."

"Maybe you should get a ring in your ear!"

"No fear. With my luck I'd get it caught on something and do myself some major damage."

"A bit accident prone, are we?"

Harry stamped his feet on the cold pavement as they waited for the bus. "You could say that. Actually, I get myself into **situations** more than accidents."

"Oh," said Emma. "And when exactly, does an accident become a situation, or vice versa?"

"Well, for example, there was the time at my mother's office. She works for the fire department in Barnsley, and two years ago they were repairing the canteen floor. Somebody had put some chairs around the hole to make a sort of barricade. Anyhow, during the couple of years I was living at home I used to pick her up from work with the car, and I'd often go up to the fire station canteen for a cup of tea while I was waiting for her to finish. On that particular day I went up there, saw the chairs, thought they looked untidy and stacked them up. A couple of minutes later the fire chief came roaring into the room and fell straight through the hole into the basement. Broke his leg. It never occurred to me that the chairs were there for a purpose. I was only trying to be helpful. Mum told me never to go up to the canteen again but everyone else thought it was a huge joke, except the fire chief. I don't think he ever liked me much after that."

"I can't imagine why!"

"Well, anyway, that's what I mean by a **situation**. It was the fire chief who actually had the accident."

"I see."

They both stared down the darkened road for a glimpse of Emma's bus. This time it was late. Why couldn't the wretched thing have been late on their first date?

"Terry sounds to be a bit of a bad lot," Emma said, making conversation while maneuvering herself out of the biting wind.

Harry first nodded, but then for some reason found himself trying to excuse his workmate. "He's a bit full of himself, but otherwise he's not such a bad chap. Definitely not ready for marriage, though. Life's never dull around Terry. He's Welsh."

"Does that make a difference?"

"Probably not to most people, but Mother once told me that Yorkshiremen and Welshmen never get along. They scrap like cats and dogs, apparently."

"Do you two scrap like cats and dogs?"

"No. Not yet at any rate. But he can be pretty irritating at times. He's always right. Can't stand people who are always right. And when he's telling you something he sounds like a damned clergyman. I've never been able to make up my mind whether he cares for me very much. Any chance he gets he's having a dig at me. But then, on one or two occasions he's helped me out with the boss, so I don't know."

Emma nodded from somewhere beneath the turned-up collar of her coat. She was wearing a long woollen scarf bundled around her neck so that just her nose poked over the top. With their breath steaming in the chilly air, they both stamped their feet to keep the circulation going.

Two other people were at the bus stop, a middle-aged man and woman who lived in Winster. Emma knew them and they chatted back and forth until the bus came rattling around the corner. It was practically empty, the windows fogged up except for a few small circles here and there where passengers had tried to peek out. Harry could make out the conductress, swathed in a large brown company-issue overcoat with her ticket clips, punch, and leather money bag slung, bandolier fashion, over her hunched shoulders. She was standing at the front of the bus, warming her bottom against the large round heater that protruded directly out of the engine, and smoking a cigarette. Those overcoats reminded him of the winter uniform used by Russian soldiers: heavy, warm, and totally uncompromising. He looked closer to see if it was the same conductress who had been on the Sunday bus, but couldn't decide. They all looked alike in those coats. The older couple boarded. Expressionless, the young woman waited while Harry pulled Emma close to kiss her. The warm smell of her perfume drifted into his nostrils.

"I'll see you tomorrow," he said, emboldened by the evening's events.

"Come over at lunch time," she responded. "I know you all take lunch at twelve o'clock over there. Me and Mrs. J. alternate ours. Tomorrow I usually take mine at one o'clock but I don't think she'll mind swapping with me. She owes me a few favours anyway."

"I'll be there." He waved as the bus, belching blue exhaust smoke, disappeared into the darkness. He could hear the driver grinding his way through several gears before crossing Matlock Bridge. The smoke lingered momentarily, then dissipated into the chilly air. Turning to walk back to Derwent House, he ducked under an adjacent streetlight to look at his watch. It wasn't even ten o'clock, ridiculously early even for Matlock. Still, despite their brief four hours together, nearly all of it in the company of someone else, he decided it had been a successful second date, by his meagre standards at any rate. There would be more dates with Emma, he knew that. But somehow he had to find a way of freeing them from the tyranny of a nine-thirty bus.

FIVE

The Duffield Incident

Early one dismal Wednesday afternoon, the office phone rang. Harry ignored it, partly because it was closer to Bill Lewis's desk than his, and partly because there were more important things to worry about. Three weeks had passed since he and Emma had first gone out together. This was only the middle of the week. Payday didn't happen until Friday, and until then he was broke. So he wouldn't be seeing Emma again until Saturday and this annoyed him considerably. Half listening to the shrill rattle of the telephone, he contemplated his gloomy financial situation. Pecuniary difficulties plagued Harry like an albatross stalking a doomed ship. He couldn't remember ever having enough money to do the things he wanted. It had begun with the death of his father, ushering in a life of what could best be described as genteel poverty. Boarding school, work as a gardener's apprentice, and a stint at the farm institute: they all dictated an asceticism which was finally beginning to rankle. This job had begun with the promise of riches beyond his wildest imagination. But to his chagrin he discovered that as incomes rise, so do expenses. The cost of living away from home had come as both a shock and an unpleasant revelation. Moreover, he found himself paying for a thousand and one things his mother had normally bought. The appearance of Emma in his life, while a happy enough development, was also serving to further sharpen a gradual realization that the move to Matlock had fallen far short of initial expectations.

Bill answered the phone and passed it on to Clem, which was unusual since Clem rarely received telephone calls in the office. Harry heard him repeatedly telling the caller that he would be there as soon as possible. Then he hung up, briefly returned to his table, and then went back to talk to Bill. The two huddled for a moment, Bill shaking his head and Clem attempting to change the other's mind about something. Whatever it was, Clem appeared to be unsuccessful. So once more he walked slowly back to his draughting table, sat down, and for a minute or two fiddled with a pencil.

Finally he looked towards Harry's corner. "Can I talk to you for a minute, Harry?" he asked quietly.

Barely able to conceal his curiosity, Harry went over.

"That was the boss," Clem said in a confidential whisper. Even so, the ever-vigilant Terry, quickly sensing there might be something going on, strained to catch the conversation.

"The police stopped him again and he tossed his keys out of the car. He's as drunk as a skunk and now he can't remember where he threw the damned things."

This had become a *tour de force* all too familiar to the Landscape and Playing Field Section. Dickie was, if nothing else, innovative in his impaired driving habits. When stopped by the police for driving on the wrong side of the road, over somebody's lawn, or through a shop window, he would turn off the road, stop the car, remove the keys from the ignition, and hide them. Since he had no keys in his possession, he couldn't be accused of driving the vehicle, could he? No keys, no evidence. Simple. Dickie prided himself on this childish bit of deceit, even bragging about it on occasions. No matter that he might kill or maim somebody, it was all a game to him, a chance to beat the police at their own tactics. His wife Joyce, and for a while their daughter Rachel, had lost count of the sleep and meals they'd sacrificed in retrieving him from the highways and byways of Derbyshire.

"Where was he calling from?" Harry asked.

"He said he was in a call box just north of Duffield. That's on the A6, north of Derby." Clem looked glumly at his colleague. "Trouble is, these rescue sorties cost me money and he hasn't once paid me for the petrol I've used. I'm getting a bit fed up with it."

Harry listened intently. While fully aware of Dickie's shenanigans, he had always understood that Morley and Bill shared the task of bringing him home. Why would Clem now be doing this, and how often? From what he had just said, it obviously wasn't the first time. Thinking back, Harry could recall one or two occasions when Clem had been absent from the office. But since all the draughtsmen were expected to supervise their own contracts, he had assumed that, like practically everyone else, Clem's absences were site visits. This business was all the more strange since the two appeared to have little contact with each other. Why hadn't word of Clem's involvement leaked out before now? There must be more to this than met the eye.

"Do you have a driver's licence?" Clem asked.

"Yes, as a matter of fact I do," Harry replied.

"I wonder if you could help me look for his keys. Two of us might get done a bit faster and besides I'll probably need someone to drive my car back while I drive his. Bill helped me last time, and the time before come to think of it, but he says he doesn't have time today. Actually, I don't think he wants to be bothered any more. Can't blame him, it's a real pain."

Harry cast a glance at the office window. Rain spattered against the glass, streaming in broad rivulets down the large rectangular panes. A broken drain pipe somewhere high above added to the torrent. Barely past lunch time, it had become so overcast that the office lights were already on. Not one of the most attractive days for a car ride. But on the plus side it would provide some respite from from Terry's constant pontificating about Maid Marion. Compensation enough, perhaps.

"Well, I..."

Clem smiled. "Oh, come on. Look at it as an afternoon outing!"

"Okay, sure. I'm not that busy. So long as Bill doesn't mind."

"Oh, no problem there. Believe me, Lewis is quite happy to be off the hook."

"How long do you think we might be?"

Clem shrugged, "Haven't a clue. In this instance, assuming we can find his keys, maybe three or four hours. Could be longer."

"I'd better give my landlady a ring, just to let her know I might be late for dinner." Harry didn't need to worry unduly. Miss Twigg's unyielding resolve for mealtime punctuality seemed to have rapidly crumbled with her new boarder, for whom she had a particular soft spot. Not to worry, she said, she would keep something warm, just in case. A nice gesture to be sure, except that the longer his food stood around in her kitchen, the more likely it was to have been sampled by Biggles the cat, who enjoyed special status well beyond that reserved for ordinary pets.

"Where exactly did the boss throw his keys?" Harry asked as they wound their way through a maze of corridors to the parking area.

"Ah, that's the catch. He hasn't a clue. At first, before my time, he used to hide them **inside** the car, but the police got fed up with being jacked around and one day they found them under the floor mat. After that they searched his car every time. Pissed him off no end, so he started chucking them out of the window. Usually they're close by because he can't throw them that far. In fact the coppers often find them for him. I'm not sure what happened today. I guess we'll find out."

The rain had joined forces with a biting cold that cut to the bone. Below them, Matlock appeared to be buried beneath a thick, winter mist. Only one or two roofs and a church spire escaped its grip, riding above the greyness as though they had been cast adrift. Harry shrank into his coat, pulling up the collar and tightening his belt. Clem's car turned out to be a white, two-door Ford Anglia of roughly the same vintage as one that Harry's mother had nearly bought three years ago, before deciding to buy a brand new Morris Minor instead. They had taken the Ford Anglia for a test drive. It was a boxy vehicle which rode like a brewery cart and made twice as much noise. Inside, its uncomfortable seats offered scant compensation for the bumpy ride. Among its numerous shortcomings, Harry couldn't get over the gear lever. It snaked out from beneath the dashboard like a bamboo cane and flexed so much that finding the right gear often amounted to little more than pure luck. But unlike the model they had test-driven, this was a sorry-looking spectacle. The front bumper was badly damaged on the right-hand side. One of the wing mirrors, at some time broken off, had been stuck back on with electrical tape. And all over the body a rash of dents was now blossoming into rust pustules. This didn't seem like Clem, Harry thought as he carefully moved a pile of rumpled clothes from the front passenger seat into the back.

It was only the beginning. Clem's driving habits also proved to be in marked contrast to his careful unassuming style in the office. He drove like a maniac. Moreover, the car's wishy-washy gear lever appeared to bedevil him as much as it had Harry. Accompanied by a loud clank, he shot backwards into a tree. Without even getting out to assess the damage, Clem furiously wiggled the magic wand into a forward gear. The car lurched forward, out of the parking lot, into the town centre, and down Dale Road towards the A6.

"It's about fourteen miles to Duffield," Clem yelled above the noise.

Harry hoped he would live to see Duffield. His mother was forever complaining about his driving too fast; she should spend a day motoring with Clem. He could see little of where they were going, since the rubber on the passenger-side windscreen wiper had disintegrated, leaving its metal arm scratching back and forth against the glass. Frequently the car careened to the right, and some slower-moving vehicle would disappear behind them in a wash of spray and dirt.

The A6 was a busy, winding, cluttered road in 1961, with none of today's motorways to relieve the congestion. Harry could see why county-office commuters from Derby had been so insistent upon getting a dedicated bus service. Once clear of Matlock Bath and the Heights of Abraham, there didn't seem to be much countryside left, and that which remained wasn't particularly attractive. It presented an unpleasant contrast to the open wildness of the northern peaks, which he and his mother had occasionally motored around. The dirty and decaying landscape they were racing through on this day had a run-down tiredness reminiscent of Harry's birthplace. Only a little farther south, closer to Derby, unrepaired bomb damage from the last war added to the dreariness. Above them, street lights, triggered by the overcast, burned sulfurous yellow through the driving rain.

"Do we know **exactly** where to find him?" Harry asked again, this time with a touch of anxiety. He could see their mercy mission becoming a headlong flight into hell.

"Exactly? No," Clem replied. "The main road goes through Duffield. Boss said to look for a signpost pointing to Ashbourne just before we start getting into the shops. I think he said it was the B50... something or other, and it's on the right hand side. Wish it wasn't pissing it down so hard. Can't see a damned thing. I gather if we turn up that road there's a call box on the opposite side near some houses and a church. That's all fine and dandy but Dickie's only part of the problem; we have to find the car, too. Hope it isn't in a ditch like it was last time. Obviously we'll have to find him first to find out."

Harry hadn't considered the possibility that Dickie might not necessarily be with his car. What if he couldn't remember where he'd left it? Then they would be forced to look for the car **and** the keys; more Scarborough warnings that this might not be the pleasant excursion he had anticipated an hour earlier.

Suddenly they were in Duffield, and no signpost to Ashbourne had leapt out at them. Harry felt a sense of frustration at being unable to help much. His side of the windscreen afforded such limited vision that he could barely see the front of the car, let alone anything else.

Clem pulled over, turned around, and drove back up the road. "There it is, the B5023!" he cried, wheeling the car to the left. "I remember that's what he said. Now, if we can just find the call box we'll be making some progress."

They nearly missed that, too. It stood on a street corner, under the overhang of a very large tree, its red paint almost blending into a solid looking brick wall behind. In the poor light they strained to see if anyone was inside. Condensation covered the glass windows, suggesting that the call box might be occupied. But well over an hour and half had elapsed since Dickie called.

"He wouldn't still be in there, would he?" said Harry, naively. "Seems to me it would make more sense for him to be looking out for us, or at least making himself visible."

Clem said nothing. He turned off the car's engine and they both got out with Harry intently watching the call box windows. Half way across the road he noticed a hand rubbing away the condensation on one of the panes. Once it got roughly to the diameter of a teacup, an eye briefly appeared.

"You know, I think he **is** in there!" Harry exclaimed, his heart beginning to pound a little.

They both slowed to get a better look, but the eye had vanished.

Clem squinted again through the rain at the tiny hole. "Why on earth would he be standing in there?"

"Beats me. You seem to be more familiar with his antics than I am."

Clem reached for the call-box door handle and cautiously opened it. Sure enough, Dickie was inside, leaning against the telephone. The smell of beer and urine wafted out into the damp air. Upon seeing them he grabbed the receiver to make it appear that he'd just completed a call, lost his balance and fell against the other side. "Jeshus, what fuckin' kept ya?" he snarled. Noticing Harry, he added, "Why d'ya bring him? Why don't we have the whole fuckin' department down here? I told ya last time I don't want every Tom, Dick and Harry flapping their lipsh about this."

"Bill couldn't make it today. Harry offered to drive my car back," Clem said evenly.

Looking at his boss and the source of the smell, Harry could see that he had wet his trousers. A huge dark stain spread down both inseams, almost reaching the ankle of his left leg. Had the police scared him so much he'd wet himself? Harry wondered. Or was his bladder finally giving out? Clad only in a light sports jacket, Dickie was shivering uncontrollably. If there had been a coat, there was no sign of it. How could the silly man have stood for nearly two hours in a space measuring less than four feet square? Why hadn't he found somewhere a bit warmer to wait? Perhaps he hadn't been there all that time. Perhaps he had just returned to make another phone call. Littered all over the floor of the call box were spilled cigarettes, some crushed to a brown pulp by Dickie's lurching feet, and the empty packet half stuffed into his breast pocket. Hanging back to allow Clem to do the negotiating, Harry looked at the mess with a mixture of dismay and revulsion.

"I think your car would be a bit warmer place to wait while we pick up your keys," Clem said.

"Sure it would if I could remember where I left the bloody thing," Dickie snapped back while pushing his way out of the call box.

This revelation sank Harry's spirits even further. It would be miserable enough finding a set of keys on a day like this; wandering the streets looking for a lost car could be worse, considering how far Dickie might have wandered after abandoning the wretched thing.

But Clem refused to be rattled. "Okay, not a problem, Boss. Mine's across the street. Any idea, **roughly**, of where you left it?"

Dickie offered an indifferent shrug. "When the coppers got on my tail I dodged down a shide street. It'sh around here shomewhere. Why the fuck would I be calling you if I knew where it was?"

"That's alright, we'll find it," Clem replied. "Where did you throw the keys?"

"Over the bloody wall." Dickie nodded his head backwards.

"Oh dear," said Clem. Oh Christ, thought Harry.

The wall, roughly six feet high, skirted two sides of what looked to be an old house that sat deep in its own grounds on the same street corner as the call box. There didn't seem to be any way of getting around either end, since from where they were standing both walls appeared to join up with adjacent properties. Harry left Clem to manhandle Dickie into the car and after randomly picking the street to his right, went to look for an opening or a gate. Halfway along he found one, a solid wooden door set into the brickwork. But after tugging and pushing at the rusted handle for a few minutes, he concluded that it must be either locked or jammed. In any event the door didn't appear to have been used for some time. Through a narrow gap on the hinge side he peered into the gloom. It was indeed a very large Victorian house, built also of brick, with stone mullioned windows and a pair of ornate chimneys on the side nearest his vantage point; the kind of place that would have suited the Munsters to a tee. No lights shone from its windows, no sounds came from within its shadowy walls. Nothing at all except an occasional whisper of wind through the surrounding trees.

After giving up on the gate, he returned to the car in time to hear Dickie demanding a cigarette. Without saying anything he went over to the call box and retrieved a few from the floor. Ordinarily he might have had some of his own. But the battle to quit had been given fresh impetus by Emma's dislike of smoking, and he had recently decided to further reduce temptation by not carrying any with him. A packet lay, barely touched, in his bedroom.

Dickie accepted the cigarettes ungraciously. "You two can find the car," he said, lighting up with shaking hands. "I'm not going out in the fuckin' shtreet looking like thish." And with that he slammed the car door on them.

"Our noble boss never went to charm school, did he?" Harry whispered, reeling a little from the stench.

Clem pursed his lips. "No, he certainly didn't. But then, we all have to pay the piper sometime."

It seemed an odd remark, and one that Clem had made before. But like before, he had never explained himself. Harry waited for some elaboration; none was forthcoming. Clem lapsed into silence, staring vacantly up and down the road as the rain continued unabated. Finally he looked at Harry. "What I want to know is, do we look for the keys first, or the car?"

"Seems to me we'd be better off looking for the keys first," Harry replied. "They're smaller and the light's fading quickly, and in any case we can't do much with the car without them. I don't know how to get into the garden, but I think the easiest thing to do would be to hop over the wall. To be honest, I think we're wasting our time. I don't see how he could have thrown them that far in his condition, do you?"

"I'm surprised he even remembers chucking them over the wall, considering he can't even remember where he left the damned car."

Harry eyeballed the height and shrugged. "Okay, we'll have a look. I'm getting soaked just standing here. Scrambling over a wall isn't going to make things much worse. Come and give me a leg up."

He flung himself at the bricks, pushing his foot into Clem's clasped hands. Fortunately the wall didn't have any broken glass cemented into the coping bricks, a popular intrusion deterrent in those days. Rolling over the top on his stomach, he landed on a lawn, ankle deep in a sea of soggy leaves that practically covered the area. Finding a set of keys would be like looking for the proverbial needle in a haystack. However, it was just possible that Dickie might have tossed the keys before entering the call box. In which case they should be close by, assuming they fell on the ground. Above Harry's head a thousand tree branches dripped water; he prayed that the keys hadn't got caught in one of them.

"What do they look like, Clem?" Harry called out in a loud whisper.

"What does what look like?"

"His keys."

There was a pause. "Like keys, I guess. What else would they look like?"

"No. I mean, are they on a ring with anything else, like a key fob or something?"

"Haven't a clue. Look for something shiny."

"Thanks. That's a lot of help," Harry grumbled. By that time, he was having difficulty seeing his feet, let alone a key ring, shiny or not. It was getting darker by the minute.

Suddenly a loud bellowing from the side of the house jerked him upright. He looked up in time to see a large furry object propel itself out of nowhere and across the lawn, fangs bared. It looked like an Alsatian, all black and tan and no sense of humour. Harry froze on the spot. He didn't fancy becoming the dog's late-afternoon tea. Nor, for both his and Emma's sake, did he want to wind up missing some vital parts. It paused a few feet away, growling softly.

"Okay, boy," Harry said, trying to estimate the lapse time to the wall. "Nobody's going to hurt you."

The dog evidently knew that, for it continued to growl menacingly, pacing a few steps to one side, then to the other, tail curled under its hind legs. To hell with the keys, Harry decided. He leaped towards the wall, managing to get both hands on the coping bricks. But the dog was faster. In a split second it had clamped its teeth onto his left trouser leg, grazing the calf and tearing the cloth. The more Harry struggled, the more the dog hung on.

"What's going on?" Clem asked from the other side of the wall.

"I'm being eaten by a bloody dog," Harry squawked. "For Christ sake, try and find the owner. Go down the road, see if there's another entrance."

"Will do," said Clem in his usual unflappable monotone. "Hang on. Don't get the dog upset."

"The dog's not upset. I'm the one who's bloody upset. And I'm going to be even more bloody upset if it takes my goddamn leg off!"

He could hear Clem's feet splashing off and around the corner. Unsure whether to continue his quest for the top of the wall or get down, he hung in the middle, hands still clawing the top bricks and his right shoe wedged into a crack. He started kicking, hoping to dislodge his attacker, but the heavy dog remained undeterred, shaking its captured chunk of trouser leg with the enthusiasm of a ferret. After a few more minutes, thinking that perhaps his frantic struggling was only making matters worse, Harry went limp, like a load of spilled laundry. It might have been a good idea in theory, but the dog had obviously read a few manuals, too.

Soon the grazed skin started to smart, and he worried that the animal might be rabid. By this time there was little doubt in his mind that the entire trip had been a ghastly mistake. He could be sitting down at Miss Twigg's, enjoying his evening meal in solitary splendor. Instead, he was halfway up a brick wall in the pouring rain with some mastiff ripping his clothes to shreds.

After indulging himself in a round of self-pity and reaching a total stalemate in the tug-of-war, Harry heard the sound of voices coming from the same direction as the dog. He looked over his shoulder to see Clem rounding the corner accompanied by a shorter person wearing what seemed to be a cape. As they got nearer he could see that it was an older woman, in her sixties as far as he could estimate, and she was indeed wearing a cape, plus an odd-looking hat and a large pair of rubber boots. Harry could also see her gesticulating wildly with a cane as she strode forcefully across the lawn with Clem trotting half a length behind.

"Well, you can't blame the dog, you can't blame the dog," the woman was saying in a loud county voice. Instantly she reminded Harry of their school house matron: portly, masculine, and possessed of a voice which brooked no dissent. Like matron, she would have made an excellent drill sergeant.

Coming to a halt a few feet away, she briefly surveyed the scene, legs apart, and the cape doing its best to cover her ample frontage. "Alright, Roger," she commanded, "you can come away. I don't think this chappie is going to hurt you."

"No, I'm not. Honestly," Harry babbled.

The dog instantly let go of its prize, ambled over to the woman's side and sat with its tongue hanging out. After eyeing Harry and Clem again for a moment she said briskly, "I find it hard to be too sympathetic. If you fellows haven't the courtesy to knock on my door first, then you must accept the consequences. You could have been burglers. These days there is so much crime. So much destruction. Certainly not the world I grew up in, I can tell you."

Back on the ground, Harry pulled down the remains of his trouser leg. "I'm sorry, Madam," he apologized. "But I couldn't see any lights on, and I also wasn't sure where the front of the house was."

"Well, **he** found it," she snorted, looking at Clem. "It's just around the corner, for heaven's sake. Have you two been drinking?"

This struck Harry as rather humorous considering the circumstances. "No, no, we haven't, really," he assured her. "We were trying to find some car keys that were accidentally thrown in here."

The woman snorted again. "So your friend here says. Tell me, how can someone **accidentally** throw some keys over a wall, eh? Damn silly if you ask me. Have you found them yet?"

"I'm afraid not," Harry said, half-heartedly swishing his undamaged leg among the leaves. "We don't even know for certain if they're in here."

"Roger," the woman commanded again, pointing with her cane. "Find keys!"

The dog glanced up at her, then trotted over to one of the trees, sniffed about for thirty seconds, then stuck his nose into the ground. Back he came with the keys in his mouth. Harry and Clem stood with their own mouths open like kids at a magical show. The woman took the keys, wiped them against her cape, and handed them to Clem. The dog, tongue still hanging out and its breath steaming in the downpour, was obviously pleased by yet another triumph of detection. It sat, poised expectantly for further orders.

"How did you... I mean... how did it know...?" Clem spluttered.

The woman smiled for the first time. "Actually," she said, "I tend to lose my own car keys quite a lot. Although certainly not over walls. I trained him to look for them. Doesn't take long to train a good dog to do things. You just have to be a strict disciplinarian."

Harry couldn't imagine anyone better equipped than her. Feeling it might be finally safe enough to get on better terms with Roger, he moved to give the dog a pat. His timing couldn't have been worse, for at the same time he bent down the woman raised her cane again to point the dog towards the house. It caught Harry squarely under his nose. With a yelp he staggered back, blood streaming. After a brief numbness his face felt as though it had been stung by a thousand wasps.

"Oh, good heavens!" she exclaimed, dropping the cane and rustling about among her numerous layers of clothing for a handkerchief. "Dear boy, I'm most terribly sorry. Come into the house and let me attend to it."

With the flow of blood temporarily stemmed, they made for the back door with Harry clutching his head and a tattered trouser leg flapping uselessly around his ankle. Roger trotted happily alongside, apparently convinced that all this pain and anguish was part and parcel of the afternoon's adventure. For Harry, the afternoon had become yet another of those **situations,** and another occasion for wishing the ground would swallow him up.

Clem was stumbling behind them making some concerned clucking noises when he suddenly remembered that Dickie had been sitting in the car for nearly half an hour.

"Harry," he said, peeling off towards the front gate, "while you get your nose fixed, I'll see if I can find the car. Meet me back at **my** car."

The woman stopped in mid-stride. "You mean you've lost a car as well?" she asked incredulously. "Well, no one could have tossed **that** over the wall or we would certainly have spotted it." Grabbing Harry by the arm she said, "Come along, young man, we'll see what a cold pack and some salts will do for that wound."

The thought of having some salts shoved up his throbbing appendage was almost too much for Harry to bear. But at least it would be out of the rain. He wondered how Emma would react when she found out he'd got himself another soaking; laugh her socks off, no doubt. In some ways it all seemed a little unfair. While he couldn't deny a proclivity for disaster, he could hardly be held responsible for the weather.

They made their way round some outbuildings to a brick-paved terrace. In the centre sat a concrete birdbath, choked with blackened leaves. Around it, weeds and grass had begun to sprout through the bricks.The area was so thick with trees that the perpetual shade had reduced the garden to a carpet of moss. Outside a door to the house, a large potted plant in the late throes of demise, had been unceremoniously dumped. It sat, sulking and rejected. Harry could see that the lawn where he'd met his Waterloo with Roger was at the side of the house, well away from the woman's living area. No wonder she couldn't see or hear them. The dog, on the other hand, unchained and free to roam about her large grounds, certainly had.

"By the way," she said, ushering Harry into her high ceilinged kitchen, "I'm Margaret Hamsterly. What's your name?"

"Harry Michaels," he wheezed through the handkerchief she'd lent him. "My friend is Clement Walker. We work for the Derbyshire County Architect's Department."

"Are you an architect, then?"

Harry shook his head. "No, we're draughtsmen. We design playing fields."

"Playing fields? I didn't think there would be anything to design in a playing field! Can't you just flatten out a bit of ground and sow some grass seed? That's what they did in my day, I'm sure."

Harry smiled weakly and shook his head again. "They need drainage."

"Drains? Why on earth do they need drains? Why can't you make 'em on a slope and let the water run off? Damned sight cheaper than drains. I think you chaps must spend most of your time dreaming up ways to waste our taxes."

"Ah..." He began to mentally construct a technically sound response, then decided that such an exercise would be a complete waste of time. He put the handkerchief back up to his face.

"Well, I hope you're not thinking of building a playing field in my garden," she snorted. "I like it just the way it is, thank you."

She bustled about, removing her cape and helping Harry off with his raincoat. Then, after hanging them behind the door she stood back and contemplated him. "So," she said, "what exactly were you doing leaping over walls in the pouring rain?"

It was tempting to be flippant, to tell her it had simply been a boring afternoon. But he guessed she wouldn't be a woman to be trifled with. And he didn't want to get whacked with the cane again. The last time was accidental. She looked perfectly capable of doing a lot more damage if she really tried. In any case, explaining Dickie's antics might be a lot easier than explaining playing-field design, especially since he didn't possess much of an understanding himself. So he decided to relate the entire sequence of events.

A cheery blaze burned in her Yorkshire range, a huge monstrosity made of cast iron, with a fireplace on the left, a large oven on the right and warming shelves above. Hinged, metal hobs could be swung close to the fire for heating kettles and pans. Like her kitchen, the range was spotless, its trim burnished with steel wool and the rest freshly blacked. She sat him at the kitchen table and patched him up while he wove his way through their afternoon's experience. It all must have sounded odd, he thought, since he was still bleeding profusely and had to talk through his mouth while pinching his nose between two fingers.

Half listening, or so it seemed, Mrs. Hamsterly ran a face cloth under the cold tap. "Alright, we'll kick off with this," she said. "Pop it on top of your nose, over the bridge. That's it. And keep it there."

That ended Harry's rambling explanation. The combined effect of holding the end of his nose with one hand and the large cloth to his face with the other was to shut off most of his oxygen supply. While waiting for the cold compress to do its work, she brewed some tea in a gigantic brown Betty, pouring boiling water from a kettle that seemed to be in perpetual readiness on the hob. After making the tea, she dropped a pretty woollen cosy over the teapot and pulled the hob back from the fire a little. It then became clear that she'd been listening more closely to his tale of woe than he had assumed.

"My late husband was a bit like your Mr. Dickie," she began sadly. "Probably worse. It killed him. But he didn't have any excuse. He didn't detonate bombs in the war. He was too old for active service. No, he was an ordinary bank manager with the Westminster in Derby. And one day he started drinking and never stopped until his liver blew up. That was the closest he got to detonating anything. Selfish bastard. I'm just glad we didn't have any children. The only thing he left was this house, which I mostly paid for out of my own money anyway. My family had a little wealth, which I inherited when Mother and Father died; otherwise I would be quite destitute. So, now there's just me and Roger. And he drinks only water, thank God."

From a cupboard she produced a bottle containing some white crystals, removed the cap and set it down on the table in front of him. "Hold the bottle under your nose and breath up," she commanded, "It'll ease the pain."

Harry took a deep sniff, and it felt as though someone had plunged a red-hot poker up his nostrils. The stuff smelled of ammonia. He wanted to ask what the crystals were, but decided against it.

"Well, how's that?" she asked.

"I'm not sure," Harry replied with his eyes watering, "I think my nose fell off."

Mrs. Hamsterly laughed so vigorously that her bosom wobbled like a huge blob of jelly. "Nonsense! It'll work wonders. Keep sniffing, but perhaps not so hard."

After several minutes of sniffing and eye-wiping, she took the bottle away and poured him some tea. During all this time Roger had sat by the fire, watching them with interest. After Mrs. Hamsterly removed the smelling salts he wandered over and sniffed at the rip in Harry's trousers.

"Oh, my dear young man," she said spotting the dog's actions, "in all the excitement I nearly forgot about your poor leg. Let me have a look at it."

Harry stuck it straight out and Roger sniffed at it again.

"Doesn't seem to be much of a wound," she declared. "Shouldn't be. He's been trained to grab only clothing... trousers, sleeves, anything he can get his teeth into and hang on. Perhaps he misjudged a little. He's like me, a bit past his prime. Anyhow, we'll get it cleaned off with some Dettol. Sorry about the trousers though. They really are rather ruined. What is your waist size?

"Thirty-two," said Harry, puzzled.

"And where do you live?"

"In Matlock."

"And whereabouts in Matlock?"

He told her.

She said nothing more about his trousers and proceeded to pour some more water from the kettle into a small cooking bowl, adding some Dettol to it. Just like Mother would have done, he thought, as the powerful odor wafted upwards. It stung, but no more than the smelling salts. For all her size and masculinity, Mrs. Hamsterly attended to Harry's leg with the deftness of a trained nurse. And for the first time since vaulting the wall, he began to relax.

The first-aid completed and cleared away, she poured the tea. As far as he was concerned, a cup of tea was infinitely preferable to the bells and whistles of her medications; to begin with it tasted better. But he had hardly put the cup to his lips when a knock at the back door announced Clem's return. His raincoat was soaked and he looked close to tears. "The wretched man barfed all over my car," he told them. "It'll stink for months."

Harry's temporarily lifted spirits sank with the realization that it would be his job to drive Clem's car home.

Mrs. Hamsterly's brow furrowed in anger. "That is absolutely disgraceful," she said, pulling Clem closer to the warmth of the fire. "And most inconsiderate. Why on earth you put up with him is beyond me. The man should be horse whipped."

Putting up with the boss had never occurred to Harry as being a negotiable situation. One either put up or found a new job. Perhaps things like that were also different in Mrs. Hamsterly's day. He turned to Clem. "Did you find **his** car?"

"Oh yeah. It wasn't that far away but for some reason he'd left the damned thing in someone's delivery yard. I walked past twice without seeing it. I swear he's getting dafter all the time."

"Where is the car now?"

"I parked it behind mine. Trouble is, we're on a main road so I have to leave the side lights on, and my battery's not all that good."

'How's the boss feeling?"

"Still pissed, and pissed off. What else is new."

"Well, we can't leave things like this," Mrs. Hamsterly said, wading into the fray. "But before we do anything else, take off that coat and have a cup of tea. I have some biscuits, too. Your supervisor can wait a while longer. It'll do him good, and in any case he can't go far because we've got his keys. Afterwards I want you to bring the cars into my driveway and we'll see if we can tidy yours up a bit."

Clem started to protest. "That's very kind of you but I can't put you to all that—"

"Nonsense, a few bad smells aren't going to kill me. And while we're at it, I'm going to give that man a piece of my mind."

Punch-up on the way, Harry thought to himself. That should cap off the afternoon nicely.

So they had their tea while Mrs. Hamsterly went and got a bucket and various cleaning *accouterments*. Then they went back to the cars.

"Boss ain't going to be amused by this," said Clem. "He looks atrocious, and he knows it. If that woman—"

"Mrs. Hamsterly."

"If Mrs. Hamsterly pitches into him, he's going to explode and he can be pretty nasty when he loses his cool."

"Who cares? Seems to me he's done that already," Harry replied. "All over the inside of your car. And frankly I don't feel like driving it back to Matlock in that condition."

Clem found it difficult to argue. He was every bit as fed up with the situation as his colleague.

"By the way," Harry asked, "did you find out **where** he'd been boozing?"

"No," Clem replied. "But it was probably in Derby. Bill Lewis said he had a meeting scheduled there. And that's his old stamping ground. Lots of pubs in Derby."

Harry chuckled. "Not as many as in York, though!"

"How do you know that?"

"The farm institute I attended was just outside York. Little village called Askham Bryan. They say York has more pubs per capita than any other British city."

Having vomited all over the front seat of Clem's car, Dickie had now moved into the back. Harry could see a slumped form through the fogged up glass, smoking the last cigarette that Harry had scavenged off the call-box floor. As Clem had noted, he was still intoxicated but not enough to escape a rapidly blossoming hangover.

"What the hell are you two doing?" he snarled, when Clem opened the car door. "I'm sittin' in here fuckin' freezing while you're buggering around. You found the keys and the bloody car. Now for Chrissakes, get me back to Matlock, otherwise I'll drive the goddamn thing myself."

"Wouldn't be a good idea, Mr. Dickie," Clem said. "I think the police are still watching you. One of them drove past as I brought your car here. They were going to stop but they saw **me** get out of it." This was a lie, but Dickie would never know. "Anyway, a lady across the street wants to give us a hand to clean up the car a little," he added. "And you can wipe up a bit, too."

"No fuckin' way!" Dickie replied. "I'm not parading around in public looking like this. So forget it."

He tried to slam the door again but Clem held on. "Sorry, Boss, I have to insist on this one. It smells pretty bad in here and I can't ask Harry to drive the thing to Matlock in that condition. It won't take any more than a couple of minutes."

"Won't take more than a couple of minutes," Dickie mimicked. "Jeshus. Here I'm sitting with a fuckin' headache and a wet fanny and you two want to wash out the bloody car."

"That's about it. We're just going across the road." Clem replied firmly. Then, turning to Harry, he asked, "Which car do you want to drive?"

Harry had noticed that Dickie's car was a dark green Morris Oxford. Its chunky design told him that it must be three or four years old. Being somewhat accustomed to Morris cars, he opted for that one.

Clem grabbed him by the sleeve as he handed over the keys. "It's a bit smelly in there, too," he whispered.

Harry discovered he wasn't kidding, but at least it didn't smell as bad as Clem's vehicle.

They drove the cars down the road, round the corner, and into Mrs. Hamsterly's sprawling driveway where she stood waiting for them. With military precision she signalled them to go around the side where a wooden garage, in an advanced stage of falling down, sat under some more trees. By now it had been dark for nearly an hour, but the garage had a light over the door which she had turned on. Dickie's face looked ashen as Harry and Clem got out; the dark ferret eyes, normally full of vitality, seemed to have sunk into his head.

There was vomit on the front passenger seat, the floor, and hand brake area of Clem's car. Harry caught its raw smell and felt nauseated himself. After fumbling for the door latch, Dickie stumbled out, blinking in the light. Mrs. Hamsterly strode up, bucket in hand and Roger trotting not far behind, and made straight for him.

"My goodness you look a mess!" she said.

"Yes, madam, well, I don't normally look like thish. Bad beer." Dickie muttered cautiously, avoiding her piercing gaze. The woman's opening salvo had clearly put him off his stride, and his pounding head wasn't helping either.

"Bad beer, nonsense," Mrs. Hamsterly scoffed. "Any beer's bad if you drink too much of it. And you've obviously had enough for ten people." She handed off the bucket and cloths in order to give herself better physical positioning. It was evident that after years of married life with a now-dead alcoholic, she was just waiting for a live surrogate to wander into her gunsights. It was the wrong place and the wrong time for Dickie.

"What does your wife think about this?" she demanded.

Dickie bristled. "What the hell's my wife got to do with her...with it?"

"What has she got to do with it? Everything I'd say. She's the one who has to try and make ends meet while you're out spending all your money in the bars. D'you have any children?"

"None of your damned business."

"I take it, then, you have. And judging from your age they must be young adults. How do you think they feel, eh? I'll bet they left home as early as they could. You know what's so sad about people like you? They think everybody's out of step except them. You probably tell your wife that your drinking is your concern alone, and that it doesn't affect her or anyone else. Right?"

For Dickie, shivering in the cold night air, the wind had been completely taken out of his sails. He stood in silence, glaring balefully.

"Well, my friend," Mrs. Hamsterly continued. "I was married to someone like you. But I was lucky, he eventually killed himself. Your family still has to put up with **you**."

The two were facing each other like a couple of wild-west gunslingers. Harry and Clem had quickly scampered out of the crossfire and were busily cleaning the inside of Clem's car while trying their best to hear what was going on. Despite the garage light, it was difficult to see much, but the mixture of Dettol and carpet shampoo, apparently always on hand for Roger's occasional accidents, certainly made the car smell sweeter. Harry's nose had begun to throb painfully again, especially when he put his head down. And again he wished he'd never volunteered for this trip.

"Look, you old bag, I don't have to shtand here and be spoken to like a schoolboy," Dickie said, and with a loud belch started towards his own car. "If you want to harangue shomebody, do it with those two twits."

"Oh boy," muttered Clem from beneath the dashboard.

Mrs. Hamsterly still stood her ground, refusing to be offended by his language. "If you behave like a schoolboy, you deserve to be treated like one. Come with me!" she commanded in the same tone that she used on Roger.

"Stuff it," said Dickie. "I'm freezing my arse off, so if you don't mind I'm going to sit in my car until we're ready to leave. If that ever fuckin' happens."

"Nonsense. Come along and I'll make you some tea. When did you eat last?"

"Madam, I don't want anything to bloody eat."

"Then you will have some tea. Or would you prefer coffee?"

There was another short pause. "I would prefer coffee," they heard Dickie say.

Still on their knees inside the car, Harry and Clem looked at each other in astonishment. This affair was taking on all the proportions of a farce. They both peered over the dashboard in time to see Dickie meekly following her into the kitchen.

"I don't believe this," Harry said.

"Me neither," said Clem. "Hope he doesn't kill her in there."

"She's more likely to kill him."

But to their surprise the shootout never occurred and there was no loss of life. They got Clem's car cleaned out, then wiped over the driver's seat of Dickie's vehicle and emptied the bucket down the drain. Mercifully the rain had stopped, or at least declined to a slight drizzle. With ears stuck out like jug handles, they listened for the sound of breaking furniture. To no avail. All was quiet inside.

"Only problem is," Clem said, alternating his gaze between the house and their handiwork, "the seats are a bit damp to sit on."

"It's okay. If my raincoat's dried, I'm just going to turn it inside out and sit on that."

"Speaking of coats," Clem continued. "I haven't found the boss's. I wonder if he left it in Derby?"

Harry shrugged. "Could have. It's certainly not inside his car, and I checked in the boot."

Clem looked at his watch. "Well, its nearly seven o'clock. Let's see if we can get underway. You still want to drive my car?"

Harry nodded.

"Alright. When we get into Matlock, follow me to Dickie's house. Once we get rid of him, we're in the clear. Then I suppose the least I can do is buy you a meal. I don't think there's much open after seven or eight in the evenings, is there?"

Harry thought about Miss Twigg's promise of food kept warm. Then he thought about the cat. "There's the *Blue Bird* cafe on Dale Road. It's open until nine and they're not expensive. There's a waitress there I'd like you to see."

"We should get in before then," Clem said. "And we don't have to worry about Joyce asking us in. Poor woman's so embarrassed she doesn't even come to the door. She's seen this so many times before. I'm very sorry the rescue mission turned into a bit of a fiasco," he added. "On previous occasions we've simply picked him up and driven him home. This is the first time he's barfed up on me and believe me, it'll be the last. You were unlucky enough to be in on it."

"That's okay, it's not your fault," Harry replied. He looked towards the kitchen. "It's awfully quiet in there. What do you think they're doing?"

"Almost certainly not humping each other."

The kitchen door was slightly ajar. After knocking, they went inside and stood dumbfounded at the spectacle. There sat Mrs. Hamsterly and Dickie, side by side on a couple of kitchen chairs in front of the fire, talking quietly. She had a cup of tea; he was clutching a mug of coffee. Dickie's jacket, freshly wiped, hung from the back of another chair, drying in the warmth. Both looked up as Clem and Harry came in.

"It seems that Bob knew my late husband. George was manager of the branch where he banked when they lived in Derby," said Mrs. Hamsterly with a smile. "Small world, isn't it?"

Dickie grinned cheesily, but said nothing. Hunched over his steaming mug he still looked pale and unsteady. Watching him, Harry couldn't help a pang of sympathy for this pathetic little man, trapped in a world he couldn't cope with. Despite the bravado, his face this evening had betrayed the desperation of someone rapidly coming to the end of his tether. Perhaps the signs hadn't gone unnoticed by Mrs. Hamsterly. After all, she'd had plenty of past experience.

"We're ready to go, Boss," Clem said. "Thanks for the use of the cleaning stuff, Mrs. Hamsterly. I think that's the first time the inside of my car's been cleaned since I bought it!"

"We can't find your raincoat, Mr. Dickie," Harry added. "We've searched your car, including the boot."

"Might have left it in Derby," Dickie said sheepishly. Then he peered closely at Harry. "What the hell did you do to your nose?"

"Just caught it on something. It'll be okay." He could see by shutting one eye that both nostrils had become swollen and discoloured.

"Thanks, Margaret. Goodnight," Dickie said as they left.

'Thanks, Margaret'? 'Bob'? What had happened to the two combatants who an hour ago were poised to shoot it out? Instead of clenched fists and bared fangs, they looked more like a couple going off to renew their wedding vows.

To call this an anticlimax would be the understatement of the century. Harry and Clem stood at a respectful distance, lost for words.

Mrs. Hamsterly followed them onto the terrace to see them off. Roger stood patiently by her side. "Goodnight, Bob. And remember what I said," she called out to him.

"I will," he replied in the same meek voice that had expressed a preference for coffee an hour earlier.

What on earth had she said to him, Harry wondered as he drove Clem's car up the foggy A6 to Matlock. Dickie's transformation couldn't have been more startling if he'd received a lobotomy. One minute he was raving like a lunatic, and in the next he was acting like Scrooge after witnessing the three ghosts. And why had she bothered to become involved with them in the first place? Perhaps, having lived with an alcoholic husband, she felt some strong empathy with Dickie's problem. Perhaps the experience had fired some missionary zeal in her. But Harry also recalled the look of sadness on her face as she waved good-by. The thought occurred to him that she might be a very lonely woman. She hadn't mentioned when her husband died. But families with alcohol problems tend to gradually retreat into themselves. Socializing becomes difficult; friends don't call anymore, and going out is often a nightmare of uncertainty. For the spouse left behind, picking up the pieces can be a long process of painful adjustment. Sometimes it proves impossible. This afternoon's adventure could have been the most exciting thing to enter her life in months, maybe years. Perhaps Mrs. Hamsterly had momentarily re-discovered herself, only to see the experience quickly snatched away .

The road was busy with early Christmas shoppers. Harry worried about losing Clem, since he didn't know where Dickie lived. However, Clem made sure he stayed on his tail. On a couple of occasions he pulled over to allow Harry to catch up. Fortunately the Ford had a good heater, which offered some compensation for the dampness seeping into his backside. In almost an exact replay of the day he moved to Matlock, he had been overly optimistic about his raincoat's usefulness as a water seal. Notwithstanding the heater, he found it a wretched car, and he was glad his mother had decided against buying one, even though it cost less at the time than the Morris Minor. The road noise was incredible and the steering had a mind of its own. But Harry could also see that many of the car's shortcomings were as much a legacy of poor maintenance as shoddy manufacturing. Clem clearly didn't believe in spending money on minor things like tune-ups and repairs.

Dickie lived less than a quarter of a mile from the office, in a fairly new development of mostly semi-detached houses. Unlike the older homes of Matlock, these were built with a sandy-coloured brick, and all with the same cookie-cutter monotony of lower-middle-class housing estates. Each had a recessed porch with a narrow full-length window next to the front door. Both upper and lower front rooms sported a bay window. A low brick wall ran the length of the street, punctuated by identical wooden gates. Behind the wall tiny patches of grass were adorned with concrete cupids and other ugly monstrosities, most of them liberally stained with algae. The only relief from this architectural tedium lay in the provision of a garage; some houses had one, some didn't, including Dickie's.

Why, he wasn't sure, but Harry had expected to find the house neglected. To his complete surprise it shone like a new pin, the paintwork fresh, lawns trimmed, and the now-empty flower borders dug over and the weeds pulled. Who did all the work? He couldn't see Dickie getting off his fat backside. Surprises were proving to be the order of the day.

He drew up in front of the house behind Clem. After a few seconds Dickie got out, ignored Harry, went into the house, and slammed the door behind him. A few seconds later it opened again and Joyce appeared. After making sure the Morris was locked up, Clem ran up to the front steps and exchanged brief words while giving her the keys. He could see her looking suspiciously over Clem's shoulder in Harry's direction.

Then Clem came back to his own car and they changed places.

Shaking his head, Harry cast another glance at Dickie's house. "Can you believe that?" he said in disgust. "The man never even said goodnight, let alone thank you. That's the last time I go trailing around the countryside for him. No wonder Bill Lewis called it quits."

"Oh, his ego's a bit bruised," Clem replied. "He doesn't like people to know that he gets into these messes, especially 'junior' staff! Which is all a bit silly because everybody this side of Sheffield seems to have heard about him. But isn't that the way with alcoholics? They always fool themselves that nobody knows."

"I suppose so. By the way, any idea what 'Margaret' told him not to forget, just before we left?"

"Dunno, he didn't say. What time is it?"

"Just after eight-thirty."

They roared down to the *Blue Bird*, only to find it had closed early for some reason.

"Shit!" said Clem. "It really ticks me off when places do that."

"How about fish and chips?" Harry suggested. "The Snitterton Road one's not bad."

Clem smiled. "Are we a connoisseur, then?"

"No, I wouldn't call myself a connoisseur, but I have great survival instincts. Once or twice I've missed my landlady's meal deadlines and fish and chips are better than nothing! They also stay open late. At least, this one does."

They got their fish and chips and, eating them as they went along, walked back over the bridge to where Clem had parked his car. Rather than pollute the inside again with the smell of fried food, Clem suggested they continue on to the park. Perched on one of the benches, Harry savoured the fatty aroma of the chips, wrapped in their insulating layer of newspaper. For the first time since leaving Duffield, he forgot about his sore nose. Despite the chilly air it had turned into a fairly nice evening. The rain had finally stopped and the stars were out. Down the road towards Matlock Bath, the Heights of Abraham stood out as a black, brooding hulk. They talked about the office, about Emma, and about Dickie. But not once did Clem talk about himself.

On the way back to Clem's car, Harry asked, "You seem to know Dickie fairly well. How come?"

Clem smiled and said simply, "Actually, I **don't** know him all that well."

Harry wasn't about to give up that easily. "Then how did you get selected to do these rescue missions?"

"No idea. Perhaps everyone else had run out of patience with him. Think about it. Lol's never around, Bill doesn't bring his car to work and Terry doesn't have one. That just leaves Morley and Angus. As you probably know, Morley helped out before I arrived, and Bill used to go with him now and again. I don't believe Dickie has ever asked Angus. There isn't much love lost between those two." He paused and then corrected himself. "Actually, I think the boss envies Angus more than he dislikes him."

"Why would he envy Angus, for heaven's sake?"

Again, Clem smiled his sad little smile. "For being content."

Harry thought of the perpetually dripping nose and the gloomy little rain cloud that always seemed to hang over Angus and wondered how Clem could possibly come up with a statement like that. "I wouldn't say Angus ever looked the picture of happiness," he protested.

"I didn't say 'happy,'" Clem replied. "I said 'content.' Happiness and contentment are two different things, especially to a Scotsman!"

Ten days later Harry received a parcel at Derwent House. Inside, he found a pair of expensive casual slacks, waist size 32, and a note from Margaret Hamsterly apologizing for their not being finished in the leg. Reading the short note over and over again, he wondered if there had been some mistake. But the note and the parcel were both clearly addressed to him. The slacks were a similar style to those he had been wearing that day in Duffield. Miss Twigg, a fairly accomplished seamstress as well as a good cook, obligingly sewed them up and they fit perfectly. Emma liked the slacks but sulked about some mysterious woman sending him clothing out of the blue. She couldn't know Mrs. Hamsterly was in her sixties, and Harry made a point of not telling her when the topic arose. Their little joke came to an abrupt and sad end when, several months later, Dickie casually informed him that Margaret Hamsterly had died of cancer. He never mentioned her again.

SIX

The Christmas Party

A week before Christmas, Dickie waddled in to tell everyone present that the office party would be held Friday night at the *Hanging Gate*. Aside, perhaps, from drawing attention to the fact that the festive season had officially arrived, it was a totally redundant announcement. Neither the venue nor the date ever changed. Each year Bill Lewis grumbled that the boss must be getting some sort of kickback from Arthur Bassett for holding the party there. In reality Dickie didn't need support from his underlings to get free drinks. Arthur knew a gold mine when he saw one, which was probably why he sent a few pints Dickie's way once in a while, and cheerfully put up with his abuse.

While everyone else in the office seemed to regard the Christmas party as a repetitious grind, it provided Harry with an opportunity to formally introduce his new girlfriend. Dickie had hardly spoken to him following what had become known as 'the Duffield Incident.' But once the memories had receded to the back of his addled brain, he began making off-colour remarks about Emma, usually in front of the entire office staff. Poor Harry, hardly in a position to tell his boss to button up, had decided to undercut Dickie by showing her off as soon as possible at some office function. The Christmas party fit his requirements perfectly, and as an added bonus he would get to cast eyes upon Terry's fiancee, the yet-unseen Maid Marion. Five days a week for a month and a half he had been regaled with detailed accounts of her multitudinous virtues. They left little doubt that Marion was at the very minimum a ravishing beauty. And in case Harry still harboured any misgivings about the claim, a well-thumbed photograph taken at Llandudno or Colwyn Bay, or somewhere, would be shoved in his face as a *coup de grace.* In fact, the snapshot didn't prove anything since Terry had taken it just as Marion was taking a lick at an ice cream cone. Why Terry would use such a silly photograph to publicize his fiancee's looks, Harry couldn't understand. Why didn't he shoot the photograph **before** she'd started on the cone? Or afterwards? Or picked some other occasion altogether? The more Harry looked at it the more Marion resembled a character from *The Wizard of Oz*.

Bill Lewis assured him the entire Landscape-and-Playing-Fields section would be at the get-together, presumably with their wives and lovers. Harry was curious to find out what they all looked like. So far he had met only the Angus-McGregor family, and even then only briefly when Mary dashed into the office one day with the two kids in tow and attempted to pry ten shillings out of her husband. Like most people, Harry was familiar with the conventional wisdom about Scotsmen being tight with their money, but until then he hadn't taken it too seriously. However, the performance put on by Angus had made him an instant believer. The man was almost in tears by the time Mary left. But she did so with the ten shillings, proving perhaps that it takes a Scotsman to know a Scotsman.

Both Bill Lewis and Lol Dobson were married. Harry hadn't met either spouse, although he'd once talked to Bill's wife, Pat, on the telephone. Apparently they had one child, a boy who, at twenty-six, could hardly be described as a boy anymore. Lol and his wife, Carol, had no children. Lol seldom mentioned her, and Harry couldn't help wondering what she thought of her husband's bevy of female admirers. Perhaps she got to do a bit of fancy footwork herself, especially if Lol spent as much time at home as he did at the office. Lewis, who usually could find something derogatory to say about nearly everybody, commented once that Carol was as thick as two lavatory seats. Why two seats and not one, or three, or half a dozen— was never explained. Carol sounded like a very interesting woman.

Nor did Harry yet have the acquaintance of Dickie's wife, the long-suffering Joyce, apart from the fleeting glimpse when they brought Dickie back from Duffield. But all he could make out then was some greying hair and a sour-looking face. People had differing opinions about Joyce Dickie. Characteristically, Bill Lewis described her as a whiner who, according to him, should have kicked her husband's backside up to his shoulder blades a long time ago. Terry, who dined at Dickie's house now and again, was more inclined to elevate Joyce's loyalty and perseverance to sainthood. "It takes a very special person to put up with someone like him," he would proselytize in that thin, whining voice. "And Joyce is undoubtedly a very special person." Morley once made an observation that the only reason for Joyce's acquiescence lay in the fact that most of the time she was as plastered as her husband. Harry wondered how much truth there might be to Morley's claim. Clem, who obviously knew the Dickies better than he wanted to admit, had never mentioned that she drank. Nor had anyone else for that matter.

Morley Singleton remained, as his surname coincidently punned, steadfastly single. Too much in love with his car to have any left over for a wife, said Bill Lewis, with the customary hint of malice. It came as no surprise to Harry, who couldn't imagine any female in her right mind putting up with anyone so utterly boring. Admittedly there wasn't much to do in Matlock, but here was a bachelor whose idea of a fun evening amounted to changing engine oil in some drafty garage. Bill figured Morley would drive his Riley into the sunset one day and never be seen again. While Harry couldn't argue with this as a great final statement to the world, it would be only if the world missed Morley afterwards, which didn't seem likely.

Then there was Clem. If he had anybody in **his** life no one would ever know. Harry couldn't recall his ever saying anything about himself, except that he'd done National Service and had once worked in his father's printing firm. And it was fascinating how he could skillfully deflect probing questions by turning them against the inquirer. But with every conversation Harry had with Clem, he became more convinced that there was something in his past he wanted to forget. It wasn't just Clem's evasiveness; Harry could sense it in the way his eyes always seemed to be looking for a place of refuge, darting from one distant object to another, anywhere except the person he was talking to. Then there had been the Duffield incident, during which Clem claimed that he hardly knew his boss. Harry felt certain this was a lie. Clement Walker presented himself to the world like the moon, keeping only one side in perpetual view. But as everyone knows, the moon has a dark side. Did Clem have a dark side, or was he simply keeping part of his life away from the light?

Whenever Harry and Emma wanted to go out for the evening, that last bus to Elton had become a perennial and irritating problem. Frequently they found themselves in a mad scramble to reach the bus stop before nine-thirty. On more than one occasion they had rounded the corner of Crown Square to see the bus leaving. Harry would race after it, yelling like a lunatic. Emma suspected that the bus driver could seem them perfectly well, for he usually let Harry canter alongside for about a hundred yards before stopping in a great clashing of gears and squealing brakes. Harry agreed; the smirk on the bus driver's face confirmed it. Nine-thirty was a ridiculous time to call it a night, even in a Matlock entering the 1960's. Once, in an uncommonly magnanimous gesture, Morley drove them to Elton after an evening get-together at the *Hanging Gate*. Harry had been more than grateful, but also a little amused at the sight of his colleague, looking for all the world a gentleman's chauffeur, patiently waiting outside the farmyard in his shiny car while Emma got her goodnight kiss at the door.

For a couple of reasons the office party would mark a turning point in Harry's relationship with Emma. First, he was fed up with the nine-thirty curfew and he had resolved to find some way of keeping her in Matlock that night. Secondly, his overactive hormones were telling him that it was about time his virginal status came to an end, preferably before he went home for Christmas. These two issues preoccupied Harry for about a week until one morning, while shaving, he solved the first, and theoretically the second, with a brilliant stroke of genius. It was so simple he wondered why he hadn't thought of it before. Morley had made the observation that those who lived in Derby ought to stay at Miss Twigg's for the night of the office function, and then drive home the following morning. As he pointed out, Derwent House wasn't short of bedrooms, it would be better than driving afterwards on a skinful of beer, and Miss Twigg could undoubtedly use a little extra money for Christmas. Unfortunately, since Morley had overlooked the fact that Bill Lewis was the only person in the office still making the daily commute from Derby, no one paid much attention. Nevertheless, it gave Harry an idea. That evening he described Emma's problem to Miss Twigg and asked if she could put her up for the night. No problem, said Miss Twigg, eager to see what Harry's new girlfriend looked like. A terrific cook was Miss Twigg, but nosy. No charge this time, she said, although there would be on future occasions. Future occasions? Of course. Why hadn't he thought of that? It opened up tremendous possibilities, assuming some cooperation from Emma's mother, not to mention Emma herself.

"This means I finally get to stay in Matlock after nine-thirty?" Emma asked with a sly smile after Harry laid out his great scheme.

"Not only that, we can walk home to **my** place for a change," he said, casting about for more selling points. He needn't have made the effort. When it comes to plotting strategy, women are light years ahead of men. Emma had got this plan worked out before Harry started explaining it. They were sitting in the shop storeroom during Harry's lunch hour the following day. Boxes and junk filled most of the space, but at least they could eat their sandwiches there and be alone for a hour. In one corner a small countertop held an electric kettle and the usual paraphernalia for brewing tea or coffee. Long ago someone had salvaged a couple of secretarial chairs to sit on. They were old, the vinyl cracked and torn. and one had a castor missing.

"It'll work out very well," Emma said with the smile still flickering across her face. "I'm not working this Saturday." Pressing a tiny hand against his chest she added, "I'll tell Mum. So long as she knows where I am there won't be a problem. In any case, I **am** twenty-one... nearly twenty-two, and I should be able to stay out at night without having to ask! It's just that Mum worries... ever since Dad died. You know."

Harry agreed wholeheartedly, and with considerable relief. "I gather kick-off is around seven-thirty," he said. "We can have a bite to eat after you finish work and then go up to the *Hanging Gate*. You'll be thrilled to know we finally get to meet Maid Marion. Apparently she's arriving tomorrow, staying for a few days and then going back to Swansea with Terry for Christmas. I think they were going to look at houses while she's here. That should be an interesting exercise. I wouldn't like to be in the salesman's shoes."

"Speaking of Christmas, I don't suppose you've changed your mind about spending it in Barnsley?"

"Sorry. I really wish I could spend it here with you but my mum's in the same boat as yours. She always looks forward to Liz and me coming home once in a while, and especially at Christmas. She finds it pretty lonely when we're not around. It wasn't too bad when my sister lived at home. But then she got that secretarial job in Sheffield. She tried commuting every day but it didn't work out too well. The train kept running late and then she'd get into trouble for being late into the office. Actually, I think Liz would be quite happy to be back at home. Her digs are pretty crummy."

He knew Emma was disappointed. "That's alright," she said. "It's just that we have two birthdays to celebrate on December twenty-fifth, remember? And it would have been nice to share at least one of them with you."

"I hadn't forgotten, honestly," he replied. If there had been any honourable way to get out of going home, he would have jumped at it. But he'd made the promise before he met Emma and he could hardly renege on it now. This year

Emma would have to celebrate her birthday without him. Next year, however, would be a different matter.

Emma made an exaggerated sigh. "Well, there's nothing to say we can't celebrate a little bit ahead of schedule, is there?"

"I suppose not." He wasn't sure what she meant by the remark, but it sounded encouraging.

After work they deposited Emma's small suitcase at Miss Twigg's. As usual, Sarah was in the kitchen, halfheartedly mixing something in a large bowl. Seeing Harry first, she flashed a pimply smile, which faded rapidly when Emma came into view. Grabbing the bowl, she retreated to Miss Twigg's rocking chair without uttering a word. Battleship Bertha was at her charming best, although Harry noted that she had carefully put Emma in a room on the floor above his. It was an extremely large room but, like the others at Derwent House, had all the old-world charm of a bus shelter.

"Did Mr. Harry tell you that breakfast is at 7.30?" she asked pleasantly.

Emma assured her that Mr. Harry had given her all the necessary details. Besides, she said, she normally got up earlier than that on work days in order to catch the bus to Matlock. Harry was relieved to see that Miss Twigg liked her. Hadn't she, he would no doubt have got the message very quickly. As they stood in the kitchen the smell of simmering stew reminded him that he had earlier told Miss Twigg he wouldn't be home for dinner. Perhaps that had been a mistake. Since Emma's room obviously included breakfast, maybe Miss Twigg would have thrown in an evening meal, too, and saved him some money. Things like that were not an insignificant factor in Harry's chronically cash-strapped world.

Still, he enjoyed taking Emma to restaurants, even if they were, more often than not, the baked-beans-on-toast variety. So they headed once again for the *Blue Bird* cafe. Still no sign of Bogart and Bacall, but the candles were lit and the tablecloths recently changed. The *Blue Bird*, Harry had found out some weeks before, was a husband-and-wife venture, with some part-time help. Georgie and Yolanda were Greek. Twenty years before they had traded the sunny hills of the Peloponnese for rural Derbyshire and a spot that got more rain in a month than they had been accustomed to seeing in a year. Instead of opening a Greek restaurant, they opted instead for the mundane fare cherished by working-class Britons. That made sense to Harry, but emigrating to Derbyshire didn't.

They were beginning to recognize Harry and Emma as regular customers. One evening Georgie sent them a complimentary glass of wine with their meal. It might not have been the most appropriate accompaniment to sausage and eggs, but his heart was in the right place. On this night, however, Georgie had gone home early, leaving his patrons in the tender care of a part-time waitress Harry had nicknamed 'Lulu.' She must have been around seventeen, with a very large bust, equally large bottom, and bleached-blonde hair. Blessed with the I.Q. of a carrot, she flounced about the cafe in a short skirt and halter top, breathing seductively at every male she set eyes on. And God help them should they fail to reciprocate. Harry failed, of course, because he hadn't a clue how to deal with someone like her, and he paid dearly each time their visit and her shift coincided. Initially oozing with charm, Lulu's attitude changed rapidly once she realized her winning ways had not worked their usual magic. Various minor irritations were visited upon their table, including spilled coffee, cold soup, and on a couple of occasions someone else's bill. But even at her worst, Lulu provided very good entertainment value.

They finished their meal uneventfully with Lulu haunting the table of a smitten male old enough to be her father. The man's wife was clearly unimpressed by all the attention, and demonstrated this fact by casting their overly-endowed waitress a look that would have turned porridge into stone. Undaunted, the single-minded Lulu kept up the pressure for the entire hour and a half Harry and Emma were in the cafe. Her victim *du jour* looked to be having a good time of it all but doubtless had to face a reckoning afterwards.

"I think," said Harry as they were leaving, "we should sell 'Lulu-effigy dolls' and sell them to all the women who come in here with their husbands or boyfriends. And of course we'll have to sell them the pins, too. A bob apiece. We'd make a fortune."

The cheerless, drizzly day had turned into a dry but cold evening. Telltale signs of a ground frost were everywhere, on church railings, doorsteps, and among the beds of emaciated wallflowers that waited hopefully for spring in front of the town hall. They hurried up to the *Hanging Gate*, hoping Kath had got a good fire going. She had. It was blazing merrily as they entered the lounge. One of the things Harry noticed that first winter in Matlock was that the Bassetts burned logs rather than the ubiquitous sooty coal of the industrial midlands. There was something rather civilized about a log fire, he thought, and what a pity the British had literally burned their inheritance in less than a thousand years. He remembered reading somewhere that the entire country had once been a gigantic hardwood forest.

The pub didn't seem very busy for a Friday night.

"Captain Bob's in the snug," Arthur called out from behind the bar. "Some's arrived. You're not the first."

"Hello, Harry!" Arthur's wife called out from somewhere. Kath must be clairvoyant. How did she know it was him?

Dickie, flushed and perspiring, was well under way, leaning against one of the tables with a pint in one hand and a packet of cigarettes in the other. Once again he appeared to have lost his silver cigarette case, although it invariably showed up sooner or later. Sandwiched between Terry and Angus was old Frank, a picture of contentment as he followed the chatter. Upon seeing Harry and Emma enter, he happily waved an arthritic hand at them. Emma immediately recognized Mary, since she was another regular customer at the shop. Dickie spotted Harry and Emma at roughly the same time as Frank, called them over and made the introductions without once taking the cigarette from his lips.

"Well, my friends," he cried, the cigarette ash growing longer by the second, "I think there are some people here you haven't met before. First of all, there's my good wife, Joyce." He stretched out his arm to embrace a woman sitting against the wall with a pained expression on her face. "My dear," he continued, "this is Harry Michaels, one of our newest recruits. And thanks to a bit of intrigue on my part, the charming young lady with him is Emma."

Harry could tell that Dickie was sizing her up.

Joyce said she was pleased to meet them. They both said hello. Harry noticed that his brief glimpse during the Duffield Incident had been fairly accurate. She did have greying hair and a rather sour countenance. But it was a face burdened more by sadness than hostility.

Dickie's fat fingers pointed again. "Emma, sweety, you may have already met Mary. The fellow behind the snotty handkerchief is Angus."

"Och," said Angus with his wistful little smile.

"Well, yes," said Mary, raising her hand like a schoolgirl in class. "I believe I've met Harry before, although very briefly. And Emma and I see a fair bit of each other because I'm regularly in to Madison's to get prescriptions filled. Glad to see you without your white uniform, Emma!"

Mary's sublime disposition was a mystery to Emma. With a couple of children who seemed to be always screaming their heads off, and a husband constantly ill with some malady or other, she cruised serenely through the mayhem as though it were all nothing more than background noise. Nevertheless Emma liked her. With a personality as transparent as glass, Mary was one of those refreshingly honest people who wouldn't know the meaning of self-interest. What you saw was what you got. And if she liked you, she liked you, no questions asked.

Dickie poised himself to introduce the girl sitting close to Terry, but she broke in before he got started.

"I'm Marion," she gushed at Harry, blossoming into a wide toothpaste smile that revealed a set of appropriately perfect teeth. "Terry has told me so much about you, I feel we've already met." The smile wasn't quite so wide for Emma. "Terry tells me you live on a little farm," she continued. "It must be wonderful to be surrounded by fields and cows and lambs, and all sorts of animals. Alton, isn't it?"

Emma could tell immediately that Maid Marion would not be on her list of favorite people. "Elton, actually," she acidly replied.

As Harry had suspected, Marion fell far short of a ravishing beauty. In fact, he decided, the ice cream cone did more justice to Terry's holiday snapshot than she did. Marion gave the impression of being a child much doted on by her parents. She had large Barbie-doll-blue eyes, the kind that one sees on billboards. Honey-blonde hair billowed about her round face like a huge feather boa, framing a small fortune in makeup which looked as though it had been put on with a palette knife. Like Mrs. Johnson, too much of everything. And always posing. Watching her, Harry wondered if she posed in bed. Her surname turned out to be Williams, about as rare among Welshmen as fleas on dogs. Marion's problem, he concluded, lay in an acute lack of self-confidence brought about by some discrepancy between her social aspirations and the reality of a working-class background.

If nothing else, Marion was obviously accustomed to having a captive audience, for once she had introduced herself she completely ignored Emma and, tossing back her hair every couple of minutes, launched into a favorite topic: herself.

"I don't know whether Terry told you," she said, "but we've decided on June 10th for the wedding. As you know, I'm presently attending an exclusive secretarial college in Swansea and I finish next spring, so everything clicks wonderfully. Of course, we'll be buying a house here. Terry has a very promising future with the County Council, and he tells me that quite a bit of the deadwood will be retiring soon."

Those within earshot shifted uncomfortably in their seats. Terry grinned sheepishly at his boss. If Dickie hadn't been already half-inebriated, it would have been obvious, even to him, that Marion's remark hit perilously close to home. Harry thanked providence that Bill Lewis, another key plank in her 'deadwood,' hadn't arrived yet.

"We had originally thought of renting a flat for a while," Marion prattled on. "But as Mummy pointed out, it's important to remember that people recognize our social standing by the way we live. I told Terry a flat would be sort of letting the side down, if you know what I mean. Anyhow, tomorrow we're going to look at a new development called 'The Limes.' I think that's such a wonderful name." 'Wonderful' appeared to be one of Marion's pet adjectives. She hardly uttered a sentence without it.

"We looked at The Limes," said Angus, shaking his head. "They're not too wonderful, lassie. One of the first houses they built had a wee problem with the footings. It bloody fell down. Ken ye imagine something like **that** getting past the building inspector! And another thing, all the inside walls are breeze block. Ah don't like breeze-block walls. Give me honest-t'-goodness bricks any day. We decided to give the place a wide berth." He shook his head again. Mary sneaked a look at Emma and smirked.

Marion wouldn't have known a breeze block from a pencil sharpener, but that didn't matter; she had an audience. Dickie, captivated as always by a young female face, listened indulgently with a silly look on his face. After pouting at Angus for having the audacity to question her intuition for fine living, she resumed. "Well, that was only one house," she said contritely. "And I don't think it could have entirely fallen down, do you Terry?"

Terry murmured something inaudible.

"And besides," she concluded, "I'm sure it had a guarantee or something. Anyway, Terry thinks the development has wonderful character and of course Terry has very good taste. So we shall see."

Harry suppressed a smile at her last remark. Judging from the way Terry behaved while Marion was safely out of sight in Swansea, his 'good taste' extended about as far as his appetite. But it was very clear who would be calling the shots in that marriage, so Terry's indiscretions might be excused as a final fling. Those who live by the sword, die by the sword, as they say.

"Where are ye staying, Marion?" Angus asked innocently.

She sat up stiffly, as though someone had just stuck her with a hot poker.

"Staying..? Where?" she stammered.

"While ye are here," Angus said, clearly enjoying her embarrassment. He and everyone else knew perfectly well that Marion was staying with Terry, but he also reckoned, correctly, that she would be most reluctant to admit it.

"Oh, I'm staying, er, here... in Matlock... in town..., you know..."

"She's staying at Slater's, Angus," Terry interrupted, visibly rattled by Angus's little joke. "They have a spare room."

Her composure restored, Marion continued to hold court for another twenty minutes with a dwindling audience. Both Joyce and Mary had quickly sized her up as a social-climbing blowhard and were now earnestly debating the pros and cons of hysterectomies. Emma listened in for a while before deciding that the topic might not be too relevant for her age group. At the same time, Marion's claptrap was starting to grate, so she sat close by Harry, picking up bits of both conversations.

Suddenly, Lol Dobson arrived, but so quietly that at first no one realized he was there. Harry assumed the woman trailing behind him must be Carol. And the first time she opened her mouth confirmed it. Lol was strangely subdued. Far from the self-confident, wise-cracking man-about-town who cruised the county office building, he behaved almost as though he'd just suffered a hernia. Even the celebrated Lol-Dobson smile, while still a mile wide, seemed forced and unsure. Harry gazed upon this transition in astonishment as Lol introduced his wife. It became immediately apparent that Carol originated from the same part of the country as her husband. But unlike Lol's soft, almost singsong patter, Carol was cursed with one of those high-pitched voices which could penetrate six-inch armour plate as though it were butter. She sounded like a rusty door hinge, which was unfortunate because, like many people who can empty a crowded room faster than a skunk in heat, Carol had obviously identified herself as a conversational diva. Mangled metaphors were a particular specialty, guaranteed to have Lol and anyone else within earshot squirming in agony. Some were so mangled, in fact, that Harry had a tough time identifying them.

She was considerably taller than Lol— a gawky woman with mouse-coloured hair tied up in a bun. Steel-framed glasses perched on the end of an unusually narrow nose. Once somebody attracted Carol's attention, she would fix them with watery-blue eyes that never seemed to blink. Harry found it difficult to avoid that stare, as did most victims of her verbal tyranny once they realized the minefield they had blundered into. His older colleagues, Harry noticed, had learned various defensive strategies around Carol. On this particular evening they all nodded at her and then stuck their faces into whatever they were drinking.

"Well, here we are again," Carol rasped as she strode into the middle of the gathering. "Hardly seems five minutes since last year's bloody wake." Hearing the noise, others in the snug looked around for the source.

Dickie, determined to be the model host if it killed him, gave her one of his thin-lipped, cigarette-punctuated smiles, introduced all the neophytes, and called out to Arthur for more drinks. "It'll be your usual?" he said to Carol without actually asking. Long ago she had adopted the 'Wembley' as a sort of signature cocktail, and she could down these little liquid bombs comprised of Scotch, vermouth, and some pineapple to protect the glass, faster than they took to pronounce. She claimed the Wembley reminded her of home. There might have been a measure of truth to this since both she and Lol were raised within walking distance of Wembley Stadium. However, Lol, who wound up paying for her liquid-nostalgia trips, would doubtless have been much happier if she'd picked a souvenir ashtray as a memento.

"Wembley for Carol, Worthingtons for Lol and myself."

Harry noticed a growing collection of empty glasses in front of his boss.

Carol turned and wagged a finger at Arthur. "Remember, mate," she cautioned. "There's at least a third of Scotch in 'em. I can get all the bloody pineapple juice I want from the greengrocer's!"

Always quick to temper, Arthur frowned at the slight against his integrity and disappeared, leaving Lol and Dickie laughing uncomfortably. As usual, they had been talking shop, possibly Lol's biggest social weakness, Harry discovered. Whenever he joined them for coffee or a beer, albeit infrequently, the topic inevitably turned to one of Lol's latest construction triumphs. There were disasters, too. But according to Lol, those were never his fault. Apparently most happened because some 'door knocker' had failed to grasp his explicit instructions. A staunch disciple of the 'if you can't blind them with science, baffle them with bullshit' school of thought, Lol reveled in obscure jargon. The more complex the project, the more bullshit it generated. His car, a dilapidated Vauxhall Wyvern with a length of wire coat hanger substituting for a radio antenna, bristled with theodolites, survey rods, chains, pegs, tapes and rubbish. For the unlucky passengers who accompanied him, riding on the car's roof could often be preferable to finding a spot inside. Harry had a sneaking suspicion that Lol rather despised him for being a mere landscaper. Lol managed to convey the impression, without actually saying so, that unless a job were underpinned by sheets of mathematics and a dictionary's worth of bureaucratese, it wasn't quite up to snuff.

"I told 'im, the bleedin' grade is three inches off," he was telling his boss. "'E says, 'so what?' 'So what?' I says. 'The bleedin' tiles aren't going to run unless the grade is right on, that's what'. Christ, everyone who 'asn't got 'is 'ead up 'is arse knows we get enough rain in that area to float the Titanic an' 'e should 'ave known that, otherwise 'e shouldn't be in the business. Bleedin' door knocker. Got to be around these fellas all the time. Not necessarily standin' over 'em. I mean, just in the background so's yer don't phase 'em. But, y'know, it was one of them bloody days when I wasn't everywhere all at once. Yer try ter be, but it's 'ard, even when yer the best."

No one challenged Lol's modesty.

Frank, who had been listening, screwed up his face. "Ah can't see fer the life o' me 'ow yer can tell wot's level by lookin' through a little spyglass," he said. "Seems like a lot 'o mumbo jumbo."

"*En Tout Cas* should've got that job," Dickie murmured, ignoring Frank. "At least they don't rob you blind when your back's turned."

Carol, who was also half listening to this conversation while at the same time scrutinizing the two newcomers to the group, scooped up one of Dickie's cigarettes and sniffed. "Y'know what they say, Lol," she asserted. "Walk softly and carry a big dick."

"'Stick', darlin'," Lol said. "It's 'stick.'"

She sniffed again. "Stick, dick. Whatever."

While the group waited for Carol to come up with a metaphorical encore, Bill Lewis and his wife joined them, with Morley Singleton close on their heels. He looked fatigued as usual, lamely waving an arm as he turned on his heel to order some drinks. Bill was usually the last to arrive at any office gathering and nearly always the first to leave. In fact, he was usually late for everything except the bus back to Derby after work, and if Dickie's predictions proved correct, he would be late for his own funeral. Nothing seemed to bother Bill in life. Daily he suffered the slings and arrows of Dickie's wrath and the scorn of his colleagues with complete indifference, outwardly, at least. Harry had seen him visibly angry only once so far. And that, predictably, was when he missed the bus home one evening. It represented a learning experience for Harry, who had never heard anyone swear in Welsh before. He was so impressed that he had resolved there and then to get Lewis to teach him some of the words.

Both Harry and Emma instantly took a shine to Pat Lewis. Like her husband, quite short, slightly built, and very softly spoken. But Pat had some very obvious qualities that Bill lacked. She radiated a quiet energy which seemed to infect anybody with whom she came into contact. When she laughed, her entire face lit up as though a spotlight had been turned on it. As Harry would learn as the evening wore on, Pat was in an entirely different league than the other wives. And no one could have appreciated this more than she. Yet, on any occasion when he briefly tuned into their chatter, she would be in the midst of it all, neither dominating nor shunning the action, turning the most inane nonsense of those around her into something intelligent. Since Lewis never mentioned his wife at work, Harry learned to his surprise that she had been a teacher at Moss Road Grammar School in Derby for the past twenty-five years. But no one could have been less pedantic, less like a school teacher, largely because she had a refreshing way of not taking herself too seriously. Seeing them together, it was evident that Lewis was very proud of his wife. Unlike many males, who tend to become defensive when their fragile egos are threatened, Bill seemed content to take a back seat to her when she had something to say. That evening was the beginning of a long process in which Harry would come to see the full depth of his senior colleague. He would find a very different person beneath the sublime, chain-smoking cynic at the office.

"Hey, William," Carol shouted across the table, glasses poised on her beaky nose for a verbal strike. "I 'ear they're goin' ter cancel the buses!"

She was referring to the commuter buses that ferried the Derby dwellers up to Matlock every day. And she knew this always tweaked Bill's tail because he was one of those who had campaigned most vigorously for the service.

"No more buses after Christmas, William!" she said again, and grinned through thin, rouged lips.

Bill reacted like he did in the office when woken up. He sat bolt upright, just as he had that day when Terry told him his tie was on fire. "How d'you know?"

"From an unpreachable source."

Lol cleared his throat. "I think that's 'unimpeachable', precious."

Carol ignored him.

"Come on, where d'you get the information from, Carol?" Bill persisted, beginning to suspect that she was just trying to get a rise out of him,

"From the 'orse's mouth, William, from the 'orse's mouth," she replied coyly.

Morley, who had said hardly a word so far, and had been listening to this, smiled his vacuous smile and said, "More likely from the opposite end, I think, Carol."

Pat Lewis wanted to talk to Emma. Since she and Bill lived in Derby, she rarely visited Matlock, and unlike some of the wives, had never shopped at Madison's. After exchanging season's greetings with the others in the group, Pat quickly moved over to where Emma and Harry were sitting.

"I've heard about you," she said in the same lilting Welsh accent as Kath Bassett. "And most of it is very good! But I'm sorry that you had to get mixed up in one of Bob Dickie's little intrigues. That man is a bit of a trial." Then turning to Harry she added, "However I'm very glad Bob carried through on his promise to get some new blood in the department. Do you know, there are seven hundred people in that building down the street, and the average age is forty-two. That's awful! If they all creaked at the same time they would bring Smedley's Hydro crashing down!"

The thought of that Victorian edifice with its silly flag tower, shaking itself into Crown Square, tickled Emma's funnybone.

"Are you planning on staying with the Derbyshire County Council for any length of time, Harry?" Pat continued, lowering her voice below earshot of the others.

Just two months into the job and happy to have it despite the poor salary, he was startled by the question. "I'm not sure, Mrs. Lewis," he replied truthfully. "It's a much better job than I had before. In fact, it's the first real job I've had. The only problem is, I'm a horticulturist by training, not a surveyor, and I'm finding that most of the emphasis is on playing-field construction."

She nodded. "I'm not being nosy. I only ask because of the experience we've had with Bill. He's been with that department for sixteen years, since 1945, and he's still in the same position he started with. I don't suppose you know he's a qualified surveyor?"

"No, I didn't."

"That's one of the big problems in your department. Bob gets all the attention. The whole building knows he was in bomb disposal during the war. And everyone is so sympathetic because he had a rough time of it that they make allowances for his antics. We hear so much about Bob. Bob this, Bob that. But Bill served in the war too. I don't suppose he told you that either?"

Harry shook his head.

"In many ways he had a much rougher time of it than Bob Dickie did. Bill signed up like thousands of others, even though he was in his late thirties and we'd been married only six years. They shipped him to Singapore and he was there when it was overrun by the Japanese. He spent the entire war in a concentration camp. Most of his friends died. The Japanese nearly killed him, too. By the time the camp was liberated he weighed less than eighty pounds and I hardly recognized the poor man when he got off the ship. Our son John— he was ten by then— wouldn't have anything to do with his dad for weeks. Bill was so crushed. He hadn't seen John for six years. Although we can laugh about it now I feel rather bitter about things once in a while. Life sometimes doesn't seem very fair."

Emma and Harry found themselves looking at Lewis who, with legs crossed and a beer nestled in his lap, was quietly chatting with Joyce as though he hadn't a care in the world. He spoke in such a soft voice they could see only his lips move. In a couple of minutes Pat had explained a lot about her husband. Most people with traumatic wartime experiences behaved much the same way as Bill. They simply wanted to get on with their lives. Dickie seemed to be an exception. For some reason he couldn't leave the past alone, or maybe it wouldn't leave him alone. Either way they made a destructive combination.

"I suppose what I'm saying," Pat continued, lightly touching Harry's hand, "is that a person can have all the talent under the sun, but if you're in the wrong place, it won't do you any good."

Her comments held no malicious intent. They were simply a gentle warning from a wife, and mother of a son not much older than Harry, not to be lulled into a false sense of security by a job whose substance derived almost entirely from workplace social relations. She had shared the painful experience of her husband's moribund career. And although she had never mentioned it to Harry and Emma, she was seeing it again in a son also languishing in a meaningless government job. Nevertheless, the conversation hit a raw nerve in Harry. While Emma and Pat chatted, he sipped his drink and silently watched his colleagues. True, they were a decent lot who did their jobs adequately. But none of them seemed to be going anywhere. For that matter, none of them, with the exception of Terry perhaps, seemed remotely **interested** in going anywhere. Even the energetic Lol showed no visible enthusiasm for breaking out of the insular, self-approbatory environment he had created for himself. They all seemed smugly content, happily squabbling in that tiny departmental sandbox; secure in the knowledge that, whatever happened, there would be a pay cheque at the end of the month. He knew he should feel the same way, but he didn't. Instead, there was always a restlessness he could never quite identify. For as long as he could remember it had been this way. Something inside Harry, his alter ego perhaps, couldn't bear to see him get too comfortable. On the rare occasions this happened, he could hear a persistent voice urging him to move on, to dismantle what he had just built and do it all again, somewhere else, some other time.

So it was with this job. He knew he should be grateful for the opportunity. And he was, to some extent. But at the same time he could hear the siren voice reminding him of a big world that could still be his. How long had he been with the department? A couple of months. In some ways it seemed a lot longer. Did he want to be like these people twenty years from now, bored with life but too comfortable to do anything about it? Did he want his mind to slowly shrink, like a stomach which becomes agreeably accustomed to less food? Part of him said "Why not? This isn't such a bad life, don't knock it." The other part quietly demurred, reminding him of others, like those around him at the office, who once so easily satisfied themselves and woke up later in life feeling cheated and unfulfilled.

The evening wore on, with the women gradually gravitating into one circle and the men into another. After a brief flush of patrons the pub had emptied out again; with over a week to go before Christmas, it was still a little too early for most office festivities and in any case the *Hanging Gate* catered largely to locals with plenty of time to celebrate at their own pace. By ten o'clock the Bassetts were beginning to tidy up. Clem hadn't appeared, but no one expected him to. Bill Lewis and his wife left early, as they usually did. Pat made a point of inviting Harry and Emma for tea if they were ever in Derby during a weekend. She was sincere about it, too. Emma promised she would let them know next time she and Harry were there.

"So, 'ow are things up at Elton, then, Missy?" Frank asked from behind his beer tankard.

Emma laughed. "Oh, you know, Frank, it's a whirlwind of activity up there! That's why I have to come down to Matlock, to take a breather!"

"Ah remember when ah wor a young lad," he said, taking advantage of a lull in conversation, "One o' them mine shafts caved in an' trapped a feller. An' as far as ah know, they never did get 'im aht. They say 'is ghost can be seen sum nights at th' shaft entrance."

"Come on now, you don't believe in ghosts, do you, Frank?" Emma replied, giving him an affectionate nudge. But she could see that he was quite serious.

"Ah don't know," he continued, running his fingers beneath his cap, as he always did when pondering some weighty problem. "Yer allus feel a bit daft talkin' abaht things like that, but ah've seen sum very rum things in my time, that's fer certin."

"They haven't taken any lead out of those mines for a long time, from the look of it," Harry said. "Emma and I were wandering around the Elton place just a few weeks ago."

"Ooh, no. Them's was doin' business long afore my time. But ah remember once in a while somebody would open up a shaft or two, unofficial like, an' 'ave another go at it fer a bit. That wus when the young feller got killed. Around 1882 or '3, if ah remember rightly." Frank lowered his voice. "Ah'm bettin' mi' pension that's there's more than just one bloke buried around them parts," he said, taking a long swig of beer. "We used ter hear stories, y'know. Lots o' stories. Lads goin' up ter the mines an' nobody seein' 'em any more."

With Dickie becoming more and more inebriated, Joyce, wearing the expression of someone who knows the roof is going to fall in because it has fallen in so many times before, began trying unsuccessfully to get him off the beer and into a cup of black coffee. Unfortunately for her, Dickie had found a captive audience in Marion who, abandoned by everyone else and having exhausted her own repertoire, now hung on every word he uttered. Had he known her better, he would have realized that Marion's indulgence extended only as far as its usefulness in promoting Terry's ambitions. She listened intently, the painted lips parted in affected awe while Dickie recited some of the travesties of justice he'd endured in the army and since. A favorite theme was his inexplicable lack of success in building the Landscape and Playing Field Section into a bureaucratic empire. Other heads of department had succeeded. Why hadn't he? It was, he declared like a broken record, nothing short of discrimination based on jealousy over his wartime achievements. To his disgust, the section hadn't appreciably grown in size since its inauguration, sputtering along instead as a half-forgotten satellite of the mighty architect's department. Still, he had won one or two minor battles, even though it must have become clear, even to him, that he would eventually lose the war.

"You always have to make your position clear," he roared through a cloud of cigarette smoke. "If I'd rolled over and played dead we'd never have wound up with a section of our own. We'd be stuck in a corner of the main draughting office and I'd probably be sharing space with a bunch of bloody fire extinguishers." He omitted to mention that his current hole-in-the-wall office had been built for precisely that purpose. "But they didn't know who they were up against. I didn't spend six years blowing up bombs without learning a few things about human nature, you can bet your arse on that."

"You must have had to be very strong," said Maid Marion breathlessly.

"I think we should be going, Tarzan," Joyce interrupted.

"Damned right I had to be strong. One occasion I remember I'd had it up to my pecker. I said to 'em, 'do you know who I am?'"

"Doesn't say much if yer had ter ask somebody!" said Carol.

He blustered on, completely ignoring the interference. "I told em, 'I'm Captain Robert Anderson Dickie, Royal Engineers, and I was doing this shtuff before some of you were wiping your own—" He let out a loud belch. "'Scuse me... bottoms.'"

"That should've won a few friends!" Carol interrupted again. After a trayful of Wembley's, she wasn't feeling any pain either. Dickie irritated her even more than her husband's ingratiating deference to him. After ten years, these office functions, with their endless shop talk, had become a bore and a waste of time, other than providing an occasion to get up some Dutch courage and fire a few cheap shots. She listened to the outpouring of self-aggrandizement with barely concealed disgust, waiting for him to take a breath.

"Robert, yer so full of shit yer eyes are brown!" she concluded, when he finally did.

There followed a pregnant pause while the rest of the group waited for the fallout.

But it proved to be an anti-climax. As always when he had a new audience, Dickie was doing his best to portray himself as a man of dignified authority. He couldn't afford to let himself be drawn into an unseemly scrap with Carol. Unfortunately, encumbered by rotund build and florid complexion, the image he generated for most observers came closer to that of a vacuum-cleaner salesman. Not that these shortcomings bothered him unduly. Inspired by the conventional wisdom that incomprehension can be overcome by shouting, he would press his point by sheer decibel force. At every collective opportunity, Radical Bob strove to gain the high ground by bellowing his skeptical audience into submission, and hanging onto it by the same virtue. He usually won. Even Carol at her shrillest couldn't compete.

Emma had said very little throughout the evening, except to Frank, and to Pat whom she found by far the nicest of all the wives. After she and Bill left, Emma contented herself with sitting and observing. Carol and Joyce had virtually ignored her, and so had Marion within five minutes of their arrival. Emma wasn't a drinker; she'd made a pint of shandy last all evening. Harry had deliberately kept his intake to a couple of pints, partly because he hated going outside to the lavatory, and partly because he had some plans for later. His watch said eleven o'clock.

"Those nasty bombs must have been awfully dangerous," Marion continued in a last-ditch attempt to earn some more brownie points for herself and her soon-to-be-betrothed. "I mean, what if someone accidentally lit a match too close, or smoked a cigarette, or something terribly silly like that?"

Dickie, fully aware that everyone else was having a tough time keeping a straight face at such a stupid question, momentarily grappled with the task of explaining to her, without looking like an even bigger fool, that bombs weren't exploded by matches or cigarettes. He decided on the classic Radical-Bob feint to one side.

"My dear," he replied in a voice noticeably losing its coherence. "When one of those little beauties deshided to go up, you'd need fuckin' matches and cigarettes as much as a fairy needs a set of balls."

"Oh," said Maid Marion, trying hard to recall whether she'd ever read anything on folklore anatomy. Terry writhed in agony. Morley excused himself and went to the lavatory.

"I thought fairies were always females," said Carol.

Lol abruptly finished his drink and stood up to put on his coat. "Time we went 'ome, dearest."

Watching the pair depart, it once again struck Harry that this man had to be the most unlikely Casanova he'd ever set eyes on. A pair of shapeless trousers, baggy at the back and stretched at the knees, hung in wrinkles around his ankles. The jacket he wore, like the others Harry had seen, would have handily fit two people at once.

Piqued at losing his captive audience before he'd had a chance to air all of his lifetime achievements, Dickie scowled at his remaining subordinates. As the years rolled by, ready listeners were becoming harder to find, unless he was willing to buy their attention with drinks.

"Jesus Chrisht!" he complained. "You lot are a right bunch o' Sunday school teachers. Arthur's not goin' to throw us out for at least another bloody hour. It'sh Saturday tomorrow, for Chrisht sake. Saturday...we can all sleep in..."

His protests fell on deaf ears. Terry frowned slightly at his fiancee and they both got up, put on their coats, and left. Morley never came back from the lavatory. It seemed to Harry that this might be as good a time as any to bail out. Only Frank stayed put, silently enjoying Dickie's fruitless protests.

"Goodnight, ladies and gentlemen," said Arthur as everyone filed past the bar. "And thank you!"

"Goodnight, Harry!" said Kath from somewhere in the back.

Emma gave Harry a long suspicious look.

"I think she likes me," Harry whispered.

Outside the pub they caught sight of the Dickies, heading down the lane to their car. Joyce had obviously convinced her husband to call it a night.

"I'm driving, Robert," they heard Joyce say flatly. Bob Dickie was too preoccupied with the task of getting his coat sleeve turned right side out to argue. Terry and Marion called out their goodnights and soon disappeared into the shadows of Smedley Street. Emma pulled up her coat collar, gently pushed her arm around Harry's and they, too, set off down the street. But they hadn't walked more than a hundred yards before a plaintive wail split the silence. Joyce's voice could be heard above the slamming of car doors.

"For Christ sake, Robert, why did you leave the bloody parking lights on?"

Her husband offered a muffled reply and more doors slammed.

"I thought the whole idea of leaving the damned car here was so we didn't have to leave the flippin' lights on," Joyce resumed. "You know the battery's weak. I don't see why we can't get a new one. If you pissed less of our money down the lav we could... I'm sick of this bloody thing, damned sick of it... How the hell are we going to get it started at this time of night? All the garages are closed..." Her voice faded for a moment.

"Thass alright, dear," they heard Dickie say. "We'll jus' push it down the slope and throw 'er into gear. Piece of cake. Done it a thousand times before. Piece of cake."

"We're not pushing it anywhere," Joyce replied testily. "Look at you, you're bloody gassed. As if that was anything new. And I'm buggered if I'm going to walk home. We'll telephone for a taxi. Just stay here while I go back inside to use the phone. Why can't we ever go anywhere without you getting plastered. I'm fuckin' sick of picking up after you, Robert, I really am."

Harry and Emma stood, mesmerized, as the voices waxed and waned, echoing thinly around an otherwise deserted street.

"You're making a teacup into a tempesht... a tempesht out of a teacup...a teacup...You push and I'll—" Dickie began again.

"Oh, shut up. Just sit still while I go inside."

There was a clacking of high-heeled shoes and Joyce came steaming round the corner. Dickie's voice followed her. "Dammit, Joyce. There'sh no need to fuss...I'll jus' give it a little push...thatsh all it needs...a little push, for chrissakes."

Casting an angry glance back at her husband, she yelled, "Leave the bloody car alone 'till I get back. Just sit there and do nothing. Understand?" Spotting Harry and Emma in the shadows, she broke into a shambling trot towards them. They walked over to meet her.

"Looks like the boss is up to his usual tricks," Harry said softly, squeezing Emma's hand.

After spending the past four hours with them, Emma didn't feel too enthusiastic about getting involved in a late-night husband-and-wife squabble. Besides, her agenda, which she suspected might be similar to Harry's, called for getting back to Miss Twigg's before the night was completely spent.

"Just see what she wants and then let's go," she whispered back.

Joyce wore the same expression they had noticed earlier in the evening: a chronic weariness borne of living with someone who couldn't be left alone for more than ten minutes.

With a tired smile she gestured into the lane. "Bob left the side lights on and now the battery's flat. I was going to call a taxi, but the car's facing downhill so perhaps you could give us a push while I put it in gear. I don't want him to do it... he can hardly stand up. Honestly, I don't know what to do with that man, I really don't. Emma, do you think you could take him inside and get Arthur to give him a cup of coffee? I hate to impose on you, I really do." And to ensure that Harry didn't develop any second thoughts about helping, she grabbed his sleeve and steered him towards the car.

Emma thought it odd that neither Arthur nor Kath had come out to see what was going on. Surely they heard the noise? Like Harry, it irritated her that

Arthur seemed keen enough to sell Dickie enough beer to get him totally plastered, and then went into hiding afterwards. He was a large, muscular man, and, although now a bit flabby with age, it was difficult to imagine him being afraid of a confrontation.

They all hurried around the back of the pub, whereupon Joyce let out another long wail. Predictably, Dickie had decided to take matters into his own hands. After briefly stumbling round in an alcoholic fog, he had managed to open the driver's door, release the hand brake and push against the door frame. But putting the car into gear took more dexterity than he could muster. Lunging for the steering-column gear stick, he missed, sprawling face down across the seat as the chubby Morris Oxford gathered momentum down the incline. Having nothing to hold onto he quickly slid onto the floor and became hopelessly jammed under the dashboard.

"I'll have it in a minute, dear..." said a slowly waning voice inside the car.

"Oh, my God, he's going to kill himself!" Joyce cried, while they ran in hot pursuit. Partly illuminated by a cloud-streaked moon, the vehicle presented an eery sight as it silently pursued its apocalyptic mission past rows of cottages flanking the narrow lane. All they could see of Dickie was a pair of wiggling feet sticking through the open door. It was then that Harry realized the potential seriousness of the situation. He had been down this lane several times and knew it had no exit. Even worse, below the lane a rocky cliff tumbled twenty feet into some allotments. A low stone wall had been built across the lane end to prevent unwary souls from accidentally falling down the rocks. Only a couple of weekends ago he and Emma had sat on that wall to admire the winter view, the same wall towards which Dickie's car was now heading with uncanny precision.

Running as hard as possible, he came abreast and grabbed the door in a futile attempt to slow it down. The Morris Oxford was not a big car, but too big to be stopped by someone weighing less than a hundred and fifty pounds.

"Don't let it go!" Joyce yelled at him.

Harry hung on. Tripping and stumbling over Dickie's protruding feet he found himself galloping ineffectually alongside while his boss flapped about on the floor. By this time they had reached a speed of about eight miles and hour and the car had clearly decided upon a kamikaze finish to its trials and tribulations. Harry looked up in horror as the stone wall loomed ahead.

"Don't let go!" Joyce repeated.

"I'll have it in jus' a minute... shoon as I get my bloody hand free..." said Dickie, unaware of the impending disaster.

"We're heading for a wall, Mr. Dickie!" Harry panted.

Dickie continued to thrash about beneath his tangled raincoat. "Jus' a jiffy. We'll have her fired up in no time," he babbled.

In a split second Harry's brain subconsciously calculated the distance remaining and the time it would consume, and he knew there was no time left. Somewhere in the back of his head an alarm bell rang. The hell with this, he told himself. I'm not ready for martyrdom yet. Letting go of the door frame, he lost his balance, staggered several more feet and then fell heavily onto a narrow grassy strip in front of a house. Emma was quickly by his side. They both looked up in time to see the driverless car, with Dickie's legs still sticking out, plunge through the rickety stone wall as though it were butter. Slowed somewhat, it clattered noisily down the rocks, through a wooden fence, reduced a homemade cold frame to kindling, and finally came to rest with its bonnet buried in a pile of compost.

For a moment Harry forgot his aching knee and badly stained trousers. He and Emma stood in their tracks, staring dumbfounded at the gaping hole in the wall. For a moment there was total silence. Then a voice, carried by the still night air, wafted over the edge.

"There we go, m'love. She's in gear. Told you... piece of cake..."

"I don't think he has any idea what he's done," said Emma.

Together they craned their necks towards the sound of Dickie's voice. "At least he's still alive," Harry replied.

Joyce arrived at the breached wall, uncertain whether to rejoice in her husband's survival or pelt him with some of the loosened stones. By this time the noise had aroused several local inhabitants and they quietly shuffled into viewing position. One, an elderly man with a coat thrown over his pajamas and wearing a pair of worn-out slippers, looked down in disbelief at the sight of Dickie, covered in mud and compost, attempting to close the car door as though he might have just parked in his driveway.

"'E went through the bloody wall," said the man.

"Why would 'e want to do that?" said another. "There's a sign up yonder that says no road aht."

"'Ow bloody daft can yer get," added the first observer.

"Ah knew Arthur 'ad a parking problem but ah never knew it wor this bad!" joked another man as he joined the group.

"'E must be pickled, the daft bugger," piped up someone else in the background.

Despite his soiled trousers, Harry couldn't help feeling a twinge of pity for Joyce, who paced back and forth across the breach with her hands gesturing uselessly. He wasn't sure whether to scramble down and help his boss up to the road or wait for him to climb up under his own steam. Dickie didn't take kindly to anything that smacked of charity, and Harry suspected that a helping hand would achieve little more in this instance than it did during the Duffield incident. In any case he felt in no mood for thrashing about in a quagmire of mud and rotting vegetable scraps. His ankle hurt and once again he had spoiled a pair of perfectly good trousers in the process of being a good samaritan. So he stayed put. For her part, Emma had already decided that discretion might be the better part of valor. She stood silently behind Harry and Joyce while the scene unfolded below.

"What the hell are we doin' here?" rumbled Dickie. He had managed to close the car door but in so doing had trapped part of his coat. Now, with as much decorum as could be mustered, he was trying to extricate it. But despite the bluster, an observable hint of sheepishness had crept into his voice. He was still drunk, but not too drunk to realize that he had just made a complete ass of himself. Looking up at the little crowd he made a silly bow which merely served to amuse the spectators and further infuriate his wife.

"You've gone and done it this time, Robert," she snarled, kneeling and extending a hand towards her husband after he had finally freed himself and begun crawling up the rocks. "You've finally done it this time, chum."

Flailing about, Dickie said unconvincingly, "Nothing's damaged, dearesht. Don't get your knickers in a twisht."

"Nothing's damaged? Nothing's damaged?" Joyce shrieked at the top of her voice. "For Christ sake, you've destroyed a fuckin' wall, wrecked the car, flattened a bloody cold frame, and plowed up somebody's vegetable garden. And you're telling me nothing's damaged! Look at it down there! James Bond couldn't have done a better bloody job."

Wiping mud from the side of his face, Dickie again grinned self-consciously at his audience. Then turning to his wife he murmured, "Come on, Joyce. We have insurance."

"Damn the bloody insurance. I've never been so humiliated in my entire life. Do you realize we'll have to report this?"

"What the hell for? It was jus' a little accshident. Anybody can have a little accshident." He fumbled in his coat pocket for a cigarette.

Joyce wasn't finished. "Look at the car, for Christ sake! It's ruined. We'll never get the smell out of it."

Head lowered and muttering to himself, Dickie continued searching among his clothing for his smokes and lighter. Harry could see that the man's hands were shaking uncontrollably. He was missing a shoe, presumably left behind in the mud, while his raincoat looked as though it had been trampled by a team of horses. It was hard to believe that all this mayhem had taken less than twenty minutes; it seemed more like two hours, and Emma was beginning to wonder how long their latest fiasco would drag on.

Joyce had started to launch into another tirade when the faint squeal of bicycle brakes announced a new arrival. Dickie blanched slightly as the police constable, who had been called by someone in an adjacent house, swung his leg with practiced ease over the frame, parked his steed against the section of wall that remained intact, rearranged his dark-blue cape, and ambled over. He looked to be in his late forties, a heavy-set man with a large stomach that the cape, and the bicycle clips around his ankles, only accentuated. From a distance he resembled an inverted pear. Pulling out a notepad, he first surveyed the gathering, then walked over to the wall and peered at the destruction below.

"Oh, God," Joyce said, noticing him for the first time.

"Oh, dear," said Emma.

Harry's heart sank to his shoes. He'd been in Dickie's section less than two months but it was long enough to know that the boss's antics were common knowledge among local constabularies. Many regarded Dickie as a sad joke, but others, recognizing the serious public risk that he posed, would have been happier to see him permanently removed from the streets. Around Matlock, Dickie's evasive tactics while driving impaired had evolved into a cat-and-mouse game with some police officers who, like the cat, derived more satisfaction from the chase than from eliminating their prey. It was bureaucratic inconsistencies such as these which had enabled him to retain a driver's licence through nearly two decades of chronic alcoholism.

"G'd evening, officer," Dickie said, still ridding himself of compost and mud. "Jus' a little problem with the battery...heh, heh. We'll have it shtraightened out in a jiffy." He poked a wobbly finger at Joyce. "This is my wife. She was driving."

But this time his game-plan came unstuck. "What?" cried Joyce. "The bloody hell I was! You handle your own problems, Robert. I'm sick of protecting your backside." Dickie, caught off balance by his wife's candor, looked as though someone had kicked him in the crotch. He could tell that things were not going to go as smoothly as he had hoped.

"I assume that yonder is your car?" the constable asked, pushing his pencil in the direction of the allotments. Then, looking pointedly at Harry's boss, he said, "And you'll be Mr. Dickie?" It was a rhetorical question which left little doubt that he knew perfectly well to whom he was speaking. Dickie blanched again, brushed some more debris from his coat, then glared at the constable, his fuddled brain scrambling to formulate a better explanation than the first effort. He looked a pathetic sight, the normally slicked-back hair disheveled, clothing crumpled and smeared with mud, and a soggy cigarette squeezed between purple lips. Before he could open his mouth, Joyce interrupted.

"Actually, no one was driving, Constable. We left the parking lights on and they flattened the battery. Then we tried to push the car and put it in gear so the engine would start, but my husband fell and we lost control and the car went through the wall." She forced a smile at the constable. "That's all."

"That's all?"

Joyce nodded vigorously. "Yes, that's all. Just an accident."

"Well, now," said the constable thoughtfully. "Let's see. From the look of your husband's apparel, he 'as just come from down in them allotments. Is that correct?"

All within earshot nodded.

"So, I 'ave to ask," he continued, "'ow did 'e get there unless 'e wor in the vehicle? It don't seem likely that 'e would 'ave gone fer a walk in that muck fer the good of 'is 'ealth."

Everyone nodded.

"Ha, ha," said Dickie nervously.

"So I can only conclude, sir, that you was in the vehicle. Am I correct?"

Dickie glared at him, temporarily at a loss for something to say, and then started to push past them.

The constable stopped him with outstretched arm and said in a deadpan voice, "I also 'ave reason to believe you've been drinkin', and you must know it's a serious offence to be in charge of a motor vehicle while under the h'influence. Moreover," he added with emphasis, "you've caused considerable property damage, which makes this a very serious situation. A very serious situation indeed."

"I washn't driving the bloody car," Dickie exploded. "The fuckin' engine washn't even switched on. I was jus' trying..."

"He was just trying to **get** it started," Joyce interrupted him. Almost immediately she realized her mistake and lapsed into silence. The policeman scribbled in his notebook.

While this exchange had been going on, the owner of the cold frame arrived on the scene, irritated at being aroused from his bed by an insistent neighbour, and determined to make it worth his while. In one hand he clutched a few bits of splintered wood as evidence.

"Tewk me two days to built that frame," the man lied. "Not to mention the five quid spent on materials an' contents. And 'e drives through the soddin' thing, just like that." He searched around the audience for moral support. "I tell 'e, yer not even safe in yer own garden these days." What the 'contents' of an unheated cold frame might possibly be in December, he didn't say. From that distance Harry couldn't see the remains too well, but there didn't appear to be anything inside except weeds, and the manure that now adorned his boss in copious quantities.

"Who's goin' ter pay fer it, that's what ah'd like ter know?" the man demanded.

Dickie, who by now was beginning to lose patience with the entire affair, scoffed loudly, the cigarette bobbing violently. "Call that piesh of rubbish a fuckin' cold frame?" he snarled. "It'sh nothing more than some bloody plywood and old window. I've blown up better stuff than that. You can shove your cold frame up your arse, you little runt."

Fearing that he might be sidelined by a fist fight, the constable quickly put away his notebook and pulled Dickie to one side. "Now look 'ere," he resumed briskly, "that partic'lar aspect of the case is a civil matter. A more important issue, which I 'ave to deal with, is the motor vehicle accident to which you, Mr. Dickie, were a party, and damage to municipal property, for which I believe you wor responsible."

"What bloody munishipal property?" Dickie snorted.

"That wall. The wall that your vehicle 'as demolished. The said wall belongs to the town of Matlock."

"Well, whoopee fuckin' doo! Who the hell cares about a broken down old wall? What about my bloody car? What d'you think we have insurance for?"

"Yes," Joyce whined. "Our insurance will cover that."

The constable let out a long sigh and then sucked in his cheeks to underscore the weighty decisions being heaped upon him. He knew he couldn't prove that

Dickie had been actually driving his car, but he didn't like this arrogant little man who so often thumbed his nose at the police. One way or the other he was going to get something from the criminal code thrown at him.

"That might be so," he replied. "But I strongly suspect you were driving your motor vehicle while under the h'influence of alcohol, and at the very minimum without due care and attention, either of which, as you should know, is a criminal h'offence. A **criminal** offence." He repeated the last words to make sure everyone heard. "Consequently, Mr. Dickie, I will 'ave to ask you to proceed with me to the Bank Road police station where this matter can be further pursued. Your vehicle will 'ave ter remain at the scene of the accident until after it 'as been inspected tomorrow. Now, we can walk there or I can call for a squad car."

Joyce let out another wail and covered her face.

Another "oh dear" could be heard from Emma.

Dickie's reaction to being backed into a corner was entirely predictable. He flew into a rage. After calling into question the constable's legitimacy, he put on the most extraordinary performance Harry had yet seen. Hurling abuse at everyone within hearing range, he paced up and down with short, springy steps, his beet-red face stuck out, a bit like a chicken pecking for food. Later, Harry would recall the temper tantrum with amusement. But at this moment his boss appeared capable of killing somebody. As they all hastily backed off, it became ever more obvious that the constable had dealt with people like this before. He stood impassively, waiting for the commotion to die down.

After a couple of minutes which seemed like hours, Dickie's ranting and raving diminished to some unintelligible muttering, then abruptly stopped. He stepped to within inches of the constable's face. "I'm not coming to your bloody police shtation for a little inthidence like this," he said, spitting out the words with as much venom as he could gather. "S'ho, what are you goin' to do about that, eh?"

The constable cleared his throat, then adjusted his helmet strap as if preparing for a major confrontation with a street mob. "Now, look, Mr. Dickie," he began. "I don't want to 'ave ter call fer assistance but I will if I 'ave to—."

"I will if I have to," Dickie mimicked sarcastically, as he often did when brought up on the losing side of an argument. "Will if I have to, will if I have to. Bring reinforshments and I'll kick your arse, you silly twit."

This tactic might have worked on a younger, less experienced constable. And if Dickie had been completely sober and more perceptive, he probably wouldn't have even tried it. In this instance, however, it was a bad mistake. Harry, Joyce and Emma watched helplessly as the situation rapidly deteriorated. The others waited with expectant relish. After once again clearing his throat the constable attempted to take Dickie by the arm. Dickie pulled away, unleashing another torrent of invective as he did so.

"Don't do anything silly, Robert," Joyce pleaded.

That bit of advice just seemed to aggravate her husband even more. He glared at the crowd, then looked over his shoulder, spotted the constable's bicycle, and hobbled over to it.

"I must warn you not to touch that bicycle," cautioned the constable, uncertain about what was going to happen next but wise enough to know it wouldn't be anything good.

Horrified, Joyce knew perfectly well what was coming next. "Please, Robert. Just do what the constable says," she pleaded again.

Unmoved, Dickie grabbed the bicycle with both hands, with a grunt lifted it high above his head, and then threw it over the wall. A gasp rose from the crowd as Her Majesty's property sailed through the air, bounced off the rocks and clattered into the side of Dickie's car. Everyone watched numbly as pieces of the bicycle's battery-powered lantern flew in all directions. Then there was silence, broken only by the forlorn rattling of a detached bicycle pump and some broken bits following the rest of the machine down the slope. A few spectators moved closer to the edge to get a better look at the latest damage. The bicycle had made a readily visible dent in the passenger side door. It lay with its mangled front wheel half buried in the mud.

"Oh, God," Joyce sobbed.

Harry couldn't believe what he had just seen. Neither could Emma. She was tugging on his sleeve. "We should go," she whispered urgently. "I think Mr. Dickie's going to get into a lot of trouble for that."

Harry nodded but he couldn't take his eyes off the spectacle.

"**Now** take me to the bloody police shtation," said Dickie, gasping from his exertion.

Evidently the constable had been greatly attached to his wheels. With tears welling up in his eyes, he gazed briefly at the remains and then lunged again at Dickie. The pair thrust and parried around in circles while the crowd swayed back and forth. This was far more entertaining than anything on television, and besides, the B.B.C. had gone off the air for the night. Dickie had his fists up and was poking unsteadily in the constable's direction.

"Want to make shumthin' of it," he babbled. "Come here, I'll take you on. Fight like a bloody man, don't jusht stand there like a piece a' shit."

"He's such an arsehole," Joyce wailed above the scuffling of feet and muffled curses.

"Come on, Copper. Show 'im who's boss!" cried a voice from the crowd.

"Give 'im a knuckle sandwich," shouted another.

The crowd rumbled approval.

Suddenly, the constable appeared to tire of this demeaning game. He stood motionless for a second or two while Dickie continued to stagger around. Then, with a surprisingly agile sidestep for such a clumsy looking man, caught Dickie's arm and swung it up behind his back in a half-nelson. Dickie wriggled helplessly, but the more he squirmed the more it hurt.

"Sorry, Mrs. Dickie," the constable apologized as he steered her husband, still cursing and swearing, up the lane towards Smedley Street. "Your 'usband 'as left me no choice. I'm afraid we shall all 'ave to go down to the station."

"I'll be in tomorrow t'see abaht me cold frame," cried the cold-frame owner.

"It's in my report," snapped the constable. Then turning towards the crowd he said, "Nobody touch the bicycle or the car. As of now they are both police h'evidence."

At this point Dickie became aware of his frozen left foot. "I'm not walking down to the polis' shtation on one fuckin' shoe," he roared. "Try it and I'll get you for assault, you son of a bitch."

Joyce looked around. "Oh, Jesus, now where's his bloody shoe gone?"

"It's probably stuck in the mud," said the constable, wondering how to handle this latest development with both hands already full.

Without saying anything, Harry climbed down the rocks. He had no idea where to look, and the light was poor, but he reckoned Dickie's missing footwear must be somewhere close to the car. Stirred up by all the activity, the ground had become a minor quagmire. Even worse, it smelled strongly of horse manure. Harry's attempts to keep his own shoes clean were of no avail; they immediately sank to their uppers. After a few minutes of searching in vain, he noticed a half-buried lump close to the right-hand-side rear wheel. With a triumphant flourish he waved his trophy at the crowd.

Joyce took the shoe and began to clean the inside with a handkerchief but Dickie snatched it from her with his free hand. "What's the bloody good of doin' that? The other shoe is still full of shit."

"Well, I can try to clean— "

"Oh, shut up," Dickie snapped as the constable resumed his arrest.

Distraught, Joyce trotted after them. "I've never been so embarrassed in my whole life," she could be heard repeating over and over. Dickie, still with his arm in the half nelson, continued to heap abuse upon his captor until they disappeared round the corner. One or two spectators debated the short-lived fight's tactical merits while the remainder slowly dispersed, leaving Harry and Emma standing alone in the silent lane. During all this time, Arthur Bassett had never showed his face.

"That's the most ridiculous thing I ever saw," Harry said, as much to himself as anybody else. Emma nodded. They both peered once again at the shadowy mess below. "The boss is in quite a bit of trouble, a lot worse than the Duffield incident. Probably the worst yet. I'm very worried about him, even although he did deserve to get arrested. One of these days he's going to get sacked, if he doesn't kill himself first. I wonder if we should follow them to the police station and see if there's anything we can do."

"No," said Emma, firmly. "You've already tried to help and all you got for it was a sore ankle, some stained trousers, and now a pair of smelly shoes. That's enough. Every time you get close to your boss something awful happens. I'm beginning to think he's bad luck."

Harry looked down at his clothes. "Maybe you're right, but at least the trousers aren't the ones Mrs. Hamsterly sent me." As they walked slowly back to the street, he added, "I feel a bit sorry for Joyce, though."

"So do I," Emma agreed. "But there really isn't much we can do. He's **her** husband, thank goodness. I wonder what they'll do with the car?"

"I suppose some garage will come and tow it out. Probably another job for Slater's! They could afford to retire on the money they've made out of the Dickies." He looked again at his watch. "It's late, but at least there's one consolation: Miss Twigg will have gone to bed." He vehemently hoped she **would** have gone to bed.

"That's handy! How will we get in?"

"I don't think she ever locks the front door. At least, I've never found it locked. It's funny, but I still don't know where that woman sleeps."

He did know where Sarah slept though, and she could be an even bigger problem than Miss Twigg. Every time Harry turned around she seemed to be there, her round pimply face devoid of expression, eyeing him silently. He was sure she stalked him and he found the experience surprisingly unpleasant. Having the bedroom next to his provided her with an uncommonly good surveillance position, and he had no doubt she would use it when given the chance.

However, for Harry the big unanswered question of the moment was whether Emma would sleep with him. Had he been Terry Jones there would be no uncertainty. Terry lined up his prey with cat-like precision. If he wanted a night in the sack with some girl, there would first be some time spent assessing the odds. Harry never ceased to be impressed by the speed with which his colleague could accomplish this task. Then he'd crank out one of his witty but carefully crafted enjoinments, to which the girl would say yea or nay (usually the former). And that would be that. Terry made it seem so infuriatingly simple. These skills eluded Harry. But had he wanted to be honest with himself, it was largely because he couldn't stand the thought of being rejected. In essence, it all came down to a willingness to gamble. Harry had never been a gambler. Terry was, and like all successful gamblers, he was prepared to lose, shrugging it off with the same nonchalance that characterized his approach to women in general.

Harry's self-conscious clumsiness came up now and again in conversation. Terry would laugh and say, "Harry, my boy, your problem is that you're too damned serious! They think you want to marry 'em! And that's enough to scare anybody off. Just remember," he added crudely, "it's cheaper to buy a rubber than an engagement ring!" Always thinking, was Master Terry. Why any self-respecting female would want to marry a snake like him, Harry couldn't imagine. But then, after seeing Maid Marion, perhaps he was getting what he deserved.

After one last look behind them, they headed off to Miss Twigg's, following the same route that the constable and his reluctant prisoner would have taken minutes earlier. Harry briefly debated whether to retrieve the bicycle but decided against it. It was very wet and muddy down there, he'd already soiled his shoes and stained yet another pair of trousers, and in any case the constable had told everyone to leave things alone.

Emma slipped her hand into his as they walked quickly past the county offices, down Bank Road, and even more quickly past the Bank-Road police station. Neither could resist a quick glance through the glass door, half expecting to hear Dickie inside, hurling more vitriol at his tormentors. But all was quiet. Neither Joyce nor her husband was anywhere in sight.

They found Derwent House in darkness, its limestone walls bathed in the moonglow that had persisted off and on all night. Emma thought it looked spooky, which Harry found odd, considering the bleakness of her own village. After wiping most of the mud off his shoes, they tried the door. It was unlocked as usual, the hallway empty and silent. He wished again that he knew where Miss Twigg slept. It would help avoid any unwelcome encounters later on, or in the morning, assuming of course, that everything went according to plan. Rather than turn on the hall light, they made quietly for the staircase.

"Breakfast at 7.30, you two. Goodnight!"

Emma nearly jumped out of her skin. Harry cursed silently. How the hell did Miss Twigg know they were there? And where was she? They paused. Harry peered into the shadows. Then through a gap beneath the dining room's serving hatch, he spotted a faint glow in the kitchen. Perhaps she slept there? It made sense since she spent most of her life cooking, baking, and cleaning, and the kitchen was unquestionably the warmest part of the house. He hoped she wouldn't come out to greet them. With equal fervor he hoped that pimply Sarah would be fast asleep by now. Occasionally during the past two months he imagined hearing someone, or something, moving outside his bedroom door while getting ready for bed. But since his boarding-school days he had always slept naked, so he was reluctant to fling open the door in case someone might be standing there. If there had been, he was pretty certain who it would be.

"I'll see you to your room," he said to Emma, cursing himself for not having the guts to say what was really on his mind.

She gently squeezed his hand. "That would be very nice, love," she whispered. "And perhaps you could wait while I pick up my things."

"Oh, yes...I...ah..." He could hardly believe what she'd just said. Like an expectant father he waited outside her room while she rummaged in her suitcase for a few odds and ends. Then, with his heart pounding, they crept quietly back to his room. Before entering, he put his ear to Sarah's door and listened. No sound. While that could be good or bad news, it would be a good night to be optimistic.

Once inside and the door closed behind them, she stood on her tiptoes and kissed him on the nose. "We have to decide on something very important, Harry," she said solemnly.

Now what, he wondered.

"Which side of the bed do you sleep on?"

Harry could hear his heart pounding. "Well, I, er...usually on the left if we're looking from the headboard...but I suppose it would be the right if we were looking from the foot of the bed...well, nearest the washbasin..." In the light of the bedside lamp he could see her giving him that look again, the one she gave him the first day he showed up at the chemist shop. Why did young women seem so much more self-assured and mature about these things? Males were such hapless clots.

"What you're trying to say, Harry, is that I sleep on your right. Right?" She put her arms around him, her head pressed against his chest. "Either side is fine. I just want to go to bed with you tonight. I can go back to my room in the morning before Miss Twigg gets up."

That might be a nice idea in theory, he thought, but judging from Miss Twigg's habits to date, it could turn out to be five o'clock. Tomorrow was Saturday, and Emma's Saturday off. Why did they have to get up **that** early?

"I have to go to the bathroom," he said as she began to pull off her coat.

"Serves you right for drinking so much beer!" Emma replied with her usual cheeky smile. "Before you go, can you unzip my dress?"

He gladly obliged but found her remark a little ironic since he had deliberately avoided drinking too much beer in case, for once, his carefully laid plans worked out.

As her dress fell away, she shivered. "Is it always this cold in here?"

"Actually, no," he replied, wondering whether to unhook her bra as well. "Sometimes it's colder. Perhaps the place will warm up in spring."

He slipped silently across the landing and down the corridor to the bathroom, putting his ear once again to Sarah's door as he passed by. Still no sound. None on the way back, either. Emma seemed to take up a very small amount of room in his bed. A mop of curly auburn hair and a small nose protruded above the quilt. He noticed her carefully folded clothes on the chair, dress hung over the back; slip, stockings, panties and bra piled neatly on the seat. Someone had once told him that a lot can be found about a man's character by looking at his shoes. Perhaps similar insights could be gleaned from the way a woman prepares for bed, he thought, peeling off his own clothes. Emma's delicate perfume drifted tantalizingly in the frigid air. He wished he'd bought an electric heater, but battleship Bertha had been very firm about that the first day he arrived. Did Miss Twigg have any heat in her own room or did she set an example for the other shivering souls in that house? If so, it could be a notable virtue in more ways than one, since she might be less inclined to get out of bed if she heard something.

He turned off the bedside lamp, deliberately leaving the curtains open so that some light from the moon shone into the room, and pulled back the covers. Emma watched him silently. Her skin, smooth as alabaster, felt cool to the touch. She had small breasts, nipples tilted delicately upwards. As he gently pulled her over they pushed firmly into his chest.

"I'm not using anything," he whispered apologetically, hoping he was going to do this right.

"It's okay," she whispered back, "I think I'm safe for this month. That's why I wanted it to happen tonight."

Harry rolled on top of her, fumbled clumsily, wanting it so badly that he hadn't the patience to indulge in any foreplay. He was conscious of Emma's fingers squeezing tightly into his buttocks. It didn't feel comfortable.

She winced slightly as he penetrated. "You'll have to take it a bit easy, love," she said, her lips trying to find his mouth. "This is my first time."

He thought about telling her it was his first time, too, but the animal instinct of achieving some physical satisfaction now consumed him. She winced again and he could feel her abdomen tighten. The bed, which probably had not received that much exercise in years, squeaked abominably. He wondered whether Miss Twigg could hear the noise in her kitchen below and hoped she'd finally taken herself off to bed, wherever that might be. Glancing to his left he could see a dim outline of their heaving bodies in the wardrobe mirror, Emma's legs pulled back and his bottom rising and falling in short jerks. Finally, an orgasm appeared from nowhere. As it did, the wardrobe door slowly swung open as if on cue.

After several seconds they both lay still, in silence. He felt unfulfilled, as though someone had offered him a chocolate bar, then given him only the wrapper. And he couldn't believe Emma felt anymore satisfied than he did. Surely sex was supposed to feel better than this? Maybe it was his fault? Maybe he had gone about it the wrong way? In fact, he **knew** he'd gone about it the wrong way. He felt just as badly for Emma because she obviously had been looking forward to this night.

"I'm sorry, Emma," he apologized, rolling onto his back. "I don't think you got much out of that. I blew it, didn't I?"

She giggled very softly, shifting herself on top of him with her legs straddling his thighs. The cheeky grin pursed into a kiss. To his surprise she didn't seem in the least bit upset.

She moved her head back a little, studying him closely. "You men!" she scolded lightly. "Don't you know it's never much good the first time. Things have to.. you know.. **adjust** inside. I talked to my sister Anne about it. She said it would hurt, but it didn't really hurt all that much. Mrs. J. always used to talk about 'losing her cherry' and for the longest time I wondered what she meant! I don't think Mrs. J. had a very big cherry to start off with. Anyway, they both told me that after the first time its gets better and better. So, in a little while we'll see!"

In a little while? He desperately wanted a chance to redeem himself. Could Emma be that much of a masochist? She laid her head on his shoulder. Seconds later he could feel her hand searching the area where they had just been lying. "Actually," she whispered with some concern creeping into her voice, "Our biggest problem may be a bit of mess to clean up in the morning. Mind you, it's not all my mess!"

Damn! He hadn't thought of that. How would he explain bloodstains to Miss Twigg when Sarah changed his sheets next weekend? The wretched girl would undoubtedly draw it to her aunt's attention. But at least he had a week to get try and get the stains out.

"I have to go to the lav," she announced in the same whisper.

As soon as she scrambled out, he realized how cold the bedroom had become. "Use my dressing gown," he told her.

"Don't worry, I was going to," she replied with chattering teeth.

It reached almost to her ankles, the sleeves flowing a good three inches below her hands. As she stood at the foot of the bed, wrapping the gown around her, a faint tinkle of falling glass came from outside the door. Emma jumped in fright. It was a sound Harry had heard so many times before. Putting a finger to his lips, he motioned her to move away. Then he got out of bed, tiptoed to the door, and listened. Apart from a moaning draught in the hallway he could hear nothing. The tiny piece of frosted glass had indeed once again fallen out. Or had someone pushed it out? It was a very tiny piece of glass but a surprisingly large area of the bedroom could be seen through the hole. Opening the door to see if the coast was clear, he thought he heard a muffled movement inside Sarah's room. It was so fleeting that he couldn't be sure. Had Sarah been spying on them? His stomach churned at the possible consequences. Would she tittle-tattle to Miss Twigg? If she did it would almost surely ruin his plan to have Emma stay overnight on future occasions. Miss Twigg might even kick him out. If only dear little Sarah would move back to her mother, or father, or anywhere other than Derwent House.

While Emma was in the bathroom he turned on the bedside lamp and quickly examined the sheets. She had been right. There was a small blood stain but it could have been worse. He would try to get it out, or at least fade it, tomorrow. He could tell Miss Twigg he cut his leg or something. A few minutes later Emma came padding back to the bedroom, peeled off the dressing gown, turned off the light and nimbly jumped into bed. She snuggled against him, making sure that all the vital areas touched his skin.

"Was anybody out there?" he whispered.

"Who were you expecting, love, the Queen?"

"I thought Miss Twigg might be skulking about, that's all."

"Nothing out there except a lot of cold air. An awful lot of cold air as a matter of fact."

Despite her assurance he couldn't help feeling Sarah's presence. They wrapped themselves around each other under the heavy quilt.

"I think we should try it again," she said, lightly caressing his lower torso and thighs. "I don't believe much my sister tells me, but this time she might be telling the truth for a change. Anyway, it's worth finding out, don't you think?"

It was the sort of redundant question that barely merited an answer. Already aroused, he let her thoroughly work him over before reciprocating. This time she was so wet he could hardly feel himself enter her. No more wincing, no more knotted abdomen. Like before, her fingers dug into his buttocks, but this time she was pulling him down. Those delightfully hard nipples again pushed against his chest. Emma groaned with pleasure. This was the way it should be. The bed squealed even louder, and longer. He never noticed it, or the wardrobe door, which this time preempted his orgasm. Afterwards, lying exhausted and covered with perspiration, he knew that Emma had become a turning point in his life. They went to sleep in each other arms, oblivious to the plummeting temperature outside.

The following morning Harry awoke to find the room so cold that water left in a glass on the washbasin had turned to solid ice. Outside his window the pale dawn revealed a landscape crusted with frost. They would have an interesting time getting Dickie's car out of the vegetable garden in this weather, he thought to himself. Naked and shivering, he quietly slipped out of bed without waking her, and washed up. For some reason, the hot-water tap had frozen but the cold tap still worked. The icy water felt refreshing, but mid-summer would have been a better time for it.

Emma had hardly moved during the night. She slept on her right side in a fetal position, head lowered as though examining something under the blankets. All he could see was a bit of tousled hair and a tiny mound that outlined her body. So this was what it was like to go to bed with a woman! No longer a virgin, he felt good. Cold but good, and happy he'd done it for the first time with someone like Emma. He wished they could do it again before breakfast but it had turned seven o'clock, and anyway, she might not be in the mood that early in the day. Terry had once told him that when it comes to sex, there's a big difference between males and females. Males always have the pilot light on; in females it needs to be lit. Terry ought to know.

Why, he wondered as he towelled himself dry, had the wretched hot tap frozen while the cold one still worked, and especially when both pipes surely came through the kitchen below? Not that anything very hot came out of the hot tap; the 'H' etched into its handle seemed largely symbolic. Usually he was lucky to even get warm water. He glared through the window. Beyond the rime covered roof of Miss Twigg's outhouses, the River Derwent lazily wound its way through rocks and fallen tree limbs. Winters were for the birds, at least for those foolish enough to stay around. He didn't appreciate sleeping in a bedroom so cold that he sometimes couldn't bear the thought of getting up in the morning. In fact, he had decided, he would be quite happy never to experience an English winter again. These were only two of the many aspects of life in a spent and exhausted Britain that were beginning to irritate Harry. People seemed to put up with mediocrity as though it had been ordained by God. Surely, there must be countries with mild winters and warm homes, and populations which got on with their lives without waiting to be prompted by an overweening government.

His ankle still hurt, although there didn't appear to be much swelling. He briefly examined it, and then Roger's teeth marks higher up. It hadn't been a good month for left legs, no doubt about that. Then another thought occurred to him. Where was Sarah? Had she knocked out the piece of glass last night? Even if she hadn't, he had no desire to bump into her before they got downstairs. Most mornings she got up quite early to help her aunt get the kitchen going. But she might come back to her room for something, and with him Murphy's Law usually prevailed. Only two weeks earlier, on his way down to breakfast, she had passed him on the landing. On the other hand, since Sarah spent the odd weekend at her mother's, it was entirely possible there might be no one in the adjacent room to worry about.

Emma stirred. A nose poked over the blankets. He quickly pulled on his dressing gown and went to sit at her side. Sleepy-eyed, she gave him a wide smile. As she stretched her limbs the warm smell of perfume once again caught his nostrils.

"Good morning, and welcome to Derwent House," he quipped. "The only boarding house in Matlock which serves ice in the hot water taps."

"How did you sleep?" she asked.

He grinned. "Oh, very well. Very well **indeed**. Amazing what a little exercise can do for you!"

"Me too. I've never shared a bed with anyone before. Not even Mum when I was little." She sniffed the air. "It **is** a bit cold in here, isn't it?"

"I think that's putting it mildly. However, you'll be happy to know that, according to my landlady, this is the warmest room in the house!"

She sniffed again. "I don't think I'd like to sleep in the coldest. This is almost as bad as our farm. Doesn't matter though, it was nice and warm in here."

He slipped his hand under the bedclothes, running it gently over her stomach. She flinched. "Your hand is like ice!"

"As I just said, I got it from the hot tap!"

She held the now-warm hand against her. "What time is it?"

"About a quarter past seven. Why?"

"Because..." She began to climb out of bed, her naked body immediately blossoming in goose pimples. "I have to get up to my room."

He peeled off his dressing gown and handed it to her.

"I though perhaps if I messed it up a bit," she said, obviously enjoying this bit of conspiracy, "then at least it'll look as though I slept there. I can bundle my clothes and take them up with me."

"What are we going to do if you run into Sarah or Miss Twigg?"

"I shall say, 'Good morning! Bloody cold isn't it?'"

Harry grinned. "Sounds good. Take my dressing gown with you. I can fetch it later."

The grey-green eyes briefly scanned Harry's lanky frame. "You're not that skinny, you know. You're just very slim!" she said, looking him over again. "I wish we had a little more time. But there's always another day, I suppose." Then she slipped out of the door.

Yes, indeed, Harry thought to himself, let us hope. He still couldn't believe that finally some of his carefully laid plans had worked out. He could write a book about the disastrous failures he'd had in the past, but they paled into insignificance with this triumph. After all, this was 1961; premarital sex still ranked highly on a long list of moral no-no's. While Harry worried about getting Emma pregnant, he resented the thought of using condoms. Birth-control pills had been on the market only a few short years, and young women requesting a prescription were routinely subjected to probing questions about their marital status. The only alternative would be to wait for Emma's 'safe' times, which could be frustrating. He had never been much for postponed gratification. After one last glance at the crumpled sheets where Emma had spent the night, he made up the bed and got dressed.

She joined him a few minutes later downstairs, explaining that she'd decided to take a bath. She'd done it, she said, to add to the illusion of spending the night in her own room. Harry wasn't sure how much of all this she had preplanned, but he was beginning to see in Emma a very resourceful girl. If Emma wanted to do something, he would find in the months ahead, Emma would find a way of doing it. Best of all, she did it in the nicest way, at least where he was concerned. They were much alike in some aspects; both possessed a deep-seated toughness which refused to give up on things of importance.

Miss Twigg served them breakfast with her usual early morning gusto. If she had heard anything the night before, she gave no indication of it. Sarah, who obviously had not gone to her mother's for the weekend, was another matter. Harry had never seen her so attentive, grinning broadly at them both while shuffling in and out of the dining room. Harry found the look disquieting, since he had learned early on that Sarah's mind ran on opposing tracks to those of everybody else. He wasn't sure if this reflected a perverted sense of humour, or whether she was just plain stupid. Situations which aroused alarm or disgust in most people, Sarah often found uproariously funny, but she would frequently sit, stony-faced, while everyone else had a good laugh about something.

"Yer Harry's girlfriend," she said, plunking down the coffee pot. "I seen yer, y'know," Harry silently hoped it would turn out to be an occasion when Emma was wearing some clothes. "Me mum once sent me to Madison's fer sum cough stuff," she continued. "Didn't work, though."

Emma smiled at her. "And you're Sarah. I've heard a lot about you, too, although I don't remember seeing you in the shop."

"Yer 'ave? Wot 'ave yer 'eard?" she demanded, her curiosity freshly kindled.

Emma wasn't about to be put on the spot. "Just things in general. Mostly nice things!"

"Oh," she said, obviously catching the word 'mostly' and trying to decide whether it should be taken literally. "Are yer stayin' anuther night?"

"Not this weekend. Perhaps another time."

She continued staring at them in silence for several seconds, then abruptly retreated to the kitchen. Harry heard her talking to Miss Twigg but couldn't make out what she was saying. Whatever it might have been, the conversation didn't spark a violent response. Miss Twigg bade them a cheery farewell when they left. Sarah watched them through the serving hatch until they had closed the front door.

"That girl gives me the willies," Harry said as they marched arm in arm up the frosty street.

"She's probably got a crush on you!"

"God forbid! Anyhow, you know what we're going to do first this fine morning?"

"Oh, yes," Emma replied. "But I wonder if it might be a bit early yet."

"Maybe, maybe. Still, it's a nice walk."

Was Dickie's long suffering car still standing on its nose in the vegetable garden? That was the burning question. Watching the mechanics trying to pull it out on a day like this should be quite entertaining. Bank Road was so slippery they could hardly stand. Smedley Street, lying in the shadows of the county offices, even more so. All appeared quiet at the *Hanging Gate*, although Kath and Arthur would have been up hours earlier, Kath baking bread rolls and lighting the fire, Arthur getting the bar ready for a busy Saturday. They immediately spotted the imprint of several sets of tyre tracks on the frost-covered lane behind the pub. Sounds of an idling engine and busy voices confirmed that something was going on.

A flurry of activity surrounded the breached wall. A policeman, his car parked near the spot where Harry had taken a tumble, was scribbling on a clipboard while two men slowly winched Dickie's car out of its overnight resting place. It appeared bent on taking with it as much of the vegetable garden as possible. Harry noted with some satisfaction the name *Slater's Garage* on the breakdown-lorry's door panels. It was obvious that the overnight frost had not prevented everything in sight from becoming covered with wet, sticky mud and horse manure. Neither of Slater's two employees was wearing gumboots, and as a result were stomping about, ill-tempered, with their shoes and overalls plastered with the stuff. As the winch groaned, Dickie's car protested this latest indignity by noisily dragging its rear bumper against the rocks. Several times the driver had to pull the lorry forward because it had slid backwards down the icy road.

Then Emma stopped and tugged Harry's sleeve. There was Joyce sitting, hunched over, on a part of the undamaged wall, staring vacantly up the lane with her back to the rescue effort. She had thrown on a faded brown coat which seemed several sizes too big. A scarf covered her unkempt hair. She looked totally exhausted.

"Shouldn't we ask her if there's anything we can do?" Emma said quietly.

Harry shrugged. "I'm not sure if we should. I don't want her to think we're spying on her."

But Joyce saw them and settled their dilemma with a half hearted wave. "I hope we didn't spoil it for everybody last night," she said when they reached her. "Robert's at home sleeping it off. There wasn't enough evidence for the police to charge him with drunk driving, but thanks to his silly temper tantrum they've charged him instead with destroying government property." She pointed to the remains of the constable's bicycle. "That thing. They told me they could have charged him with assaulting a police officer, but one of them down there knows Robert, so they've stuck him with resisting arrest instead. So that's another fine we'll have to pay," She sighed. "That man is the bane of my life. I don't know, I really don't know. It gets worse and worse."

One of the garage attendants came over. "Yer won't be able ter drive yer car, Missus," he said with barely concealed satisfaction. "If yer 'usband 'adn't hit that cold frame he would 'ave been alright. But a piece o' wood pushed the front left mudguard right into the wheel. It'll need straightenin' aht an' some paint. That copper's bike made a right old dent in the door, too. All in all the car's a bit of a mess. We'll tow it ter Peak Motors, since that's where Mr. Dickie usually takes it fer body repairs."

Joyce nodded, then got up to leave. The man walked back shaking his head. "Rum job is this 'un," Harry overheard him say to the other attendant, and they both laughed.

"Would you have time for a cup of coffee, Mrs. Dickie?" Harry asked with sudden inspiration. "The *Hanging Gate* should have opened up by now. We could dodge in there."

She brightened for a split second and then shook her head. "Thanks, Harry, that's very kind of you," she replied. "But if you don't mind I'd rather not show my face in there for a while."

"We could go to Amber's," suggested Emma. "I've been there just for coffee once or twice. They don't seem to mind if you don't order anything to eat."

With her spirits rekindled, they trudged off to Amber's, another fish-and-chip-shop up Bank road from Madison's. Unlike many, which offered only a take-out service, Amber's had a few tables and chairs. The oldest fish-and-chip shop in Matlock, it was still owned and operated by the original family. Old George Amber came from Grimsby, where he'd worked as a deckhand with the North Sea fishing fleet. In 1895, fed up with harsh working conditions and low wages, he came to Derby to work in the textile mills. Two years later he married a girl from Matlock who worked as a cook at Smedley's Hydro. Since she wasn't keen on leaving her family to go and live in Derby, George, the enterprising young Yorkshireman, decided to turn that problem into an asset. With his savings he set up a fish-and-chip-shop in rented premises which he ultimately purchased. They had two sons. One died of tuberculosis; the other went into the business and eventually bought out his father. He married and had three sons. All three served in the Second World War. The youngest and the oldest went into the R.A.F. One was killed in a raid on Essen in 1943, the other died a year later in a mid-air collision with another bomber. The middle son went into the army, survived the war and re-entered the business. In 1961 Les and his wife, Millie, were still operating from the same location and enjoying a well-earned reputation for high-quality food.

It became obvious that Joyce hadn't eaten anything for a while because, once inside the busy shop, she decided she was hungry. Harry ordered her a plate of chips, and then, with Emma by his side, sat with her, sipping coffee while she opened the floodgates of a disastrous marriage. Listening, he couldn't help wondering why she would put up with the man for all those years, particularly since they appeared to have had problems right from the start. According to Joyce, Dickie turned out to have been a womanizer before he got married, and had continued the grand tradition afterwards with barely an interruptive hiccup. Between mouthfuls, Joyce recalled the thousands of pounds lost to alcohol. They were constantly in debt, and that was largely the reason for not having a telephone; she couldn't take the constant harassment from creditors.

Her husband would periodically disappear for several days, no one knew where, but for some unknown reason he had always been able to get away with the absences from work. It wasn't as if the County Architect was an old wartime pal; none of the upper management were for that matter. Perhaps it was Dickie's bluster, or perhaps his superiors sympathized with the man's problems and simply looked the other way. Whatever the reason, Joyce considered it a lucky break since she, more than anyone, knew that if he lost this job he would never get another supervisory position. He might be lucky to get a job at all. For a while she had been able to count on the support of her parents, even though they counselled against the marriage. But they had both died a long time ago, leaving her to fight on, alone.

Dickie's one steadfast devotion was to their daughter, Rachel. He worshipped the ground she trod. Sadly, her affection for him began to wane once she grew old enough to appreciate the damage he was inflicting upon the family. In her mid-teens, Rachel silently endured the embarrassment of her father showing up drunk at school functions, the teasing and snide comments from teachers and classmates, and the regular skirmishes with police. Ultimately the embarrassment boiled over into frustration, with Rachel adding her voice to her mother's frequent outbursts. It surprised and shocked Dickie that his daughter would turn against him, since he had always felt they enjoyed a special relationship. But rather than risk a confrontation with her, he directed his anger toward Joyce, who eventually wound up bearing the brunt of all the squabbles. Dickie's angst over Rachel's disillusionment only seemed to aggravate the situation, and by the time she turned eighteen she had already left home. Two years later, without telling her parents, she suddenly married a young man she had known only for a couple of months and moved with him to Manchester, where he found a teaching position. That was seven years ago. To Dickie it had been seven years of painful silence, with only a card at Christmas and no grandchildren to bridge the impasse. Both he and Joyce were deeply hurt by Rachel's secrecy, but he still could not bring himself to think ill of her. So it was perhaps to be expected that the only photograph adorning Dickie's untidy desk at work showed a young girl with dark brown hair and a frightened smile. Harry concluded that it must be Rachel.

"I don't know what I'm doing here babbling away like this," Joyce said as she dipped the last chip into a small puddle of ketchup. "You must find me a bit tiresome." She smiled self-consciously. "But it was nice to get a few things off my chest, and it was sweet of you to listen." She reached for her handbag.

"No, please, it's on me," Harry insisted. He didn't know what else to say. At twenty-two his experience with domestic conflict wouldn't have filled the back of a postage stamp. His own father, according to Mother, loved his family, barely drank at all, and for his pains died before Harry was old enough to remember what he really looked like. Granted, there were a few sketchy vignettes, most of them etched into his memory by a moment of crisis. He could still see a tall, slim man hopping around on one foot in the garden after young Harry had dropped a rock on his ankle. And he could see the same tall, slim man looking incredulously into a tree that had suddenly unleashed a torrent of water upon his head. It turned out to be one of Harry's failed attempts to create a waterfall with a watering can. Harry could still remember his father demanding to know from the boy's equally perplexed mother why anyone would want to build a waterfall up a tree. The fact that Harry had survived to adulthood suggested that Father, in addition to his other attributes, must have been an infinitely patient man.

Joyce touched his hand appreciatively. "You're a nice young fellow, Harry," she said. "And you've got a good companion. Take care of her." She pulled on her coat, stuffed the papers she'd brought from the police station into her pocket, and left. They watched through the window as she hurried down the icy street, pulling her scarf over her head. Emma looked silently at Harry for a while. He stared into his coffee cup.

"What do you think will happen to Mr. Dickie?" she asked.

Harry shrugged. "Beats me. He's got away with it this long, maybe he'll squeak through until he retires. Who knows."

"I don't understand why anyone would stay with somebody like that for so long."

"Perhaps she doesn't have any other choice," he replied thoughtfully. "I think most of us would do something different if we had a chance. As old Frank would say, that's life."

"Would you do something different?"

"Oh, I don't know. Maybe, maybe not."

"Well, she was right about one thing," Emma said.

"What's that?"

"You **are** a nice young man!"

"Of course I am," Harry modestly replied. "The best!"

SEVEN

An Unhappy Event

Harry went home for Christmas a week after the office party. They belatedly celebrated Emma's birthday when he returned after Boxing Day, much of it in the same fashion that had followed the office party. And once again the little piece of glass fell out of the bedroom door. With some money he'd managed to put aside, he bought Emma a slender gold bracelet as a combined birthday and Christmas present. He had asked the sales clerk to have Emma's initials engraved on the piece, then realized to his embarrassment that he didn't know her middle name.

Christmas at home did not go well. Emma's appearance in Harry's life had been met with polite enthusiasm until he mentioned that her family farmed. Upon hearing this, his mother's attitude changed abruptly and for the remainder of Christmas she either made catty remarks or sulked every time Emma's name came up. He told her about the gift he had bought; she sarcastically warned that unless it were 18 karat gold 'anything less was just throwing good money after bad.' As their squabbles went, this wasn't much, but Harry had hoped for a happier response. It angered him that she would presume to judge Emma before she had even met her. Did she dislike farming people in general, or was it something about **Emma's** farm? Certainly, he hadn't helped his cause by mentioning that they had only a smallholding on the Derbyshire moors. The possibility that his mother might be a closet snob came as an unpleasant surprise, considering her own working-class background. True, there had been the occasional warnings in the past about 'how easy it was for lower class people to drag us down to their level, but how virtually impossible it was for us to pull them up to ours.' Harry had dismissed it as typical parental rhetoric. After all, she had been saddled with the responsibility of raising two young children on her own, and she was doing it more or less alone in a dominantly blue-collar town.

Dickie, not the least contrite about his pre-Christmas antics, pulled a stunt similar to the Duffield episode in January. And once again Clem was called upon to retrieve him. But this time he didn't ask Harry for assistance, and only mentioned it during lunch a couple of weeks later. It had been a fairly simple procedure, he explained wryly, since the car keys didn't become airborne. A rumor began to circulate that Joyce was threatening to leave, encouraged, apparently, by Rachel. If this was true, it must have been a particularly hard blow for Dickie. However, nothing observable materialized, and the boss remained his usual ebullient self in the office.

Gradually it was becoming apparent that landscape design was indeed the Cinderella in the larger business of designing outdoor-sports facilities. Since landscaping was much closer to his heart than playing fields, Harry had made a deliberate attempt to get himself assigned accordingly. Dickie seemed content to let this happen, but Harry noticed that the perks, few as they were, invariably went to staff who worked on the major playing-field contracts. For the most part this was Lol and the self-styled rising star sitting at the draughting table across from him. Not that any of this could be justifiably considered cause for discontent, but the more Harry thought about it, the more he could see Pat Lewis's concern.

One Monday morning in early February, Clem didn't show up for work. The following day he still had not appeared. Since Clem kept very much to himself and seldom revealed his activities, no one paid much attention. Besides, since everyone did site inspections, periodic absences were expected. True, the amount of time people spent away from the office varied widely. Lol, for example, hardly ever came into the office, whereas with few exceptions the only time Bill Lewis left was to catch the bus home each day.

Late Tuesday morning Harry sneaked a look at Clem's daily planner. It showed no scheduled absences from the office that week. No site visits. No doctor or dentist appointments. He couldn't have gone chasing after Dickie because the Boss was at that moment sitting in his office.

After lunch on Tuesday, Bill Lewis, upon completing his football pools, sauntered over and asked Harry if **he** knew where Clem was. Harry said he didn't. Bill nodded and walked away. This deepened the mystery; if the office's senior draughtsman didn't know where he was, who did? To be sure, Clem had been away only a day and a half, but Harry felt uneasy about the entire business. It wasn't like Clem. Ever since arriving in Matlock he had been a fastidious worker and it was totally out of character for him to take off without recording it in his planner, even if he didn't actually tell anyone. The previous Friday, Harry recalled, Clem had complained of not feeling well. He hadn't paid much attention because, despite a perpetual pallor, his colleague never seemed to catch anything serious. Indeed, Clem and Angus made an interesting contrast, with Angus coughing, dripping, and wheezing from a face as cherubic as Santa Claus.

The day wore on and still no sign of Clem. It irritated Harry that no one seemed to be the least bit interested in his colleague's disappearance. Very slowly, Clem had come out of his shell as he got to know Harry better. Harry wasn't sure why he had been able to hit it off with him more than the others. Perhaps it was by allowing Clem to open up at his own speed. But even so he had little to say, preferring to let Harry do most of the talking, which Harry did, if only to keep the conversation going. While the other staff members continued to treat Clem as something of a pariah, to Harry's knowledge he had never quarreled with any of them. Indeed, he would be a difficult person to take issue with since he seldom said enough to provoke a confrontation.

A couple of hours later Bill mentioned that Dickie had no idea where Clem was either. And that was that. By the end of Tuesday afternoon Harry decided to find out if Clem's landlady had seen him. But only Morley had Clem's address and he was in Derby for the day. So Harry waited impatiently until the following morning. As usual, Morley was late in, although it is likely that everyone would have preferred to be late on that day. Wednesday dawned cold, miserable and rain-swept, buffeted by an icy wind that roared off the peaks and down through the Derwent Valley. And it stayed that way for the rest of the day. Harry's only reason for being on time was to get Clem's address.

"He's in a bed-sitter off Church Street," Morley said, hanging up his coat with his usual sigh of fatigue. "You'll have to head down Causeway Lane towards Matlock Green and then turn right. He's actually not far from where you live. On your left, halfway down Church Street there's a butcher's called *Graftons* on a dead-end road. They let out three or four so-called 'self-contained flats' above the shop." He sniffed. "Damned things are nowhere close to being self-contained. In fact the entire building ought to be condemned. I stayed in one when the county offices first relocated here. Stuck it out for a whole fortnight! There are two floors above the shop so I've no idea which one he would be on, although I suspect if might be the top floor. You'll have to pop in and ask the owners. They're a husband-and-wife team and one of them is always there when they're open. It's usually the wife; he spends most of his time at the race track."

While Harry knew his way around Matlock reasonably well, Matlock Green was uncharted territory. He'd ventured in there only once, just before Christmas in an unsuccessful bid to find a shoe-repair shop. From a distance it looked to be a mixture of largely run-down old houses, garages and yards. The people who lived there seemed to be a rough lot. Certainly not an area he would want to hang around in. Besides, nearly everything in Harry's life— the chemist's shop, the road to Elton, the Hanging Gate, and the county offices— were all towards the other end of town.

The puzzle had to be resolved.

"Bill, I'm going to check up on Clem," Harry called out as he went for the back stairs. "It's nearly three days since he's been in the office. I don't care what anybody says, it's not like him to just disappear." He'd deliberately raised his voice on the chance that someone might go with him. That notion was quickly dispelled. Lewis nodded uninterestedly and went back to what he had been doing. Terry looked up with a pained expression as if to say, "Why bother?" Angus and Morley simply buried their heads among their drawings. The hell with you all, Harry thought to himself. I'll go alone.

The wind was still blowing, although it had briefly stopped raining. Angry clouds, streaked with black and grey, scudded overhead. Down the valley, the high cliffs bordering Matlock Dale were cloaked in a thick mist. Harry was glad of the lined raincoat his mother had bought him for Christmas, and he pulled the belt tighter as he set off down Bank Road.

Once past the Causeway Lane football grounds an untidy jumble of dilapidated buildings told him that he was entering the nether world of Church Street. On one corner, what had once been a millinery shop stood empty and half-derelict, its ornate front window boarded up and smeared with graffiti. The entire area looked for all the world as though it had grown utterly tired of itself, and, like a small child bored with its toys, had fled without cleaning up. Litter swirled about, clogging drains and attaching itself like little wet pieces of billboard advertising to any handy surface. Most of the street was lined with row housing, a grim legacy of Matlock's former textile heyday. They huddled in clusters, their front doors and parlour windows opening directly onto the pavement. Farther down the street was a cul de sac containing a gaggle of shops, including one with the name *H. Grafton, Quality Meats and Poultry* barely legible above its window. Harry could see another floor above the shop, and then what looked like an attic above that. To the left of the door into the shop was another. He wondered if that led up to the flats, but since he couldn't find any name plates, went into the shop to find out.

A short, overweight woman leaned against the back counter nursing a mug of tea. The place was empty, save for an emaciated cat snoozing on top of the glass-covered meat display. The woman made no effort to disengage herself from the counter, choosing instead to communicate from where she stood.

"Yes, young man, and wot can we do fer you today," she said in an expressionless monotone.

"Do you have a Mr. Walker living in one of your flats?" Harry asked.

The woman thought for a few seconds. Surely she couldn't have forgotten the names of her tenants?

"Which Mr. Walker would you be looking for? We 'ave two. One's an older gentleman, a commercial traveller, ah think. T'other's a youngish chap 'oo works up at Smedley's Hydro."

That would explain the hesitation. "The last one," Harry answered.

The woman stuck her thumb at a forty-five-degree angle towards the grimy ceiling. "'E's on't first floor. It's the door on the right at 'top of the stairs. I 'aven't seen 'im fer a day or two so 'e might not be in." She shrugged and resumed her task of dragging a large slab of bacon to the slicer. "But ah' reckon yer might as well give 'im a knock," she added. The same thumb jerked towards the door. "Just go ahtside and then through't door next to it."

So Clem lived on the first floor, not the top one, as Morley had predicted. At least he'd got the address right. Harry made his way up the stairs to the first floor landing, stopping for a moment at the top to catch his breath. It steamed in the frigid air. It had to be colder in this building than outside, he thought. Even colder than his own bedroom. But unlike Miss Twigg's, this place stank of backed-up drains. Brown paint which had been hastily slapped on many years ago was flaking off, revealing an even older application of wallpaper. Who would want to decorate a hallway in brown paint, he wondered. And why would they paint over the wallpaper? It all smacked of the money-grubbing expedience of slum housing.

None of the three doors indicated who the occupants were. No directory. No nameplates. All were tightly shut. One looked as though it had been kicked in.

For a change, however, the door jamb had held firm, with the door partly disintegrating instead. A thin piece of plywood was screwed over the splinters.

He knocked on the door which the woman downstairs had described as Clem's. There was no reply. Somehow, though, intuition told him Clem was there. He could sense the man's presence in much the same way one can tell when there is someone else in a darkened room. He put his ear to the door and listened.

"Clem, it's Harry. Are you okay?

Again, there was no response from inside, just the sounds of an old building gradually falling apart.

"Look, Clem," he said, putting his mouth as close to the door jamb as possible, "just tell me you're alright and I'll bugger off. It's just that we haven't seen you for three days and Bill Lewis is worried."

What a bald lie. Lewis wasn't in the least bit concerned about Clem. Or if he was, he could have fooled anybody. But then, no one else seemed to be in the least bit concerned either.

For a split second he thought he could hear the faint sound of someone coughing. After a minute or two it was repeated. So there was someone there. In desperation, Harry turned the knob, expecting to find the door locked. To his surprise it wasn't. Inside, Clem was lying on a camp bed in the corner. As Harry walked in, he made a feeble move to draw a dirty blanket around himself. Although the room was in semi-darkness, it didn't prevent Harry from seeing that Clem was seriously ill. Both he and the bed smelled of stale perspiration, and it mingled with a score of other foul odours that come from poor sanitation. Stifling an urge to retch, Harry pulled back the ragged curtains and tried unsuccessfully to open the window.

Clem smiled, wagging his finger mockingly. "You shouldn't have come, Harry. You'll get the sack for missing work." Then his head rolled slightly towards the wall.

Harry was appalled at the man's condition, and no less disgusted by the conditions under which he was living. He'd always considered Miss Twigg's establishment to be somewhat spartan, but it was Buckingham Palace by comparison with this hovel. Across one corner an old bed sheet had been slung over a wooden pole and was serving as a wardrobe. Next to it, a dilapidated gas ring sat on an iron wash stand, attached by its umbilical rubber hose to a coin-operated meter. The gas was turned off but a saucepan half filled with tomato soup suggested that Clem had tried to eat. Bread, what looked like margarine, and a few other odds and ends littered the rest of the wash-stand surface. On the other side of the stand a dirty sink rounded out the accouterments of this 'self-contained' flat. It looked as though the building owners must have got the deal of a lifetime on brown paint because the room, like the corridor outside, was smothered in it. Above Clem's cot, neglect had combined with gravity on a patch of the ceiling plaster, leaving the wooden lath exposed like the bleached ribs of some prehistoric mammal. Harry glanced uneasily at the rest, half expecting it to come crashing down, too.

Clem appeared to be running a high fever and he was scared. Staring out from sunken sockets, his eyes betrayed the fear everyone experiences when they find themselves succumbing to insidious forces beyond their control. Harry could see that the man's skin, now the colour of wet flour, was coated in sticky sweat. His hair, lank at the best of times, stuck to his head in wet streaks. Breathing with difficulty in short grunts, he lay flat on his back, still clutching the blanket. In Harry's short life there never had been a situation like this. He had to do something..

"How long have you been in bed, Clem?"

Clem opened his eyes and put up five fingers.

"Christ! You've been in bed five days?"

"Yup," Clem wheezed. And then after a short silence, he said, "I don't seem to be able to stand up any more."

"Did you call the doctor?"

He slowly shook his head.

"Are you registered with one here?"

The head again rolled from side to side.

"I'll get one to come and look at you," Harry said. It was a bold gesture, and a rather empty one, since he had no more idea who to call than Clem. The last time he'd needed a doctor was years before, after gashing his arm on some broken glass. Unfortunately Dr. Walker was a Barnsley physician, and that didn't do Harry much good in Matlock.

Sitting on the edge of the cot, he mulled over the options. It was more than likely that Clem should be in hospital. If he rang 999, an ambulance would come and take him in. But that would create a big scene, and Harry had an instinctive aversion to ambulances. His father's first and last trip to the hospital required an ambulance. He could still remember them carrying him out of the house, paralyzed from the waist down, in a chair; people standing around outside on the pavement, gawking. And his mother, shocked and confused, trying to get her dying husband out of the spotlight with as much dignity as she could muster. Then there was that afternoon a few days later, when she came in to the living room and told them that it was all over. Dad had died in the iron lung. It was the first time he'd ever seen his grandpa cry. He wept softly, covering his face with his large callused hands. Grandma just sat, staring out of the window for a long time. He would never forget that day.

Clem rolled his head again and looked at Harry with wide-open eyes. "Please don't send for a doctor," he pleaded.

"But, Clem, dammit, you're very ill. Look at you. You're running a fever and you're covered in sweat. At least we'll be able to get a prescription..."

"Harry, please!" Clem's face flushed with anger and he turned away.

Harry could barely hear him.

"Please don't send for a doctor," Clem repeated, very softly.

"Well, I can't just sit here and do nothing," Harry snapped. Looking about him he spotted a half-empty aspirin bottle. "Here, take some more of these," he said. "Maybe they'll get the fever down." He jiggled out three and fetched a glass of water from the sink. Clem made a pathetic effort to sit up. Harry helped him. After the aspirins he moistened Clem's face cloth and wiped off his face and neck. The cloth smelled as bad as he did. With an audible sigh of relief Clem flopped back on his pillow.

The two sat in silence for about five minutes. Harry was bewildered. Why didn't this strange man want to go to hospital, or for that matter, to even see a doctor? He couldn't be that scared. There had to be some other explanation. He kept thinking about past conversations with Clem over the Christmas season. They hadn't been angry or hostile conversations. Nothing like that. In fact, he'd never seen Clem get really angry. But on a couple of occasions when Harry had talked to him about the future, he would become sullen and withdrawn and the subject quickly dropped as though it held no relevance. For Clem, there just seemed to be the past, and a fleeting, finite present. He would smile when others in the group laid out their hopes and dreams, but his eyes revealed very different emotions. Someone or something had snatched away Clem's future, and he knew he could never get it back. He'd once said that he preferred to draw on his yesterdays because no one could take **them** from him.

Clem made such a contrast to some of the others in the office, who would seize upon the smallest excuse to babble endlessly about themselves. Angus, for instance, bared his soul, and those of everybody else in his family, on a daily basis. Someone should have provided him with a bulletin board. Then there was Terry who behaved, as Bill Lewis once put it, as though he had a bicycle pump shoved up his bottom. Not Clem. It would have been a little more understandable if he were trading quantity for quality. But there was nothing to trade.

"Do you hurt anywhere?" Harry asked him.

For some reason Clem considered that an amusing question. He managed a short laugh as his head again moved slowly back and forth.

"I mean, does it hurt when you breathe?"

"A little. But it'll pass," Clem replied.

Harry wished Emma was with him. She would handle this situation much better, despite her professed dislike for Clem. But this was Wednesday; half-day closing for most of Matlock's shops. He glanced at his watch. It was nearly 1 PM. Emma's bus left Crown Square at 12.30. She would be gone.

He felt himself shivering. The room was miserably cold and Clem's single thin blanket totally inadequate. There didn't appear to be any source of heat, other than the gas ring. He didn't want to leave but in view of his friend's intransigence on the issue of medical attention, there was little more he could do. Perhaps the fever would subside in a while. Then he'd come back and make some soup, if he could find any; the stuff in the saucepan was spoiled. He flushed it down the sink, cleaned things up, and looked around. A couple more cans of tomato soup sat on the shelf. Was that all he ate? It seemed pretty meagre fare but probably sufficient for the present situation. One of his mother's many homilies came to mind: 'starve a fever, feed a cold.' Or was it the other way around? Either way, soup would be hardly likely to create a problem. Clem wasn't in any condition to eat at that moment, and, with his lunch hour practically gone, Harry decided to come back later.

"Clem, I'm going back to the office," he said, straightening out the bedsheets. "But I'll come after work and make some soup. Do you have any more blankets? It's bloody cold in here. Sweating like that you're going to catch pneumonia."

Clem shook his head again. "I'll think warm thoughts," he said with another feeble grin.

Harry got up to leave, then as an afterthought grabbed Clem's overcoat and spread it over the blanket.

"This might make you sweat more," he said, tucking the sleeves under the mattress, "but don't throw it off."

"No doctor, please," Clem's voice trailed off behind the closing door.

"Okay, no doctor. For the moment, anyway," Harry said, ducking his head back inside.

Outside on the street he glanced back at the butcher's shop. It was now closed for the half-day. Did they have a telephone? Probably, although even by 1962, many small-town businesses were without phones. Why was it always raining? The chill dampness put him in a foul mood as he trudged back to the County Offices. His shoes would be wet again. They'd already been ruined by ugly tide marks from previous soakings and accidents, and try as he might, the stains wouldn't polish out. Sloshing through the puddles, he tried to remember the name of the Roman fellow who landed on British soil eons ago and promptly dismissed it as 'a land of mist and fog, and entirely unfit for human habitation.' Or something like that. Anyway, the man was absolutely right.

"Well, did you find our errant colleague?" Bill Lewis asked, with only a modicum of interest.

Harry shook out his raincoat in the hallway, then tossed it onto one of the pegs by the back-stairs exit. As he walked over to his draughting table he noticed that Bill had burned a large hole in his tie with cigarette ash. How bloody silly. One of these days he was going to set the office on fire, just as Dickie had predicted, unless Dickie beat him to it.

"He's at his digs," Harry replied. "God. What a miserable place. I'm surprised Morley even stuck it out for two weeks. I think Clem's got the flu. Anyway, he's running a fever and he's been in bed since the weekend. I'm going back at five o'clock to see if I can get some food down him. By the way, where **is** Morley? I wanted to ask him if he knew whether those people who own the butcher's shop have a telephone."

Bill shrugged. "I suppose they would be in the telephone directory if they did. Why?"

"So I can ring for help if he gets worse."

"Must have been some hangover Clem had."

"He's not hung over, Bill," Harry retorted. "He's ill. And what I can't understand is why he wouldn't let me pack him off to hospital or even fetch a doctor. I don't know what to make of him. It's almost as though he wanted to be left there."

"Maybe he's atoning for his sins."

"Atoning for **what** sins?"

Bill answered the question with only a flickering smile and shambled back to his drawing board.

At five o'clock Harry set off again to Clem's digs, this time armed with an old umbrella his mother had given him. It was of little value. An icy wind was again gusting up and down Bank Road, threatening to turn the brolly inside out. Within five minutes he had more water dripping down his neck from inside the umbrella than from the outside. By the time he got to Church Street it was getting dark, and for the millionth time he cursed the miserable weather. He longed for spring and the promises it always brought: warm days and sunshine. Would those frozen wallflowers in front of the town hall ever bloom? Perhaps more importantly, would he still be around if or when they did? A terrible dreariness hung over the empty pavements and buildings. He couldn't imagine this place ever wearing a summer mantle. The enterprising industrialists who spawned these hellish suburbs were possessed of a singular purpose. In short, it precluded anything that failed to contribute directly towards the task of housing as many people as possible in the smallest space. Yet, a few pathetic sticks passing as trees had managed to sprout and survive in the dismal little back yards. Their barren branches crackled restlessly in the wind, as though they might be yearning to escape and seek a more hospitable environment. He hurried to the shelter of the door leading up to Clem's flat.

Earlier he had decided he would try to get Clem to swallow some soup and a couple of slices of bread. Perhaps there was tea in one of the canisters littering the washstand. He hadn't examined the contents of them all. It would be too bad if Clem took milk with his tea; he was pretty certain there was none of that lying around. And lighting the gas ring might get some warmth in the room. Fumbling in his pocket for coins, he fished out some pennies and a one-shilling piece. They would suffice. Climbing the stairs reminded him of Scrooge's house in the film 'Christmas Carol.' These stairs were narrower but every bit as chilling. The light bulb on the first landing had failed, leaving only a shadowy glow from the main floor. As before, no one appeared to be around.

The room was now in total darkness. Harry fanned the wall with his hand for the light switch and a tiny bulb over the sink lit up. Someone had fashioned a lamp shade from a length of Christmas trim. It had once been red but had turned orange with age; brown stains showed where the paper had come into contact with the light bulb. There's a place looking for a fire, Harry thought as he pulled off his wet raincoat. Clem still lay motionless on his back with his arms above the blanket and extended down his sides.

"Well, Mr. Walker. Feeling any better?" He called out while shovelling some pennies into the gas meter. There was no response. He lit a match and the gas ring blossomed into a halo of blue flame.

"I reckon we'll toast up the room a bit and then we'll warm some soup. D'you think you could handle a bit of tomato soup?" Harry asked.

There was still no response from the cot.

He walked over, sat on the edge of the bed, and looked closely at Clem's ashen face. The greasy film of perspiration had gone from his skin, together with the look of terror in the open but now sightless eyes. For the first time since they had met, he looked completely at peace with the world. Harry reached for an exposed arm, intending to give his friend a gentle tug. It was as cold and unyielding as the street outside. He recoiled from the shock, paused for a moment, and then leaned forward to see if he could hear any breathing. There was nothing. Finally, plucking up some courage he vainly probed the arm again for a pulse. Apart from the pounding of his own heart reverberating to the tips of his fingers, there was nothing.

Clem was dead. But it took several seconds for the reality to sink in. Even worse, Harry had left him and he'd died alone in that cold and dreary little room with no one at his side. The panic rapidly spiraling in Harry's throat quickly became joined by an explosion of anger and remorse. Why had Clem stubbornly refused to be helped? This couldn't have been an everyday case of flu. He must have known how desperately ill he was. No less culpable was Harry's behavior. Why didn't he stay, instead of going back to the office? In all likelihood there was nothing he could have done, but at least Clem would have had someone. Perhaps he might not have died had someone stayed with him. It was incomprehensible. How could someone just give up like that, without even a struggle? What had killed him? What on earth was he going to do? The jumble of thoughts danced about in his head. Dickie was the only person familiar with Clem, and the logical person to call. Then Harry remembered they didn't have a telephone. Damn. How could a grown man be such an irresponsible clod? Should he find a telephone and call 999? Was one supposed to call 999 in these situations? He'd never called that number in his entire life. What would happen if he did? He'd feel pretty silly if the operator didn't consider this an emergency. One thing was certain: he couldn't sit here and do nothing.

Outside, the wind badgered and blustered. Inside, only a hissing gas ring broke the stillness as Harry grappled with his predicament. Clem's worries were over. His had just started. He'd seen a corpse only once before in his life, and that had been his grandfather. The loss of his father had brought many changes, mostly unpleasant. After packing Harry off to a boarding school in Hertfordshire, his mother had sold the house and moved in with her parents. It hadn't been very satisfactory arrangement. Frictions soon developed and to make matters worse, Grandma became senile. For nearly five years she forgot, remembered, and forgot again, wandering out of the house at night and flying into temper tantrums by day. She finally fell down the stairs, broke her hip, and died several days later of pneumonia.

By the time Harry left school and started work at the parks department, a rapprochement of sorts had evolved, and Harry came to understand and respect his grandfather. A division of labor was defined: he and Mother went to work, Grandpa cooked meals and looked after the house. One day Harry was summoned to the superintendent's office and told that his grandfather had died of heart failure. There had been no suffering; Grandpa had gone upstairs for his afternoon siesta and simply dropped down dead. Just like that. Full of remorse, he cycled home to find the doctor leaving, mother sitting silently by the fire waiting for an ambulance to arrive. He desperately wanted one last glimpse of the surrogate father he'd barely got to know, and went upstairs to his grandfather's bedroom. Unsure what to expect, Harry pushed the door ajar. They'd lifted him on to the bed and he was lying on his back, the wrong way round, feet resting on the pillow. The silence in that room was deafening. He recoiled at the sight, as he had just done with Clem, and hurried back downstairs. Grandpa had died in the same style that he had lived. In some ways Clem had done the same.

That was Harry's first experience with a corpse. But this was different. He'd seen only a glimpse of his grandfather. Clem was inches away and he'd touched the cold and rapidly stiffening body. There was an atmosphere of unreality about the entire thing. Staring at Clem's lifeless face, he half-expected him to open his eyes and say something. There should have been much to say, too, even if it were only to shed some light on this man's mysterious past. Now, unless someone else spoke for him, he would be taking most of his secrets to the grave.

The confused and muddled thoughts came and went as he kept his lonely vigil at Clem's uncomfortable cot. Fifteen minutes passed. New shivers drew his attention to the gas ring, which had gone out. Having no more pennies for the meter, he finally decided it was time to summon help. He had no idea who normally responded to these situations. Was it the police? Or the fire and ambulance department? Or someone else entirely? The best strategy, he decided, was to firstly see if there was anyone at home in the other flats and, if not, run back to Miss Twigg's. She would certainly be there because it was dinner time. Miss Twigg seemed to have solutions to most of life's dilemmas. She would probably know what to do.

He pulled up Clem's blanket, tucking it tightly under the dead man's chin and around his sides before realizing the futility of what he was doing. Shoving his arms through his raincoat he turned off the light, carefully closed the door, and walked the couple of steps to the other flat on Clem's floor. No one answered. Quickly he clambered up the stairs to the flat that occupied the attic and met with the same success. The hell with it, he decided; Miss Twigg would be a better option anyway.

She was in the kitchen with the ever-present Sarah, and looked up in surprise as Harry burst in from the hallway. The look on his face was enough to tell her that something was wrong. In any event, he wouldn't be bursting into her kitchen unless there was, since she had made it clear from the outset that boarders were not welcome in her private domain. Harry had always respected this edict for a variety of reasons, not the least of which was the obvious fact that kitchens, and especially Miss Twigg's kitchen, were places where physical work was done. And cleaning up was the type of physical work which didn't appeal to Harry one little bit.

"My goodness, you're looking a little flustered, Mr. Harry," she said, looking over her glasses in mock sternness. "Did you think you'd missed dinner?"

"My friend's died," Harry blurted out, choking back a flood of tears. "And I haven't a clue what to do. I think he had the flu. He was alright earlier today. Or at least he seemed alright. But when I went back to his digs an hour ago, he was dead."

She looked at him for a moment. "Come come, now. Are you sure he was dead? He wasn't breathing? No pulse?"

"I know he's dead. He's stiff, and stone cold."

"So are my feet at this time of year, but I'm not dead. Yet," Miss Twigg retorted.

"He's dead," Harry repeated. "I know it."

Miss Twigg suddenly became all seriousness. "Was this the strange fellow at your office you once talked about?"

"It was Clem Walker." Harry paused and then added, as though regretting he'd ever mentioned it, "He really wasn't all that strange."

"You poor boy. Where is he now?"

"Still at his digs. I left him there. Under a blanket."

"No, I mean, where is he staying?" Miss Twigg asked as she made for the hallway and the telephone.

He told her and she let out a loud groan. "My God. Why on earth would he want to stay there? That place is nothing more than an overpriced rat trap."

"I've no idea," he replied. "This is the first time I've been to his digs."

"And probably the last, I think."

Sarah, who was listening to the conversation with wide eyed curiosity, approached Harry, eager for more gory details. "Yer mean, yer saw 'im and touched 'im, an' 'e was really dead an' everythin?" she asked.

"Never mind that, Missy," Miss Twigg snapped. "Put the meat and vegetables in the oven to keep warm. And don't burn them; we might be a while. First thing we'll do is ring 999. Then we'll go over to Grafton's and wait for the ambulance."

Sarah pouted. She pouted a lot. But on this occasion he had too many things on his mind to pay much attention.

"Did he have a doctor?" Miss Twigg called from the hallway.

Harry shook his head. "No. He wouldn't let me fetch one either."

"Really? Did he say why? That's very odd."

"He didn't say why," Harry replied. "He told me he didn't want a doctor and he wouldn't let me send for an ambulance. I did as he asked. Now I wish I hadn't. Perhaps he'd still be alive."

The phone call completed, he and Miss Twigg hurried through the wet streets to Matlock Green.

"What about his family? Can they be contacted?" she asked along the way.

"I know absolutely nothing about them, except that his parents live in Devon. He once told me his dad was a printer. But he may be retired now. Clem never said much about himself."

"Perhaps you should have telephoned your supervisor?"

"He doesn't have a telephone."

Miss Twigg shot a puzzled glance. "Doesn't have a telephone? That's most unusual for a man in his position."

"He's a rather odd fellow," Harry replied without elaborating.

"I presume your friend wasn't married?"

"Apparently not. At least that's what my boss says."

"You don't sound convinced."

Her question once again aroused memories of past conversations. "I don't know. He's said some odd things when we've been out for a pint. Almost as if he was hiding something."

She silently took all this in, and they stumbled up the darkened stairs to the flats.

Clem was exactly where Harry left him, with the pathetic rag of a blanket still tucked under his chin and the icy-cold room shrouded in the same terrible stillness as that bedroom where his grandfather had died. But for all the similarities, there was something different about Clem's death. Grandfather, he remembered, had looked utterly composed, as if he had readily come to terms with his other-world destiny before collapsing on the floor. Superficially, Clem did, too. But beneath the physical stillness, Harry could sense a furious clamouring, in the same way that a thousand disturbed barn swallows might try to escape all at the same time. And for a fleeting moment he experienced an overwhelming urge to grab Clem and take flight with him, to leave the confines of that awful room and that wretched cot and to see his friend finally win the nirvana that had eluded him on earth. Wherever Clem was now, it must be far from where he deserved to be, Harry felt certain of that. Suddenly feeling lightheaded, he went over to the chair by the sink and sat down.

Miss Twigg quickly confirmed that Clem had no pulse. "You're right," she said, "he's gone." With that she gently pulled the blanket over Clem's head.

In a dull voice Harry asked, "Who will be coming?"

"The doctor and an ambulance. If the doctor suspects foul play he calls the police. In your friend's case I think they'll just take him to the mortuary. I do wish your Mr. Dickie had a telephone."

With her nose wrinkled at the smell, Miss Twigg began examining the room. The more she looked, the more disgusted she became.

"Disgraceful. Absolutely disgraceful," she fumed. "A friend of mine told me that these flats were bad, but I never thought they were as bad as this. I hope they decide on an autopsy. That means someone would probably inspect this place. Then the Graftons are going to catch it," she said with satisfaction.

Harry nodded approval. Morley had said earlier that the Graftons owned the building, which, judging by its design, might at one time have been a single residence. Looking around at the cracked plaster and peeling paint, Harry couldn't help thinking it seemed like a shabby way to treat a part of Matlock's Victorian heritage. While Miss Twigg tidied up, he went over to the silent gas ring and turned off the control knob. It was essentially a make-work exercise since the meter had to be fed with more pennies before the ring could be used again. In any event, Clem wouldn't need it any more.

After about twenty minutes which seemed like eternity, a short, stocky man clutching a well-worn leather bag scurried in, announced that he was Doctor Midgely, took Clem's vital signs, pronounced him dead and pulled the blanket back over his face. Then he spotted the aspirin bottle.

"How many of these did he take?" he asked.

Harry and Miss Twigg both shook their heads. "The bottle was half empty when I first saw him at lunch time. I gave him three before I left," Harry replied.

"What time would that be?"

"About twelve-thirty."

The doctor stood silently for a moment, apparently deep in thought. "Hm," he said, as much to himself as to anyone else. "In all likelihood, pulmonary edema." Then, noticing the puzzlement in their faces, he explained, "Double pneumonia in layman's language. I'm not totally certain at this point that the pneumonia killed him, but it was definitely a contributing factor. When both lungs fill with fluid they..... Anyway, the medical examiner will have the final word. It's my guess he died about three hours ago."

Harry and Miss Twigg accepted this information with the deference normally accorded medical professionals. Why argue? If the man had told them Clem died of an ingrown toenail, they would have little choice but to believe him.

He eyed them both through heavy-rimmed glasses. "Are either of you related to the deceased?"

They advised him that they weren't.

That caused Doctor Midgely to frown. "Then, do you know, perhaps, where his next of kin can be contacted?"

They both shook their heads again.

"I work with him," Harry explained. "We're with the County Architect's Department. I think his parents live in Devon, or at least they used to. Actually, the only person who knows anything about him is our boss."

"Have you telephoned him?"

"He doesn't have a telephone."

"Doesn't have a telephone?"

Here we go again, Harry thought to himself. "No, he doesn't have a telephone."

"Oh, dear," the doctor said, scratching his head. "Oh, deary dear. Do you know where he lives, perhaps?"

"I'm afraid not," said Harry, wishing the good doctor would ask him a question he could answer, even if it happened to be only one. "I do know he lives here in Matlock, and he's up in one of the new housing estates, but I don't know the address."

"That's alright," said the doctor, trying to hide his exasperation. "We will root him out one way or other."

Dickie would be delighted to hear that, Harry thought to himself.

"The ambulance people will have to take his personal belongings. You know, clothes, wallet. That sort of thing. Perhaps you be so kind as to hang on for a little while longer until they get here. I'm already late for a delivery."

Harry and Miss Twigg nodded, and the doctor left.

Five minutes later an ambulance arrived. Clem was carefully transferred to a stretcher along with his clothing and personal effects, and removed, the attendants' boots clattering loudly on the stairs as they went. Then it was all over. Clem was gone as though he had never existed. In some ways, Harry couldn't help thinking, he never had.

"I think we should go home now," Miss Twigg said, buttoning up her coat.

Harry nodded again, looked around the room one last time, and they left, closing the door behind them.

The following morning, Harry imparted the previous day's events to a half-filled office, then waited impatiently for Dickie to arrive. Only Terry, Bill Lewis and Morley were in. Lol Dobson was in Belper, trying to determine why a newly built tennis court turned out to be several feet too short. It was just as well; Lol had less time for Clem than anyone. Angus, who had been wrestling with post nasal drip for the past week, had decided that day to drip at home. It was a decision roundly applauded by all, since the incessant snarfling was beginning to get on everyone's nerves.

Clem's death was received with polite concern by all present. Bill wanted to know the nature of Clem's illness. But Harry couldn't tell him any more than what he had seen and what the doctor had said. Morley offered the opinion that Clem's wretched living conditions had probably killed him. Terry agreed with a sniff and went back to his work.

By nine-thirty Dickie still had not arrived so Harry sneaked over to the chemist's to tell Emma what had happened. The news shocked her, although not nearly as much as the experience had shaken him. He was well aware that Emma didn't care too much for Clem, which puzzled him because she never really said why.

"It must have been awful for you." she said, clearly revealing where her own concerns lay.

Mrs. Johnson was obviously not in the shop; otherwise she would have been in on this event like a dirty shirt. Perhaps she was with Dickie; maybe that would explain why he was late. Harry would like to have stayed and chatted but they could get together at lunch time as they usually did. He went back to the office to find that Dickie had finally showed up in his absence. As he entered the room, Bill was in the process of passing along Harry's information. Dickie stood, leaning against Bill's drawing board, the customary cigarette stuck to his lower lip, gazing silently at the floor. Given the circumstances, this was uncharacteristic of his boss. Normally a very excitable man, he could, and often did, quickly fly off the handle over the smallest crisis. Today, for a change, he was surprisingly subdued, as though the event had touched him personally.

Glancing up when Harry entered the room, he said, "So that's the end of it for Mr. Walker, eh?"

This seemed such an odd comment that Harry was lost for a reply.

"Are you going to get in touch with his family, Bob?" Bill asked.

Dickie nodded. Then after another short silence he went to his office.

"See, that's what you get for checking up on people," Terry said sarcastically while Harry pulled the dust cover off his drawing board.

Right now Harry wasn't in the mood for Terry's flippant remarks and ignored him. In addition to this business with Clem, he was having another bad time with some playing-field design. Terry occasionally gave him a hand, but in such a condescending fashion that Harry invariably regretted asking. He tried to concentrate, but the image of that dismal room, and the cot with its lifeless occupant covered by a blanket, wouldn't go away.

After about fifteen minutes, Dickie reappeared. "Can I see you for a minute, Harry?" he asked.

This request, albeit couched in the politest tones, usually presaged a dressing-down for something, real or imagined, that Harry had done, or hadn't done, on the job. However, on this occasion, he thought he could detect a different tone in Dickie's voice. Accompanied by Terry's sly grin, he meekly followed Dickie into his office.

"Sit down, my friend," Dickie said, closing the door. That wasn't a good start; normally his use of the term 'my friend' meant precisely the opposite. But, again, a slightly different inflection in the command hinted at some other reason for being called in. This time his boss wasn't flushed and excitable, as he normally was when Harry had done something particularly stupid. With a sense of relief, he knew this morning wasn't going to be an occasion for getting his backside chewed off.

Dickie lit another cigarette, leaned back in his chair, and eyed his young assistant for several seconds.

"Since you were closer to Clem than the others," he began, "I think you should know something about him." Leaning forward, he added, "But this is highly confidential and you must not tell a soul. Not even Emma. Okay?"

Harry gave a nod, flattered and a little surprised that Dickie would impart anything of importance to him.

"During the war, Clem's father was my commanding officer. Jack Walker is a fine fellow and I have a lot of respect for him."

"I thought he was a printer," Harry interrupted.

"His family owned a printing firm in Torquay. They still do. Very wealthy lot. Jack went into the business after university but when the war broke out he joined up, like the rest of us idiots." A slight smile flickered across Dickie's face. "He kept my arse out of a sling once when I disobeyed standing orders and defused a parachute mine. Those things were the Navy's domain. Mind you, after the hearing he privately gave me the drubbing of my life! But that was Jack. He'd never chew you out in public." He became serious again. "Clem had been married, you know."

Noticing Harry's look of surprise, he added, "And he has two children. Clem was a big disappointment to his father. He was an only child. Jack and Mildred wanted more but she miscarried on the second and that was the end of it. They wanted him to go to university, then join the firm, just like Jack. Well, to begin with, Clem never had any aptitude for school. Couldn't get into university." Dickie pursed his lips. "Christ! He never really tried, and only went to work at the firm to keep his parents quiet. Left after a few months to do his National Service. They assumed he would return to the family firm afterwards but he didn't. Joined an advertising agency instead. God only knows why. Anyway, he was there less than a year before they sacked him. After that I gather he disappeared for months on end, doing odd jobs here and there. Jack gave him a monthly allowance, which in my view was a mistake. He met this girl, Melinda, and before you know it they got married. Jack and Mildred were very much against the whole thing. I'm pretty certain she only married Clem for the family's money. And she got that nailed down tight by having a couple of kids in fairly rapid order. One day about four years ago the police knocked on Jack's door and told him that Clem had been charged in connection with some counterfeit-currency scam. They claimed he was involved in laundering the stuff. How the hell he got involved in that I haven't a clue, unless it was through contacts he made in the army. I didn't follow the trial very closely, although it was in the newspapers. It cost Jack and Mildred a bundle for his defence. But he was convicted, along with three others, and he went to prison for three years."

Harry couldn't believe his ears. This was the Clem he'd almost come to know? The quietly spoken fellow with the soft, brown eyes and self-deprecating humour? The same pathetic lump lying still and lifeless under that blanket? How could anyone carry that kind of a secret so insouciantly, knowing full well that he was misrepresenting himself to the entire world? This would be a watershed in Harry's young life. He shifted uncomfortably in his chair, certain that he would never, ever again, take anyone at face value.

"Anyway," Dickie continued, "good old Melinda saw the writing on the wall and immediately set about divorcing him. I'm not sure if the decree absolute was through or not. Mildred has never forgiven Clem and refused to see him to the end. Jack came around a little. Mind you, Mildred was always very socially conscious, and I think if the truth be known she was a lot more concerned about what Clem's conviction had done to her position in the community than what it might have done to him."

After a pause, Dickie's tone changed again. He spoke much more slowly while looking directly at Harry. "Of course, most of that is history. The point is this. I put my neck on the block for Jack. I felt I owed it to him. The poor chap's health wasn't that good after the war, and this mess nearly killed him. When Clem was paroled six months ago, Jack asked me if I could get his son a job. That's how he came to be working for us. I covered up for Clem, plain and simple. I made sure there was no note of his prison record on the application form, otherwise he wouldn't have had a hope in hell of getting the position. And he'd picked up enough draughting experience in some of his previous jobs to qualify, minimally at any rate. The County Architect usually defers to the section heads for final decisions on lower-level appointments, so I recommended him. I rammed it through."

Dickie's cigarette had burned down. He lit another from the butt of the old one and exhaled a long stream of smoke. "So now you know," he said. "But if any of this gets out I'm in a lot of trouble. And if it does, I'm going to know where it came from. Right?"

Harry nodded again.

Looking down at his desk pad, Dickie said, "In some ways I'm rather glad Clem's gone, although of course I wouldn't wish this terrible thing on him. Just gone, that's all. I interviewed better candidates for the position and it was a frustrating business knowing I wasn't going to pick any of them. A bad business. Really bad business."

The relief at finally getting this sad affair off his chest was palpable. He let out another long stream of cigarette smoke and once more lapsed into silence. Harry, his head full of some very mixed emotions, remained on the edge of his chair, digesting it all as best he could. This was the kind of stuff one could easily find in a suspense novel. Dickie had lied to help an old friend. The friend's son turned out to be an ex-convict who finally died a lonely death in a run-down flat. It happened all the time in fiction, but he never expected it to happen in real life, and even less to wind up being a part of it. Dickie had been remarkably frank. Although Harry now knew a lot more than he did yesterday, there were still some unanswered questions.

"I think Clem wanted to die," he said.

Dickie raised his eyebrows. "Really? What makes you think so?"

"Because otherwise he would have let me help him. I could have sent for a doctor or an ambulance and we could have got him to hospital. But he wouldn't let me, he really wouldn't. I think he saw it as a way out, so he just lay there and died. He gave up."

"That was one thing I didn't like about Clem," Dickie replied. "He was pleasant enough, but spineless. He always took the easy way out." Then he thought for a moment about what Harry had just said. "You may be right. I **do** know it really shook him when Melinda and the kids left. I think he'd assumed she'd stick with him. In some ways that destroyed him more than the prison sentence."

Whether Harry was right or wrong about Clem's death wish, his final hours did help to explain some of the seemingly ambiguous comments he'd made on various occasions. Perhaps they had been his way of easing the turmoil inside his head. It must have been agonizingly difficult to live with so much inner pain and be unable to share it with others. Even if he hadn't been sworn to silence, Clem could hardly have gone around telling everyone shortly after getting a government job that he was an ex con. Dickie would have been the first to stick a knife in him.

But despite all this, despite Clem's weaknesses, Harry found himself wanting to believe that he was basically a decent person. Perhaps the man's failings were simply the product of being an only child of over-indulgent parents. Perhaps he'd been pushed too early into an unwanted vocation. Perhaps there had been too much money and too little initiative— certainly not an uncommon scenario. A lot of perhaps's. But whatever the truth might have been, Clem had finally run out of chances to prove himself.

"The worst part about all this was a few minutes ago when I telephoned his father," Dickie said as Harry got up to leave. "I could tell from Jack's tone of voice that he thinks I let him down. He could be right. Maybe I did."

"I always thought Clem had a guilty look about him," Emma said during lunch hour later that day. "You could see it in his eyes. Did you ever notice that he never looked directly at you when he spoke?"

"No, I didn't," Harry replied truthfully. "All I know is that he had the patience of Job when I went with him to Duffield before Christmas. I mean, Dickie was just bloody rude. But Clem never got upset... well, just a little bit when Dickie barfed all over his car. I'm not sure if **I** could have put up with that crap. And that wasn't the first time he'd gone to bail out our noble boss. Apparently he'd already made one or two trips to fetch him back from God knows where after the police got on his tail. It's a darned sight more than I would have done."

Emma was sitting on his knee. "Good for Clem," she said, "but it seems to me you got knocked around more than he did. It was you who got your leg chewed by a dog, and your trousers ripped, and a walking stick shoved up your nose. He just had to clean out his car... which you and that woman helped him with. All Clem lost was some time— which he got paid for anyway— and a little petrol."

For a split second her casual remark made him angry. "I just think Clem got a rather raw deal, that's all," he snapped.

Startled, she looked at him. "You really are quite upset about all this, aren't you? Did you like him all that much?"

"Oh, I suppose not. But there was something about Clem that reminded me of my boarding-school days. I was a bit like him then, locked up inside a little world that I couldn't escape from. And nobody could understand why I was so miserable." He absently kicked at the chair they were sitting on. "No, I can't say I liked Clem all that much, but the memory of that awful little flat, and Clem lying there staring at the ceiling, is going to stay with me for a long time. What I found really sad was the doctor asking if we knew where his family was. Can you imagine, he died all alone and his parents didn't even know about it? Dickie was saying he felt he'd let Clem's father down. Well, I think I let Clem down. I should have stayed with him instead of going back to the office. I know I wasn't family, but I would have been better than no one at all."

For reasons Harry never understood, Clem's parents refused to take his body home to Devon, although his father came up to Matlock for the funeral. Clem was buried the following Saturday in Matlock's municipal cemetery, the same one that old Frank had laboured in for so many years. Only eight people came to pay their last respects, and that included the clergyman. Other than Dickie and Harry, no one else in the office showed any interest. "After all," Terry had said, "it is the weekend. Who wants to go to a funeral on a weekend?" The remark struck Harry as similar to that made by Dickens' wealthy banker, who informed his colleagues that he wouldn't attend Ebenezer Scrooge's funeral unless he were fed.

Emma accompanied Harry, even though she didn't like funerals any more than she liked Clem. But, as she admitted, it was a terrible way to die, and she wouldn't have wished that on anybody. It was a bitterly cold day, with rain periodically turning to sleet and a biting wind from the north. Even their heavy coats couldn't keep them warm. The occasion represented two firsts for Harry. It was the first time he'd ever seen his boss wear a hat, and the first time without a cigarette in his mouth. Slouching beneath his chapeau, which appeared to be too small for his head, he looked distinctly uncomfortable. Nevertheless, Harry could tell that Dickie was grateful he and Emma had made the effort to attend.

He had already arrived when they got there, and they found him in deep conversation with a tall, balding man whom they assumed to be Clem's father. Harry had expected to see a latter-day martinet, complete with handlebar moustache and perhaps a swagger stick for good measure. Instead he saw a man with gentle features and a soft-spoken voice that belied his army career. Dickie introduced them.

"I'm very sorry, sir," Harry said, shaking the man's hand. "In fact we all are."

With head slightly bowed, he smiled. "I owe you a debt of gratitude, young man, for helping my son. Bob told me what you did."

"I wish I could have done more," Harry replied, "But he just wouldn't let me."

"You did everything you could. I think it's us who wish we had done more. I'm not sure if you know, but Clem was our only son and the past few years have been very difficult for my wife and me."

"Yes, so I..." Harry started to say before noticing Dickie's brow crease into a furrow. "Yes, I'm sure it has."

After a short service in the cemetery chapel, Clem's tiny entourage trudged through the mud to where the hearse was parked with its engine still running. Staff from the funeral home were waiting impatiently for the word to lower the cheap coffin so they could leave. As they all huddled under umbrellas in a futile attempt to keep dry, the clergyman pronounced the ashes-to-ashes-dust-to-dust, his voice almost lost in the sound of the rain and wind.

Harry leaned over to Dickie, who was standing next to them. "Did Clem's ex-wife come?" he whispered. Two young women who looked to be in their late twenties were standing opposite and he had wondered if Melinda might be one of them.

Dickie shook his head. "Not bloody likely. Jack wouldn't want her here anyway. I've no idea who those two are, unless they're cousins." Then nodding in the direction of a man standing between the two women and Colonel Walker he added, "That chap works in Walker's firm. I think he's their general manager. Jack has a heart condition so he didn't want to drive by himself."

Finally, Clem was laid to rest. Not far, Harry learned afterwards, from the young girl's grave where Frank had told them the flowers always shrivelled up and died. A few weeks later they dropped by the cemetery, curious to see what kind of a memorial had been placed on Clem's grave. There wasn't one; just a small flat stone bearing the inscription:

Clement Douglas Walker
Born 13 March, 1930
Died 7 February, 1962

No one had placed any flowers. It was just as well; they probably would have died anyway.

There was another minor postscript to Clem's tragic end, one which gave Harry reason to think there may be some justice in this world after all. A year later almost to the day, a gas ring in one of the other flats set fire to a newspaper carelessly left close by. Within three hours the entire building burned to the ground and in addition to their losses the Graftons received a stiff fine for failing to comply with safety regulations.

Somewhere, Clem must surely have been smiling.

EIGHT

The Hayloft

Spring came to Matlock. The frozen wallflowers in front of the Town Hall survived, as did those spread about Hall Leys Park. Harry and Emma walked past them daily, casting an approving eye at their vibrant colours and cheerful optimism. But springtime in England's peak district tends to be a fickle, fleeting thing; soon it was early June. On this particular day the Derbyshire moors were bathed in a warm summer glow crisscrossed by miles of limestone walls. Stretching as far as the eye could see, these shoulder-height creations cobbled the small lumpy fields into a patchwork quilt of hazy, muted colours. Typically, like those found in Harry's native Yorkshire, they were dry stone walls, and most were suffering from years of neglect. No one, it seemed, had either the time or the inclination to repair the walls. Perhaps they had been there for so long that so one noticed them anymore. Many had partly collapsed, while others leaned drunkenly into the narrow lanes.

With one or two exceptions, this wasn't prosperous agriculture, the peak country soil being too thin and stony to support cash crops. Consequently most farmers in the area eked out a living with small dairy herds. Some grew a little subsistence corn or hay. The area around Emma's farm was, for the most part, almost devoid of trees. A few emaciated elms and sycamores could be found huddling for shelter in the lee of farm buildings. Others, in clumps of two or three and bent by the wind, straggled across the cow pastures like shawled peasants searching for kindling. At dusk, their thin finger-like branches drew a stark silhouette against the darkening sky.

But it was the wind itself that intrigued Harry. He couldn't recall a day when the air was totally calm. When winter closed in, it would roar down from the north, tearing off tree limbs and tossing about stone roof tiles as though they were playing cards. Emma's brother spent half his time nailing the truant slabs back into place. Every year, particularly during the wild months of January and February, there were tales, retold with great relish, of unfortunate villagers being dismembered by flying debris. In the gentler days of summer, however, the wind usually died to a whisper, fanning the ripening hay and moaning softly through cracks and crevices.

Scores of stone haylofts littered Derbyshire's peakland pastures. Sometimes square but more often rectangular, these uncomplicated structures were open from floor to roof and normally had a large double door at one end. They simply served to keep the weather off the hay or straw that was piled inside. Harry was familiar with several around Emma's farm but not, it should be stressed, in an agricultural context. Ever since her brother had spotted them through her window over a month ago, busily doing what comes naturally between couples, in bed, Harry had decided that the farm house was a bit too public for close encounters of the carnal kind. Haylofts, they had found, were a good alternative during the summer months, especially if the building in question happened to be stuffed with hay.

On this mild, late Sunday afternoon that was where he and Emma were headed. Mrs. Callingwood, with customary half-heartedness, had invited Harry for tea. That finished, they decided to spend a little time on their own before the last bus. There happened to be one semi-derelict loft belonging to a neighbor about half a mile from the house. They had used it before, against Emma's better judgment since the hay inside was old and had a rather bad smell to it. Its main advantage was that no one ever seemed to go near the place— hardly surprising under the circumstances. The moorland air was still mild; roadside flowers were struggling through the long grass in full profusion. All in all it made a good day, Harry had decided, for a romp in the countryside.

The lofts, more correctly called field barns, were, in many ways, a reflection of the marginal agriculture on these bleak moors. A few farmers, particularly those with scattered pastures, still used them. But to all intents and purposes they had become obsolete, relics of a bygone era before tractors and lorries replaced horses and carts. They stood, sadly neglected and largely abandoned. Like the dry stone walls that surrounded them, most were in a state of semi-collapse with their roof rafters sagging like a swayback horse under the crushing weight of the stone slates. Mortar crumbled from between the rough-hewn stones, leaving gaping holes through which grass, weeds and the ever-present wind pushed their way. Late at night, when Harry found himself padding back to Matlock after missing the last bus, those he passed seemed to lean menacingly, casting their shadows about him in an attempt to foil his path. They reminded him of the old public air-raid shelter around the corner from his mother's house, whose interior blackness behind the flash barriers always hinted of sinister deeds.

"I think Mum knows we're doing this, love," said Emma trying to keep up with Harry's loping stride as they made their way down the winding lane to the loft.

"I doubt it," Harry replied. "Unless your brother's been telling tales again."

"No," Emma persisted, "She made a funny remark the other day".

"That would be a first. I don't think your mother has made a funny remark in her life."

She poked him in the back. "I really wish you'd try to understand Mum. She means well. It's difficult for her, you know."

This was an appeal that Emma had found herself making increasingly over the past few months as Harry had begun to resent Mrs. Callingwood's barely concealed distrust of him. It wasn't as if she actually disliked him. She'd never thrown him out of the house or anything like that. In fact she quite liked Harry, but like a lot of rural folk she regarded people who lived in towns and worked in large offices, especially government offices, as a breed apart and not entirely above suspicion. Harry naturally fell into that category, and it irked him.

"What was the 'funny' thing your mum said?" he asked.

"She said if we ever got caught in the rain we could always dodge into a hay-loft."

"That was it?"

"Well, yes. But Mum's never mentioned the haylofts before. I just thought it a bit strange that she would do it now."

Harry chuckled. "Maybe she doesn't want me to catch pneumonia! Very thoughtful of her, I'm sure."

Despite the warm weather the hay inside the loft had a damp, musty smell, but at least it was softer than straw. They clambered up the sloping pile into the rafters, Emma first and Harry giving her a push with his hand. He pulled off his jacket and slipped it behind her. She rolled backwards, slipping her dress under her bottom and placing it neatly to the side. Quickly her panties, bra and shoes were on the same pile. She's getting very good at this, Harry thought as he removed the rest of his own clothes. As a delicate smell of perfume rose from her skin, he cast an approving glance at the outline of her body nestled in the straw. Emma had been claiming recently that her bust size was increasing, but Harry couldn't see much evidence of it. Even the smallest size bra seemed to be too big. He had once suggested that push-ups might improve things, and for a couple of months after Christmas Emma dutifully did ten minutes every morning. But to Harry's dismay the bulges showed up in her arms instead and the experiment was abandoned.

Always before having sex, Harry briefly worried about her becoming pregnant. And he worried even more afterwards. Since he still refused to wear a condom, he'd lately been badgering Emma to get a prescription for birth-control pills, but she didn't want to risk her mother finding out. Fortunately the impasse was relieved to some extent by Emma's clockwork regularity. They simply tried to avoid the 'risky' parts of the month. So far it had worked. Fatherhood was not, as far as he was concerned, a responsibility to be countenanced at his age. He'd seen that happen to someone he knew at the teacher's college and it had been a disaster for everyone concerned. A shotgun wedding with tears and recrimination on all sides. And now mom and dad were holed up with baby daughter in a miserable little flat above a dry cleaner's shop. Nobody wanted the wedding. Nobody wanted the child. A bad situation, no doubt about it, and one that reared its ugly head every time Emma's period was due.

In a narrow shaft of sun which poked through one of the many holes in the loft wall, Harry could see Emma studying his face as he lowered himself on to her. She enjoyed foreplay, a lot more than Harry had patience for. But he went through the motions anyway, squeezing his hand beneath his crotch and into hers. Once inside he was never very fast. Not that Emma minded; she wasn't very fast either. As usual her nipples quickly hardened with the friction of their bodies; Harry could feel them pushing delicately against his chest. Beneath them his jacket covered about as much of the straw as a postage stamp covers an envelope and bits jabbed uncomfortably into Emma's back. Another problem with haylofts, Harry had quickly found the first time, was that they were home to a multitude of wildlife, some large, some very small, and quite a few which got into places they definitely did not belong. As Emma's legs heaved under him he could feel a legion of much tinier legs scaling his buttocks and thighs. They tickled and itched relentlessly.

Their love-making finally over, they lay still, listening for a while to the birds chattering among the rafters. Halcyon days like these sped quickly and the waning light reminded Harry that it must be getting close to last-bus time. Even during the summer months its run into Matlock passed the lane end at a quarter to nine, sometimes a little earlier. If he missed it he would again have to hoof into town. Emma's mother wasn't keen on him staying over, which Harry found odd, since she didn't seem to mind Emma staying at Miss Twigg's on the odd occasion. He had on occasions wondered if the problem might lie more with Emma's brother, who gave every indication of disliking him from the start. Even worse, the man had an ugly temper, which seemed to cast a pall of gloom on the family every time he showed up. Harry wasn't about to push his luck for the sake of honour.

There were worse fates than having to walk into Matlock. Since that disastrous trek to Elton on their first date there had been others, some in bad weather, some in fair. In fact, it proved to be a pleasant daytime walk during the summer months, provided it didn't rain. But at night, the shadows played games with Harry's imagination, and he often found himself scuttling along, glancing furtively at the darkness. These were country roads. No street lights, no pavements, and many water-filled ditches to stumble into. For the most part the only company he encountered were a few cows. Now and again a rabbit would pop out of the long grass and after quickly observing the human intruder, continue its nocturnal foraging.

"You'll have to roll off, love," Emma whispered. "I think I've got a kink in one of my boobs and I'm getting a bit chilled."

"What's the time?" Harry asked.

She was getting accustomed to this futile request, since he asked practically every time they visited the haylofts. Why he would think she any more idea of the time than he, she couldn't understand; neither of them were wearing a stitch of clothing or anything else. Besides, her watch was small and had been one of the few gifts her father had apparently taken the trouble to buy her himself, so she usually left it at home.

"Why ask me? You've got the watch," she replied. "Where did you drop it this time?"

For some reason, perhaps a legacy of his manual labour days at the parks department, he always took off his own watch, along with his clothes, dumping it in the hay close at hand. Propping himself up with one arm he cast about with the other, expecting it to be there, but the watch lurked in the fading light, beyond his grasp. Cursing, he ran his free hand beneath Emma's wet buttocks and into his jacket pocket, groping for the cigarette lighter that might help find his reclusive timepiece. It burst into flame at the first flick, and Emma's startled face jerked slightly to one side.

"Good grief, Harry, be careful! You nearly took off my nose."

"I think my damned watch has sunk into the hay," Harry growled. "Hold the lighter for a minute." He pushed it towards the hand she had brought up to protect her face. But Emma's timing was off and the lighter made a small arc as it slipped behind her right ear. Almost immediately they both could smell something burning as a narrow coil of smoke mingled with the staleness of the loft.

"Christ! That's my hair!" Emma yelped, clutching the side of her head. "Why didn't you bring a torch? I had this lot permed only two days ago."

Harry didn't reply; Emma's scorched coiffure could turn out to be a trifling concern. He had other matters on his mind, not the least of which was the lighter which had now disappeared along with his watch. Unfortunately, it was of the type that had to have the lid closed to extinguish it, and one didn't need to be rocket scientist to appreciate what could happen if the thing had remained lit for a few seconds after it landed. His worst fears were quickly realized when a much more pungent aroma of smoldering grass began to overwhelm the smell of burned hair. As they both sniffed around themselves like a couple of bloodhounds, it dawned on him that he had just set the loft on fire.

Trying to sound unconcerned, he said, "There's some hay burning somewhere."

"Oh my God!" Emma squawked, struggling to disengage her legs from his while flapping vainly at the smoke which by now was quickly spiralling into the rafters. The two rolled and writhed, each trying to rescue as much clothing as possible before sliding down to the floor. Still searching for his watch, Harry looked below to see Emma, hopping on one foot, attempting to pull on her panties. Finding they were on backwards, she began to pull them off again.

"For heaven sakes, Emma, do that outside,' he called. "Just grab your stuff."

"I can't go out there stark naked!"

"Who the hell's going to see us? We're in the middle of a bloody field! Besides, you've got your underpants on, that's better than nothing."

They flapped around in confusion while the smoke rapidly thickened. By now it had become so dense near the roof that Harry was obliged to abandon his search. He slid down the pile on his bare bottom, choking and laughing foolishly as he did so. Emma's sense of humor had deserted her at this point in time. He could hear her half-talking, half-crying to herself as she wrestled with her underclothes. Reaching out to push her through the door, two of his fingers connected with the top of her panties and the elastic snapped back against her stomach with a loud crack. Emma let out an angry gasp. She didn't know whether to hit him or run. The acrid smell of smoke and a rapidly rising panic in her stomach told her that running would be the better idea.

"Honestly, Harry, of all the bloody stupid things to do," she panted angrily. "That was right up alongside with lighting a match to look for a gas leak.

There's a perfectly good torch sitting in our kitchen, but oh no, we have to use a lighter. A lighter, for Christ's sake in a pile of hay! This is it, this is the last time I'm coming into a loft with you, Don't ask me again because I won't come. What the hell am I going to tell Mum?"

Harry was less concerned about her mother's sensibilities than the crisis at hand. "Never mind your mother just now," he gasped. "Let's get out of here. Run!"

Holding hands, they stumbled like two escaping convicts over an apron of sun-baked cow cakes and loosened stones, then raced for a low stone wall in the distance. Emma, with her panties back on for the second time but only half way up her legs, waddled like a duck, trailing small pieces of grass which were now coming loose from her scorched hair. Trying desperately as she ran to formulate a plausible scenario should someone link them with the destruction of their neighbor's property, Emma knew her brother would be one of the first to put two and two together. In the lee of the wall they stopped to catch their breath and peered anxiously through the darkness towards the loft. Smoke was already billowing into the sky. After several more minutes small tongues of flame could be seen flickering through holes in the sagging roof.

While Emma fussed over her ruined clothing, Harry watched the escalating conflagration with a certain amount of detachment. Maybe, perhaps, he had some sort of destiny with fires. His mind flashed back to childhood, to the large comfortable home they had briefly owned before Dad died. The house was flanked on one side by fields which rolled down a gentle incline to the sleepy village of Stainborough. Harry particularly loved the field immediately next door because it was bordered by beech thickets under which, in one spot, he had fashioned a den. In those days it was fashionable for kids to have a secret place, complete with secret passwords, where one could hide from girls and entertain one's peers. It was a convenient spot to experiment with the taboos of youth, such as cigarettes, and the lethal wheat wine which their teetotaler relatives in Thurgoland brewed for 'medicinal purposes.'

One hot summer day, while Harry crouched in his den having a quiet puff on one of his mother's *Craven A's*, Mr. Walton from over the hill showed up unannounced to mow the hay. Harry was only eight, but savvy enough to realize that rising cigarette smoke might be as good as a signpost in the calm air. Tossing the still-burning butt into the field, he beat a hasty retreat back to the house. Half an hour later Harry's neighborhood reverberated to the sound of fire engines pounding up their quiet street. With sinking heart, he watched a dozen firemen dash into Mr. Walton's field, dragging large hoses and heavy blankets and making loud adult noises. The hedges echoed to the sounds of people yelling instructions, running into each other, and Mr. Walton coughing and cursing. It was five hours before the blaze was under control, long enough to arouse the curiosity of both his mother and the neighbors. Harry wore his guilt like a neon sign but swore that the blaze the firemen had traced back to his little den was caused by sun shining through a broken bottle lying on the ground. Mother, of course, knew better, partly because she knew Harry better, and partly because he smelled of smoke and she was missing some cigarettes. When Dad came home from work there was further interrogation and Harry's guilty marquee flashed more brilliantly than ever. But to his astonishment Mother quietly repeated his story, and it sounded so much more credible coming from her. So credible in fact that Dad bought it with hardly a protest. From that day, he realized there was much more to his mother than the parent who cooked meals and packed him off to bed every night.

The cooling evening air brought him back to reality. And a shiver reminded him that he was still half-naked. By now, Emma had pulled on her dress and was attempting to knock some of the dirt off her underskirt. Ever since their first night in bed he'd found her to be something of a contradiction. While she had a healthy appetite for sex, she could be surprisingly conservative in public. Harry could swim; she couldn't but had agreed to let him teach her at the public pool. To his astonishment several weeks of cajoling had been needed to get her into a bathing suit. And even then she managed to make Harry feel as though he'd asked her to sign up for amateur night at the local strip club. Clearly the clothing issue was troubling Emma's Bourbon mind.

"My bra's still in the loft," she said testily.

As she spoke he became conscious of another presence. Some object out there in the darkness, beyond the wall, rustled and swished. Footsteps splashed among fresh cow piles and the noise came closer. He shot a nervous glance at Emma, but she either wasn't listening or didn't consider it cause for alarm.

"Never mind your bra," Harry hissed. "Somebody's here. Get down!"

Quickly bobbing up, he could make out a dark shape. Advancing slowly, it rustled and sniffed and then stopped. After a few seconds he again cautiously raised his head above the top row of stones to be met by a large and very wet muzzle and the curious gaze of two dark eyes.

Emma cast a sidelong glance at the Jersey cow and beyond to other shadows as a gaggle of her friends shambled over to join the get-together.

"Is that what you were worried about?"

Harry mouthed an affirmative.

"It's just Jessica," she said curtly, as though she might be enumerating somebody for the latest census. "She belongs to the Haithwaites. And she's not dangerous. Not nearly as dangerous as you, anyway."

"I'm sorry. I didn't mean to set the bloody loft on fire!"

"Well, it **is** on fire, and my bra's in there along with one of my shoes. Mum will want to know where they went. What am I going to tell her?"

"You mean your mother checks all your underwear?" Harry asked sarcastically, adding, "You don't need a bra anyway."

While it wasn't meant to be a cruel remark, on this occasion it simply added insult to injury. Emma began to cry. He'd never felt this wretched since that first date when he walked her home in the rain. After standing awkwardly for a few more minutes, with Emma still sobbing and the hayloft blazing merrily, he did something that totally defied common sense. He decided to go and have another look for his watch. Perhaps *decision* would be the wrong word; it was more of an impulse. Later he would tell Emma that something told his subconscious that he couldn't just leave it there. The watch didn't keep very good time, but, like Emma's, it held considerable sentimental value. It had belonged to his father and to Harry it represented an important link with the parent he had never really known. He had to make one last effort. If Emma's bra could be located at the same time, so much the better.

With his shirt half-buttoned and wearing only his briefs, Harry raced back across the minefield of cow dung towards the loft. He could hear Emma's plaintive cry of dismay, but her words were lost to the wind in his ears. As he ran, his bare feet splashed plumes of muck up his legs and clothing. Although the structure hadn't yet become completely engulfed, thick grey smoke was now pouring through every hole it could find. He had no idea of where to look, just an overwhelming sense of purpose. And how he expected to find anything that small in the smoke and darkness he had no idea. Perhaps he'd put it too close to the edge and it had fallen onto the floor? Perhaps the shiny metal would attract his attention? The fact that he could be dead in a few minutes never entered his mind.

Inside the loft the acrid smell of smoldering hay hit his eyes and nostrils like a shock wave. Tears streaming down his face and choking violently, Harry vainly began to claw through the loose material at the foot of the pile. Looking up, he could tell from the faint crackling and red glow that the actual fire was still limited to the area where they had been lying. He knew he wouldn't burn to death, but the smoke was another thing entirely. It grew thicker by the minute, mingling with a strong stench of ammonia. Now he cursed his stupidity, realizing that not only could he see less than six inches in front of him, he couldn't breath either. As he blundered about on his hands and knees, reality took flight and delirium quickly took its place. Gasping for air, he began to giggle uncontrollably at the silliness of trying to fight a pile of burning hay dressed in nothing more than a shirt and a pair of briefs. As his breathing became more laboured, Harry suddenly felt the straw beneath him open up and he experienced the sensation of drifting in space, of being shielded by some invisible force from the smoke and fumes. His eyes no longer streamed; he was no longer choking. The frightening chaos was still there, he could hear the noise, but it was as though he were watching it all on a screen. For what seemed like an eternity he revelled in a transcendental cocoon of cosy, muggy silence. It was too good to last. The tranquillity abruptly ended in a cataclysm of new sounds and smells.

"Why's the lad wearing only 'is underpants?" a loud authoritarian voice asked above the noise of heavy engines and the crackle of flames.

Someone else asked, "'Ow long was 'e in 'ere?"

Another voice could be heard in the far-off distance giving commands, such as, "Get yon wheel off the bloody 'ose, ah could piss faster than this; don't get the engine too close," and so on.

Concerns were being expressed about having enough pitchforks, whether some timbers would collapse, and a variety of other technicalities which held little relevance for him at that moment. Half of him felt a compelling urge to offer assistance but the other much superior half told him not to bother. Besides, something was stuck firmly onto his mouth and when he tried to speak all that came forth was a sort of rubbery wheezing. He decided he didn't really care all that much. Nothing mattered at all. People were obviously lifting him up because his body could feel a gentle rocking from side to side. Activity was all around, yet he couldn't see anyone. Footsteps shuffled. Voices waxed and waned like a weak radio signal. They weren't familiar voices except for one which sounded like Emma's, and it seemed to be at least a couple of octaves above normal. Something was definitely going on. There were a lot of people rushing about, and he seemed to be the focal point of all the activity. A blanket was being wrapped firmly around him. "Don't worry about it," the heavy half told him. "It's not your concern." So he didn't worry about it; he just lay there and let everything wash over him like warm surf.

Emma's squeeky voice continued. "I've got his trousers. He left them at the wall. I know they're all filthy. Oh God! He left his watch in there but I told him he shouldn't go in. We were just walking. Just walking and we stopped for a rest. Did you find a watch? No? Oh my God, he's not going to die, is he?"

Die? Was he going to die? Not there. Not then. He was feeling much too good to die at that moment. What a silly thought.

Emma's babbling trailed off amid the rustle of oilskin jackets and the sound of equipment being moved around. A pervasive smell of smoldering hay hung about him. He could feel himself becoming airborne again. The noise of diesel engines became louder, more men were grunting and giving instructions. They sounded very angry.

"Don't tell dad," he heard himself trying to say. But the thing attached to his mouth wouldn't let him. There was more bumping and maneuvering, with Emma once again assuring the multitude that she had his trousers. Doors clanged shut, and Harry drifted happily in and out of consciousness while the ambulance bounced down the country lanes into Matlock.

Whatever other faults she might have had, Emma's loyalty was indisputable. When Harry came to later that night in the hospital ward, she was sitting by the bed, a frightened little soul fidgeting with her purse. Hospital beds were high, the chair short, making it almost impossible for Emma to see over the sidebars. Craning her neck, she looked intently at Harry's every stirring, fearful he might still suddenly expire. She hadn't had time to do anything with her hair; it remained a mass of tangled curls and bits of grass, with the singed part glaringly obvious. A pale yellow cardigan she had worn when they first set out for the loft was pulled over her shoulders, blotched with mud and cow dung. Clearly self-conscious about her grubby condition, she kept wiping a sleeve across her dirty face.

Harry peered blearily over the top of his sheets and searched her face for signals. There was absolutely no doubt she was upset, but at the same he could detect a trace of relief. For her part, Emma didn't know whether to kiss him or hit him.

"How did **you** get here?" he asked, trying hard not to make the question sound like a criticism.

"With you in the ambulance. As we went passed the house I ran in and told Mum what had happened. Didn't you see me? They drove really fast."

Harry groaned. "Oh God, I'll bet your mother was thrilled."

"Well, it would be an understatement to say she wasn't very pleased, but the ambulance men didn't give her any time to get into it."

"Where are we?"

"Matlock hospital. You swallowed a lot of smoke, love."

That came as no surprise. But while he could smell the stuff down in his lungs and still had difficulty in taking a deep breath, he still felt strangely detached from the situation; the last vestiges of some medication had manifested itself in a lingering grogginess that somehow alienated him from his physical body. Voices and sounds seemed to be coming from another planet. He found himself half-expecting to hear someone intoning, "Harry Michaels, your time is up. Come with me!"

Weakly propping himself up with his elbows, he looked about him, noticing only his sport jacket hanging over the back of Emma's chair.

"Where's my clothes?" He had no idea why he'd asked that question. It really didn't matter much at the moment where his clothes were since he wasn't in a position to use them.

She nodded downwards to a brown paper bag on the floor, containing his shirt, trousers, one sock and his shoes. "I collected everything I could find, including what you were wearing. Most of it needs washing and your trousers are a complete mess. Looks like a cow pooped on them. Jacket's not bad though. I've no idea where your undershirt and tie went to, and I saw one of the firemen using one of your socks to wipe something. I don't think you'll get it back." She made a wan smile. "I don't think you'd **want** it back; it got soaked in oil. Oh, and my mother is probably trying right now to explain to the Haithwaites how we came to be passing their hayloft when it caught fire."

"You didn't tell her I **set** it on fire, did you?" he asked.

"No, of course I didn't," she assured him. "I gave her the 'official version.'"

"What, pray, is the 'official version?'"

"That we were walking past when we saw smoke and you raced in to see if you could put it out."

"Great, except that it doesn't really explain why I would be running around the bloody place without my trousers on, does it?"

"No, it doesn't. And I don't think Mum believes the official version but it's the best I could do at the spur of the moment. She said she's beginning to think you're mad!"

For the moment, Harry wasn't too concerned about the Haithwaites' reaction to losing one of their buildings, or, for that matter, whether her mother thought he'd lost his marbles. He was, however, beginning to appreciate the legal magnitude of their summer-afternoon caper. Fire engines, ambulances, hospital. So many people involved; so many people soon to be asking questions. What had happened? The thought suddenly occurred to him that he might have been burned or maimed in some other horrible fashion. He couldn't feel any pain, but that didn't mean anything. Perhaps, he was now scarred for life; after all, he'd not had a chance to look in the mirror or check himself over. Perhaps, by that single act of folly, he had committed the rest of his life to social exile, to the desperate existence of an abandoned recluse. A latter-day Elephant Man.

"Am I, er, badly hurt?" he asked, poking about beneath the sheets.

"Only your pride. And mine," she replied. "You didn't come out, so I put on as many clothes as I could find and started to run home for help. But one of the Utley boys... they live down the way... he took me out a few times last year but I don't like him very much... I met him in the lane, coming the other way. He'd already noticed the smoke and called the Winster fire brigade. So then I ran back to the loft with him. I told him you were inside but he couldn't get in for the smoke." Tears briefly welled up in her eyes. "I thought you were dead. I honestly thought you were dead."

She stared silently at him for a moment while wiping her face, this time with the corner of his bed sheet. Streaks beneath her eyes told of tears shed while the ambulance raced into Matlock.

"One of the firemen said that if you had been there just a few more minutes you would have suffocated," she continued. "He said he couldn't find your pulse. I told him I didn't know where he could find one either. Paul Utley ran home and his dad rang for an ambulance because they said you'd have to have your lungs cleaned out or something. Anyway," she concluded, "I told everybody the official version, but I'm pretty sure Paul knows what we were doing, so it'll be all over Elton by tomorrow. He's got a grudge against me because I wouldn't go out with him anymore."

The conversation lapsed again. Then she said quietly, "I think I'd like to hide for a week or two. You've really put me and Mum in a spot, chum. I hope you know that. Everybody will be laughing at us."

Harry started to say something.

"Another thing," she interrupted. "The firemen were really pissed off. They hate haystack fires because they have to pull all the stuff out of the loft and spread it on the ground, otherwise it smolders for weeks. I know because we once had a fire in one of our haystacks. It took them over a month to get it all out. I don't know whether the Haithwaites will be too upset about their loft.

It's really old and so was the hay. But they're a miserable family . Mum and Dad never got along with them, so they might create a fuss just to make a point. Mum's worried they'll call the police."

Harry groaned again.

"Thing is," she added, "They can't **prove** we set fire to it."

"Did the entire place burn down?"

Emma gave him a long look. "'Course not, It's made of stone so it couldn't all burn down. But the roof caught fire and some of the slates have fallen in. It's a real mess. The firemen poured water on top of it, and then they said they were going to start pulling all the hay through the door with pitchforks. I don't blame them for being ticked off."

While Emma had been talking about **her** mother, Harry wondered whether to tell his own about this latest escapade. It seemed pretty certain he wouldn't be getting out of hospital this day. So he decided to wait until the doctor did his rounds tomorrow and then he would see what the prognosis might be. Tomorrow! Tomorrow was a Monday, a work day. Lewis and Dickie would be wondering why he hadn't come into the office. First Clem, then him. They would be thinking that sudden disappearances were becoming an epidemic. He didn't mind the idea of missing a day or two of work. But a hospital bed wasn't a particularly desirable place to spend them. Although he'd visited people in hospitals, this was the first time he had ever been admitted to one, and he wasn't impressed with the experience. There seemed to be something about command-driven health care which robbed it of all inspiration. And nowhere was it more dramatically reflected than in the nation's public hospitals. While a few new edifices had been built since the war, alas, this wasn't one of them. It must have been at least a hundred years old and possessed the comfort and charm of a public lavatory, albeit a very clean public lavatory. Looking around the large ward, he wondered whether British hospitals, like modern fast-food restaurants, were deliberately designed this way to discourage patients from lingering too long. They all seemed to smell the same; they all had impossibly high ceilings, and those who made such weighty decisions obviously had a fascination with green paint. The walls were green, the linoleum floors were a sort of green— more a brownish green— and so were the cotton privacy curtains around each bed. Even the patients showed a certain similarity of appearance. Most, whose faces he could see, had the look of someone suddenly stricken with flatulence in a crowded room.

He counted twenty beds in his ward: heavy, white-painted iron contraptions, which would have been state-of-the-art during Florence Nightingale's day. Melted down for scrap, each could have easily made half a Lancaster bomber. The windows down one side of the ward faced into a grimy brick wall. The other two walls? Who knows; it was nighttime. Over half the beds were unoccupied, including the one on his right. A senile old lady was installed in the bed to his left. Her head and shoulders supported by a couple of pillows, she looked to have been there for a very long time, and by all appearances, wasn't too happy about it. On the other hand, it could be that she just didn't like green paint. Harry reckoned that she must have out-talked her welcome a long time ago because everyone, including the staff, took considerable care to avoid her.

"He weren't gettin' in my bed," she was rambling on in a thin, reedy voice to no one in particular. Her watery eyes roamed the ward while one hand waved an old bus ticket from side to side. Harry and Emma turned to see who was making the noise. She eyed them suspiciously.

"No, Mister," she continued. "Last time I spread my legs for the bugger I wound up with five kids. Not this time. Not this time. I'm keepin' my bloody legs closed." To illustrate her point she clamped the bus ticket between her teeth and pushed her knees shut with both hands.

"Who's she talking about?" Emma whispered.

Harry shook his head. "Beats me. Maybe her husband."

Emma stared wide-eyed at the old crone. "You mean someone like that would have a husband?"

They both studied her while she muttered along to herself.

"She reminds me of my grandma," Harry finally said. "She went senile and Mum and Grandpa had a hell of a time with her for three years."

"What happened to her?"

"She finally fell down the stairs, broke her hip, and died of pneumonia."

His melancholy tale did little for the old lady, who apparently overheard some of it. Tears briefly welled in her eyes and she gave out a little sob. Then, just as abruptly, her mood changed and she began to sing in a high-pitched voice:

"Daisy, Daisy, give me yer answer do, I'm 'arf crazy, all fer the love of you..."

"Do you think we should join in?" Emma asked, finally starting to shed some of the stress of the past few hours.

Harry shook his head. "I don't know the words."

"Freddie's got a parrot," the old lady burst out again without explaining who Freddie was. Her lower lip curled down and she turned towards her new audience. "Disgustin' thing an' all, chuckin' its feathers abaht an' fartin' all the time." There was another pause as she tried to remember the tangled threads of her past. "We went to Freddie's for Christmas. 'is parrot was there, too, but it waren't fartin'. Usually we'd be all gassed out before 'e got ter carvin'. But not this time. It wor' very strange. Then 'arfway through the main course the bloody bird starts up:

Lucky little turkey. Lucky little swine,
'e's got stuffin' up 'is backside,
but I've got chewing gum up mine."

Somebody at the far end of the ward gave a slow handclap. Harry and Emma looked at the old lady, then at each other. Then they began to giggle uncontrollably. It was infectious, spreading like the rustling leaves of autumn throughout the ward. One man let out a great belly laugh; a younger women in the far corner tittered cautiously. In an instant it became the therapy they both badly needed. Tears of a new sort rolled down Emma's cheeks to mingle with the streaks left by those earlier. Harry wheezed until his chest hurt. Everyone got a laugh except the old lady. Far from being flattered, her face turned almost black with rage and she started wagging her finger around the ward.

"'Ow would you like gum shoved up **your** backside?" she demanded. The ward hurriedly lapsed into silence.

"She's off her rocker," said Harry. "Completely off her rocker."

Emma looked at her watch. "I have to go, love. It's a long time past visiting hours and I'm awfully tired," she said, getting slowly to her feet.

"How are you going to get home?" Harry asked, aware that her last bus would have gone hours ago.

"I'm going to take a taxi. I don't think I've got enough money to pay for it but I'm sure Mum will help me out. This'll be the first time I've ever been all the way home in one. Posh, eh! I'll ask the taxi driver to go by Miss Twigg's so I can let her know where you are; otherwise she'll worry. She's going to worry anyway. And in the morning I'll ring Mr. Dickie and tell him what happened... or at least the official version at any rate. If they let you out tomorrow, let me know, otherwise I'll come down after work. Your jacket's okay but you'll need some clean underwear, some more socks and another pair of trousers. I'll take these dirty things to your digs and pick up the clean stuff at the same time. Be good." She kissed him on the nose and left, leaving Harry to contemplate his latest folly. It turned out to be a short recap; the lights in the ward were turned down and he once again drifted into unconsciousness.

He didn't get much of a chance to sleep. Between incessant outbursts from the old lady who knew somebody named Freddie who had a parrot, and a very muscular nurse sticking a thermometer down his throat at various times, the night seemed to be a never-ending succession of interruptions. He learned that the woman's name was Daisy, who, according to the beefy nurse, had outlived her husband by several millennia. She had gone completely senile but had been admitted to hospital on the handy justification of a bowel infection. There, both the state and her relatives seemed to have abandoned her. Daisy had two married daughters, neither of whom wanted the responsibility of her. Day in, day out, she repeated her silly little songs and rhymes to the point of distraction. It was sad because physically she was quite sound for a seventy-eight year old; the body was still willing but the mind had fallen apart. The muscular nurse, undoubtedly echoing the sentiments of everybody else, said she sometimes felt like breaking a plate over the old lady's head. And she looked perfectly capable of doing it.

"You really must try to stay out of burning buildings, Mr. Michaels," said Dr. Metcalfe as he did rounds early the following morning. "You were in a bit of a mess when they brought you in and you very nearly wound up with a pair of very useless lungs. That would have been most unfortunate," he smiled indulgently, "since we make more money out of live patients than dead ones!"

Taking their cues, the doctor's cheering team of an intern and two nurses also smiled broadly. One nurse was young and very attractive, with deep blue eyes and dark curly hair. The other, also young, might easily have passed for Popeye's girlfriend. As for Dr. Metcalfe, he reminded Harry of the actor James Robertson Justice, at that time enjoying immense popularity for his starring role in the 'Doctor' series of films. His full sandy beard, precisely clipped, framed a round and ruddy face that bristled with efficiency. His stethoscope, Harry noted, was not tucked into a pocket or left to dangle, *de rigeur*, but instead slung jauntily over his shoulder.

"How's your throat?" he asked, scribbling on his clipboard.

"Much better. I think," Harry replied, offering a fruity cough as evidence.

"You think? Hm. Good. As you might recall, we had to shove a tube down it to drain your lungs. You wouldn't believe the muck we brought up. Looked like the inside of a chimney!"

Harry wouldn't have been any wiser if they had shoved the kitchen sink down his throat. But the doctor's comment puzzled him, nonetheless.

"How could that happen?" he asked. "I must have been in there only a minute or two."

Metcalfe slowly shook his head. "Actually, old chap, we reckon you were in there between fifteen and twenty minutes, which is quite long enough for your lungs to have been badly damaged. You were lucky, the ambulance attendants told me that some burning roof timbers had missed your head by a couple of inches. Still feeling a little woozy?"

"Just a bit," Harry replied.

He nodded. "We gave you a sedative. Takes a while to wear off. Y'know, you're going to have to train your girlfriend to run a little faster! If she'd been sharper at fetching help, you might not have even had all this inconvenience."

Oh, God, he thought. They know everything.

Noticing the look of embarrassment on Harry's face, Dr. Metcalfe hurriedly added, "Just joking! Actually, it's a good thing she was there. She saved your hide. No offence, I hope?"

The apology did nothing to ease his acute sense of being the butt of some amusement among the staff. Feeling a strong urge to lash out, he replied peevishly, "No, of course not. but do you **have** to wake us up in the middle of the night to take our temperature?"

The doctor just laughed and said, "Of course we do! We all worship at the shrine of mindless bureaucracy. The National Health System is no exception. In fact, my dear chap, I think we may be a role model for the entire government!"

He turned to the nurse who looked like Popeye's girlfriend. "His vitals okay?"

"I think our patient may survive," she replied.

He then studied Harry over his reading spectacles with a barely concealed grin.

"By the way, did you ever find out how you came to be missing your trousers?"

Damn him. The man just couldn't resist getting in one last jab. The familiar flame of embarrassment seared up his neck. "Er, no," he said weakly, "I think they fell off and got lost... or something."

"Fell off. Ha, ha, ha!"

The medical team laughed uproariously, obviously delighted that a patient could muster such a sense of humour so early in the morning.

"Not to worry," Dr. Metcalfe concluded with a conspiratorial wink and a tap on the steel bed frame with his pencil. "If you ever do decide to come out with the real version, I'm sure the *News of the World* will publish it! In the meantime we'll keep you in today for a routine X-ray, and I'll put you on a bit of penicillin to discourage any lingering bugs."

After more laughter all round, the entourage left, leaving Harry propped up in bed with a sickly grin on his face. Several pairs of eyes from the other beds burned deep painful holes in him. What should he do— crawl out of sight, or leap out onto the floor yelling, "It's true, it's true! I lost my trousers while banging my girlfriend in a hayloft! Satisfied?" This time, however, cowardice played the better part of delirium and he meekly slid beneath the sheets. There, prostrate and with his eyes fixed on the high ceiling, he thought about the things that had happened to him since moving to Matlock. For some illogical reason many of them involved his trousers; at every opportunity they seemed to get damaged in some way or other. First there was the Duffield Incident, then the Christmas episode with Dickie's car, and now this. Perhaps his trousers were jinxed, although he couldn't think why. Perhaps, unknown to him, God had ordained that he should never wear trousers.

After breakfast, a nurse took him for his scheduled appointment with the X-ray laboratory and that proved to be the only break in a very monotonous day. By the time evening arrived, he was ready, willing, and eager to help the muscular nurse split Daisy's head with a plate. Or anything else they could lay their hands on. Daisy never ran out of breath, and seldom slept for more than an hour or two at a time. It had crossed his mind that the half-empty ward might be half-empty for a reason. After a day or two with Daisy, patients were probably desperate enough to buy their way out.

Around six o'clock, Emma poked her head into the ward. Gone was the streaked mascara, the tear-stained cheeks, and the bedraggled hair. She looked more rested, although the previous night's trauma was still showing in her face. Harry saw that she was wearing a pale blue, cotton dress he had bought her a few weeks previously on a day trip to Derby. As always, it fit her perfectly.

"Hello, love," she whispered, brandishing another bag. "Here's some clean things and another pair of trousers. Mrs. J. let me off a bit earlier so I could go and pick them up. When I told Miss Twigg what happened, she nearly had a fit. I gave her the 'official version' so now she thinks you're some sort of hero! Remember to give her the 'official version' yourself. I also rang Mr. Dickie but he wasn't in. What else is new? So I talked to Morley and he said he would pass along the message. I don't think you're going to get much sympathy from that lot. Morley laughed his head off right there on the phone!"

"Maybe you should have told him I also lost my trousers. He might have died," Harry said grumpily, eyeing the bag. He was tempted to comment that the replacement trousers might have looked better if she'd put them on a clothes hanger but changed his mind. She had enough problems without putting up with his churlishness. He'd got out of bed during the night and almost fallen on the floor. Trying it again he felt the same floating sensation and decided to sit on the edge of the bed instead.

"Are you alright?" she asked, concern turning quickly to alarm.

"I'm okay. just a little bit dizzy. I'll be okay." He looked at her more closely. "What happened to the burned hair?"

"Not bad, eh?" she said, pleased that he had noticed. "Mrs. J. gave me a real ragging, but then she gave me a bit of time off to go to the hairdresser's. They trimmed it and gave me a wash and set. It'll soon grow back. I don't think Mrs. J. believes the 'official reason' any more than everybody else does."

"I'm not surprised," Harry said. "That woman's got a very dirty mind."

Three of the other patients also had visitors, and for a while the ward brightened with chatter which almost, but not entirely, drowned out Daisy's solo marathon. She seemed to think Emma had showed up for her benefit so they both got yet another rerun of 'Freddie and the Parrot.'

"I got a real third-degree from Mum when I got home last night," Emma continued through Daisy's noise. "She says the Haithwaites are going to the police. They think somebody deliberately set fire to the place because a few months ago their milking shed was vandalized. So Mum's all upset. She thinks the police are going to make a big fuss and that she's going to get dragged into it."

"That's the last thing we need," Harry said gloomily. It was bad enough being the laughing stock of Elton. Being charged with arson wasn't funny.

"Mum says the police might want to take a statement from us. So far they haven't been around. Do you think they will?"

"Your guess is as good as mine. But if they do, we'll just stick to our 'official version'. I went through it all in my mind again last night. Unless they find my lighter there's no way they can pin the fire on us. And even if they do find the lighter, they can't prove it's mine. It's all pretty silly, if you ask me. The bloody hayloft was already falling down. We did the Haithwaites a favour by demolishing it before it fell on someone."

Emma pondered the expedient logic. "I'm not sure the Haithwaites will see it that way."

"Well, do we **look** like arsonists," he demanded.

"I suppose not."

After a couple of minutes of silence, she changed the subject. "When are they going to let you out, love?"

Harry shrugged. "Maybe tomorrow. I'm not sure."

"Okay, well, if you do get out, ring me at the shop; otherwise I'll be down after work again tomorrow afternoon."

She left after an hour. Harry endured another noisy night with Daisy providing the background noise and the muscular nurse arriving at 2 AM with his penicillin. Shortly after that a new patient was admitted, a young woman with a lot of tubes sticking out of her. He was thankful once again for his own lucky escape. Then, at eight-thirty in the morning the jovial Dr. Metcalfe and his cheering team re-appeared at the foot of the bed. Overall, he thought to himself, there hadn't been much time to get bored.

Once again the doctor gazed at Harry in amused silence before scribbling more words on his notepad. Then he asked, "How are you this fine morning, Mr. Michaels?"

Fine morning indeed. It might be fine for him, especially since he must be earning at least five times Harry's paltry salary. He felt like saying, "Exactly the same as yesterday morning, Doc," but instead assured all present that everything was on the up and up.

He should have known that the medical profession dismissed these sorts of assurances as nothing more than fluff because the words had hardly left his mouth before Dr. Metcalfe whipped out his stethoscope. "We'll have a quick listen, I think," he said.

Whatever the sounds were, they evidently pleased him. He grunted with satisfaction. "Well, the X-ray indicates no scarring on your lungs, so we'll keep you on the penicillin for a week as a precaution. Any other aches or pains?"

Harry assured him again that there were none.

The doctor gave his notes a final perusal.

"In that case, then, I see no reason to keep you here any longer. Actually, we could have sent you home yesterday but I thought you might appreciate the chance to sample some of this establishment's fine food!" He laughed heartily again at his own joke. The other three followed suit, although their laughter was somewhat tempered by the experience of having to eat more of it than anybody else.

The foursome turned to leave. As they did so, Metcalfe looked back and said, "I sincerely hope you've managed to find a replacement pair of trousers!"

"Yes, I did, thank you," said Harry, beet red from the toes up.

Amid giggles and loud guffaws, they departed.

"They know. They bloody well know," he silently cursed while waiting for a nurse to officially escort him out of the ward.

Two hours later, no one had come except the breakfast wagon. He wolfed down a small plateful of lukewarm scrambled eggs and cold toast, then waited again. A couple of nurses visited other patients in the ward, but he might have had smallpox for all the attention they paid to him. Time dragged on. Lunch time came and went. The deviled-egg salad was nice but like breakfast, not very filling. He spent the better part of the afternoon reading some very old editions of *Reader's Digest* and dozing off.

His slumbering was rudely interrupted just before six o'clock by a sharp voice from the foot of the bed. "What are **you** doing here?"

He opened one eye to find the head nurse staring at him with a perplexed frown. "Weren't you discharged this morning?"

Harry struggled to a half-sitting position. "That's what Dr. Metcalfe said, but I thought someone had to come and get me up and..."

"Dress you? This isn't the Ritz Hotel, Mr. Michaels. We assume that when you're fit enough to be discharged you are also fit enough to dress yourself and leave without maid service. Now, be a good fellow and leave as soon as you can. We may need this bed at any time."

Looking around, he very much doubted that claim. Barring some major catastrophe the ward appeared to be in no immediate danger of being swamped. The woman's voice irritated him. For a split second he considered informing her that various staff people had been in and out all day without one of them noticing there was anything amiss. For that matter, where had **she** been all day? She was supposed to know about all things that went on in the hospital. But why bother. Head nurses, like other career bureaucrats, always seemed to be imbued with an iron-clad self-confidence that defied any assault from outsiders, particularly mere patients. He began to haul himself out of bed as she drew the privacy curtain. Just before it closed he caught sight of a familiar bob of auburn hair out in the hallway. He could hear Emma's shoes briskly clicking across the bare floor.

"Your husband was discharged this morning but he doesn't seem to want to leave," he heard the head nurse say. "Must be the food."

There was a rustling of paper bags and Emma said, "I wasn't sure if he was getting out today so I brought him some fruit. And actually, he's not my husband, he's my boyfriend."

She might as well have talked to the wall. The head nurse had assessed the situation and certainly wasn't going to be contradicted by a visitor. "Ordinarily we keep smoke-inhalation patients in for forty-eight hours or more," she continued, flinging open the privacy curtain. "But your husband is young and in good condition, and there was no permanent damage." Then, as they both peered at him, she added, "All the same, it's a good thing you're here, Mrs. Michaels. Perhaps you can get him organized."

So saying, she briskly left. Emma and Harry sat on the bed and for a few minutes munched on some grapes before pulling out the clothing Emma had brought in the day before. Harry looked with dismay at the crumpled trousers and shirt. The tie she had hurriedly pulled from his wardrobe didn't match anything else. But at least they were all clean and free of the odor of burned grass.

"Miss Twigg took the dirty clothes and they went straight into the wash," Emma informed him. "And she says she'll sew on a couple of buttons you lost."

They re-drew the privacy curtains and he dressed quickly. Emma sat on the bed and affectionately stroked his bottom as he pulled up his briefs.

Daisy's eyes followed them as they both left. "Freddie's comin' tomorra'," she cried. "But 'e in't goin' ter diddle me no more, no more. 'E'll 'ave ter buy a tart, that's what e'll 'ave ter do."

"She's a looney, is that one," Emma murmured.

"I wonder if Freddie really does have a parrot?" Harry mused, closing the ward door quietly behind them.

They were greeted by Sarah when they got to Miss Twigg's twenty minutes later. Looking up from her task of setting the dining room table, she grinned at Harry and pouted at Emma. "Auntie Bertha says yer put out a big fire all by yerself. She says yer nearly got killed. Did yer?"

Harry had started to formulate a response when Miss Twigg bustled around the corner, her face a picture of anguish and concern. She threw up her arms in theatrical surprise. "Oh my goodness! Oh my goodness!" she burst out. "I was so worried when Emma knocked on the door the other night. And I wasn't expecting you back for a few more days. I had a friend once who got a frying pan on fire and they kept her in for nearly a week. In fact, I was going to pop over to the hospital tomorrow to see you."

Harry couldn't imagine a frying pan generating enough smoke to choke a canary, let alone a human. But, like his boss, Miss Twigg always said things with great conviction and he had found it best not to argue.

Wiping her hands down her apron, she beckoned them to follow and retreated back into the kitchen to resume the serious business of whipping up an evening meal. Miss Twigg might have been a big ungainly woman, but she had a caring disposition, especially when it came to her boarders. And she had an extra-soft spot for Harry, partly because he ate up everything she set before him. As far as she was concerned, that was the ultimate compliment for a landlady.

They followed her into the kitchen. It had been another warm day and the kitchen door was flung wide open. The cat was in its usual position on top of her vast table, surveying the food.

"Does your mother know about this?" Miss Twigg asked, her rosy cheeks quivering.

Harry shook his head. "I haven't had time to tell her yet. We don't have a telephone so I would have to call her at work, and in any case..." he trailed off, wondering whether his mother would buy the 'official version' either.

"Well, never mind for the moment," said Miss Twigg, once again wiping her hands down the soiled apron. "You're alright and we're all very proud of you. It's a pity there aren't more public-spirited young people around. Most of them are so selfish these days... and lazy. My goodness are they lazy! They're not going to set the world on fire, I can tell you."

It was a poor choice of words for the occasion. Harry gulped and Emma blushed. He wondered if this was how Brutus felt before knocking off Caesar. Sarah walked over to her seat in the kitchen corner, sat down with a thump and continued staring intently at him. Emma and Harry pulled out other chairs and watched preparations. He couldn't help reflecting how much Miss Twigg's attitude had changed during the short time he had been there. He remembered the first day when she told him in no uncertain terms that boarders were not allowed in the kitchen. Nowadays she seemed almost glad to see him in there.

After a few more minutes she announced that dinner was ready.

"I'm setting a plate for you, too, Emma," she added. "Poor thing, you must be exhausted, all the dashing about you've been doing. Sarah, go and set another plate for Emma. And hurry up."

Emma gratefully accepted. She wasn't so much exhausted as she was upset, knowing full well that their escapade would quickly find its way around the neighborhood. Paul Utley would see to that, the weasel. But she also knew that her mother had a shrewd idea what they had been up to, and it would do little to upgrade her opinion of Harry.

Sarah pouted again at Emma, slowly got to her feet, and disappeared into the dining room. They could hear a rattling of cutlery being thrown about. A plate fell to the floor with a crash. Harry winced. Miss Twigg roared around the corner and for a few seconds a heated exchange echoed down the barren hallway.

"That Sarah will be the death of me," she grimly announced upon returning the kitchen. "I'll be glad when her mum and dad sort things out and she can go home, I really will." Lowering her voice, she added, "Her sister Darlene is even worse. Out all the time, smoking and running around with who knows who. Mind you, at least she has a job. I have my suspicions that young Sarah here plays truant from school, although no one has said anything to me. It's a poor situation but I can't do much about it. I'm just too old for this sort of nonsense."

As if on cue, Darlene suddenly flounced up the kitchen steps. Although he'd been staying at Miss Twigg's for at least nine months, this was the first time Harry had been able to get a good look at her. Before, she had been a little like Emma's sister Anne, merely a fleeting shadow, racing in or out of the house. Most often, however, she simply wasn't around. He had often wondered what hours she worked, and for that matter, what kind of work she did. Sarah had once told him that Darlene was a waitress. Then a couple of months later she had apparently switched to hairdressing. From her appearance on this occasion, it looked as though hairdressing might still be in. Wobbling precariously on stiletto heels, she grabbed the door jamb for support before propelling herself into the room.

The girl's sallow face, plastered with too much makeup, was crowned with a bleached coiffure which looked like onion rings piled one on top of the other. Harry couldn't believe the contrast between the two sisters. Darlene was as tall and slim as Sarah was short and fat. What a difference a couple of years make, he thought to himself. Soon Sarah would blossom. Then, like her sister, she would probably fade as quickly, hastened by the trappings of marriage, kids, and a meaningless job.

To his relief, Harry had been given a clear indication that he wasn't Darlene's type. He suspected that, like a lot of working-class girls, she preferred hairy chests and the long greasy look. He failed on both counts, keeping his hair cut fairly short and sporting not a single bit of fuzz anywhere on his chest. From what he could gather from Miss Twigg, Darlene had formulated a fairly narrow agenda for life: men. And by all accounts she pursued that agenda with considerable zeal. In many respects, Harry had concluded, she was a juvenile version of Lol Dobson's wife.

Ignoring everyone in the room, Darlene waved a finger at Sarah. "Come 'ere, ah want a word wi' yer," she said tersely. Sarah obediently sauntered over and the two huddled in a corner. They could see that Darlene had a serious problem, although no one could hear what they were saying. Sarah kept shaking her head, growing more agitated as Darlene persisted.

The conference abruptly ended with the older sister once again pushing past them to the door. "If ah find aht yer 'ave 'em, yer'll get it, ah'm tellin' yer," she hissed as a parting shot. Sarah, flushed and tight-lipped, went back to her chair and resumed her silent observation of Harry. He hated that look. Every time she did it, Harry became more convinced that she knew everything. At least, everything he and Emma did up in his room. It was as if those wide, staring eyes could penetrate his clothes. He felt naked, and strangely insecure. Perhaps if Sarah had been older he might have been flattered by the attention. But this wasn't a pleasant sensation. For all her cherubic innocence there was something disconcertingly dark and adult about the way she faced life. Dear little Sarah, he firmly believed, was quite capable of causing him considerable discomfort if she so desired.

"Well!" exclaimed Miss Twigg, with eyebrows raised. Wiping her hands down her apron again, she looked at Sarah and said, "I'll talk to you later, Missy." No one else said a word.

She had cooked up a meal of pork chops, roast potatoes and the tiny canned peas that she knew Harry loved. Sarah disappeared, probably to escape her aunt, so they were able to finish dinner and have their coffee without further scrutiny. Afterwards they went for a short walk in Hall Leys park. The air was still mild and languid. For a change the restless breeze which squeezed through High Tor and into the town had died to a murmur. Several beds of hybrid tea and floribunda roses were in full bloom, their scent permeating the air about them. It was a pretty park, although not maintained to Harry's standards— the grass long and unkempt in some places, and rubbish left in piles to decompose. That would not have happened, he told himself, in Barnsley's Locke Park, where he had spent those wonderful years of apprenticeship. Some people were examining a large carpet-bedding display depicting Matlock's coat of arms. It was a colourful effort, painstakingly planted up with a variety of low-growing annual flowers and clipped to perfection.

Soon it was almost nine o'clock, growing dark, and Harry was tired. Despite the fatigue he wanted Emma to spend some time in bed with him. But it was too early in the evening to sneak her upstairs. Miss Twigg would still be about and even if **she** didn't intercept them, Sarah undoubtedly would. It was yet another occasion when he wholeheartedly joined with Miss Twigg's wish that Sarah's domestic environment would sort itself out and she could go home. Harry's sex life would be far less complicated without her.

After sitting on a bench for a while, they slowly walked, hand in hand, back to Derwent House.

"I'll have to catch the nine-thirty bus," Emma said reluctantly. She had the same idea as Harry but knew it wasn't practical that evening. In any case, they both needed some rest.

He said, "I can walk you down to the bus stop."

She put her arm around his waist. "We're going in the wrong direction for that, love. Besides, I think you should turn in if you're going back to work tomorrow. And to be honest, I could do with a good night's sleep myself."

He had to admit she was right. After kissing her on the nose, he went inside and Emma went to catch her bus. Sarah was still nowhere in sight. Miss Twigg saw him through the dining room hatch and inquired if there was anything else he needed. Nothing that she could provide, he assured her. Perish the thought.

Despite the mild evening air, his bedroom was surprisingly cold. Shivering slightly, he stripped off his clothes, wondering again as he did so why he'd ever been stupid enough to develop a habit of sleeping naked. Sliding beneath the cool sheets, he lay on his back and speculated on the kind of teasing he would be in for at work tomorrow. Morley had said he was going to tell Dickie, and Dickie would have told the entire office— and everybody else everybody within a ten mile radius.

He was beginning to doze off when there was a knock at the door. Before the words 'come in' were out of his mouth, Sarah was in the room, cradling something in her arms.

"Auntie Bertha said yer might need a clean towel," she said, negotiating her way around the foot of the bed to the wash basin. She hung the towel on the rail and then stood, contemplating him for a moment.

"Are yer really tired?"

"Well, yes, a little," Harry replied suspiciously.

"Oh." She made her usual exaggerated sigh but after a short silence suddenly reached out and flicked on his bedside table lamp. Harry could see that in addition to the towel she had brought up some magazines. They were well-massaged and the front cover of the top copy had been half ripped off.

"Ah thought we could 'ave a look through these an' mebbe yer could explain a few things. Move ower a bit."

"I, er..." he began.

With surprising agility she jumped up on the bed next to him and began to spread the magazines over his stomach. The sense of impending doom surged again. She got as close to him as she could without actually sitting on top of him. It quickly became apparent that whatever Sarah might be looking for, it wasn't explanations. The magazines appeared to be those which Darlene's boyfriend had lent her, and they were very explicit.

"Look at this," she said, thumbing a full page photograph. "There's two fellas in 'er at the same time. Now **that** must 'urt, don't yer think?"

Harry reared up on his elbows to make sure he wasn't hallucinating. Sure enough, it showed a very well-endowed young girl lying on top of an anemic male, looking sublimely at the camera while another equally weedy looking male was poised, like some trapeze artist, on top of her. He found himself trying to figure out how the photographer had taken the picture.

"An' look at this 'un. 'e's got it stuck in 'er bum!" Sarah continued, her fat thumb working feverishly.

By now he was beginning to get aroused, even though he tried hard to prevent it. The magazines spread in front of him twitched and then rose slightly. This did not go unnoticed. Sarah looked at the small hump, a cheesy grin spreading from ear to ear, and reached out to feel it. Harry felt as though he had been electrocuted. What if Miss Twigg came up? And why was it that most females who showed an interest in his body were either too old or too young? Somehow he had to get out of this predicament, and with all possible speed.

"Ah told yer a've done it before, wi' Len. 'E showed me 'ow but ah think ah could do it better wi' you."

He couldn't imagine a more distasteful prospect. And in any event, she was under-age. How on earth had he got himself into this predicament? It was a totally ridiculous situation.

"Look, dammit, Sarah..." he babbled.

"Yer must be interested 'cause yer've got an 'ard on," she persisted, stroking the growing lump. "Ah'll bet yer not wearin' any underpants."

Harry made a grab for the quilt. "Yes I am."

She grinned again. No, yer not!" And with that she yanked off the bedclothes. There was a short pause as they both contemplated the source of the lump.

"It isn't very big, is it?" she said slowly. "But ah reckon they go in easier when they's smaller."

"This one isn't going anywhere, Sarah," Harry shot back, unaware that his voice had taken on a peculiar falsetto. And he wasn't sure which had been more severely wounded: his dignity or his pride. "For starters you're not old enough, and for another I'm not interested. Do you realize what's going to happen to me if your aunt catches us in here? I'll be out on the street in two seconds. So pack up your magazines and go see Len. Better still, wait for a year or two before seeing Len again."

He attempted to pull the sheet, the blanket, anything, over his nakedness, but Sarah had a firm hold on them and wasn't about to let go.

"Ah told yer, ah don't like Len much," she pouted. "'E's too rough an' 'e smells. You smell nice. An' ah won't get in the fam'ly way 'cause ah took Darlene's pills."

So that was what the crisis in the kitchen had been all about. She'd stolen Darlene's birth-control pills! No wonder her sister was in a flap. The poor girl must have had to pull some strings somewhere just to get the prescription, and without the package she couldn't even get a refill. Sarah was living very dangerously. So, probably, was Darlene without her pills. He wondered how Sarah had found the opportunity to steal them. Since Darlene apparently lived most of the time with her current boyfriend, the two sisters would see very little of each other. However, it was obvious that an opportunity must have presented itself somewhere at some time, and Sarah had availed herself of it.

As she waited for this little bombshell to sink in, Harry noted with some relief that his youthful assailant hadn't begun to shed any of her own clothes, although she was tentatively playing with the top button of her woollen cardigan. He prayed she would hold off long enough for some brilliant solution to surface.

In his most authoritative tone and still tugging on the quilt he said, "Look, for the last time, I'm not interested. And you shouldn't be taking somebody else's birth control pills. They might not suit you. In fact, they might not even work." Then, realizing that he might have stumbled upon a key line, he repeated what he had just said.

"Why not?" she demanded.

"Er, because... Because I've got three women pregnant already, and they were all using birth-control pills."

"She looked down at his crotch in amazement. "Wi' that?"

"I wasn't using my toe."

She thoughtfully eyed Harry's erection for a few more seconds while weighing up this major setback, gave it a quick fondling, then allowed him to pull the bedclothes back over himself. Inwardly, an enormous wave of relief swept over his naked form, even though he'd had to give himself a reputation he would probably never get a chance to live up to.

Sarah, however, wasn't quite ready to concede defeat. "D'yer 'ave any rubbers?"

"For Pete's sake, Sarah, I'm not going to have sex with you!" he exploded. "Now, please, get off my bed, get out of my room, and let me go to sleep. I've only just got out of hospital and I'm tired, really tired."

After another deep sigh, Sarah scooped up her magazines, shuffled off the bed, and left.

"Ah still like yer, Harry," she said as she quietly closed the door.

"And I still like you too," Harry lied, turning off his bedside lamp after making sure she had really gone.

That was one experience he probably wouldn't tell Emma about.

He went to work the following morning, although by the time he reached the top of Bank Road he felt weak and had started coughing. At the office, Morley, Bill and Terry greeted him with the kind of knowing look that suggested they had either come to their own conclusions or had received information other than the 'official version.' The only possible informant Harry could think of was Mrs. Johnson, who could have, probably **would** have, told Dickie. Emma hadn't really said what she had told Mrs. J., but it wouldn't need to be very much; Mrs. J. could easily invent the rest. As Harry's mother always said, word travels fast, and in this small town it seemed to travel fast indeed.

"So, Harry, my boy," Bill Lewis said from behind a cloud of cigarette smoke, "doing a little fire-warden duty on the side, are we?"

Terry waited for his colleague to pull off the dust cover of his draughting table.

"Risky places, those haylofts," he grinned. "All that straw just waiting to catch fire all by itself!"

"It can, it can," Harry blustered. "Under the right conditions, it can."

His colleagues roared with laughter.

"What did you do, try to blow it out?" Morley asked after making a mammoth effort to sit upright in his chair.

"Nothing worse than a layloft fire," Bill continued. "Enough to scare the pants off anybody!"

Now Harry **knew** someone had been telling tales out of school. As usual, he could feel the heat creeping up the back of his neck. But there was no alternative. He had to sit and brazen it out, if only for Emma's sake.

"Honestly," he protested unconvincingly, "it was already on fire when we passed."

"Who said it wasn't?" said Terry, sounding like a chess player who has just checkmated his opponent.

"Ha, ha," chuckled Morley.

"What puzzles me is why you stayed inside the place when it was so full of smoke," said Bill.

"I lost my watch."

There were more knowing looks all round.

"It just fell off your wrist?" asked Morley with another chuckle.

"Yes," Harry replied, grasping at this small straw. "The strap was worn. In fact I was going to get it replaced."

"Hope you found it, after going to all that trouble?" Bill said.

That, of course, had been the most upsetting part of this fiasco. "No, I didn't," he glumly replied.

At that moment, Dickie came in, replete with the ever-present cigarette. Seeing Harry, he stopped in his tracks and let out a mirthless cackle. "Well! Our fire warden has returned!" he cried. Then turning to the others in the room he added, "So we didn't lose him after all, fellas, although I hear he nearly lost his shirt!"

Everyone had another good laugh while Harry grinned and squirmed in his seat. His windpipe was still sore from the tube the doctors had pushed down it, so when he tried to laugh he broke into another coughing bout. In spite of the discomfort, this turned out to be a lifesaver. They were all for a good laugh at someone's expense, but the older staff had developed a great affection for their youngest assistant, whom they looked upon as the baby in the department. The merriment turned to concern.

"Maybe you should have stayed home for another day, son," Bill said, getting off his stool.

"Oh, get off the pot, Lewis," Dickie snapped. "He's a strapping young lad. A little smoke won't kill him."

All maintained a respectful silence while Harry made some loud and disgusting noises in the back of his throat.

"Anyhow, my young friend," Dickie resumed when the hacking had died down. "We're glad you're in one piece. You can thank Emma for letting us know what happened. Who knows, I might have found myself looking for two replacements instead of one!" He was referring to Clem's position which, after three months, still had not been filled. Rumour had it that the position might be abolished as a cost-saving measure.

Dickie was clutching some papers, obviously intended for Harry's attention. Ambling up to Harry's draughting table, he dumped them down.

"Harry, we've had a complaint about the Derby-Road-School project. For Chrissakes, did you really think two tons of dirt would fill a bog that size?" He glared at his assistant for a moment. "Well, it didn't. You bloody underestimated again, and by a country mile. First time they tried to play on it, half the poor buggers sank up to their arses in wet mud. Not very Pukka. Not very Pukka at all. It's stuff like this that makes us all look like unprofessional clods."

"The ground must have been softer than I thought," said Harry, seeing his hopes for a quiet first day back at the office disappearing into thin air, "You're right, we probably need a little more fill. Problem is, the contractor's going to come back on us for an extra."

"Nonsense," Dickie replied, lighting another cigarette by the usual expedient of shoving it into the remains of the old one, "everybody is trying to get rid of fill dirt. Tell your chappie to find someone who's excavating nearby and tell 'em to go dump it in our hole."

There were two problems with Dickie's suggestion. First, Harry didn't really consider it to be 'their' hole. There wasn't a hole to begin with. Just rather soft ground. It had only become a hole later, when it sneakily appeared after they got the playing field seeded. No one should have been too surprised. A lot of government buildings were being built on reclaimed land. And God only knew what lay below the surface. Some sites were bombed-out developments that had been bulldozed. This particular area had been a row of run-down tenements and allotments. The second problem was that, contrary to Dickie's optimism, very few contractors were prepared to do anything for nothing, especially for the government.

Unfortunately for Harry, this project had also once again drawn attention to his woeful ineptitude. While he did get to work on purely landscaping projects,

Dickie once in a while would assign him to a playing field, and the outcome was always the same. The mathematics of precision grading and levelling were anathema, and as foreign to his brain as Latin. He was, after all, a horticulturist, not a surveyor. Shrubs and trees and flower beds made much more sense. Losing those down sinkholes seemed somehow less catastrophic than half a soccer team, although his boss probably wouldn't see it that way.

"I'll talk to the contractor tomorrow," he replied, pulling out the drawings and placing them on top of his draughting table. "But even if he doesn't charge us for the fill, we'll still get stuck for his hauling costs."

Dickie fixed him with his beady eyes. "I hope for your sake, my boy, he doesn't charge us anything."

As they both leaned over to examine the location of this latest disaster on the drawing, something reddish-coloured and very small landed on the paper and headed north as fast as its little legs could carry it. Harry noticed it. Dickie, grunting though cigarette haze, also noticed it but initially paid little attention. They continued their discussion. A minute later another insect appeared in front of them and was quickly joined by half a dozen of its relatives. They reminded Harry of a tiny squad of paratroopers landing behind enemy lines. Without pausing, they scurried off in all directions, trying to find cover from the glare of his cantilever lamp. As they both watched, he realized to his horror that they were jumping out of his tweed jacket, the same one he'd been wearing on Sunday. He had no idea what they were, but it was obvious they had come from the hay in the ill-fated loft. For the first time he was getting a close look at the invisible creatures which made life so miserable for him on those clandestine occasions.

Dickie, glasses perched on the end of his nose, peered at them in silence for a few more seconds. "Hiring a bit of cheap help, are we?" he asked sarcastically.

For the hundredth time in the past couple of days, Harry wished he could die. As he tried to sweep them aside, more and more appeared until the draughting table was alive with insects. Some began crawling over Dickie's papers while others scaled the lamp. A few which had wandered too close to the edge fell haplessly to the floor and began racing for the door. Terry, ever vigilant when it came to someone else's business, craned his neck to see what was going on. It wasn't difficult to put two and two together. He and Dickie both knew. And Harry, with sinking heart, knew that his 'official version' had just been blown away by some dumb creatures which hadn't the sense to stay put.

"My, my," said Terry, "I'm sure there's some rule about bringing pets to work. Can they do tricks?"

"Must get my jacket dry-cleaned," Harry mumbled between renewed coughing bouts. Unfortunately, the more he coughed, the more insects he shook free. Soon Bill and Morley came over for a look at the miniature circus. For a while everybody stood around in a tight circle while the desktop pandemonium continued with full fury. Finally, Harry took the jacket off and started to hang it on some pegs by the main entrance.

Dickie looked at him darkly. "I think, my young friend, the sooner that jacket goes to the cleaners the—"

"—less we will all itch," Bill interrupted.

"Maybe Emma will take it in for me," Harry said, grabbing it off the peg again. "Can I nip across the road for a moment?"

"Oh, please do," Dickie said, gathering up his papers and flapping away a few hitchhikers. "And hurry back. It's not lunch time yet."

A warm sunny day had developed. He sprinted across the road to the chemist shop, where Emma and Mrs. Johnson, sitting on stools behind the counter, looked at him in surprise. Mrs. J. broke into her toothy grin.

"Well, here's our new— "

"Fire warden," Harry said without smiling.

Emma, immediately spotting what he was wearing, hurried round the counter and pulled him towards the door. She knew what the problem was before he even opened his mouth.

"Why on earth did you wear **that** jacket to work?" she whispered frantically.

"There's a button missing on my other one," he lamely replied. "Besides, you told me in hospital it was alright."

"I only meant relatively speaking. It's got things in it, hasn't it?"

Harry nodded, shedding the jacket and thrusting it at her. "It's got **lots** of things in it. Can you run it over the dry cleaners? They know you and I thought you might be able to get it back a bit quicker."

Emma held it at arm's length. "Don't tell me things came **out** of it?"

Harry nodded again. "Oh, yes. All over my bloody draughting table. And everybody got a good look. And a good laugh, I might add."

"Oh my God," she said slowly. "You realize that this jacket of yours has nackered our 'official version?'"

"I'm afraid so."

To the considerable relief of them both, not to mention Emma's mother, the Haithwaites never contacted the police about their suspicions of vandalism. Why, no one ever found out. Mrs. Callingwood dismissed Harry's speculation that the loft might have been abandoned as wishful thinking, suggesting instead that the Haithwaites' lack of concern stemmed from the fact that it wasn't insured. But it didn't stop the gossip, and Emma had to endure months of snickering from people in the village. She stuck to her word though; they never had sex in a hayloft again. For Harry, it meant playing cat and mouse with Sarah and her aunt more often. It was worth it. Eventually the incident, embellished over time, went into local folklore around Elton. Harry's traveling menagerie enjoyed a similar fate in the Landscape and Playing Fields Section.

NINE

Wheels

Terry and Maid Marion were married, as scheduled, on June 15th, in Swansea. In an uncommonly magnanimous gesture, they invited Harry and Emma to the wedding. Dickie had received an invitation long before they did. Harry declined, not from a lack of interest, but more on account of a higher priority: that of buying himself a car. After less than nine months with the Landscape and Playing Field Section it was becoming glaringly obvious that his job held very little future, aside, perhaps, from a measure of security. On his miserable salary he couldn't even afford his own flat. However, with a bit of conniving there might be a possibility of getting himself a set of wheels. In some ways it was as much an act of defiance as a lifestyle decision; if he couldn't afford most of what everybody else in the office had, at least he would have a car and the hell with it.

By now he knew that he wouldn't be staying with the Derbyshire County Council for very long; there appeared to be almost no opportunity for advancement, at least in his little backwater. Terry remained firmly entrenched as the golden boy in Dickie's eyes and would automatically be first in line for promotion. But promotion to what? Bill Lewis's position as senior draughtsman at a few more pounds a month? Or Dickie's job, which resembled the centre of a six-way intersection equipped with faulty traffic lights? He wasn't sure if even Terry would want that. No, the next hill had begun to beckon, but he could always take his car with him.

Declining Terry and Marion's wedding invitation got Harry and Emma into another spat. Should he have accepted it, he argued, they would have had to buy the couple a wedding gift, take the train to Swansea, stay in a hotel for at least two nights, possibly three. And in separate rooms, which would be frustrating as well as expensive. Adding it all up, Harry decided he wasn't sufficiently fond of either of them to jeopardize his car-buying project. Emma didn't quite see things his way. She hadn't been to a decent wedding in her life, and was decidedly put off by the prospect of missing this one. Not that she didn't want Harry to buy a car. To the contrary, it would be a welcome change from using the bus to go everywhere. One day in the shop she had tried to calculate how many hours a year were spent on the bus. It came to roughly a thousand hours, or forty-two days. It seemed like a lot of wasted time. Trouble was, the car would be Harry's, not hers. She would have been happy to go Dutch on the cost of the trip. Harry wouldn't hear of it. Terry, possibly trying to stir up trouble, invited Emma to go on her own although he stopped short of offering to pay her way. Emma seemed to sense what he was doing, and politely declined.

So the wedding struggled through without them, and also without Dickie, who announced at the last minute he couldn't attend. By Marion's account, when they returned from their honeymoon on the Isle of Sky, it had been a posh affair, as might be expected. There had been only one fight at the reception, caused, apparently, by some riff-raff (her term) who became so plastered he fell head first into the punchbowl. Her younger brother, interpreting this behavior as an insult to the entire assembly, had taken it upon himself to loosen a couple of the fellow's teeth. Harry could imagine, with some amusement, the anguished look on Terry's face as the unseemly brawl broke out. Terry had what might be described as a negative smile, which was a sort of smirk in which his thin mouth curled down, rather than up. It was the type of look most people reserved for identifying bad smells.

Harry not only wanted to buy a car, he wanted to buy one before Terry. It was, for Harry, a rare display of one-upmanship. Terry and Marion had bought their new semi-detached house in the Limes. Contrary to Angus's cheerless predictions, it hadn't yet fallen down. The purchase, Harry had been told, was made possible by a generous contribution from Marion's father, a self-made success story in scrap metal. Presumably Terry would hear about that for a very long time to come. Nevertheless, he now had a home of his own and Harry didn't. And the prospects for acquiring one did not appear good. A car, on the other hand, was theoretically within reach.

He was still fuming over the two days it took Terry and Marion to move in. Two days in which he moved a lot of furniture, some of it very heavy. It was also the first and last time he had been invited over. And if that hadn't been bad enough, Terry could now be heard around the office dropping loud hints about getting the garden fixed up. No way. Terry could get someone else to break his back on that one. Mulling over these events, Harry decided that getting a car now, while Terry was still reeling from post-nuptial shock and a ravaged bank account would be, at the very least, sweet revenge.

The great decision to buy a car occurred while Harry was limping home from Elton very late one August night. Both feet were badly blistered, and like Emma he was beginning to feel that a large part of his life was revolving around a bus schedule. He had a driver's licence. In fact the driving examination was just about the only thing he'd ever passed with flying colours, and at the ripe old age of seventeen to boot. Mother had insisted he take proper lessons, so Harry spent several happy months under the watchful tutelage of a fire inspector who worked at her office in the Barnsley Fire and Ambulance Department. Benny Fastwell was a diminutive little man, with fierce black eyes, perfect white teeth, a magnificent moustache. and an acerbic wit which, with lightening speed, could turn to withering sarcasm. There was always some conjecture about Benny's ethnic origins, since his features stood in sharp contrast to the pallid complexions of his fellow Yorkshiremen. In his perfectly pressed uniform, Benny cut quite a dashing figure. Apart from a near pathological loathing of the fire chief, almost nothing ever upset him. His explosive laugh and flashing smile were everywhere. He loved dancing, and the Department's annual Christmas party usually dissolved into a grim wrestling match among the women, married or single, for a chance to do a turn around the floor with Benny. His wife, a large woman at least six inches taller than he, reminded Harry of the Mona Lisa, since she, too, always gave the impression of being privy to a secret. Perhaps it was the knowledge that any time Benny stepped out of line, she could quite easily beat him to a pulp.

Notwithstanding his many attributes, Benny's greatest talent lay in avoiding anything, other than dancing, which involved physical work. Whenever such occasions arose in the line of duty, Benny had a bad back— more specifically a slipped disk which slipped almost upon demand. And it slipped often. Everybody knew about 'Benny's Bad Back.' He could thank that disk for helping to elevate him from lowly fireman to his current position. Fighting fires was dirty work, occasionally dangerous, and not particularly well-paid. Fire inspectors fared much better and they got to wear a snappy uniform and stay clean. Benny's unfailing charm and streetwise common sense made him a perfect candidate. Moreover, he had survived his fire-fighting days as something of a celebrity. Five years earlier, the Empire cinema had burned to the ground in a spectacular late-night blaze. Benny, with uncommon disregard for himself, had charged into the projection room and rescued the film *du jour*. Afterwards a grateful theatre chain sent a letter of thanks and Benny received a commendation from the hated fire chief. For Harry this conjured up a delightful image of the pair smiling between their teeth at each other during the ceremony. Later, Benny went on to ace the fire inspection training program and soon had custom designed an enviable work schedule for himself. To the puzzlement of his superiors, who really should have figured out his game plan a long time ago, he spent an inordinate proportion of his time with restaurants and cinemas, whereas other institutions such as schools and libraries hardly ever saw him.

Benny liked Harry, and the two got along right from the start. Just as much, he liked riding around in a new car while someone else did the driving. If Harry had been a poor pupil, the situation would have been different; after several years of driving fire engines, Benny fancied himself as a professional driver with very exacting standards. But Harry took to driving like fleas take to dogs. It was smooth sailing from day one.

"If tha remembers nowt else, Harry, lad," Benny would often say in his broad Yorkshire dialect, "it's ter spend as much time lookin' in th' mirror as tha does lookin' ahead. Check fer feet under parked vehicles. An' treat everybody on't road as a bloody nincompoop."

Harry did just that, and passed his driving test before his mother, who had bought the car a few months earlier in anticipation that Harry would be able to do the driving while she herself took lessons. Benny was pigeonholed to teach her, too, but the arrangement didn't last long. They drove back to the house one day with Benny looking flushed and out of sorts.

"Harry, my lad," he said in an agitated voice while pulling his former pupil to one side, "ah think you'll 'ave to handle your mum from now on."

"What's the matter?" Harry asked, knowing full well. The problem was that Mother, ever the cautious soul, drove too slowly. So slowly, in fact, that she seldom needed to get out of second gear. After suffering several weeks of abuse around town from infuriated drivers who got stuck behind her, Benny had decided to try the country roads where there was less traffic. At least, that was the theory. Unfortunately, like many theories, it ignored reality; in this case the fact that spring was in the air and many people were out enjoying the countryside after a particularly miserable winter. They crawled back to town along narrow roads, followed by a lineup of honking cars that could have put a celebrity funeral to shame.

To make matters worse, Mother was having difficulty with the clutch. No matter how many times Benny explained it, she got the sequence backwards, trying to drive with the clutch depressed and change gears while it was engaged. Needless to say, this idea did not work. Each time they set off, Benny shrank into his seat, red with embarrassment, as the loudly suffering Morris Minor jumped down the road like a frightened rabbit. It wasn't long before he started complaining of a sore neck on top of his back problems.

"Ah experienced the ultimate 'umiliation today, I'm tellin' thee," Benny sniffed. "A bloody bicycle passed us! Can yer imagine? A bloody bicycle. Any'ow, ah think she's got the basic 'ang of drivin'. She just needs practice now, and you can sit wi' 'er for that just as well as me. Mebbe by the time she takes 'er test she'll be able t'get up ter thirty miles an hour. Assumin' she 'as any gears left."

Eventually his mother did manage to get up to thirty miles an hour but never completely mastered the intricacies of a gear box. The car didn't need a horn, even if she could ever remember where it was. Mother's presence announced itself at least half a mile away as she vigorously sampled the gears in hope of finding one which would propel the vehicle forward. Combined, it produced the kind of noise that might have brought tears of joy to an *avant garde* musicologist. What puzzled Harry and astounded Benny was that she passed her driving test the first time. Without intending to offend, Benny speculated that the examiner must have simply been thankful to get out of the car in one piece.

A major obstacle to buying a car was a lack of sufficient funds. Harry had saved up about £150, but he anticipated needing twice that amount to buy something reasonably reliable. Then there was the question of what to look for. In the early 1960's Britain still had a wide range of makes and models, even though many were glaring examples of how-not-to-build-a-car. He remembered when his mother bought her Morris Minor, the car heater was an optional extra. After spending the first frigid winter with the windows rolled down in a vain attempt to keep warm, Mother relented and took the car back to have a heater fitted. Even then it was the most useless thing he had ever seen. It sat under the dashboard like a small torpedo, the only adjustable mechanism being a small plastic knob in the middle which was supposed to control the speed of the fan. But no matter how far, or in which direction, this knob was twiddled, the ridiculous contraption kept up a noise similar to a clogged vacuum cleaner. And all with a conspicuous absence of heat. Harry suspected that the knob was merely a placebo put there to give passengers something to do.

A few weeks after the marriage of the century in Swansea, Harry and Emma had noticed a light-brown Hillman Minx in the showroom of Ernshaw Motors while they were walking up to Elton. It looked to be around five or six years old. He liked the look of Hillmans. This one was a four-door model, with beige upholstery and a bench-type front seat. They had both agreed that it was a friendly looking car. But Harry's relatives had on occasion said some rather uncomplimentary things about Rootes-Group products, which included the Hillman, the Humber, and Sunbeam sports cars. Uncle Tom, for one, utterly despised them as overpriced junk. One person who would undoubtedly know something about this machine was Morley Singleton, so the following day Morley was cornered at lunch time.

"Actually, they're not bad cars," he said with a sniff. "One thing I don't like is the Bendix brakes on older Hillmans. They tend to seize up and then you burn your brakes out... or even worse, slide off the road into a ditch. And Rootes Group cars are expensive to repair, unless you do your own work, like I do of course."

Bendix brakes? What were Bendix Brakes?

"They're cable brakes. Quite a few British cars used them up until the early 1950's. These days most manufacturers have gone to hydraulic brakes. Much more reliable, and with hydraulic brakes you can have a backup system. When a cable snaps, poof! That's it."

Going 'poof' while on a Sunday drive wasn't an encouraging prospect.

"Would this model have Bendix brakes?" Harry asked the oracle.

Morley sucked air through his teeth and let it out slowly. "Dunno," he replied. "You haven't yet found out what year it is, but I would say if it's pre-1952, there's a fair chance it'll have cable brakes. And personally I wouldn't touch it."

On the strength of that piece of wisdom, Harry and Emma went down the following Saturday morning to Ernshaw Motors on the Bakewell Road. He had gambled that Mother might be good for the extra hundred pounds or so, if for no other reason than getting him out of the habit of using her car for all his special occasions. But even if that settled the financing issue, there still remained the road-fund licence and the insurance to buy. However, a ray of hope again presented itself: Uncle Clifford, Mother's brother, was an insurance agent so he might get a break on that item. Not to worry now, he decided. Those bridges would be crossed if and when he came to them.

"I wonder if the car will still be there?" Emma puffed, just before making the usual 'slow down' tug on his sleeve.

Harry was feeling philosophical. "If I'm meant to have it, it'll be there," he said loftily. "But I wish they would put prices on the windscreens so you'd know where you stand."

"When we went past last time I saw something tucked under one of the wipers."

"I think it was the model year, although I'm not sure. Of course, they don't want you to have too much advance information. They would rather get you into the showroom first. Sneaky devils. At least this firm has a better name than the dealership where Mother bought her car. It was called Smart and Batty. Can you imagine one fellow introducing himself as Smart, and then saying his partner is Batty. Doesn't inspire confidence, does it?"

Emma poked him in the ribs as they trotted along. "You're joking. Aren't you? You just made that up!"

Harry smiled, innocently. "No, honestly. She really did buy her car from Smart and Batty. When we go to Barnsley I'll show you the place. Actually, they were quite nice people to deal with."

It was a beautiful Saturday morning, the road bustling with motorists, but Ernshaw's could not be described as busy. In fact, apart from a man in his mid-forties whom they spotted leaning against a door at the back of the showroom, the place appeared to be deserted. For one fleeting moment Harry wondered if they were closed. However, seeing them turn off the street and into the forecourt galvanized the man into a frenzy of activity. After straightening his tie and buttoning his hounds-tooth jacket, he whipped over to the showroom entrance, waiting for them like a buzzard who has just spied its next meal.

"That's a terribly loud jacket," Emma whispered.

"Not to mention the fact that it's at least three sizes too big," Harry added. "At least he'll never get run down by a bus."

Emma wasn't sure what he meant by the last remark. She didn't ask.

"Good mornin, gentlefolks!" the man cried, leaping from the building, his large protruding teeth flashing in the summer sunlight. "I'm Ed Glumley. And 'ow are we today?"

Harry had a thing about the use of *we* when asking a question of somebody else. It smacked of indulgent paternalism. And indulgent paternalism reminded him of their family doctor who would peer down at them in their sickbeds and ask much the same question. Doctor Walker had a long thin nose stuck onto a long thin face. The whiskers that blossomed from the end of his nose would quiver excitedly as he spoke. As a child, Harry was so mesmerized by those whiskers he would often forget to be scared.

And another thing: why did used-car salesmen always seem to look like used car salesmen?

"We are well, thank you," Harry replied, trying to sound a bit older than his just-reached twenty-three years. "I'm Harry Michaels and this is my friend Emma Callingwood. We came to see about the Hillman Minx over there. Noticed it the other day as we were passing by."

"Ah, yes," Mr. Glumley said enthusiastically while walking backwards to the car. Not an easy feat but he did it on his toes in a sort of fox-trot, and he did it very well. He patted the car's roof. "She's a real beauty if I do say so myself. Well, what can I say about her?"

There was a pregnant pause while both men looked at each other to see who was going to speak next. Situations like this always presented a dilemma for car salesmen. He wasn't sure how much effort to put into this sales pitch since the hopeful car buyers standing in front of him were obviously very young. They would be lucky to have driver's licences, let alone enough money to buy a car. Still, it had been a poor month. Come to think of it, he'd had a rotten year so far. What did he have to lose? Things were so much better in the old days when he sold appliances.

"Ah, yes," Mr. Glumley said again. "Well, young man, I can tell you she's a 1956 model, which, as I'm sure you'll be aware, was a very good year for Hillmans. They changed the design in 1957. Shouldn't 'ave, if yer ask me. Not nearly as classic as this 'ere model. And luckily this one is a deluxe version—"

Which means it came with a heater already installed, Harry thought to himself.

"—Which means that it is fully equipped with such refinements as a powerful heater, cigar lighter, not one but **two** windscreen wipers, wing mirrors..." He tugged on one to prove his point. "And very clean. Very clean. Only one owner. Retired lady. Found the car too fast for her liking. Traded it for a Sunbeam Alpine, I believe."

A Sunbeam Alpine? Emma caught Mr. Glumley's logical inconsistency, although for the moment it had gone over Harry's head. How could a nimble little sports car like a Sunbeam Alpine possibly be slower than a four-door Hillman sedan? Perhaps it had something to do with Mr. Bendict's brakes, she wondered. Harry, at least, appeared to attach quite a bit of importance to them.

"'As a ten 'orsepower over'ead-valve engine," Mr. Glumley continued, "which gives more power and much better petrol consumption than the earlier side-valve engines."

"I hope so," Harry replied. "Those things couldn't pull the skin off a rice pudding. How much does it do to the gallon?"

"Oh, well..." Mr. Glumley searched in his head for a suitable figure. "Ah would say abaht thirty miles, give or take a mile or two." Then he grinned sheepishly again. "Yer 'ave ter remember that the car is six years old."

Harry peered in at the dashboard. "No radio?"

For a moment honest Ed looked as if he had been asked to perform an indecent act.

"Good lord, no. No radio. Well, stands to reason, dunnit? The G.P.O. considers a car radio to be a permanent fixture so yer 'ave to buy a licence for it. But yer don't need a licence for a portable radio so most people put one of **them** in the car instead. Nifty idea, eh?"

Harry had never considered that bit of bureaucratic nonsense. "Of course," he said weakly. "May I look under the bonnet?"

They looked at the engine, kicked the tyres, checked the upholstery, and fingered the paint work. It was indeed a clean car, with quite a bit of tread left on three of the four tyres. Harry noticed a couple of large rust bubbles on the rear-left mudguard but didn't give it much thought.

There was another silence until, remembering his conversation with Morley, Harry suddenly asked, "Does this car have Bendix brakes?"

It was clearly another question that Mr. Glumley had not anticipated. His bushy eyebrows shot up. "Er, Bendict's brakes, Bendict's brakes... Let's see. I really..." he waffled. Finally, realizing that enlightenment was not on the horizon or anywhere close to it, he decided to bare his ignorance. "Er, what exactly are Bendict's brakes, young man?"

Harry felt a brief surge of power flow through him. Getting one up on a salesman occurred about as frequently as an eclipse of the sun. "Cable brakes," he replied. "Apparently quite a few British cars used them, including Hillmans. But," he frowned knowingly at Mr. Glumley, "they're bad news. They can stick and—"

"Oh, cable brakes," Mr. Glumley quickly interrupted, "No, goodness me no. This 'ere model 'as 'ydraulic brakes, look." He dove under the still-open bonnet, pulling Harry after him. "See, there are the 'ydraulic lines and yer fluid reservoir. No, this model definitely 'as 'ydraulic brakes, although I do believe that some of the much earlier models 'ad cable brakes." His relief at successfully heading off that potential crisis would have been visible a mile away. "A fine used car," he continued, emboldened by the hydraulic-brakes triumph, "and very good value at £475."

There was another short silence. Harry swallowed hard. Mr. Glumley's price was about £175 more than he could afford. And besides, while far from being an expert on cars, he knew the price was much too high. New Hillman Minxes currently sold for about £750, depending upon optional extras. Mr. Glumley sensed that the price had not gone over too well, but he could hardly back down this soon.

"Why don't we take 'er for a spin down the road, Mr. Michaels?" he suggested, fumbling in his threadbare trousers for the ignition key.

Harry shook his head. "I really don't think I..."

"And you can drive 'er!" Mr. Glumley added grandly.

So they drove down the Bakewell Road for a few miles. The car ran very well, although Harry had noticed some blue smoke from the exhaust when the engine was started. And Mr. Glumley had been careful to leave the choke button slightly pulled out. Nevertheless, there were several things Harry liked about the Hillman Minx, including the steering column gear lever, which for some reason he always considered to be a bit 'American.'

"Runs like a top, eh?" said Mr. Glumley.

Harry nodded.

Emma, sitting in the back seat, suddenly flourished a large black boot, complete with studded sole. "Who did you say was the last owner?" she asked sweetly.

"Retired lady. Original owner," Mr. Glumley repeated without looking around.

"She must have been a very large lady to wear a size-eleven boot. And a man's boot at that. Did she perhaps do a little part-time coal mining or something?"

Harry's brow furrowed when he noticed the boot through the rear view mirror, but he said nothing. Mr. Glumley, noticeably flushed, gestured with his right hand. "What the..? Where did it come from?"

"Under your seat," Emma replied.

Not another word was said. After returning to the showroom they stood around the car like relatives at a burial. Harry kept looking at it and shuffling his feet. £475 was over his head, and in any case he was now even more convinced that, nice car though it might be, it wasn't worth that kind of money.

"Well," said Mr. Glumley, hoping they might have already forgotten about the boot, "does this beauty 'ave a buyer? It won't last long I can tell you. That is a certainty."

Harry cleared his throat. "I like the car, Mr. Glumley, even though it has a few problems, but I'm afraid it's a little too expensive for my budget."

Mr. Glumley's face clouded as he saw his commission evaporate as quickly as it had blossomed. "Ah, yes, well... Yer 'ave ter remember, these 'ere Hillmans are a quality product. Yer can't expect to get 'em fer the price of a Ford Popular. But definitely worth the investment, I can assure you. That is a certainty. A twenty-one carat certainty."

"Don't you think nearly fifty-five thousand miles is rather a lot of mileage for a six-year-old car?" Emma piped up.

"Fifty what?" Stung by Emma for the second time, Mr. Glumley was becoming decidedly rattled. After glaring at her for a few seconds and biting his sizable lower lip, he walked around the car, then for some reason spent a few seconds scrutinizing the passenger-side door handle. Why the hell hadn't Ernshaw's mechanics turned back the odometer when the car first came in, as they usually did? Trust this damned girl to spot it. Women were always a pain in the arse when it came to buying cars, nitpicking this and criticizing that.

Harry felt just as foolish. Why hadn't he thought about that? While he was inwardly stewing about the price, Emma had been quietly finding as many reasons as she could to force the price down. Who said buying cars was a man's exclusive prerogative? Mr. Glumley might be a friendly soul, but he was lying through his teeth. This car hadn't been owned by a little old lady who used it to go to church on Sundays. On the contrary, the previous owner was likely a male who wore size-eleven boots. And he probably used the car for work which, judging from the odometer reading, must have been all over England.

"That's rather a lot of mileage," Harry said, remembering the blue exhaust smoke he'd noticed earlier.

"And it certainly should affect the price," Emma added.

Mr. Glumley looked as though he would like to strangle them both. Realizing he was skewered on the horns of a dilemma, he loudly cracked his knuckles, then thrust them deep into his trouser pockets and pondered the situation. He could let this sale slip by and make sure that the odometer was turned back before anyone **else** had a look at it. Or he could go, cap in hand, to old Mr. Ernshaw's son, who was now running the business into the ground, and ask permission to reduce the price. At least he might be able to pin some of the blame on the idiot mechanic for not immediately attending to the odometer. And as the old saying went, a bird in hand is worth two in the bush. Or was it three in the bush? Maybe it was a hedge rather than a bush. Either way, he would have to settle for a reduced commission but it would be better than no commission at all.

"Yes," he said slowly, "that is rather a lot of miles. An' you are right. It could affect the price. In view of circumstances I will go an' talk to Mr. Ernshaw an' see if we can trim the price a little."

"I really think it needs to be trimmed more than a little, Mr. Glumley," Emma said in the same obsequious tone she had used to point out the boots and the odometer reading.

He nodded, and with hunched shoulders went into the building, leaving Harry with a slightly bruised ego and Emma looking around the car for more compromising evidence. This was the side of Emma that had taken a while to emerge. It had always been there, but being a typical male he just hadn't noticed. On top of a lot of innate common sense, she had an inner strength that bordered on plain stubbornness. Once a cause had identified itself as sufficiently important, she would pursue it with the same zeal and relentlessness as a tax collector. To wit: the situation at hand. Harry wanted a car. She wanted Harry to have a car. This appeared to be a decent car but it had done a lot of miles and the price was too high. Therein lay an injustice which must be redressed. She also knew perfectly well that she and Harry were being viewed as a couple of naive youngsters who didn't know one end of a car from the other. Which was largely true. Nevertheless, it irritated her. She loved Harry and wasn't going to stand idly by and see him played for a fool.

"How much do you think it's worth?" Harry asked her.

Emma laughed a little at his question and shrugged. "I don't know. But if it's got all those miles on it and there's never been anything done on the engine, you might get stuck with some repairs pretty soon. We found that out the hard way with a second-hand tractor my dad once bought. By the time he'd finished, it wound up costing him almost as much as a new one. The best thing about this car is that they slipped up and forgot to wind back the thingamajig."

"The odometer."

"Right. At least we know how far it's really been."

"Yes, we do, don't we? Nice looking car though, isn't it?"

Emma nodded. "The body looks okay, and that's what I'd look for. Seems to me you can always repair an engine or a gearbox but if the body is all rusted there's not much you can do about it."

That was something else he wished he had said.

They turned at the sound of a door opening and closing. Mr. Glumley reappeared looking a little more relaxed. "Well now, Mr. Michaels," he said, flourishing a small slip of paper, "I talked to our sales manager an' he agreed with me that the car is definitely overpriced." He forced a smile. "I reckon our appraisers didn't do their job properly. Heh, heh! Any'ow, I'm told we can let this beauty go for £375. That's a very good price for a quality Rootes product as I'm sure you'll appreciate."

"How about £350?" said Emma.

Mr. Glumley glared at her again. "Who's buying this 'ere car, you or 'im?" he snarled.

"I am, actually," Harry replied apologetically. "But she's right. £350 is just about all I can manage."

"Jesus!" said a crestfallen Mr. Glumley. "You realize that's my commission?" He looked close to tears. "And ah don't make... Jesus... That's pushin' it a bit too far, y'know."

Like two seasoned poker players, Harry and Emma didn't blink.

With Mr. Glumley desperately trying to calculate whether he would make anything at all from such a transaction, she reached out for Harry's arm as though they were about to leave. "Perhaps we should go over to Pollock's and have another look at the Morris we saw the other day, love,"

Harry looked startled. "Pollock's? What? I, er..." Then finally catching on, he hurriedly nodded agreement. "Oh, yes, yes. I think we should."

It was a bit transparent but sufficient to jolt Mr. Glumley into a decision.

"Alright," he said, forcing another smile. "Alright. £350 it is then. 'Owever, we can't offer a guarantee under these conditions, yer understand?"

"What sort of guarantee would it have been?" Harry asked, wondering if he'd just shot himself in the foot.

"Six months on the engine, gearbox, and brakes."

"Well, the car ought to hold up at least as long as that," he replied. Then hesitating for a moment, he added, "Sorry, but I can't pay for it today."

Mr. Glumley's face fell again.

"It'll be okay," Harry quickly reassured him. "It's just that I don't have all the money in my bank account at the moment."

By this time the salesman was becoming weary of the entire business. "Gettin' the rest from yer dad, are yer?" he asked sarcastically.

"From my mother, actually. And she lives in Barnsley, so I'm going to need a day or two."

"Well, I'm afraid we can't hold—"

"—A quality product like this," Emma chipped in with her cheeky smile.

They could tell Mr. Glumley didn't appreciate being teased. He glowered. "Er, yes. A quality product like this. 'Owever, a deposit would, I'm sure, do the trick."

"How about £50?"

That cheered him up a bit. "That will be acceptable, I'm sure. 'Owever, under the circumstances, bein' a much-reduced price an' all, the deposit cannot be refundable either, yer understand."

That struck Emma as being grossly unethical but this time she decided against saying anything. She'd done her bit. The ball was in Harry's court from now on.

He wrote Ernshaw's a cheque, and after the paperwork they left, both giving the car a pat on the bonnet as they passed. It grinned at them, or so it seemed, from its almost oval grille. Emma glanced back as they began to walk up the street, trying to decide whether it was a benign or a malevolent grin. Later they would both find out.

By the end of the following week Harry's mother had sent him the extra money. On her instructions Uncle Clifford arranged the insurance; Mother got stiffed for the premium. Emma lent the money to pay for the road-fund licence. So, with a little help, the sun shone on Harry and everything came together. On Saturday afternoon Emma met him in Crown Square and they went down to Ernshaw's to pick up the vehicle. The car had a large 'SOLD' sign on the dashboard. They walked around it. Harry again kicked the tyres and for the first time noted the number plate: GRA 739. Mr. Glumley was there. On this day he was true to his name. Not only glum but totally uninterested. Since his commission on the deal had hardly paid for a night out at the pub, he wasn't about to put himself to any further trouble on Harry's behalf. He scowled at Emma as they walked into the showroom.

"So Dad came up with the money, eh?"

"My mother, actually," Harry corrected him again. Mr. Glumley either had a short memory or he was just being peevish. Most likely the latter.

"We do require a certified cheque," he said with a thin smile.

"I **have** a certified cheque," Harry replied evenly.

"Oh, I see." Mr. Glumley nodded his head towards the big glass windows. "Well, it's out there, exactly where you saw it last week. After we've completed the bill of sale, it's all yours. Don't forget to attach yer new licence, assumin' yer 'ave it with yer."

"Yes, I do, Mr. Glumley," he replied again. "And don't worry, I'll put it on."

They completed the final paper work and Harry, with Emma trailing behind, hurried out to the used car lot to claim his latest acquisition. Emma ran her finger along the roof as she climbed into the passenger side. The car was covered with a fine coating of road dust.

"It's roomy, isn't it?" she said approvingly.

Harry nodded, inserted the ignition key and pulled the starter button. Nothing happened. Disbelievingly he pulled it again. And again. "Now what?" he groaned.

Emma listened to the silence. "Maybe the battery's gone flat?"

"Damn. Great start this is." He looked back at the showroom. Mr. Glumley was nowhere in sight. "I hope he hasn't sidled off. Bloody fellow's going to get this thing started whether he likes it or not." Flinging himself out of the car, he tore back into the showroom just in time to catch Mr. Glumley coming out of the lavatory. Instinctively realizing there was something wrong, he tried to duck out of a side door but wasn't quite fast enough.

"The car won't start, Mr. Glumley," Harry called out to him from the showroom entrance. "I think the battery's gone flat."

Honest Ed muttered something and with a resigned shrug went into the back room to fetch a booster battery. Half a minute later he came trundling around the corner with the equipment on a small cart. He and Emma exchanged scowls.

"Probably 'cause it's been sittin' for a while," he said without conviction. "Quite often happens. Nothin' ter worry abaht. If it 'appens again, there's a crank handle in the boot."

It didn't sound very reassuring. If the battery had been in decent shape, it shouldn't have gone flat that quickly, unless the car had been there for much longer than Mr. Glumley had been prepared to admit. He was beginning to wonder if this unassuming Hillman Minx might have a few more dark secrets than just the previous owner's identity. Still, he told himself again, it was a nice-looking car. Even more important, Emma thought it was a nice-looking car.

Mr. Glumley hooked up the booster battery and the car coughed into life. Without saying a word he slammed down the bonnet and strode back to the building, dragging the cart behind him.

"Thanks. Good-by!" Harry yelled through the car window. He ignored them.

"Nice chap," Emma said as they drove off.

"Do you still see any exhaust smoke?" Harry asked.

Emma turned, craning her neck as far as she could towards the rear window. "Nope. At least, I don't think so."

It was far from an auspicious beginning. As they drove down the road, Harry thought about his bank account, now as empty as Terry's, and all the money he owed Emma and his mother. He hoped this represented the end of the car's problems since there would be no extra money to pay for repairs for months to come. And to make matters worse, he'd traded away Ernshaw's guarantee. Emma had mentioned a few days before that Anne's boyfriend might be good for some cheap repairs if push came to shove. But since he'd earlier listened to the tale about Bruce messing up one of their tractors, this suggestion didn't offer much comfort.

It didn't take Harry long to find out that his ten-horsepower pride and joy harbored more than one or two dark secrets; it had a whole cupboard full. And they kept rattling out like noisy skeletons, usually at the most inconvenient times. Emma bore the brunt of Harry's trials and tribulations. With characteristic loyalty and optimism, she joined in the battle to keep *Useless*, as they came to nickname the car, on the road.

Initially, *Useless* performed like a docile pet, opening up a new world to explore during the remaining weeks of summer. Petrol was expensive, burdened as it was with taxes, and Emma found herself pouring more and more of her pay packet into the petrol tank. She didn't mind; it was nice to see places she had never seen before. Like many rural people of that period, she had spent practically all of her young life in and around Elton. Even going to work in Matlock had been considered a bold move.

They both loved the countryside, and the Peak District, with its windswept moors and craggy hills, proved to be wonderful walking country. The car also opened up new and interesting places to make love. Since the June fiasco and Emma's subsequent edict, they had stayed away from haylofts. In fact, it was much easier to throw a thick blanket into the back of the car and have sex in some secluded spot under the summer sun. One minor problem emerged, however, and it was something Harry never considered. Since he could now drive Emma home in the evenings, she no longer had an excuse to stay at Miss Twigg's overnight, something that hadn't gone unnoticed by her mother. However, the car obligingly broke down sufficiently often to reduce the impact of this development. Moreover, Miss Twigg went out of her way one day to tell Harry what a nice young lady Emma was, and how she enjoyed her occasional visit. Harry should have had a twinge of conscience, but he didn't.

It proved to be *Useless* which, almost single handedly, doomed Harry's rapidly deteriorating relationship with his boss. The accident could have happened to anybody, but fate conspired, as it usually does. Officially, Harry and Bill Lewis were collaborating on a large landscaping project in Buxton. It would be more correct to say that Harry was doing the work while Bill provided background noise. With wheels, Harry could make much more frequent site visits, and this was starting to pay off in the form of fewer mistakes. For the first time, he felt good about this project. He and Bill had already visited the site twice, having decided that the office was a poor place to be in fine weather.

Whenever Dickie was bored, which appeared to be often, he would waddle into the office and hurl abuse at whoever was handy. During the period Harry was with the Derbyshire County Council, he never did determine precisely how his boss spent his working hours. True, a considerable proportion was consumed by liquid lunches and much publicized scraps with the upper brass, but the rest was a mystery. His tiny office, perpetually awash in paper, cigarette butts and other rubbish, presented a picture of long hours and overwork. Closer scrutiny, however, revealed that the mess frequently remained undisturbed for weeks, an undeclared fire hazard which no one dared touch.

Mondays were patently bad days for Dickie, a dilemma he regularly solved by not showing up for work until Tuesday. Often when he did come in on Mondays he was like a bear with a sore head. So, not surprisingly, Monday mornings had become prefaced by fervent prayers for his absence.

On this particular Monday morning, however, Dickie came to work curiously mellow. It might have been the weather which, like the summer before, had turned out hot and dry. Nevertheless, his attitude caught all present by surprise and the unease could be cut with a knife. Around ten-thirty he sauntered into the draughting room, positioned himself, as he nearly always did, in the centre of the room and slowly eyed everyone in turn while the ash grew long on his cigarette.

"Well, my friend," he said to Harry, "How are you and Lewis handling the Buxton job? Haven't received any howls of rage from up in the hills... not yet at any rate... so presumably you must be doing something right." He sneered, "You've probably noticed old Lewis is a hard one to keep down. Isn't that right, Lewis?"

With his back to them, Bill quietly slipped the uncompleted football pools into his inside jacket pocket. "Sure is, Boss," he said in a very quiet voice.

Taking all this as a compliment, Harry chipped in, "The contractor will be seeding this week, so I wish we could get some rain."

Dickie's ears pricked up at the remark. "When were you up there last?" he asked.

"Last week," Harry answered.

Sneaking a look through the windows at the sun-washed east wing across the street, Dickie automatically pulled out another cigarette while simultaneously stubbing the old one into a gigantic tin lid-cum-ashtray Morley had placed for that purpose on top of the filing cabinets. Normally by five o'clock it would be overflowing and filling the air around it with the stench of stale nicotine.

"Bring your car to work?" Dickie inquired, aware that his assistant had just bought one.

"Actually, yes I did," Harry replied. Normally he wouldn't have, but over the weekend he had been gamely slapping new plaster onto Mrs. Callingwood's front-room wall. Nothing had been done since last winter, when it last fell off. The prolonged dry weather had finally stemmed the rising damp and the special moisture-resistant formula she had bought was supposed to withstand everything short of a nuclear blast. He'd managed to get the base layer on by Saturday night, and this evening he was planning on going back to finish the top coat. It had taken a lot of plaster, largely because most of it wound up on the floor. Emma had assiduously removed as much of the surplus as she could, just in case her brother noticed it. Brian, ever the critic, could find fault with anything except himself, and made sure things stayed that way by doing virtually nothing around his mother's house. Harry's motives weren't completely altruistic either. It had crossed his mind that this little repair job might be a way to improve his standing with Mrs. Callingwood. Relations between them had never been comfortable, and the hayloft incident had marked an especially low point.

"Good," said Dickie. "We'll pop up there again today and take another shufty. Grab your drawings and specs and we'll get going." He looked across to Bill's table. "Lewis, you're probably not doing anything useful. You can come along too. Don't forget your digitalis; we don't want the excitement to do you in while we're out in the wilds." It was not only an unkind remark, but probably aimed in the wrong direction. Bill looked frail but in all likelihood had more stamina than his overweight boss. He smiled his inscrutable smile, said nothing, and followed them down to the parking area.

Harry would have been glad to make this trip, but not today. Putting up with Dickie was bad enough, but a bigger problem was *Useless*. Just when Emma and he were beginning to think that it must have been a **benign** smile they saw in its grille the day he bought it, the car decided to put their uncertainty to rest. It started innocuously enough with a flat tyre outside Winster. Then the steering-column gear lever decided to part company, or so it seemed, with what it was supposed to be attached to lower down. Now, every time he got into the car, it reminded him of the Ford he had so despised. The lever still operated in a fashion, but not before he'd made a spectacle out of himself trying to get the vehicle moving.

"So, how's your new toy working?" Dickie asked after relegating Bill to the back seat and shouldering his way into the front.

"Oh, not too bad," Harry said with considerable uncertainty. "A few little problems here and there. Shouldn't be surprised, I suppose, with a car that's a few years old."

Dickie grunted. "Never did think much of Rootes products. Too expensive to get 'em fixed."

You, of all people, would know about that, Harry thought.

His two passengers sat expectantly while he thrust and parried, trying to find a forward gear. Somewhere below, the transmission sounded as though it might be digesting some bones. *Useless*, it seemed, was determined to put on a memorable show for the guests.

"Quite musical, isn't it," Dickie said dryly.

"I wouldn't use this car for any bank robberies," Bill interjected from the back seat. "You'd be halfway through your prison sentence before you got to the end of the street."

Harry smiled weakly, wiped his perspiring brow, and breathed a sigh of relief as the clutch engaged. His relief was short lived. The car bucked and stalled, obviously protesting the task of starting off in high gear. He tried again, and after another minute or two of silent cursing, *Useless* finally relented and allowed them to set off. He couldn't understand why, but once the car was in motion, shifting gears became much easier, although it couldn't resist throwing a curve once in a while. The past few days had, if nothing else, given him a better understanding of his mother's gearbox difficulties.

It was a beautiful day. They made their way up the winding A6, through Bakewell and into the low peaks. Even in mid-summer the road wasn't particularly busy. Occasionally they skirted the River Wye, reduced to little more than a trickle by the drought. Harry would have liked to relax, but he was concerned, not only about the car's deteriorating gear shift but also the tyres, one of which was becoming dangerously worn. Thankfully he didn't have to buy petrol. Emma had once again impoverished herself for the sake of mobility.

Harry liked Buxton, with its solid Georgian buildings and understated elegance. It was the Romans who first exploited mineral springs in the area, but Buxton really came into its own during the eighteenth century when the fifth Duke of Devonshire poured money into the town in an attempt to outdo Bath as a watering hole for the rich and famous. It was a timely shot in the arm. Before that, Mary Queen of Scots' well-publicized treatment there for rheumatism after languishing in the Tower was just about Buxton's only claim to fame. The Duke commissioned John Carr to build the Crescent, a long curving row of graceful homes built in Palladian style. But despite the new baths and other major works, the town failed to usurp its Somerset rival. A chagrined Duke turned his efforts to Chatsworth House, where he was much more successful. To some extent, Buxton's quest for glory was hobbled by its situation. As one of the highest spa towns in England, it required the advent of railways and steam locomotives powerful enough to climb the steep grades into the town to launch another phase of growth during the mid eighteen-hundreds. Like a well-preserved senior citizen, Buxton gradually faded from eminence as a spa centre during the early decades of this century, only to re-emerge as a tourism centre for the Peak District National Park.

By the time they arrived, Bill had become as mellow as his boss, announcing that lunch would be on him. This shocked both Harry and Dickie into a few seconds of silence. Bill was almost as tight with his money as Angus, a condition he excused on the grounds of impending retirement, rather than ethnicity. The town bustled with the usual summer holiday crowd. They made their way to Market Place, where most of the restaurants and pubs were concentrated, and Harry parked the car on Compton Street. They ate at the *Cheshire Cat*, a bow-fronted establishment full of porcelain cats. By the end of the meal, Harry had counted over two hundred and Dickie was threatening to sack him if he counted another. For some reason the boss didn't seem too enamored with Bill's choice of venue either, saying he preferred the pub two doors down. But since he wasn't paying, the decision was hardly his to make.

The County Council had recently built a new nursing home not far from the town centre on London Road. It was a nicely designed building, and the site had presented excellent landscaping opportunities. On the land which fell away sharply from the left side of the complex, Harry had designed a series of rock-fronted terraces which descended into a staff parking area. Several flowering cherry trees flanked a short driveway to the main entrance, and between the driveway and the road he had graded the land into a shallow slope. This was currently being seeded with grass and he had specified several hundred daffodils to be naturalized in the lawn when autumn arrived. All in all it looked quite impressive. Even Dickie, never much interested in the landscaping side of his section's activities, offered an appreciative nod. Bill immediately headed for a newly constructed garden seat, fashioned a sun hat out of the newspaper he'd brought with him, and proceeded to complete his football pools.

"Bloody useless," Dickie rumbled as he followed Harry over to the terraces. "I wouldn't mind, but that's all the bugger does in the office, too." He was beginning to perspire in the heat. Glaring in the direction of his senior assistant he yelled, "Don't strain yourself, Lewis!"

Bill, unflappable as ever, simply smiled and continued with what he was doing.

After spending an hour at the site, Dickie was growing restless and hinting heavily at the need for a cold pint. In the meantime Harry found that his car had been boxed in on one side by a lorry delivering office furniture, by a rock wall on the other, and by some bushes in front. The future lawn lay behind him, across from the driveway. Such little space remained on either side that he could barely open the car doors. To make things worse, the inconsiderate lorry driver had parked at an angle which gave Harry virtually no room to squeeze through. It was a situation requiring some careful backing up for several feet, then pulling forward and hard left to avoid driving over the newly seeded grass. Dickie, fully aware that Harry's dilemma could have serious implications for getting out of the heat and into a drink, quickly abandoned his verbal attack on Bill and hurried over.

"Back up, Harry. I'll guide you out," he commanded, perspiration trickling down his red face and his stomach hanging over his trousers. "And make it snappy."

But *Useless* was once more in no hurry to go anywhere. Harry fought with the gear shift while the engine roared impotently. Through the rear-view mirror he could see Dickie glaring at him. Finally he succeeded in finding reverse and carefully inched the car back. After a few feet a flabby hand signaled for Harry to stop and begin moving forward to his left. After that, apparently feeling his task was completed, Dickie allowed his gaze to focus on two attractive young women who had come out of the building for their tea break. One of them saw him and gave a cheerful wave. From behind the cloud of cigarette smoke he broke into a sly grin and waved back.

Meanwhile, after the success of finding reverse, Harry was trying to find a forward gear. After a few seconds the lever seemed to tighten in the spot where first gear normally was, and he confidently pushed it up and let out the clutch. But instead of moving forward, *Useless* shot backwards again. Slamming his foot on the brake he glanced through the mirror in time to see Dickie's cigarette pop out of his face like a bullet. Both hands went to his head and then to the car's boot lid. Harry could see that he was very excited and yelling something, but he couldn't make out what until the engine had declined to idling speed.

"My foot! My fuckin' foot!" Dickie cried with great anguish. "Get the bloody car off, for Chrissakes!"

Harry leapt out of the car to find that, just as Dickie had indicated, the rear-left wheel was sitting squarely on his right foot. And in that split second he knew that his career with the Landscape and Playing Fields section, if he'd ever had one to begin with, was doomed.

"Never mind coming for a look, you moron," Dickie gasped, "Move the fuckin' car out of the way!"

Hearing the commotion, Bill came trotting down the path to find Harry frantically trying to get the car into a forward gear. It was to no avail; *Useless* wasn't about to miss out on a golden opportunity like this. The gear lever crunched and the engine continued to roar in vain.

"For Chrissakes, Lewis, do something. Get the goddamn car off! The stupid bugger's maimed me."

Harry gave up on the gears, scrambled out of the car again, and with Bill's help pushed the car forward. Outlined across Dickie's squashed shoe was a clear, dusty tyre imprint. Once free, he crumpled like a pricked balloon, but before he hit the ground they managed to push their shoulders under his arms and then half-lift, half-drag him up to where Bill had been sitting moments before. While they struggled, the air crackled with invective. Dickie's face, contorted by pain, had turned a pasty white.

"Get his shoe off," said Bill calmly. "Let's see what the damage looks like."

"I'll tell you what the damage looks like, Lewis. He's broken every bone in my fuckin' foot," Dickie hissed. "That's what the damage looks like."

Trembling violently, Harry removed the shoelace. Between them they gently eased off both shoe and sock with Dickie moaning and cursing even louder. He knew that if his boss decided to attack him then, there was little Bill could do about it. His only hope lay in the fact that he could now run much faster.

The torrent of bad language had attracted the attention of the two girls who had unwittingly got him into this mess. They walked over and stood with Harry and Bill in a semi-circle, watching the mangled foot swell to the size and colour of a small beetroot. The lorry driver also briefly joined them.

"Instead of standing around with your fingers up your bums," he snarled, "Perhaps you'd be so good as to load me into that piece of crap down there and get me to the hospital."

One of the girls parked her chewing gum somewhere inside her mouth and asked, "Does it hurt?"

Dickie, stifling an urge to kick her with his good foot, let out another sarcastic hiss. "Does it hurt, dearie? 'Course not. I let a car run over my bloody foot every day just to break up the arthritis. Why don't you go down there and let this silly twit run over **your** foot and see if it hurts. Christ almighty. I'm surrounded by imbeciles."

Reeling from the verbal assault, the girls hastily retreated. The lorry driver shrugged, adjusted his cap, and wandered back into the building.

"It hurts, it hurts," Dickie kept repeating.

"I'm sure it does, Boss," Bill replied, attempting to calm the situation. "But at least I don't see any bones sticking out."

It was the wrong thing to say. Almost anything would have been the wrong thing to say. Dickie glared balefully at his senior draughtsman. "The reason you don't see any bones sticking out, you senile old fart, is because they're all broken into little fuckin' bits,"

"You don't think either of those two girls were nurses, do you?" Harry asked, his voice practically hoarse with fear. "This place is a nursing home after all."

"Nurses? Nurses? Ha! That pair of airheads couldn't turn off the lights without a book of instructions," Dickie retorted.

"Wouldn't help if they were, the place isn't operational yet," Bill said. "We'll have to take you down to the hospital out-patients, Bob."

"Great news. First bit of fuckin' common sense I've heard so far. You've won a coconut, Lewis! Hospital. That's what I just said. And what's more, if Harry's pile of junk doesn't work, you two can bloody well carry me there."

With that unpleasant prospect in mind, Harry shot off to wrestle with the car again. This time, however, *Useless* appeared to have either tired or relented because it allowed him to find reverse in only two tries and forward in three. He drove a little closer to where Dickie and Bill were huddled. The afternoon sun shone down relentlessly. By the time they had maneuvered Dickie into the back seat, all three men were soaked in perspiration. Bill had a rough idea where the hospital was and guided Harry through the traffic with their casualty maintaining a constant babble of self pity behind them. After dropping him off, they went for a walk in the hospital grounds, read everything there was to read in the waiting room, chatted with an ambulance driver and were beginning to wonder what else they could do with their time. Finally, after three hours, Dickie emerged from the out patient's ward on crutches, clutching a small bag containing his shoe and sock, and his damaged foot buried inside a plaster cast. A stern-looking, middle-aged nurse helped him through the door.

"Well, doesn't this look bloody wonderful?" he said, thumping across the floor.

Spotting Bill and Harry, the nurse began, "Your friend has—"

"I'm not their friend," Dickie interrupted, "I'm their bloody supervisor. And the nitwit with the pimples is the one who ran over my foot."

"Your bloody supervisor... I mean, your supervisor," she resumed, "has a couple of broken bones and a fracture. He tells me you will be returning to Matlock by car. We've just given him a painkiller to make him more comfortable. And it would be helpful if he could keep his leg elevated as much as possible. The crutches can be adjusted if they don't suit him." She turned to Dickie. "See your doctor in about a week and don't forget to take the rest of the painkillers. One every four hours for the next three or four days."

"My assistant here is the one who's going to need the painkillers when I'm through with him," Dickie retorted as he pushed past them. "I'm going to elevate my leg up his arse."

It quickly became evident that the boss wasn't going to be docile patient.

"Jesus, I'm going to die in this damned heat," he complained as they once again bundled him into the back seat. "And where the hell am I going to put my bloody foot?"

Harry was tempted to tell him but had a sudden inspiration. "Why don't you stick it through the window?" he suggested.

For a moment Dickie thought he was being facetious and was about to launch into another tirade when he realized it might not be such a bad idea. With Emma's car blanket rolled into a pillow to raise his head and his left leg on the floor, they were able to rest the cast on the right-rear window so that a few inches stuck out.

"Only problem," Bill said, eyeing their handiwork, "is that his toe ends are exposed. It's a warm day but when we get on the road his foot could get a bit chilly."

"That's okay," said Harry, "we'll just pull his sock over the end. It should stretch enough."

It did. The painkiller also did a remarkably good job. They drove back to Matlock with a large, white foot protruding at a jaunty angle from the side of the car and an uncommonly subdued Dickie at the other end of it. Apart from some startled looks from passing motorists the rest of the trip was uneventful. By the time they reached Dickie's house it was nearly seven o'clock. Harry hadn't been there since the Duffield incident before Christmas. Like before, it spoke of care, the lawn cut and trimmed, flower beds now overflowing with a summer bounty of colourful petunias. Even the gate had been repainted.

The mystery was quickly resolved by Joyce. Armed with gardening gloves and a hand fork, she rose from behind some bushes and ran to meet them. Since her husband hadn't appeared for dinner, she was expecting to see him polluted again.

"My God, Bob!" she cried as Dickie, flanked by his two assistants, hobbled up the path. "What on earth have you done this time?"

The ferret eyes glared at her, then at Harry. "My pointy-headed assistant here ran over my foot."

"He did what?"

"I said he ran over my fuckin' foot."

The concern on Joyce's face suddenly cracked into a smile that seemed to spread across her entire face. "He ran over your foot? Ha, ha, ha!"

"It's not very funny, Joyce."

"Ha, ha, ha!" cried Joyce. And she laughed until tears began to roll down her cheeks. Harry had never seen her laugh before. Even Bill could remember only a handful of occasions in the past ten years.

"I'm sorry, Mrs. Dickie," Harry apologized, "My car's been giving me some trouble."

"So you ran over Bob's foot to get even! Ha, ha, ha!"

"Well, not exactly. I accidentally backed up over it."

"You backed up over it! Oh my God! It's a pity he wasn't lying down; you could have run over his head! Ha, ha, ha!"

Without saying another word, Dickie pushed them aside and stomped into the house, leaving Joyce wiping her nose and trying to gather enough composure to say good-by.

"You missed your bus, Bill," Harry said as they closed the garden gate .

Bill chuckled. "Yeh. But it was worth it!"

For a couple of weeks Harry basked in the admiration of his colleagues, who all agreed that a broken foot couldn't have happened to a nicer fellow than Dickie. It was two days before the boss came back to work, still on crutches and with a face as black as thunder. He never quite forgave his youngest assistant for that humiliating experience, knowing full well that his staff were all having a good laugh at his expense.

Unfortunately, Harry's celebrity status didn't compensate for the price he paid in the office. Suddenly he found himself excluded from the occasional lunch time sessions with Dickie and Terry, and sometimes Bill, at the *Hanging Gate*. And he also started getting into hot water for slip-ups which before would have warranted little more than a comment. Dickie began to drive him harder, which in itself wasn't such a bad thing since Harry had a predilection for indolence. But the sneering and abrasiveness made coming to work less and less enjoyable. Terry, who had initially viewed Harry as a potential threat to his hopes for pre-eminence in the department, reveled in this latest disaster and hardly bothered to hide the fact. From then on, each morning Harry trudged up Bank Road he felt the next hill starting to beckon more visibly than ever.

TEN

Well Dressings and Sunday Outings

"I'd like to take you to a well-dressing," Emma announced one day as they were sitting in the chemist shop stock room during lunch.

Albeit at some cost, Harry's car had completely revitalized weekends during those balmy days of summer. They especially loved poking around places off the bus routes and beyond walking distance. Shortly after the disastrous Buxton trip, Harry was forced to get the gear lever fixed. It cost him more than a week's wages, which meant that the burden of keeping the car on the road fell even more heavily on Emma's shoulders while Harry's finances recovered. The Hillman couldn't be fairly described as a lemon, yet. Rather, they both decided, it was simply possessed by gremlins. Every so often the gremlins would pop out of their hiding place somewhere inside the car's bowels and have some fun. And they always knew when to do it.

No sooner had the gear lever been repaired than *Useless* was at it again. This time it was a front brake pad which squealed and occasionally grabbed. And to keep it company, the battery was now proving that its lack of energy on the day he bought the car was not just a fit of contrariness. It got to the point where hardly a day went by that Harry didn't have to dive into the boot for the cranking handle. After a while they simply left it on the floor behind the front seats.

"What's a well-dressing?" Harry asked, between mouthfuls of Emma's cucumber sandwich.

"They dress up a well and dance around it. People do a lot of funny things in those small villages," said Mrs. Johnson, who had overheard the question. "Things'll change when they get television."

Emma made a face. "You've never been to one, Mrs. J., have you?"

"I've got better things to do!"

"A lot of the villages around our area have well-dressings," Emma continued. "Mrs. J's partly right, even though she's being a silly bugger! They dress up the well with flowers and the minister comes and blesses it, and they usually have a choir to sing special songs. It's very interesting. Most of them seem to be in spring or early summer. Elton's never had a well dressing but Youlgreave, near us, and Tideswell both have one. I think they're both in June. And I'm fairly sure a few villages have them in August and September. I'll talk to Mum. She'll know which ones haven't been held yet this year."

It turned out that there were five or six well-dressings during August, and a couple in September. One was at Hartington, close by the River Dove, some six miles west of Elton; and the other at Wormsley, roughly the same distance on the way to Stanton-in-Peak. Wormsley was a much smaller village and more isolated than Hartington, lying on the eastern slope of the low peaks. Mrs.

Callingwood proudly informed Emma that as a young girl she had taken part in the annual well-dressing at Stoney Middleton, where she grew up. She remembered the pretty yellow dress her own mother had sewn for her, and the elaborate daisy chain she wore in her hair. In those days, functions such as these were very much local affairs. Few people outside the village attended them, unless they were relatives, but that was changing rapidly.

Well-dressing appears to be a long-standing Derbyshire custom, dating back to at least the fourteenth century and quite possibly earlier, its purpose still debated. While many scholars believe the ritual may be rooted in early Christianity, a few have suggested pagan origins. Tissington has one of the oldest well-dressing ceremonies. It began in 1350 when the village apparently escaped the Black Death because of the purity of its well water. But again, historians point out that Tissington locals were already dressing their well long before this date. Deliverance from the plague, they assert, was merely taken as added justification for holding the ceremony. It is very likely that well-dressing began as a pagan ritual to ensure a plentiful supply of water for the village and later Christianized.

Water, or more specifically the lack of it, has always been a more pernicious problem than infectious epidemics. During the past millennia many areas of Derbyshire have been bedeviled by periodic droughts. In 1615, the Youlgreave area had no rain between March and the end of May, and local wells dried up. By way of contrast, Tissington, where the well-dressing ceremony was firmly established, continued to produce an abundant supply of water from its well. This must not have gone unnoticed. Shortly afterwards, Youlgreave began its own well-dressing ceremony and many others followed suit. Traditionally the ceremony was held on or around Ascension Day. Currently the well-dressing season runs from spring until autumn. Emma learned that Wormsley's was held the first Sunday in September, which that year fell on September 4th, the following weekend. According to Mrs. Callingwood, who knew all things pertaining to local customs, it kicked off at ten in the morning.

On Saturday, Harry and Emma went shopping. And although barely able to afford it, he bought her a dress for the occasion. It was white and yellow, with a full tulle skirt, and they only realized afterwards that it must be very similar to the dress that her grandmother had made for her mother. Emma bought herself a pair of white cotton gloves, white high-heeled shoes and a white handbag to go with the dress. Then they went back to Miss Twigg's so she could try them all on. Lately, Emma had occasionally been having dinner on weekends at Harry's digs. Miss Twigg was always delighted to see her, and the few shillings extra she charged Harry for the meals could hardly have covered their cost. Had she known what they did upstairs in Harry's bedroom, there might have been less enthusiasm. The little piece of frosted glass in his bedroom door fell out most often when they were in bed together, and that invariably coincided with Sarah's presence somewhere close by. It was hard to avoid putting two and two together. Would Sarah be able to keep such titillating information to herself? Possibly, but unlikely. After a while they stopped worrying about it. If Sarah wanted to undulge in a little voyeurism, there wasn't much he could do about it unless Miss Twigg had the door repaired.

She was busily flapping a duster about the dining room when they entered. Her face creased into a welcoming smile.

"Well, now," she said, noticing the shopping bags, "been spending a little hard-earned money, have we? You might as well. The government will be taking every penny we have before too long, I shouldn't think. Taxes, that's all we see these days. Spend your money before they can get their hands on it, that's what I say."

It didn't seem to have occurred to her in the spur of the moment that the government had already got their hands on it. They were spending the bit that was left.

"New dress," Emma said. "Harry's treat."

"My goodness now, what's the occasion?" Miss Twigg asked, wondering whether they might be heading for the registry office sometime soon.

"I'm taking Harry to a well-dressing this Sunday."

"A well-dressing, indeed! Where?"

"Wormsley."

Her brow furrowed. "Wormsley? I didn't know they had one."

"It's not a very big one, but it looks like the weather might be nice for it," Emma replied.

Miss Twigg pushed the dusting cloth into her apron pocket, parked her bulk on one of the dining room chairs, and looked up at the ceiling. "I can't remember when I last went to a well dressing... or where, for that matter," she said, smiling to herself. "I must have been a little girl. But they're pretty things. Very pretty things."

"I told Emma she could use my room to try the dress on," Harry said, nonchalantly.

"By all means, by all means. Let me have a peek at it before you leave." She watched them go upstairs with a trace of the smile still lingering.

"Mum says the well dressings are becoming too commercial," Emma said as she peeled off her clothes to try on the new ensemble.

Harry sat on the bed, watching. Emma didn't mind; other than their local doctor, Harry was the first man she had ever taken off her clothes for. A shaft of late afternoon sun flooded through Harry's bedroom window, creating a pool of golden light where Emma was doing her striptease. After putting on the new dress and shoes, she went to admire herself in the wardrobe mirror. Apart from the tulle skirt, which was a little too large at the waist, everything fitted perfectly, the colours in the dress contrasting beautifully with her auburn hair. It was times such as these that served to remind him how lucky he had been to find someone like Emma.

"I've never been to Wormsley, have I?" he asked.

Emma shook her head.

"I really can't imagine something like a well-dressing in a God-forsaken moorland village ever becoming commercialized," he said, still eyeing her figure. "Most of the world doesn't even know where Wormsley is. For that matter, I suspect a few people in Wormsley don't know where Wormsley is! Those villages aren't the most dynamic places I've ever seen."

"More goes on in our villages than you'd imagine," Emma said with a grin. She gave herself one last lookover in the mirror. "Not bad. Mum can put a tuck in the skirt."

"Seems to me the most active place in most of them is the graveyard," Harry continued. "At least there, people are dying to get in!"

"Har, har, har!"

"Seriously, though, doesn't it ever bother your mother that she's spent practically all her life in Elton? It would drive me bananas."

Emma looked slightly affronted. "She didn't spend **all** her life in Elton. She was born in Stoney Middleton."

"Which must be nearly as big as Elton!"

"I'm not sure. But at least it was somewhere else."

"At least five miles away."

"Everybody has to live somewhere, love." It wouldn't be the last time she said that.

"We have an hour before dinner time," Harry said, changing the topic to one closer to his heart— or more correctly, an area south of his heart. "We could work up an appetite."

"Sorry," Emma replied cheekily, "I've gone off you!" She proceeded to remove her new clothing, carefully packing it back in the boxes.

"You'd better be kidding."

She stood in front of him, wearing only her underclothes and nylons, the trace of an enticing smile flickering across her face. "Seriously. I've decided we should only have sex once a month, and you've already used up your quota for this month and the next six!"

Without saying anything, Harry grabbed her hand and pulled her on top of him. They wrestled wildly among the bedclothes as each tried to remove the other's clothing. Giggling, she pounded him with one of the pillows while giving him just enough leeway to do what he wanted to do.

"You rip my nylons, Robin Harry Michaels, and you'll have to buy me some more!" she said.

"Shh," Harry cautioned, "This floor isn't very soundproof. I don't want Miss Twigg up here."

"Why, do you think she might want to jump on your bones?"

"Oh God, I hope not!"

"I don't know, getting humped by one's landlady is quite fashionable!"

Harry shuddered. "Not by this landlady it isn't."

He took Emma home that night, and the following morning drove back to Elton. They had a leisurely breakfast at the farm, but not before being reminded by Mrs. Callingwood that she had been up since 4.30 AM to milk the cows. Harry had lost count of the number of times she had made that point. She was an odd woman. For all her gruffness, she had a quiet generosity which seemed to embarrass her. Frequently she would invite Harry for a meal. Several times she had washed his clothes and sewn on missing buttons. And inevitably these gestures were rejoined by some cynical comment, as though she might be trying to hide the weakness she had just shown. Emma repeatedly assured him that there was nothing personal in her attitude, and he had begun to believe her. In fact, he had come to the conclusion that Mrs. Callingwood's behavior reflected bitterness more than resentment. Bitterness at the poor hand life had dealt her despite years of hard work and thrift. Her husband's untimely death seemed to have been the final blow, robbing her of what little retirement pleasure they might have reaped. Now, to make matters worse, her son's incompetence was threatening to destroy the farm that she and her husband had sacrificed so much to build.

Harry offered to take her to the well-dressing. Typically, she declined with a short laugh, saying that farmers were the only people who had to work seven days a week. But to his surprise, this time she thanked him for the offer.

It was a beautiful day, mostly blue sky with a few tufts of cottony cloud pushed across the skyline by a slight breeze. Considering the weather, Harry thought, this might be an appropriate year for well-dressings. It had rained very little in that part of the Peak District during the previous two months, and there hadn't been much even before that. Local farmers were complaining about their pastures drying out. Conversely, it had been a good year for hay; the air was full of its sweet smell. Most fields were yielding their second hay crop, much of it lying freshly cut and waiting to be turned. Among the odd farms growing corn crops, few were able to harvest anything of value. Most of the corn had matured prematurely, and now it sat, dry and withered on stunted stalks, waiting to be plowed under.

The only potential blemish on Harry's horizon that day was his car. After playing with *Useless*'s front brake, the gremlins had gone into the car's clutch, which now seemed to be slipping. A few days before, it had made some unsettling noises, accompanied by a lack of power as he drove up Bank Road. And that morning, coming up the hill into Winster, the performance had repeated itself. Like most of the car's ailments, they came and went sporadically, adding further weight to their theory that *Useless* was possessed.

Possessed or not, it held the upper hand since no garages were open on a Sunday. And even if they had been, he had no money for repairs until the end of the month, having just spent half of his August pay cheque on other repairs. Crossing his fingers, he hoped that, for a change, Murphy's Law wouldn't prevail. To his considerable relief it got them to Wormsley without any more fuss.

"Well?" Emma asked in the car as they made their way up the B5056 and then headed north east along a series of narrow country lanes towards Stanton-in-Peak.

"Well, what?"

"Do I look alright?"

Harry could truthfully say he hadn't seen her look any better. There was something about golden summer days that worked wonders for Emma. She seemed to absorb the sun and radiate it out, despite the fact that she never suntanned.

"I was going to wear one of Mum's hats," she said. "She has a couple of wide-brimmed straw things with yellow ribbon. Thought it might keep the sun off but it made me look like a dwarf! So I decided against it."

"Oh," replied Harry, unable to contribute much to the decision since he hadn't seen her in it. The hat probably didn't make her look like a dwarf, but at the same time it would have been a shame to cover up her hair.

Out of the corner of his eye he noticed her studying him. Her eyes tracked slowly up his slacks, rather worn and scuffed at the pockets, to the checkered shirt his mother had bought him years ago, to the sports jacket that, despite being dry-cleaned after the hayloft fiasco, had definitely seen better days.

"I was thinking," she continued, "You need some new clothes, love. Some casual stuff. I know you don't like jeans but a pair of slacks and shoes would make a good start. All you have now are the clothes you wear to work, and they're getting a bit moth-eaten. Next time we go to Sheffield I'll be your fashion coordinator and we'll see what Austin Reed have in stock."

Harry couldn't really argue. His boarding-school years had ended six years ago, but he still hadn't got used to buying clothes for himself. Currently his impoverished wardrobe consisted of two pairs of trousers, two sports jackets, two pairs of shoes, three sweaters and a raincoat, and all, except the raincoat and the slacks Miss Hamsterly had sent him, in the final stages of usefulness.

"Trouble is, I'm such a funny shape," he replied, while carefully negotiating the car around a small flock of sheep being transferred to a new pasture. "All legs and arms. I can never get slacks to fit me, and looking for shirts and jackets is a bloody nightmare."

Emma grinned. "I don't think there is anything wrong with your legs. They fit quite well on me! But you're right about the arms. They **are** too long and I've noticed they get into places where they don't belong!"

Harry's skinny arms never ceased to amaze her, particularly when they were in bed together. Sometimes they felt like octopus tentacles, snaking with effortless ease down her back and between her legs. And on the ends were the coldest hands she'd ever known. Still, how did the old saying go, 'cold hands and a warm heart?'

Like most small villages, Wormsley had several wells, most of them long-since sealed up by the local health authorities. The well-dressing ceremony continued to be performed at the oldest, which stood in a small square formed by a bend in the street. Behind it sat Wormsley church, a solid mass of stone built in typically English-Protestant style. Harry noted that they had located the cemetery at a safe distance from the well, on lower ground at the other side of the church. He'd developed a passive concern for graveyards after visiting some distant relatives with his mother several years ago. The Reverend Everall was vicar of a small parish just outside Harrogate. At the time of their visit, workmen were crawling about in the vicarage cellar, vainly trying to block the incursion of foul-smelling sewage. Floorboards in a main-floor lavatory had been ripped up, leaving the toilet suspended by its plumbing. Looking at it, poised uncertainly over the black void, the thing reminded him of a Ronald-Searle cartoon. Mrs. Everall, the quintessential clergyman's wife, stoically explained that for some inexplicable reason the house, built early in the last century, had been located down-slope from the cemetery, with obvious consequences. But, despite the stench, she and her husband looked remarkably healthy.

Wormsley's surviving well was kept in working order even though it now seldom saw anything but ceremonial use. One or two locals let their dray horses drink from a pump and trough that had been installed. And when the village formed its first volunteer fire brigade in the early eighteen hundreds, the hall was shrewdly built close by.

"Let's leave the car here," Emma said, as they rounded a corner into Wormsley's main street. "Then, if it gets busy we won't have to wait for everybody to leave."

Harry raised an eyebrow. "**That** busy? This place? I doubt it's going to come anywhere close to the Changing of the Guard."

"Well," she replied with a hint of defensiveness in her voice, "it doesn't take too many people to clog up these little streets. Anyway, the view's nice from here."

"I suppose. Where's the well?"

"Just down this street and round the corner."

He looked at the new watch Emma had given him for his birthday in July. "We're a bit early. There's at least ten minutes to kick-off."

She laughed. "I don't think the time's too important. They never start on time, and even if they do somebody's late and messes everything up!"

After parking the car on a grassy verge, they both sat on the bonnet and admired the view. He could see the river not far off below, casually winding its way from its confluence with the Wye to the north, down through Matlock and into Derby. Everywhere was strewn with boulders, as though some giant had been playing a crude game of marbles. Between the rocks, uneven swaths of parched grass dotted with cornflowers shimmered in the early morning sunshine. And as always, there was the wind, reduced on this sunny day to a murmur but still there, reminding everyone that it would be back in force in a few months time.

Peak-District villages have a dominant characteristic similar to many in Harry's native west Yorkshire: they seem to huddle, like a frightened child cowering from the blows of a teacher's cane. In the shelter of a low hill, a copse of trees, or anything which might afford some protection from the incessant wind, the buildings were usually aligned so that they turned their weathered limestone backs to the north west. Wormsley village, not much more than some smallholdings, two strips of row houses, a few cottages, a pub, several shops and the fire hall and church, was no different. It crouched halfway up a shallow vale that follows a bumpy course down to the River Derwent. Out in the fields, those ubiquitous stone walls sprouted from the dry ground, interrupted here and there by a wooden gate.

After a few minutes they started to walk. On the opposite side of the narrow road, they came upon half a dozen pigs shuffling about inside a stone-walled compound that might at one time have been a building. Part of the side facing the road had fallen down, leaving the pigs just enough room to survey the outside world, which a couple were doing as Harry and Emma walked over. The cottage next to the pigsty appeared to be in a similar state of disrepair, its roof sagging, as most did, under the weight of the huge stone roof tiles. Someone had made a half-hearted attempt to patch over loosened stones at the gable end, but chunks of cement were now coming off. The building's only saving grace was a massive yellow rambler rose, still producing blooms, that smothered the front door and an adjacent window. Harry leaned over the ramshackle gate to get a closer look at it. Such extravagances were rare in these bleak moorland places, with most cottage gardens being given over to the much more utilitarian purpose of growing food. In this village, even that seemed to be done with little enthusiasm.

The village was quiet, all the shops closed and the pub not yet open. A woman with two small children and a baby in a pram were making their way in the direction of the ceremony. Stuffing the car keys into his pocket, Harry grabbed Emma's hand and they followed the woman. Quickly they joined up with several other people heading in the same direction at the same leisurely pace. As they walked, an elderly man leading a Clydesdale passed them in the opposite direction. Dressed in a grubby, collarless shirt with the sleeves rolled up and his waistcoat unbuttoned, he might have come off a postcard. In the customary fashion of working-class country folk he gave a perfunctory tug at his cap. Somewhere, a solitary church bell clanked out its call to attendance.

"Why do church bells in this area always sound so flat?" Harry asked while sidestepping a large pile of dog droppings.

Emma thought about that for a moment. Since she'd never really listened to a wide variety of church bells, she couldn't tell whether these were flat or not. "They all sound the same to me. Are they not so flat in Yorkshire?"

"I'm not sure," he replied. "But around here they always go 'clank' instead of 'bong', as though they had a crack in them. Odd."

She gave him a long look. "This wouldn't be a bit more of the old 'Yorkshire's-bigger-and-better' rhetoric, I suppose?"

"No, really! They do sound different."

Giving him a dig in the ribs, Emma took his hand again and they walked past the double row of houses he'd seen from the car. Most hadn't been painted for years. Net-curtained windows gazed out, silent but not unseeing, at their counterparts on the other side of the street. To Harry they epitomized the stuffy inevitability of English parochial life—pleasant but narrow-minded as the edge of a ruler. And try as he might, he couldn't see himself settling down to this kind of existence. He loved Emma, or at least he thought he did. But if he married her it was doubtful whether she would want to move very far away from home. The thought of ending up in one of those houses amidst a legion of prying neighbours triggered a rush of claustrophobia. Nearly everyone who lived here, he reckoned, must have been born in the village. And like Emma's family, most would spend the rest of their days in the same place.

There had to be more to life than that. His mind turned to a recent *Sunday-Telegraph* advertisement inviting applications for government jobs in New Zealand. Not that he'd been specifically looking; the ad more or less jumped out at him. New Zealand was half-way around the world, although that aspect hardly triggered a thought. Since his school days, distance had never intimidated him. For eight long years, lonely and socially isolated, he might as well have been on the back side of the moon. He could tell people a few things about distance. And loneliness. And how he had learned to live with both by turning them into an asset. No. Distance wasn't relevant. What **did** matter was being somewhere else.

"You'd never know anyone lived here," he muttered, "So far I haven't seen a soul in any of those windows."

"How often does your mum use **her** front room?" Emma asked. "Everybody around here spends most of their time in the back, in the kitchen where there's a fire. It's warmer, in case you hadn't noticed!"

At the back of the square, immediately in front of a curved stone wall topped by some iron railings was the well. A three-sided wooden screen, battered from many years of the same use, had been erected around an ornate, cast-iron pump, by the looks of it freshly painted, that sprouted from the flagstones. Its long handle had a white ribbon tied on the end. In front sat a large stone slab hollowed out into a shallow tray, deep enough to hold a few inches of water, with a spillway at one end. As Emma's mother had assured him, the pump looked to be in good working order. But all the same, Harry felt cheated. He had imagined all village wells to be similar to those depicted in children's books, complete with a wooden bucket and a cute little roof. This one had no roof, no bucket. Not even a low wall around it to sit on and toss pennies. A vertical frame, roughly five feet square and filled with moist clay, was nailed to the centre of the middle screen. Someone had carefully pushed marigolds, one or two other annual flowers, some leaves and bits of terra-cotta into the clay to create a picture depicting the head of Christ, complete with a startlingly yellow halo. Above it was inscribed part of a New Testament quotation from the Book of John:

He Who Drinks of the Water that I Will Give Him Shall Never Thirst.

Bright green vinery, which upon closer inspection proved to be made of plastic, wound through the trellis. Overall, for a small village with limited resources, the set was colourful and the artwork surprisingly well done. Harry wondered aloud who had done it.

"Mum says it's a retired lady who used to be a schoolteacher at Darley Bridge. Apparently she's done it for years," Emma said.

By the time they reached the square, about thirty people were already milling about, with a few others still straggling along. Most were older, and obviously local. Four elderly men stood in a tight group, earnestly debating some topic. All wore weather-beaten flat caps that looked to be made of the same cloth. Harry spotted one very attractive girl, who was standing with someone he assumed to be her mother. She noticed him, smiling slightly before lowering her head. Emma scowled at them both. The woman with the baby and two small children began to dispense pop and some biscuits from the pram. Her two children eagerly gathered around while the baby peered suspiciously from beneath a large gingham bonnet. Harry smiled. It brought back recollections of childhood walks with his sister and mother and the doll pram to the fish-and-chip shop. The long walks had been his mother's way of coping with their father's death. Whenever Harry and Liz came home from boarding school for holidays they would walk for miles, down into Stainborough and up into the tiny village of Hood Green, with salt and vinegar and a moistened face cloth tucked into the pram's false bottom. After picking up their food, they would continue on, eating as they walked. Those had seemed such halcyon days; he would never know the anguish his mother bravely concealed from them.

He glanced again at his watch. It was a quarter past ten. Emma was right, these things did start late. But no sooner had he come to that conclusion than a flurry of activity drew his attention to a narrow lane behind the square. A party of adults and some children of various ages came trotting through, headed by the minister in full regalia. Judging from their appearance, part of the gaggle following him were elements of the church choir. All twelve were males, of which only about two-thirds, mostly the older members, were wearing cassocks. Decked out in freshly pressed short trousers the younger choirboys looked uncomfortably tidy, although Emma noted with some amusement that one of them had spilled something down the front, and with an inadequately small hand was trying to hide the stain from his mother.

The minister was a tall, middle-aged, drooping man with wispy, sandy hair and features that vaguely resembled Morley Singleton. He looked anything but enthusiastic about the task at hand, mired as he was in a summer cold. His thin nose, reddened by a succession of soggy handkerchiefs, continued to drip unabated. Finally, like a flock of disoriented sheep, the choir got themselves lined up on one side of the screen while the minister fumbled within his robes for a pair of horn-rimmed glasses.

"That's Reverend Clomper," Emma whispered.

Harry could barely stifle a laugh. "Clomper!" he exclaimed. "You're kidding! Who could possibly have a name like that?"

"Shush," said Emma, noticing a few turned heads. "He comes to our church once in a while. Our own minister left a couple of years ago and they never got a replacement. Pity. He was cute!"

One didn't need to be a local to see that many in the audience were related to those in the choir. Several mothers could be heard whispering loudly to their young offspring to stand up straight, get to the right pages, and stop picking their noses. Two cherubic little boys started a shoving match, whereupon one of the boys' mother leapt out from the audience and soundly boxed his ears. While he stood sobbing and holding his head, the other boy began to pick a fight with someone else. A couple of the older choir members attempted to ride herd on their younger colleagues. One of them, a man in his mid-forties, who happened to be wearing a cassock, could be seen wagging a finger in all directions, to very little avail.

"I think they ought to get going before a punch-up breaks out," Harry said with barely concealed amusement.

"Hush," said Emma again. "They're all doing their best."

They evidently were. To Harry's surprise, the ceremony went remarkably well once it got going. Even more surprising was the choir's performance. Their voices, *a cappella*, and sharpened by youthful exuberance, reverberated against the barren stone walls and drifted up into the summer sky. A few daring souls joined in, including one older woman whose off-key enthusiasm pierced the harmony like an air raid siren. The Reverend Clomper put on a brave show, each time waiting patiently for the choir to finish before attending to his nose. Then a young girl of about twelve stepped out of the audience with a bouquet of flowers, placing them with exaggerated carefulness in front of the pump.

"Try ter make 'em sit up," her mother commanded from within a knot of people at the front.

With her bottom in the air, she fussed with the flowers while muttering something in reply. Her white dress, tied behind with a large bow, wiggled in semaphore fashion as she moved. The clergyman, blinking owlishly over his glasses, seemed so mesmerized by the apparition that he kept losing his place in his prayer book. After further prompting, the girl got the flowers where they were supposed to go and with a look of relief resumed her place in the crowd.

After blessing the well and intoning some fervent hopes for Wormsley's continued prosperity, the Reverend Clomper snapped his prayer book shut and blew his nose. This the crowd took as a signal that the ceremony had ended and they began to disperse. Harry moved in to have a closer look at the motif mounted on the screen; Emma chatted with someone she knew. After exchanging perfunctory greetings with one or two parishioners, the minister quickly departed, presumably to nurse his aching head. The choir seemed to dissolve on the spot, the younger choirboys running to their parents and the older males joining their wives. A few individuals also placed flowers around the well before wandering off at the same leisurely pace they had arrived. Soon the tiny square was practically deserted except for a few birds, hastily picking up scraps of food left behind. The wreaths and other votive flowers rustled in a slight breeze from the lane.

"So that's a well dressing," Harry said, taking Emma's hand.

Emma nodded. "Yep. That's a well dressing. Do you think Hollywood will soon be calling?"

"Very likely. The well was a bit disappointing but I enjoyed the ceremony."

"What was the matter with the well?"

"Well..." Harry groped for words. "It didn't look like a well, that's all."

"What's a well supposed to look like?"

He shrugged. "Dunno. I thought there might be a big hole with buckets and stuff."

She laughed. "Buckets and stuff? You mean like the one Jack and Jill had problems with?"

"Sort of."

"No, love. I don't think there are many like that, around here at least."

"Which village has the most elaborate do?"

"Tissington, according to Mum, but it's in May, I think."

They walked slowly down the main street back to the car. The morning air had warmed considerably. As they crossed over to the side of the street facing the valley, Harry removed his jacket and slung it over his shoulder. It was the type of day which put a glow on everything. But his mood suddenly changed when he stepped into the same dog droppings he'd successfully avoided just an hour before. Half a day in the sun had produced an unmistakable aroma which could have given even the flies a headache.

"Fuck!" said Harry as he limped off to wipe his shoe in the longer grass farther down the slope.

"Try to get most of it off, love," Emma said, practical as ever, "Otherwise it'll really stink up the car."

"You don't say. Why the hell don't people make their dogs go on their own property instead of crapping up the countryside. This really pisses me off."

"That reminds me," said Emma as she watched Harry's performance from a safe distance, "did you know that a chap by the name of Crapper invented the flush toilet? I think he was an American. Somebody mentioned it on the telly the other day. Just thought you might like to know."

This pearl of wisdom fell on deaf ears; Harry was still trying to pry the reeking muck out of the shoe's upper stitching.

"Fuck!" he said again. "Now I've got it on my hands. We never let our dog do this sort of thing on the pavement."

What Harry had self-righteously forgotten to mention was that their dog, a black-and-white female mongrel who had been named Timmy until she suddenly produced a litter of six pups, blemished many pavements and front lawns before being run over by a bus.

Emma casually looked at her own shoes to make sure that she hadn't stepped into anything and then rummaged in her handbag. "You can use my handkerchief to wipe your hands," she called. "It's an old one anyway. Just make sure it doesn't make its way into the car."

He looked up in annoyance.

"Why, pray, would I want to put something full of dog droppings in my car? For Christ's sake. I'm not a moron."

"Didn't say you were, love," replied a chastened Emma. "But you can be a bit forgetful."

"Not with dog droppings," Harry retorted as he finished wiping his hands. After tucking the soiled handkerchief under a rock, he scrambled back to the car. A little dog poop wasn't going to ruin his Sunday. "Let's go to Bakewell. We'll have lunch at the *Bakewell Inn*. Maybe we can sit outside. It's a nice enough day for it."

Emma frowned. "I hope you're paying for it. I've only got enough money for a couple of gallons of petrol."

Harry fished out his wallet and examined the contents.

"I am the proud owner of a one pound note and..." he stuck his hand into his trousers pocket, "about 2/6d in change. Not bad, eh!"

"Well, if you're that rich, you can buy the petrol, too."

As the car made its way towards the main road, it soon became apparent that Harry hadn't done a very thorough job of cleaning his shoe. The smell wafted gently from beneath the dashboard and seemed to linger at chest level. Seeing the look on Emma's face, he surreptitiously wound the window down a notch. That simply increased the air flow and the smell increased dramatically.

"You didn't get it all off, did you?" she sniffed.

"I guess not. Perhaps I should take off my shoes and put them in the boot."

Emma nodded, then hesitated. "Problem is, love, you have rather active feet, if you know what I mean. We could wind up worse off than before."

"You never said I had smelly feet before," Harry replied with a pained expression.

"Well, it's not something people discuss a lot. It's just that, with the warm weather and everything..."

"I'm not going to bloody Bakewell with the car smelling like a den of skunks. We'll pull over and I'll throw my shoes in the boot."

Emma gave in. "Whatever you think's best."

Harry stopped the car, took off his shoes and deposited them in the boot. And as Emma had predicted, the inside of the car soon reeked of stale socks. They wound all the windows down but it didn't make any appreciable difference. Between the smell and the narrow, roller-coaster road, it wasn't long before Emma started to look distinctly off colour.

"How long before we reach the B5056?" Harry asked. "I've no idea where we are."

"Not soon enough," Emma replied. "I haven't been down here for a long time and I think we missed a turn-off. But keep going."

"D'you think it would help if I also took off my socks?

She looked bleakly at him. "I don't think it could do any more harm."

So he stopped again, took off his socks and they joined his shoes in the boot.

"At this rate it's going to be tea time before we get to Bakewell," he said as he threw the car into gear again. This time, however, the clutch pedal came up, the engine roared, and nothing happened. He put it into neutral, then tried again. *Useless* sat stubbornly at the side of the road, surrounded by a large patch of daisies, and refused to budge.

"Oh, no," he wailed.

"Now what's fallen off?"

"The sodding clutch. I thought something was sounding a bit strange last week but it seemed to clear up. And then this morning it began to act up again."

"Is it slipping?"

"Worse than that. It seems to have disappeared. Fuck! That's all I need right now." He slammed his hands against the steering wheel in exasperation.

"That's all **I** need right now," Emma replied, acutely aware of the financial toll this car was taking on her, too. "Try it again."

He did, with the same result.

"Maybe if we let the car cool down, it might get us home?"

Harry nodded. "It's worth a try. We don't have much choice, do we?"

"No, we don't, love."

They sat silently in the afternoon heat, listening to the gentle wind and a herd of desultory cows munching in an adjacent field. A farm lorry passed them, carrying bales of hay. The driver stared at them without slowing down, and soon disappeared round the corner. After half an hour, Harry started the engine, put the car into gear, and gingerly let out the clutch. But *Useless* wasn't going anywhere. After fifty-five thousand miles, the car had finally had enough.

He looked across at Emma. It could have been his imagination but at times such as these he thought he was starting to detect the same care-worn look in her face as they'd seen in Dickie's wife, Joyce. "Well, now what do we do?" he asked as much to himself as her.

She was not amused. "I suppose we could walk home, assuming we can find the right road. Trouble is, I don't know this area very well, and a lot of these small roads don't have signposts. It's unbelievable, all the money we've spent on the car and it does this to us. I think you're right, love, *Useless* is definitely possessed."

"I'm damned sure it is," he snorted. "Breaking down's bad enough, but we're in the middle of nowhere. If we walk home I still have to retrieve the car, and I certainly can't afford to hire someone to tow the bloody thing back to Matlock. Christ!" He pushed his hand through his wavy hair. "I wonder how that little old lady is making out with the Sunbeam Alpine? Tell you something, if I ever see Ed Glumley again I'm going to kick him where it hurts."

Emma was in no mood for listening to empty rhetoric. In any case, she'd encouraged him to buy the car in the first place. "Lock the car up," she said. "We'll walk back to Elton. At least it's not raining."

So they locked up the car and set off in the direction they had come from. The area was a maze of narrow, little roads running off at odd angles, and all lined with the same monotonous dry-stone walls. As Emma had asserted earlier, none were signposted. Ten minutes later Harry realized he was walking in bare feet. His shoes and socks were still in the boot. Emma groaned.

"I don't believe it," she said. "We've walked all this way for nothing? One of these mornings you're going to show up for work without your trousers."

"You stay here," Harry ordered, "I'll go back to the car. No use both of us getting tired out."

"Of course not," she replied stiffly, hoisting herself up onto a wall. "I just wish I'd borrowed that big hat of Mum's."

He found his way back to the car, made one more futile attempt to get the clutch to work, put on his shoes and socks, and set off again to where Emma was waiting.

At least, that's what he thought. But after fifteen minutes of pounding along a road which looked like all the others, Emma was nowhere in sight. He cursed her for not staying put and plodded on. Another ten minutes passed and he knew something was wrong. The afternoon was getting hotter. Although it was now more comfortable walking, his clothes were far too heavy and he was perspiring profusely. Suddenly, rounding a bend, he spotted a familiar car parked at the side of the road. It took only a couple more seconds to realize that the car was his own. He'd spent nearly half an hour walking in a circle. Cursing loudly he climbed on top of a wall to get a better view of the distance. Squinting in the sun, he could see that the walls were a big part of the problem. There were so many of them that they bedeviled any attempt to discern where the lanes joined each other. Still, notwithstanding that, Harry had an undeniably poor sense of direction. He could get himself lost in his own back garden. After resting for a short while he set off again with no clearer idea of where he'd left Emma than he had before.

The road had some familiar features, but now he couldn't remember whether he'd seen them before getting lost, or after. Each lane, it seemed, had the same windswept tree dotted here and there— the same gates and the same tumble-down walls. Another twenty minutes of trudging resulted in yet another circular tour, although this time he could swear it had been a tighter circle.

"Emma!" he yelled in desperation. "Can your hear me?" Nothing replied except the whispering breeze and the distant sound of a tractor.

Finally, just as he was beginning to wonder if he would ever see his girlfriend again, he stumbled abruptly into a 'T' junction. Pulling his shirt out of his trousers to get some air circulating, he looked up and down. To the right the lane quickly disappeared down a hill. In the distance to his left, and in the opposite direction to what he expected, glowed a small patch of yellow. He yelled again. Emma saw him and wearily got down from the wall as Harry came towards her at a shambling trot.

"Where on earth have you been?" she demanded. "I thought you'd gone home without me."

"I got lost," he panted.

She gave one of her familiar snorts. "How could you possibly get lost? I've been here all the time."

"I'm sure you have. It's where **I've** been that caused the problem."

"It's been nearly two hours, for goodness' sakes."

"Tell me about it," Harry snapped.

"I'm getting hungry," she said, "and my feet are sore."

"**Your** feet are sore? How about mine? I think I've got blisters as big as soup plates."

"No. It's these new shoes. They're a bit tight."

He grabbed her hand and they stood in the middle of the lane. "Where do you reckon we are?" he asked.

She thought for a moment. "I reckon we're somewhere between Darley Bridge and Birchover. And we definitely don't want to go to Darley Bridge. But once we find Birchover we're as good as home."

"Woopee, that's really pinned it down!"

Ignoring him, she continued, "I think Birchover's in that direction." She pointed to a low hill to the right of where afternoon sun blazed down. He couldn't see anything to distinguish it from any other low hill in the area. And there were scores of them, all sparsely punctuated with similar looking farmhouses and barns.

"I suppose we could knock on somebody's door and ask," he said, kicking at a pebble.

Emma nodded. "We could, except that you almost need a piece of paper and a pencil; there are so many of these little lanes. Still, we can give it a try."

After a couple of minutes they came upon a farmhouse standing well back from the lane behind a large dried-out pond. The few ducks that were poking about in the mud flapped away, grunting, as they approached. Several stone outbuildings clustered to the left of the house, most of them in the customary state of disrepair. Even in September it was one of the most inhospitable-looking places Harry had ever seen. He could imagine what it must look like in the middle of winter.

"No use going to the house," Emma said, "Everybody will be outside at this time of day."

She was right, as always. Picking their way through an untidy mess of duck feathers, cow droppings and bits of lumber, they approached some noise coming from one of the outbuildings. Inside, an elderly man was tinkering with a piece of equally ancient machinery. He jumped in surprise as they came around the corner and eyed them suspiciously from under his cap.

"'ello, then," he said, "Yer got up the wrong road, eh?"

How did he know that? Harry wondered.

"Sorry if we scared you," Emma said. "Can you tell us which way is Birchover?"

On the surface it seemed like a fairly simple question. But the man's brow furrowed and he scratched his head.

"Well, Birch'erver's ower yonder," he replied, pointing up into the roof. "But yer can take three or fower roads there, if yer see wot ah mean."

"Yes, I know what you mean," Emma said sweetly, "Which one's the quickest?"

The man scratched his head again. "Ooh, ah don't know. Mebbe past Lyle's farm. Aye, that's probably't quickest. But then't little brook road'll get yer there an all."

"Our car broke down," Harry interjected, thinking that if they mentioned their plight some offer of help might be forthcoming.

"Aye," the man sagely replied. "That's allus the way wi' them things, in't it."

"Which way is Lyle's farm?" Emma persisted.

The man stood up and went out into the yard.

"Yer go dahn to a little junction, an' yer tak' th' right fork an' foller it fer a while. Then there's a turn left, which yer don't tak'. Keep going an' th' road goes on fer a bit afor it turns left. Lyle's farm's on't corner. Just keep follerin' that road an yer'll get inter Birch'erver. Ah should mention it comes aht afor Birch'erver but yer should be able ter see't village from't road end."

"Thanks. Bye bye," said Emma. And pulling Harry behind her she strode back to the lane.

"Fat lot of help he was," Harry grumbled. "And why do they always call these 'roads?' These aren't bloody roads. Some of them are hardly even lanes. I mean, look at this one. The only way two cars can pass is by one of them pulling onto the verge."

Emma was patient. "You have to remember, love, these lanes weren't built for cars. I think the silliest thing the County Council has done is asphalt some of them. It just encourages people to drive too fast and the next thing you know they've run into a cow or something."

Harry found her down-to-earth view of the world refreshing, if not always comprehensible. It takes country folk to know country problems, he thought. Most city dwellers would consider running into a cow a rather minor accident compared to hitting another car, or a pedestrian. However, he reminded himself, it's easy to forget that cows are not scenery. They're someone's livelihood.

The lane headed down a slight incline, and past the fork the old man had mentioned they could see it wind to the right farther on, before heading up another hill.

"You know," said Harry, pausing, "we could take a shortcut across that pasture. It would save us a bit of time."

"Oh, sure," Emma replied. "Ever tried walking in a field with high heels?"

"Not lately. Take your shoes off. I didn't find it too bad, and everything's pretty dried out."

"I'm wearing nylons, remember?"

"Take them off, too."

"What about the cow plops? If I put my foot in one, you're going to get it, Mister Michaels."

"Look, Miss Callingwood," said Harry, "the sooner we get to Birchover, the sooner we can get something to drink."

"I want something to eat, love. I'm hungry. It's a been a long time since breakfast."

"We'll get something to eat, don't worry. It won't be as good as the Bakewell Inn but it'll be better than nothing, assuming there's anything open. I keep forgetting it's Sunday."

Looking about as though someone might be around, Emma went over to the wall and took off her shoes and stockings, tucking them into her handbag."

"Underpants, too!" Harry teased.

"Stuff it."

They climbed over into the field. Over to one side some cows were browsing. They appeared restless.

"Those are heifers. The heat sometimes makes them grumpy," Emma said, giving them a nervous glance. "Don't wave at them or anything. They can butt you over a wall if they feel like it."

"Why would I want to wave? I don't even know them."

"Very funny."

It was a large pasture, and not so flat as they had previously thought. Walking as fast as she could, Emma gamely tried to find the dry ground, weaving here and there, with her handbag in one hand and shoes in the other. At the same time Harry was nervously watching one animal out of the corner of his eye that seemed to be following their every movement, head lowered and tail swishing. Suddenly it broke from the pack and started cantering towards them, followed by a couple of others. Halfway across the field it briefly paused, then broke into a full charge. Emma, hearing the ground vibrate, looked over her shoulder in horror.

"Oh, Christ," she said, breaking into a run.

"Oh, Christ," Harry said, doing likewise. It wasn't too far to the top of the field. At least, not for him. Forgetting Emma for the moment, he flew along, his long legs easily clearing the lumpy ground. Emma wasn't so fortunate, even without her shoes. Reaching the wall, he turned to find that she had disappeared. He froze into a crouching position, scanning the grassy hummocks for some sign of her while the heifer wondered what to do about its vanishing quarry.

"Stay down," he yelled, assuming that she had dropped to the ground and played dead. Whatever she had done, it seemed to work. After sniffing about for several seconds the animal lost interest and wandered back to the herd. With the threat removed, at least for the moment, he hurried back to where he had last seen her. Slowly, a bottom appeared above the grass as Emma struggled to her knees, looking like a low-budget-picture monster. He'd seen the low-lying soft spot in his own headlong flight, but had leaped around it. Emma hadn't. One foot sank in the mud. And while trying to save her handbag and shoes she lost her balance and sprawled flat on her face. There didn't seem to be much of her in front that wasn't coated with mud or cow dung. A fair proportion of the yellow dress wasn't yellow anymore. Her legs were black. And in trying to free herself from the mire she'd managed to wipe some of it on her face and hair.

Finally upright, she stood unsteadily, tears streaming down her face as he hurried to her side.

"Satisfied?" she cried. "Bloody satisfied?"

"I'm sorry, love," he said weakly, picking up her handbag and shoes. "I thought we could save some time."

She brushed him aside. "Leave me alone. Just leave me alone. Look at me! What the hell am I going to tell Mum this time? You get me into more bloody messes. You and your stupid ideas."

They scrambled out of the field while the heifers continued to eye them from a distance. Emma fumbled in her purse for a handkerchief, then remembered she'd given it to Harry earlier to wipe his shoes. He bit his lip, staring intently down the lane as though expecting it to offer up some solution to the latest in what seemed to be a string of disasters since they'd first met.

"Look at my dress," she sobbed. "It's ruined. Honestly, Harry, I could kill you sometimes."

At that point in time he could cheerfully have killed himself and saved her the trouble. Why did these things always happen to him? It seemed as though they couldn't go anywhere without something going wrong. Was fate trying to tell him something, or was he simply the most accident-prone clod on the face of the earth?

Emma hobbled on ahead, with Harry following lamely behind. "Well, at least you saved your shoes and handbag," he said, trying to sound upbeat.

"Great!" she muttered. "Just tell me how I'm going to wear them looking like this?" I can't even go into the pub at Birchover, I'm so filthy. Do I have any muck on my face?"

"Just a bit."

" Mum's going to kill me."

"I think she's more likely to kill me."

"She bloody ought to."

They passed Lyle's farm, also deserted. Not even a dog barked at them. Then, behind one of the ramshackle barns Harry spotted something that offered salvation. It was a large, stone trough, brim full of water and what looked to be a working pump overhanging it at one end. Why hadn't he thought of it before? Just about every farm had one, and there were others scattered around the pastures for the cattle. In fact, it was escaped water from one of them that Emma had fallen into. No animals were in sight; he breathed a sigh of relief.

"Come on," he said, climbing over the wall. "I've got an idea."

Emma spotted the trough. "Oh, no! I'm not stripping off my clothes in front of someone's farm," she said, pulling back. "I look daft enough already."

He grabbed her hand again. "For starters, it's not in front of someone's farm. It's **behind** it. The water's clean, and in this heat you'll dry off in a couple of minutes. I'll keep a watch for peeping toms. There must be hundreds hiding in the bushes!"

Reluctantly, Emma pulled off her underskirt and dress, clambered into the trough, and stood self-consciously as Harry splashed water about. The water was clean but cold, making her shiver. Quickly, goose pimples began to ripple up her thighs.

"Trouble is," he said, pausing briefly, "you've got muck all up your arms. Why don't you take everything off and then we don't have to worry about getting your underclothes wet. Better still, let me do it so you won't dirty them."

She flapped him away. "You know what you are, Harry Michaels? You're a bloody pervert. Any chance you get, you're pulling my clothes off. Leave me alone."

"Okay. Have it your way."

Harry continued, but as her underclothes started to get wet she changed her mind. Stepping out of the trough she silently let Harry do the honours and then climbed back in again. He cranked on the pump handle to get more clean water, cupping his hands at the same time for a drink. It was delicious. Ten minutes later Emma was washed off. Feeling a bit like Sir Walter Raleigh, he lifted her out and carried her to the other side of the pasture where untrodden grass covered the ground. With her arms round his neck she pulled herself up and kissed him on the cheek. Then she sat, legs pulled up to her chin, while he went back to fetch her clothes.

"I'm not going to dry out all that quickly, you know," she said, teeth chattering.

He looked at her clothes. "Why don't we use your underskirt. You can wear your dress without it, can't you?"

"I suppose so."

He couldn't remember when she had looked so vulnerable, or so completely captivating. This would have been a perfect time, but unfortunately not a perfect place. Even though the farm looked deserted it undoubtedly wasn't; someone could have walked around the corner without any warning. Besides, they were both hungry and thirsty, and it was still a mile or two to Birchover. So he wiped her off with the underskirt and she dressed, putting on her stockings and shoes as well. Surprisingly, the underskirt wasn't too wet after they finished. Harry reckoned it might be sufficiently dry to wear again by the time they reached Birchover.

"My dress is still a mess," she said, wiping at the mud with her skirt. "I'm going to look pretty silly going into a pub looking like this."

He reluctantly agreed. "There isn't much we can do about it. Maybe when it dries the smell will disappear."

They managed to get some of the loose muck off, but the stains, and some of the smell, remained. It was bad enough, but it could have looked worse.

After Harry helped himself to another drink at the pump, they set off again. Several seconds later, Emma suddenly stopped.

"Your shoes," she said.

He looked down at them. "What about my shoes?"

"You took all the trouble to wash me off in the trough. Why don't you rinse your shoes. Might get rid of the smell!"

"Good idea!" he replied, also taking off his socks to avoid getting them dirtier than they were already. After swishing the soles about for a minute or two he wiped them in some long grass and then put the shoes to his nose. "Much better!"

After what seemed like eternity, the winding lane took them into Birchover, where they arrived, hot and tired, with aching feet. Emma's underskirt hadn't completely dried, but dry enough. She ducked down the side of a cottage and slipped it on. It felt damp and clammy but it was better than carrying the thing. After walking past the *Druid Inn* several times they plucked up enough courage to go inside. Even in those days the pub served good meals. It wasn't busy, although they might have been better off if it had been. The publican had plenty of time to watch them select a table, and he continued to scrutinize Emma while Harry went up to order. Then, to the curious stares of some locals, they buried their troubles in pints of bitter and shandy, and steak and kidney pie. Despite the grimness of Birchover village, it was a cosy little pub. For a while Harry forgot about the car they had abandoned some miles away. Emma's dress, dried out by sun and wind as they walked the last mile and a half, still had an aroma but it wasn't noticeably offensive, blending with those in the bar.

"Mum says there's witchcraft around here," she said from behind her shandy.

"Which craft would she be talking about!" Harry joked.

Emma was all seriousness. "No, really. There's a place called Rowtor Rocks up behind the village where people used to make sacrifices and things."

He thought about the name of the inn. "They wouldn't have been Druids, I suppose?"

Emma shrugged. "Don't know. What are Druids?"

"I seem to remember from school that they were Celts, and I think they originated in Ireland and Wales... a long time before they came to be called Ireland and Wales. They had a thing about doing rituals in circles made of stones." He grinned. "And that, madam, is the sum total of my knowledge on the subject."

"Oh. Well, anyway, it's supposed to be really spooky when there's a full moon."

After fetching another half-pint for himself and stretching his long legs under the table, he said with a smile, "In that case, we will have to visit when there's a full moon. I'll bring my Count-Dracula costume."

They reached Elton just before five o'clock. By a stroke of misfortune Mrs. Callingwood was in the kitchen and spotted them before Emma could run upstairs and change. She stood, open-mouthed as usual, with a large question mark on her face.

"Now what?" she exclaimed, taking a closer look as they straggled through the door. "Well-dressings can't be that rough, even these days."

Emma tossed her handbag onto the table, sat down with a deep sigh and pulled off her shoes.

"We decided to go to Bakewell afterwards for lunch, but Harry's car broke down."

"What did you do, drag it all the way home?"

"No, Mother." Emma wasn't in the mood for sarcasm. "We got chased by some cows and I fell in a mud hole."

"My, my," Mrs. Callingwood said as she continued putting out the tea things. "You two can certainly pack a lot of activity into one afternoon. A lot more than **I** did at your age, you can be sure."

Emma ignored her. "We came back through Birchover and had lunch at the *Druid*."

Mrs. Callingwood squinted behind her glasses. "Looking like that?"

"Nobody noticed."

"I'll bet they didn't."

"Anyway, we're not very hungry."

"Just as well. I'm only making a salad." She looked with narrowed eyes at Harry. "You know, you're the most accident-prone boy I've ever come across. One of these days you're going to kill yourself. Just make sure you don't kill Emma, too."

Harry, stung by the remark, opened his mouth to say something and then shut up.

"Where's your car now?" she asked.

"I'm not sure," he replied. "We took some side roads. That's why we got lost. It was all my fault, of course."

Emma interrupted, "It's somewhere in that bunch of little lanes south of Stanton-in-Peak. I don't think I've ever been there before so I couldn't help him."

"Well, you can't leave it there," she said. "What's the matter with the blessed thing this time?"

"I think the clutch has gone," Harry replied.

Mrs. Callingwood nodded, without looking at him, "We'll pull it back here with the tractor."

"Oh, Mum," Emma said impatiently, "Brian won't do that and you know it."

"You forget, it's my tractor," she shot back.

"Maybe it's your tractor, but it's his time."

"Doesn't matter, you or I can drive it. We don't need him, and he won't need the tractor 'till later on."

"Who's got the tractor keys?"

Her mother smiled very faintly, as though she'd discovered a trump card. "He does of course. But I have the spare set, and there's some rope in the shed."

"Will you drive it, Mum?" Emma asked. "You can work the gears better than I can. Remember that time I nearly knocked a wall down!"

"I recall you **did** knock it down. Alright, I'll drive. Go and get changed. We'll have tea when we get back."

Harry could hardly believe his ears. But it solved only part of his problem. The tow would only get *Useless* to Elton. It still needed to be repaired and he had no idea how he was going to pay for it. He also had to get himself back to Matlock in time for work the next morning, which meant either going in on the bus with Emma or going back on the bus later that night. There was a third option: walking. However, after spending most of the afternoon on blistered feet, he didn't find the prospect too appealing.

Emma fetched the rope while her mother backed out the old David Brown tractor. By hanging onto the seat with one hand and the large mudguards with the other, they both could just manage to stand forward of the P.T.O. coupling. It was still light outside, and warm, although the days were now beginning to draw in. They bounced down the lane, out to the B5056, then turned on to the winding lane to Birchover. A couple of cars and a farm lorry passed them. The village was quiet, the pub still open and a few people milling about the front door. They rattled through, taking the same lanes that they had used hours earlier. Mrs. Callingwood knew the area like the back of her hand. Eventually, after rounding yet another bend, there was *Useless*, maintaining its lonely vigil amid the little patch of daisies.

"Don't tie the rope around the bumper," Mrs. Callingwood warned him, above the noise of the tractor. "You'll fetch it off."

Harry got down and looked under the front. He noticed that the brackets which supported the bumper, connected to the chassis; so he tied the rope around one of them.

"I'll give you as much rope as I can," she called. "Emma, you ride up with me so you can keep an eye open in case the rope breaks or something."

Harry jumped into the car, released the handbrake, and let the tractor take up the slack. Emma was up on the tractor again, making faces at him as they moved slowly down the lane. He could see Mrs. Callingwood telling Emma which way they were going so she could semaphore to Harry with her arms each time they reached a lane end. Evidently, her mother didn't want the tractor going in one direction and Harry in another.

Crawling at a snail's pace, they reached Elton forty-five minutes later, and pushed *Useless* into the farmyard where it sat in disgrace, in a corner. Emma put the tractor away while Mrs. Callingwood went inside to get tea ready. Harry thanked her for the help. She blinked through her glasses at him; a faint smile flickered and died almost immediately.

"Oh, never mind," she said abruptly. "Just make sure it doesn't sit here for the next six months."

The classic response. All the same, Harry got a sneaking feeling that she had rather enjoyed helping them out. Giving instructions and in command atop her little tractor, Mrs. Callingwood had seemed like an entirely different woman. Perhaps it was because these days she seldom got an opportunity to feel useful, as she had when her husband was still alive. Now, Brian and Beth were running the farm and making no pretense of their desire to fully control it.

After tea Emma decided it would be nice to wash the car, covered as it was with dust. He could see her mother eyeing them through the kitchen window as they fooled around with the garden hose. Finally, tired and grimy from the afternoon's adventure, he caught the last bus to Matlock with no more idea of how he was going to get the car repaired than he had before. But at least it wasn't sitting on the roadside in the middle of the Derbyshire moors.

"Would you like a surprise?" Emma asked him two days later as they walked down to Miss Twigg's after work. *Useless* still languished in Elton, and he was still wondering how to get it running again. Elton had no service garage; neighbouring Winster did, but since he and Emma were nearly broke it might as well not have had. There was another week to go until mid-month salary advance. Things did not look good and Harry was fed up. It wasn't as if he was particularly extravagant; he just didn't have enough, it seemed, to enjoy even the simplest of pleasures.

"That depends," he replied. "If it's a nice surprise, yes."

"It's a nice surprise. At least, I think it's a nice surprise. Anne's boyfriend says he'll repair the car."

Harry groaned. "You were telling me only a few days ago what a nitwit Bruce is. And that wasn't the first time. Anyway, I still can't afford it."

She put a finger to his lips. "You haven't heard all of it, love. Apparently he doesn't want anything for doing the work, but we'll have to buy the parts, and we have to get them for him."

"How would I know what to buy? Mechanic I'm not."

"He's going to have a look at the car, see what new parts the clutch needs and then he'll make up a list for us to take to Ernshaw's," she said persuasively. "Think about it. We won't need to have the car towed to Winster and labour's always the most expensive part of getting anything repaired, so it might not be all that bad."

Harry remained puzzled. "I still don't understand why Bruce would want to do it for nothing. I mean, I've only met him once and even then he wasn't exactly overjoyed to see me. In fact nobody up there seems overjoyed to see me except you. And what are we going to do if he makes a mess of it? Then we'll really be in the hole."

"We don't have too many options, do we?" she replied with a trace of irritation in her voice.

"I suppose not," he said.

"I'm going to take an earlier bus home tonight. I'll get off at Wensley and go and see him, and he can run me home in his van. Mum says he'll start right away if its alright with you."

"Mum says?"

"Yes. It was Mum who asked him. Hope you don't mind."

"No, 'course I don't mind," he replied with a shrug. "I'm just a bit surprised, that's all."

"It wasn't all big-heartedness," Emma said. "I think she would like to get the car out of the yard before Brian starts complaining."

It was nice of her to intervene. But there was something slightly fishy about this whole deal. People like Bruce didn't do things for nothing. However, not wishing to look a gift horse in the mouth, he raised no more questions. It was evident that Emma and her mother had this thing worked out.

"Bruce is going to repair it in our yard," she added. "He has some of those ramp things that you shove under the wheels. I don't think it'll take him long once he gets the parts."

Harry went over to the chemist shop the next day at lunch time. As promised, Emma had a short list of parts. Good as his word, Bruce had apparently taken the clutch apart that same evening and found that the clutch plate was completely worn out.

"Can we get these today?" she asked.

Harry shuffled with embarrassment. "Depends how much they cost."

"Alright," she said briskly. "Let's ring Ernshaw's and find out. I'm sure if we read off the list to them they can give us a price. Mrs. J. won't mind us using the telephone for a minute."

So they rang Ernshaw's and Ernshaw's told them that they didn't have some of the parts in stock. Given their experience with *Useless* and Ed Glumley, this came as no surprise. The parts salesman explained that, after all, the car was nearly seven years old and if they stocked parts for every make, model and year, well, heaven knows what kind of a mess they would be in. They'd have to build a storeroom that stretched all the way to Bakewell, etcetera, etcetera. In his mind Harry could hear all those voices which had warned him months before about the trials and tribulations of getting spare parts for Hillmans. It would take at least three days to get them in. And by the way, since this was a cash sale, they would have to be paid for in advance, if you please. Ernshaw's were taking no chances on getting stuck with a few miserable pounds worth of car innards. However, they were able to quote him a price, which totaled slightly less than £30, roughly half a month's salary before taxes. He did not have thirty pounds. Neither did Emma until the following day, when she suddenly announced the discovery of an additional ten pounds in her savings account. It was at this point that Harry began to suspect that her mother was more deeply involved in getting his car repaired than Emma had acknowledged.

The following day he and Emma pooled their resources and raced down to the dealership during lunch hour to order and pay for the parts. *Useless* continued to sit in Callingwood's farm yard. By week's end the parts were still nowhere in sight. Harry was furious. Unfortunately, since Ernshaw's were the only Rootes dealer in Matlock, he had little option but to put up and shut up. Finally, on the following Tuesday, a day that happily coincided with payday, the parts came in. Harry was able to partially pay Emma back. She took the bits and pieces, packed in a box, up to Elton on the bus.

Then it decided to rain for the first time in nearly a month and it rained solidly for two days. Bruce declared he wasn't going to work on the car until it cleared up, and he didn't. However, by Friday the rain had stopped, and by Sunday he had *Useless* working again.

Harry breathed a thankful sigh of relief. Nevertheless, running a car on his salary was proving to be a miserable experience. He could barely afford the insurance and licencing, much less any repairs. For months Emma had been buying most of the petrol and even her patience was beginning to wear thin. It was an affordable proposition on paper, of course, as many propositions are. Too late he was seeing the wisdom in his mother's advice to take the budget he had painstakingly worked out and add half as much again to it. He knew better. Now, there was little to do but to console himself with the highly publicized fact that over half the people in Britain who owned motor vehicles couldn't really afford them.

"What does Bruce drink?" he asked on Sunday afternoon as they stood in the farmyard looking at the car. Neither Anne nor her boyfriend were anywhere in sight. And while still reeling from Bruce's astonishing display of generosity, Harry felt obliged to offer some token of appreciation.

"Everything and anything," she replied. "Why?"

"I thought perhaps I could get him a bottle of Scotch or something, you know, as a sort of thank-you."

Emma patted his backside. "That would be very nice, love. Let me find out and I'll give it to Anne to give to him."

"I thought perhaps we could drop it off at his house, and then I could thank him personally. After all, he's saved me... us... quite a bit of money."

"No, no," she said hurriedly. "He's never around. It would be a lot easier if I just gave it to our Anne."

Without thinking about her remark, he said. "Okay, whatever you think's best."

Next day Emma informed him that Bruce was partial to *Bell's*— and anything else he could lay his hands on. Later, he thought it odd that she had been able to learn of Bruce's preferences in such a short space of time, particularly in view of the fact that she and Anne hardly ever spoke to each other. But Harry bought a bottle of *Bell's* anyway with some of his nearly exhausted funds, and Emma the messenger reportedly gave it to Anne to give to Bruce. Immediately afterwards Bruce disappeared from conversation as though he'd dropped off a radar screen. Harry began to get a very strong impression that neither Emma nor her mother wanted the two to meet again. He never did find out why, but that was the way it worked out. He never saw Bruce again.

A week after getting its clutch repaired, *Useless* had another weekend flat tyre, this time late at night after dropping off Emma. While fumbling about in the dark with the spare he accidentally caught the rear-left mudguard with the wheel-nut wrench. It knocked a gaping hole the size of a saucer. As he poked at the bits he realized that the metal beneath must have been completely rusted away. Someone, probably Ernshaw's, had simply sprayed over it with paint. That night marked the beginning of the end for Harry's brief era of car ownership.

ELEVEN

Time to Move On

Since he had been with the County Council less than a year, Harry received only a week's holiday that summer. He could have waited until his first anniversary, November the first, to gain another week but his mother had been unwell, and he decided to spend a few days with her. In spite of their differences, she missed him. During the two years he'd spent at home while apprenticing at the parks department,she had begun to take his presence for granted. It seemed nice to have a man around the house again, even if he did drive her crazy with an almost constant clamouring to sell it and move. A cottage in the country would be nice. In Devon or Cornwall, perhaps. No matter, so long as they moved away from that dismal coal-mining town. She resisted the temptation; it might be a mining town, but it was home, and most of her friends were there. Now, Harry was gone, as abruptly as he'd arrived after leaving boarding school.

Both were still licking their wounds after last Christmas, when her surprisingly vehement attack on Emma had almost caused him to walk out of the house. Neither had mentioned Emma since. The impasse begged for reconciliation, but his Mother was a proud and fiercely independent woman. Even though she had started the fight, it would be up to Harry to mend the broken fences. Perhaps, he wondered, if she got the chance to meet his new girlfriend, her opinion might change.

So in the middle of October, he decided to take Emma home with him. It was a disastrous mistake. Far from mellowing, his mother's intransigence only hardened, and despite Emma's efforts to ingratiate herself, it was downhill from the start. For several days they coexisted in icy politeness. Then, to compound his blunder, Harry confided at one point that he had considered asking Emma to marry him. Had he divulged a plan to assassinate the Royal Family, Mother's response couldn't have been more devastating.

"I told you last time that you can do a little better than farm girls," she snapped back. "Besides, she has thick ankles, and they'll just get thicker as she gets older."

"I don't see what you dislike in her," Harry protested. He couldn't see where thick ankles had much to do with the issue. Besides, her ankles were perfectly acceptable as far as he was concerned, along with the rest of her anatomy.

"Emma will never change," Mother continued. "These sorts of people will drag you down to their level, but you'll never bring them up to yours." Then, pulling that age-old parental ace in the hole, she added, "If you can't think of me in this, at least think of your father. He worked very hard to get us where we are."

Get us where we are? Where were they? In a dismal semi-detached house in a godforsaken coal-mining town. What sort of an achievement was that, he asked himself. At least he'd had the initiative to get away from it. That Mother would so vehemently challenge his judgment in selecting a mate was totally unexpected. He felt deeply hurt and more than a little humiliated; she had derided his choice with such scorn. After Emma finally responded to four days of acute discomfort by catching a miserable cold, they left amid tears and recrimination a day earlier than planned, with Harry vowing never to return.

In spite of his staunch defence of Emma, things were never quite the same between them after that. It was as though his mother's excoriating reception had driven a stake into the relationship. Emma never blamed him for the debacle. Or if she did, her behavior never revealed it. But almost imperceptibly the little bit of confidence that Harry had developed with her during that past year started to evaporate. And as if sensing the promise of change, his alter ego began pointing ever more vigorously to the next hill. As the weeks went by he grew increasingly restless. Thursday's child had to move on.

Work was becoming a burden. Dickie irritated him, although the feeling was clearly mutual. Terry, whom he was obliged to face across their adjoining draughting tables every work day, also irritated him with his self-righteous pomposity. Terry was going to get a pay raise. But as far as he knew, **he** wasn't. He'd picked up several colds from the ever-dripping Angus, and Lol, while an easy going sort, continued to treat him with mild contempt. The entire section, smug and parochial, had begun to irritate him. Looking back, the only person he'd felt any real affinity with had been Clem, even though he knew virtually nothing about the man. And now Clem was dead. In short, Harry was out of humour with just about everybody still alive.

Emma noticed the change, although she never said anything. But the faraway look in Harry's eyes told her that things were not the same. It wasn't as if they quarreled a lot. They never had. The change was more of degree than substance; a very slow cooling down. And although Harry knew it was happening, he felt powerless to do anything. It was an odd feeling, but not unfamiliar to him. A little like running helter-skelter towards the edge of a cliff with his consciousness telling him about the fatal two-hundred-foot drop and his alter ego yearning for the exhilaration of flight. They continued to see each other practically every day. Emma continued to sleep with him on weekends and on other occasions when he could sneak her upstairs without Miss Twigg catching them. They had given up any pretense with Sarah. She knew what they were doing but to Harry's surprise, considering their embarrassing encounter that night following his stay in hospital, hadn't told her aunt. Sarah must have been sincere when she said she would still like him. So the little piece of glass in Harry's bedroom door continued to fall out on a regular basis when he and Emma were there. To the point that he'd half seriously thought about flinging open the door and inviting Sarah in to watch. It surely would have been a bit more comfortable for her than being crouched in a drafty hallway for hours on end.

One Saturday afternoon, on Emma's day off, they were window shopping in Crown Square. The weather was mild but there were unmistakable signs that autumn was settling in. After a hot, dry summer some of the trees had begun to turn colour in September. Now they were shedding like confetti. Horse chestnuts, many tucked away behind walls and in cul-de-sacs, had dropped most of their huge, fingered leaves, revealing hundreds of conkers yet to fall. And here and there some elderly beeches were turning the colour of golden-burned butter on their ponderous way to a clear coppery red. The shops were busy, although most of the crowd seemed to be just sightseeing.

Even the stone buildings had lost some of their severity in the warm sunshine. Matlock's architecture, uncompromising in its drab respectability, reflected the essential Victorian England, many of the surviving mills and factories a monument to the industrial revolution when steam power transformed cottage production into assembly lines. Like his own home town, practically everything before the turn of the century had been built of sandstone, much of it now blackened with a hundred years of soot. Roofs and pavements were made of stone flags; even some of the streets were cobbled with stone. It was solid, dependable stuff, but to Harry it merely served as a reminder that Thursday's child hadn't yet gone very far.

Dale Road, Matlock's major shopping street, bustled with locals and a few late-calling tourists. Planning to drop into the *Laughing Dog* pub for a drink later, they wasted some time browsing a bookseller's and a furniture shop. Emma ran her hand along an elegant curved settee prominently displayed in the furniture shop window.

"*Cant's* have some nice things, don't they?" she murmured.

Harry agreed, imagining for the moment what some of it would look like in their own home. Nothing stood in their way except the cost. They looked at many things in the shop: big double beds, tallboys and dressers, armchairs and Queen-Anne dining suites. They could all come together in a cosy stone cottage, with a chimney at each end and swaybacked roof like all the others, and a fine view across the moors. But in his imagination Harry knew theirs would be different. He would have a garden and grow roses, just like his grandfather; hybrid teas and floribundas, and climbers smothering the solid sash windows. Big untidy perennial flower borders would tumble down to the garden gate. He would install central heating and an indoor lavatory and convert the outhouse into a workshop. It was all possible. It just took money, and that was when his fantasy ride landed back on earth. On his salary they would be lucky to be able to even rent a flat, let alone buy a house, and he'd all but given up on any future with Dickie's office. He'd turned twenty-three that summer. Was he ready for settling down yet? He wasn't sure. Part of him said yes but that other part, his ever present alter ego, would nudge him, saying, "It's a big world out there, Harry my boy, too big to get bogged down in a provincial town like this. Why not see some of it before it's too late?"

Harry's gaze strayed to the street. Emma, sensing that his mind was on other things, put a fabric swatch back in its rack and quietly steered him out of the shop. Next door housed a travel agent. They paused and Harry examined the destinations, some exotic, some mundane. Thomas Cook had them all. But standing there, as the sassy brochures and posters almost leaped through the window, he thought, nobody could learn anything about a country by just visiting. One had to live in a place, share in the hopes and dreams of its people, and experience daily life outside the cosseted comfort of a tour bus to appreciate the essence. Yes, it was a big world out there. Where would one start? And how would one go about getting a job all those miles away? Harry had never been aggressive or particularly resourceful when it came to job hunting. Otherwise he probably would never have settled for the local parks department after graduating. Most of his classmates had spent their final months scouring the newspapers and trade magazines, and lining up as many interviews as they could. By contrast, Harry had buried himself in the task of organizing a concert, which in some ways spoke volumes about his attitude towards careers in general.

"How would you like to live in another country?" he asked Emma as they continued on down the street.

She looked up at him for a moment. It was an innocent question. But she knew Harry well enough to know that it held some purpose. "I don't think I'd like to be that far away from home. Would you?"

"I'm not sure," he replied. "For that matter, I'm not sure where home is."

They made their way to the pub, sitting at the same table they had sat at on their first date nearly a year ago. This time the big stone fireplace stood cold and empty, awaiting the return of winter. They sipped their drinks in silence for a while, watching people outside coming and going. It was warm inside; the front door had been flung open, a gesture which a multitude of flies had taken as an invitation. Harry half-heartedly swatted at them with his hand. So many people were standing in front of the bar that it was hard to see who was serving. He caught sight of a woman wiping glasses. She was tall, in her late thirties to early forties he guessed, and wearing a thin, cotton blouse, which barely hid the push-up bra underneath. It was hard to tell whether she was married; she wore no wedding ring and conducted herself with an energetic independence characteristic of singular status. He watched her for a while as she casually slid the glasses into their overhead rack before once again attending to the customers. There was something about her that intrigued Harry. Perhaps it was the steel-rimmed glasses. He didn't know why but he had always been attracted to women with glasses. She was very trim, although not particularly attractive, her light brown hair tied into a pony tail and bangs that almost obscured her forehead. She noticed him staring and flashed him a quick smile before the crowd closed ranks again.

"She's too old for you," said Emma, who missed very little when it came to Harry's roving eye.

Harry blushed slightly. "I was just wondering whether she's one of the owners. We've been in quite a few times when she's been serving."

"That doesn't necessarily make her one of the owners."

"I suppose not."

Emma put down her drink, reached across the table and gently clasped his hands.

"Look, love, I know you're not very happy with the job up the hill and I don't blame you. Anyone who can put up with Dickie deserves a medal. But there are other options. You could try getting a job with one of the parks departments around here. Derby and Chesterfield must have good-sized departments. Or even Sheffield. Seems to me you're better qualified for that kind of work than designing playing fields."

He looked out at the street again. "It isn't just that... Oh, I don't know. It's probably all in my head but everything in this country seems so small. People even think small. They spend all their lives doing what their parents did, and their parents before them. I'm all for tradition but we have to look forward as well as backwards. There doesn't seem to be any vision. I sometimes get this urge to push everything out. There are so many countries in the world, and I probably won't see any of them."

Emma didn't understand. He knew she didn't understand.

"We all have to live somewhere. Most people are glad to have a job," she replied.

"Don't get me wrong," he continued, "I don't want to sound like a spoiled brat. This job's certainly better than the one I had before. Still, I think I'm going to make some inquiries about a few countries. See how hard it is to get work there. Just a few inquiries. Doesn't cost anything to ask, does it?"

He could tell his words had hit home. She briefly fell silent and then said, "What about us? Me?"

"We could both go."

"How long would you stay?"

He shrugged. "Six months, a year maybe. I suppose it would depend on the kind of job I got."

"Where would you look?"

"I'm not sure about that either, but it would have to be somewhere different, well, different from England... and somewhere where there's plenty of space. Canada, Australia. America, perhaps."

Quietly, she said, "I'll wait for you."

"Wouldn't you **want** to come with me?"

She smiled and shook her head slowly. "I'm not a Thursday's child, love. And I don't think I could leave Mum on her own. I pay board and room, and she relies on it quite a bit because Brian doesn't give her much except a headache."

"But she's not alone," he protested. "Brian **is** around, even if he **is** useless, and so is Anne. It's not as if she has no one else except you. Besides, you can't pay board and room for ever."

"Me and Mum are special, just like you and your mum."

That made Harry think for a minute. Were he and his mother special? He'd never thought of it that way. Liz had always said Mother thought the sun shone out of his backside. Perhaps that's why she had such lofty expectations of him. But none of that proxied for a special relationship; special relationships had to be a two-way thing. And Liz certainly had him cold on that one. She and Mother spent much more time together and shared their innermost thoughts. He and Mother had never done that. The difference between him and his sister was that this localistic lifestyle suited her. Like Emma, she had few aspirations beyond a job and warm fireplace in winter. For his part, Harry had never felt constrained by local community bonds or family ties. Not that he despised such social trappings; he was simply content to keep them alive in his mind. And sufficiently in the background for new linkages to form. There was no urgent need to be physically present. People like Emma and Liz represented the majority of Britons who were either comfortable with the status quo, or feared the unknown consequences of change. Better the devil you know than the devil you don't, they would have said.

Emma stayed with him that night, but left for home the following morning to help her mother. Conspicuously absent on this occasion were Harry's good-natured protests about her leaving him alone on Sundays. Instead, he spent the afternoon in the library, browsing through travel guides. There was very little new material, and even less that dealt with such mundane topics as immigration and finding jobs in new countries. It seemed no one had any interest in seeking a brave new world. And yet that couldn't be; he knew from newspaper reports that thousands were leaving England every year for precisely the same reasons as he.

"I think you're not finding what you want because you're not looking in the right place," a friendly librarian told him. She looked startlingly like his mother. "Libraries don't get much demand for that type of thing. You should be writing to the embassies and high commissions. And I can get their addresses from the directory we keep on file. Which countries did you have in mind?"

Standing there, he suddenly felt a bit silly. He had no idea. It seemed as though Australia and New Zealand were popular destinations for the disillusioned. And he liked the idea of a warmer climate. But from what he had read, Australian and New Zealand cultures possessed many of the qualities he found so frustrating in England. If he was going to break ties with his homeland, it had to be for something as radically different as he could get. That left Canada and the United States. For some reason the British had always regarded Canada as a poor cousin of its noisy neighbor to the south. It was a country the Matlock library had the fewest books on. And when Harry examined the atlas, Canada looked like a series of books itself: ten provinces packed side by side across five thousand miles, with two territories sitting on top. In contrast, the United States in all its complexity seemed to be a bewildering jumble of mini-countries, some as different from each other as chalk and cheese. But one thing both these two North-American giants appeared to have in common was a surviving pioneer spirit. They were countries where people and ideas were judged on their own merits, rather than how they fitted in with long-standing tradition.

He had pored over photographs of Texas and southern California, Alberta and British Columbia. Their cities rose up, new and clean and proud, in the western sunshine. Distances were mind boggling. Authors waxed eloquent about travelling a thousand miles as though it were to the corner off-licence. Everyone had a suntan, and clothes to show it off in. This was what life was all about. Somewhere, amidst all that opulence and opportunity there had to be jobs for the taking. If he emigrated, he would head west.

"Perhaps you could get me the addresses for the United States and Canada," he told the librarian. "And maybe Australia and New Zealand. But particularly the first two."

She laughed gently at his boyish enthusiasm, and got the addresses for him. The following day, at work, Harry wrote to all four embassies and high commissions. With surprising efficiency, all four replied. Canada was the first. The package bulged with all the usual tourism propaganda, but it also listed the government agencies in each province responsible for hiring staff. A week later the American material arrived and Harry pored over it with disappointment. Government workers, the secretary pointed out, had to be U.S. citizens. It would be better to try the private sector and he should write to the individual states for help in this regard.

While the flurry of letter writing had been merely an opening shot, the seeds of travel had been sown. Without being fully conscious of it, he had decided to emigrate. If not for ever, then at least for long enough to see what was over the next hill. Many factors contributed to this decision, but none so forcefully as Emma's remark a couple of weeks later.

"Something hasn't come this month, love," she said while they ate lunch in the stock room.

It was a bombshell. A chill ran down Harry's spine. Emma had just uttered the words he had always been afraid of hearing, and hoped he wouldn't hear.

"How many days?"

"Three." She offered a little smile. "It was supposed to be on Saturday."

"That's not too bad," he said, knowing full well that Emma was as regular as clockwork. "Does it feel like it might come?"

She shook her head. "Not at the moment. I don't even feel bloated or anything."

It was Tuesday. He searched in his head for something useful to say. "Is that three days including today?" The question sounded pretty stupid.

"Yes, love," she said patiently. "Three days including today."

Cursing inwardly, he thought about the scores of times they'd considered using condoms, and then decided against them. What made it all the more ridiculous was the fact that Emma worked in a chemist shop and could get them at a substantial discount. It was largely his fault for being so cavalier. But Emma didn't like condoms either and Mrs. J. threw fuel on the fire by pointing out that **her** men didn't need them. She omitted to mention that the reason they didn't was because she was too old to get pregnant. Emma wasn't.

"What do you feel like?" he asked after a pause.

"I don't feel pregnant, if that's what you mean! It's a bit early for that."

Groping for another bit of conversational balm, he asked, "Is there anything that might bring it on? Any sort of medicine?"

"Not that I know of. And I'm certainly not going to ask Mrs. J. She'd have a field day out of that one."

He fidgeted with his tie.

She put her hand on his knee. "Look, love, let's not get too excited. It might just be late, nothing more."

"Trouble is, you've never been late before. I can almost set my watch by it."

Then Emma changed the subject. Her apparent lack of concern puzzled him. How could she be so offhand about something that important? It was almost as though she had hoped to get pregnant so that he wouldn't leave. She had never said much about Harry's interest in emigrating, but he could tell that his restlessness was seriously affecting their relationship. Before, talk of the future had invariably included him. Now it didn't. She was increasingly discussing herself in singular terms instead of 'we.' Even worse, their activities together were becoming tainted with a sad inevitability, a little like watching a wild animal which knows its final moments have come. He had hoped she would agree to emigrate with him if it came to that. But she always gently brushed his arguments aside, repeating her concern for her mother. He knew that Emma's reluctance ran deeper than that. She lived in an environment she knew and felt comfortable with, despite some ambivalence. Her perceptual horizon embraced the peaks, her farm, the village and her narrow, little work world. And Harry was a part of it, but only so long as he remained there. There were times, albeit fleeting, when Harry wished he could settle for something so easily.

Back at the office, the crisis seemed even more menacing. After stewing at his draughting table for an hour, the panic began turning to anger. Why now? he fumed. Just when he'd made the decision of his lifetime. Was fate trying to tell him something? And if it was, what was it? Was he destined to rot in this country for the rest of his days, just like everyone else? Was he going to wind up like the fellow at the teacher's college, living in some squalid one-bedroom flat with a wife he despised and a baby he didn't want? Perhaps this was punishment for trying to be different, for having the audacity to get up on his flat feet and question what everybody else accepted.

Then he suddenly remembered. Warm baths! Years ago he'd seen a girl in a motion picture taking a warm bath to bring on a reluctant menstrual cycle. Or was it to prevent pregnancy after she'd had sex? Either way, it had something to do with not having babies. He also recalled someone at the teacher's college saying that drinking gallons of black coffee could also do the trick. Tossing these two dubious vignettes about in his head, Harry fretted for the remainder of the afternoon. At five o'clock he donned his coat and went for a walk until five-thirty, when the chemist shop closed. Noticing the owner making one of his rare visits behind the counter, he waited impatiently outside for Emma to finish work.

"Warm baths!" he said as she hopped down the steps.

"Yes, they're very nice, love," she replied, giving him a puzzled look at the same time.

"No, no. Warm baths are supposed to make things happen. You know, your period."

She laughed. "I think that's an old wives tale. I can't see how it would work."

"Never mind, let's go down to Miss Twigg's and give it a try."

"Harry, I'm quite capable of having a bath at my house. I have them all the time, you know!"

"Something has to be different," he insisted. "Maybe you have to stay in the bath for an hour or so. Miss Twigg's hot water heater is bigger than yours. I'll keep adding some more as it goes cold."

"Are you feeling alright, love?" She was beginning to wonder if Harry had taken leave of his senses. Maybe her mother was right.

"I'm fine. It's you I'm concerned about," he replied curtly, knowing full well this wasn't entirely true. There was more than an element of self interest involved.

"Well, if it'll make you feel any better, I'll have a bath at your digs. But I hope for your sake Miss Twigg doesn't catch us. She'll think we're both cracked in the head."

Miss Twigg spotted them through the dining-room serving hatch as they entered. There was a flurry of tea towels and she came bustling around the corner.

"Oh, my," she flustered, "you never said anything about bringing Emma for dinner, Mr. Harry. I'm not sure I've made enough."

"That's okay, Miss Twigg," he assured her. "We were just dropping by to pick up something, that's all."

"Well, I'm sure with a little stretching I can make it do," she went on. "If Emma would like to stay, she's quite welcome. It's Lancashire hot-pot."

"I'd love to," said Emma brightly. "So long as it's not a bother."

She could see the frustration in Harry's face and it amused her a little. Men were such singled-minded clods. He was bent on getting her in a warm bath as quickly as possible and until that happened, nothing else mattered.

"Thanks, Miss Twigg," he said lamely. They went to the stairs.

"I'll be serving up at six o'clock as usual," Miss Twigg called after them. "So don't go too far."

He might have already gone too far, he thought to himself.

There was no sign of Sarah. And that worried him. She had the distressing habit of materializing, like a genie, out of nowhere. However, there wasn't much they could do about the bath until after dinner. Emma would have to take another later, he calculated; and two tomorrow... and every day until something happened. What if nothing happened? It didn't bear thinking about.

When they came down at six, Sarah was in the kitchen. She pouted as usual at Emma when she brought in the coffee cups. Harry breathed a sigh of relief. So long as she stayed in the kitchen or near vicinity, all would be well. After they finished eating he swilled down his coffee, then moved to leave the table.

"Where are you going?" Emma asked.

Afraid someone might be listening he grunted, "I, er, thought we'd go up and, er..."

"Not on a full stomach, love. I'm not going to make myself sick for the sake of half an hour. Let's go for a walk. This entire thing's ridiculous anyway."

So they bundled up and went for a reluctant walk down to Hall Leys Park, with Harry peering at his watch each time they passed beneath a street lamp.

"Why didn't I think to bring an egg timer; then it could have gone 'ping' when the half hour was up," she said sarcastically. "I really am beginning to worry about you, Harry."

"For heaven's sake," he shot back. "Doesn't it worry you that you're late? It certainly worries me. Personally, I don't feel like being a father yet."

"Maybe you should have thought about that before."

He was becoming very irritated. "It wasn't just my idea not to use anything. You were all for it, too."

After a tense silence, she put a conciliatory arm through his. "Sorry, love, but it's a bit early yet to say I'm pregnant. And I'm just as concerned as you."

They went back to the house, noting with some relief that the dining-room hatch doors were closed. Harry had noticed she tended to close them during cool weather, presumably to help keep the kitchen warm. They crept up the stairs to Harry's room and while he kept a lookout for unwelcome intruders, Emma slipped into his dressing gown.

"I'll go and run the bath water," he said, ignoring her protests that she could do it equally well herself.

The bathroom was probably the most comfortless room in that comfortless house. Like his room, it had once been painted the same shade of green and had a brown-linoleum floor. And also like his room, it boasted a frosted glass door. The wash basin and bath were relics of a period when looks were considered more important than efficiency. The bath sat squarely in the corner on four, clawed feet, discoloured from years of abuse with abrasive cleaners. Located next to it, the wash basin had come loose from the wall, leaving it largely supported by the drain pipe. All the iron taps leaked— every tap in the house seemed to leak— with the result that both the basin and bath wore long streaks of brown stain into the drain plugs. To complete the cheerless decor, a solitary ceiling light glowed from its green-glass shade. Harry wondered occasionally whether the place might have looked better when Miss Twigg's parents were alive. It could hardly have looked any worse.

Not only did the bathroom excel in ugliness, it was always cold, just like all the other rooms in the house except her kitchen. Even during the summer months, he never lingered in the bath any longer than absolutely necessary. In winter he would sit in the rapidly cooling water, torn between adding a little extra hot water, and thereby postponing the inevitable, and leaping into his skimpy little towel. Frostbite, someone had told him, could be a very nasty thing.

The unusually mild days of October had abruptly disappeared. On this early November evening it was cold and getting colder by the minute from a miserable wind blowing through the valley. Turning the taps, he prayed that Miss Twigg had the immersion heater switched on. After spluttering and coughing for what seemed a lifetime, hot water bubbled out.

"'Ow come yer 'avin' a bath now?"

Harry spun round. Sarah had pushed open the partly closed door and was looking at him with a half-smile-half-perplexed look on her face. He cursed himself for not closing the door and locking it. But then, she would probably have been waiting outside for him. Damn the girl; why couldn't she stay down in the kitchen where she belonged?

"Oh, er, I'm not," he snapped, realizing too late he'd said the wrong thing.

"Then wot are yer runnin' the 'ot water fer? Auntie Bertha wouldn't want yer runnin' it fer nuthin'."

"I'm not running it for nothing. Emma's taking a bath."

That was also the wrong thing to say. Probably worse than the first thing. Sarah's curiosity became further aroused. Pulling out an old wicker stool she plunked herself down on it.

"Why's Emma 'avin' a bath?" she asked.

"Why is she what? Oh, well, er.." Why the hell was Emma taking a bath? He feverishly searched for some plausible reason. Fortunately, in Sarah's case it didn't even have to be too plausible.

"She has a rash!" he cried, with sudden inspiration. "Yes, she got a prickly rash, and we thought a nice warm bath would help."

"Is it chickenpox, then?"

Harry shook his head. "No, I don't think it's chickenpox."

"Measles, then. Pr'aps its measles?"

"No, not measles either. Might be from eating too much fish."

Sarah's eyes widened. "Dus she eat a lotta fish, then?"

"No, no, she doesn't. But she had some crab meat in a sandwich for lunch today. That might have done it. In fact, I'm pretty sure that's what did it."

"Ooh, I'd better tell Auntie Bertha about that, jus' in case she ever gets sum crabs." Sarah began to slide her large bottom off the stool.

"No, no, don't do that!" Harry pleaded. "She doesn't know Emma's here. We didn't want to worry her. Let's keep this a secret. Only you know about it. Okay?"

"Ooh, alright." She sat silent for a few seconds and then said, "Can I 'ave a look?"

"Look at what?"

"Emma's rash."

"No you can't!" he said ushering Sarah to the door. "Emma doesn't like people to see her when she has rashes."

Sarah pouted a bit but went downstairs without any more fuss.

When Harry got back to his room, Emma was sitting on the edge of the bed, dressing gown pulled tightly about her, looking thoroughly annoyed.

"Where have you been this time?" she demanded. "You're always wandering off."

"Sarah came in while I was running the bath water."

"Christ! That's all we need. Where is she now?"

"It's okay, it's okay. I got rid of her. Told her not to tell Miss Twigg. She said she wouldn't. I'll kill the little bitch if she does."

Emma got up. "For your sake, I hope she doesn't. Let's get on with this stupid nonsense."

Grabbing his towel they both padded quietly across to the bathroom in the darkness. Emma shed the dressing gown, climbed into the steaming bath, giving him a long look of disapproval as she slid into the water.

"Well, here we go once more," she said sarcastically.

"What do you mean?"

"Here I am, stripping off in public for you again. I really do think you're a little bit perverted, Harry."

"I'm only doing this..."

"I know. For my own good. Is there anything else you have to do?"

"No. Why?" he asked.

"Because I can manage the rest on my own, thank you very much!"

"I know you can, but since Sarah is roaming about I'd rather stay here and keep an eye on things. Besides, I can run some more hot water when it starts to go cold."

"You might find it hard to believe, love, but I know how to work the taps. If you recall, we have some of our own at home. Did that epic picture you saw mention how long I'm supposed to stay in?"

He shook his head. "No. Actually I can't remember what picture it was. But you must have to stay in long enough for the heat to soak through. Perhaps half a hour or more."

"In other words, until I look like a boiled lobster."

Harry said nothing, retreating to the stool that Sarah had just vacated.

Emma gave him another long look. "Y'know, I've done more stupid things since I met you than I've ever done in my entire life. Running about stark naked in a burning layloft, playing rub-a-dub-dub in a farmer's horse trough, getting boinked while some spotty kid looks on. I keep asking myself why I do it. I don't know. I think I've lost my marbles, too. You're contagious, Harry. Contagious."

She was about to tell him yet again that this was a thoroughly silly idea, when there was a quick knock on the door and Sarah burst in, flourishing a box.

"S'cuse me, Emma, I got yer sum bakin' soda," she announced. Then noticing Harry in the corner she grinned. "Mi' mum allus uses it."

Harry went beet red with embarrassment. Emma's mouth dropped open and when Harry looked across, she was trying to slide under the water as far as she could, leaving just the top of her head poking above the surface. Had the water been soapy, this attempt at modesty might have enjoyed some success. But it wasn't; Harry could see all the way to the bottom. To make matters worse, two very pink nipples and two equally pink kneecaps now poked into the frigid air like four miniature volcanoes.

"Ah can sprinkle sum in fer yer," Sarah blithely continued, pulling out the box's small metal spout. "We just 'ave ter swish it abaht a bit. Is the rash on yer chest or yer legs?" She peered into the water for a closer look.

"Do you mind!" Emma exploded, frantically covering her crotch with one hand and her chest with the other. "What do you think I am, a shop window display?"

'Ow cum yer let **Harry** see yer all naked?"

"Okay, thanks, Sarah," Harry said, taking the box from her and feigning a smile. "I'll put it in. You'd better get back to the kitchen; otherwise your aunt will be wondering where you've gone. Remember, this is our secret."

Disappointed at not being allowed to help, she pouted, backed out of the door, then leaned in again, holding a towel.

"Almost fergot. Ah sneaked an extra one o' these fer yer," she said, and disappeared downstairs.

"Of all the..." Emma spluttered, struggling into a sitting position.

"At least, her heart was in the right place," he said, sprinkling a bit of the baking soda into the water and trying to be as nonchalant as the circumstances permitted.

"What's that going to do for a bloody pregnancy?" she demanded, pushing him away. "Honestly, Harry, I sometimes think I'm going out with one of the Marx brothers. This is absolutely ridiculous."

"Actually, Sarah's right, this stuff is quite soothing. My mum used it when we were kids."

"That might be so but I don't think it's going to do much for what might be going on inside my stomach."

Harry sighed and closed the box. Half an hour and a couple of bathtub refills later, there was another faint knock on the door.

"'As 'er rash gone away yet?"

"It's going gradually, Sarah," Harry reassured her as Emma got ready to slide under the water again. "Thanks for all your help." This time Sarah didn't come in.

After another thirty minutes of sitting in stony silence while Harry dutifully added more hot water, Emma finally ran out of patience, climbed out, and looked down at herself in shock.

"Look at me!" she hissed. "I look like a bloody prune."

Harry couldn't argue. Over an hour in a hot bath had done some startling things to her skin, none of them flattering. Upset, and shivering in the icy cold air, she rubbed herself dry, threw on his dressing gown and stalked off to get dressed. They walked to the bus stop in sullen silence. He would have driven her home but the car's road-fund licence had expired and he couldn't afford to renew it until Friday's mid-month pay advance. These days *Useless* was becoming a sore point. For one reason or other, it seemed to be out of service as much as it was in. Either he couldn't get it started, or a tyre had gone flat and so had the spare, and he never had enough money to get things fixed. So it sat in front of Miss Twigg's house mocking him, or so it seemed, every time he walked past.

Had he been honest with himself, *Useless* was merely an aggravating catalyst in an atmosphere of growing frustration. This was going to be Harry's winter of discontent, following hard on the heels of a carefree spring and summer, when for the first time in his existence he had almost felt satisfied with life. Almost. Now he sensed that Emma was tiring of him. Certainly they no longer enjoyed the mutual intimacy of their past year, and it made him feel strangely ill at ease. Gone was the sparkle in her eyes which told him he was something very special. Their actions, their conversations, even their hours in bed together, had become almost automatic. He'd noticed that they didn't laugh as much anymore and increasingly their time together terminated in a similar fashion to this evening, with Emma smoldering on the edge of resentment.

She leaned wearily against the bus-stop sign and stared at the pavement.

"Have another bath later tonight," he urged.

"Oh, Harry, for goodness sake, it's not going to do any good," she replied, as though she might be talking to an errant child.

"Do it anyway, just for me."

She nodded. "Alright." The bus came, she kissed him on the nose and climbed aboard without turning round.

The rest of the week dragged by. Harry could see impending fatherhood more clearly than ever, and in his mental turmoil was wondering whether to ask Emma to marry him. If this were last spring there would have been no hesitation. He knew she loved him then, and he thought he loved her. Now he wasn't sure about anything. Even though she remained loyal, it was with an indifference that seemed almost patronizing. It had produced two very conflicting emotions: one that wanted to gather her up and make things completely right again, and another that wanted desperately to walk away and leave it all behind.

One minute he was blaming himself for the mess he'd created, and the next, furious over her nonchalance about it. Harry was slowly tearing himself apart.

Emma grudgingly took more warm baths. And drank enough coffee to keep the Brazilian economy afloat for some time. She was cleaner than she'd ever been in her life, and so wide awake that her astonished mother didn't have to pound on the door to get her up in the mornings. Every lunch hour Harry would hurry across the street to the chemist shop. Quickly the topic would turn to the question of whether anything had arrived. After three or four days he could tell that her patience was wearing thin. By Friday they got into a row, and that evening Harry went to the pub alone.

The following morning, he drove up to Elton, having finally assembled enough cash to pay for a new licence. He had almost decided not to put it on the road again for a few more months; *Useless* appeared headed into a terminal decline and he wasn't sure if the expense would be worth it. The battery, never reliable from the outset, was in extremely poor shape, regularly needing the cranking handle. More rusted metal had crumbled from the hole in the left-rear mudguard. It made him so angry that he had more or less made up his mind to sell the car. But he'd learned what millions of other motorists already knew: car ownership was like being addicted to drugs. Never mind all those years of taking the bus and never giving it a thought; taking the bus now suddenly became an inconvenient prospect. However, if Emma's pregnancy turned into a reality, his limited resources would be needed for more important things than a car.

He sat in the kitchen fidgeting as she made him a cup of coffee. "Has anything...?" he started to ask.

"Yes, love," she said, and went on with what she was doing.

"It did?"

"Yes, love."

"When, for goodness sake?"

She said, nonchalantly, "Oh, last night, but it actually started yesterday afternoon."

Harry felt suddenly drained. An enormous wave of relief swept over him, but it was quickly replaced by anger.

"Why on earth didn't you tell me?"

She looked at him. "Because, love, I didn't see you after lunch time yesterday, remember?"

"Those warm baths must have done something. I thought they would."

"I don't think the baths had anything to do with it," she said. "All I got from that silly nonsense was dry skin and some chapped legs."

And he realized, once again, she was talking to him in a way which these days was becoming more and more familiar. There was no open hostility, simply tolerant politeness. He studied her as she folded some laundry. Had she found someone else? If so, there was little evidence of it. He found himself half-wishing she would. At least it would provide sufficient grounds for self-righteous indignation and an excuse to stop seeing her. But his other half didn't want to stop seeing her. The other half wanted things to be like they had always been.

"By the way, I'm going to the pictures tonight with Anne and one of her friends. Do you want to come?" she asked pleasantly.

Harry was startled. This was the first time since they first met that she had arranged something without him, and certainly the first time she'd gone out with her sister.

"No," he found himself saying, "You go with Anne. I want to go to the library." Damn her anyway, and damn everything.

A few days later he made a telephone call to a contractor working on one of his projects. As usual the call had to go through the Matlock exchange. The operator's voice sounded vaguely familiar.

"So, are you working hard?" it asked.

"Oh, things aren't too bad," he replied, playing for time while trying to identify the speaker.

"Don't you know who this is, Harry?" it persisted.

He had to give up. "No, I'm afraid I don't."

"It's Anne. My, my, you'd never make much of a detective!"

Of course, it was Emma's sister. Oddly, this was the first time he'd ever talked to her on the telephone— at least, that he was aware of, and he'd almost forgotten that she worked as an operator at the exchange. She had a pleasant voice, quite different from Emma's, reflecting perhaps, her training and also her age. She would be twenty-six in June.

They chatted briefly about the weather. Then she asked, "What are you doing tonight?"

"Nothing particularly," Harry replied, a little taken aback.

"How about going for a drink?" she continued. "Unless you're going out with Emma."

He wasn't. And even though something told him she knew perfectly well he wasn't seeing Emma that evening, he didn't mind. Still smarting over what he perceived to be Emma's offhanded attitude toward him, Harry decided a little revenge was in order. In any case, he told himself, he and Emma weren't married, although there had been a time when they behaved as though they were. Moreover, the recent menstrual fiasco, not to mention Emma's rather cavalier handling of the situation, had thoroughly unnerved him. For her part she seemed just as enthusiastic about sleeping with him as she had always been. It was he who had become uncharacteristically cautious; fatherhood would have been a sure way of destroying any emigration plans. In his frustration and uncertainty he was even more convinced than ever that Emma was quite prepared, despite the social consequences, to become pregnant if that was what it took to keep him in Matlock.

"Okay," he said, without hesitating. "Where can I pick you up?"

She laughed. "Oh, you don't need to do that. How about if I meet you somewhere?"

He could hardly take Anne to the *Hanging Gate*. By now, everyone there knew he and Emma were a pair. They also liked Emma, so it wouldn't be five minutes before someone was down at Madison's telling her about her boyfriend's indiscretions. That would be bad enough in itself, but learning that Harry had spent the evening with her sister could put him on the endangered-species list.

"How about the *Laughing Dog*?"

"Sounds great. I get off my shift at eight o'clock, so I'll meet you there at about eight-thirty."

As he put down the phone, a small twinge of guilt rippled through him. No doubt, it was a sneaky thing to do. But what if Emma was doing the same thing on him? In any case, she had started going out without him. Two could play at that game.

For the rest of the afternoon he wondered what had happened to Anne's boyfriend. Was he still around? Emma had not said anything about them breaking up. While Bruce wasn't a big man, Harry suspected that he could be nasty if provoked. And a date with Anne wasn't worth getting into a punch-up over. Emma said that Anne and Bruce had been going out together for several years. Perhaps she was becoming tired of him. Or perhaps she'd finally realized what a loser he was.

Mulling over the events of the past month or two, he realized that this had been coming for a while. He remained very fond of Emma; the problem lay more in the implications of the relationship than in Emma herself. It would be so very easy to take the path of least resistance: get married and settle down in the area. But each time he wavered, the siren call of his alter ego beckoned in the background. Thursday's child had to go. He had no choice.

At five o'clock he left the office by the rear exit and down through the car park to avoid being spotted from the shop by Emma. It was another dismal day, dark and cold, the streets wet with recent rain. In some ways he wished it would snow; that would at least cover up some of the grime. The warm days of summer seemed long gone, and the season's fast retreat into winter had even got Miss Twigg down. She stomped about the kitchen, cursing her rheumatism and sparring with Sarah over the most trifling things.

After dinner he went to the library and spent an hour looking through the travel literature on California. There wasn't much, although nearly all paid lip service to the state's vast agricultural industry. Maps, while clearly out of date, showed a long valley, sandwiched between the Sierra Nevada and the coast ranges, stretching for almost five-hundred miles from Redding to Bakersfield. Photographs portrayed migrant workers harvesting everything from grapes to cotton. But what particularly interested Harry was the nursery trade. He loved roses, and had always hoped to work in a rose nursery. There were at least three large rose producers in California: Jackson & Perkins, Armstrong's and O.L. Weeks. J & P grew most of their roses just outside Bakersfield in the San Joaquin Valley. The other two were located in places he couldn't find on the library's maps. Other than a brief mention of these firms in one of the travel books, there was no further elaboration.

Anne was already in the pub when he got there, quietly sipping a gin and tonic and being eyed by a couple of hungry-looking males. She smiled broadly as he entered the almost-empty lounge.

"I was thirsty!" she said.

This was the first opportunity he'd had to get a good look at Emma's sister. She was an attractive girl, but with coarser features than Emma, and taller by at least a couple of inches. Judging from the bulges in her woollen rollneck sweater, Anne also had a much larger bust. She sat back, her long fingers toying with a freshly lit cigarette, and took stock of him while he ordered a pint and another gin and tonic.

"Sorry I'm a little late," he said, trying to make conversation.

She smiled again, revealing beautifully perfect teeth. "You're not. I was early!"

They talked about nothing in particular. Then she said, "I hear you're thinking of going abroad."

"Who told you that?" he asked, knowing full well.

"Emma, of course."

"Oh, I've been making some inquiries," he said. "Nothing much has come up yet."

She tapped the ash from her cigarette and looked around the lounge. "I wouldn't mind getting away from this. I mean, it's so bloody tedious. There must be better places."

Harry laughed. "That's exactly what I told myself!"

"I also hear you're not going out with my sister anymore."

He blinked. This was news to him. Who had told her **that** one?

"Well, not quite," he replied. "If I do emigrate I'd like her to go with me, but she's not keen on leaving your mum. And I honestly don't think she understands why I would want to go. She doesn't see anything wrong with England. Maybe there isn't. Maybe it's all in my imagination. I don't know. That's the difference between us. I've got an itchy foot; Emma hasn't. I sometimes wish I hadn't either. It keeps getting me into so much trouble."

Anne sipped on her drink. "I wondered if you'd got her preggers and were taking off!"

He could tell from the sly way she was looking at him that Emma's recent crisis had leaked out. And for a fleeting moment it annoyed him that a near-stranger should presume that he would consider doing such a thing.

"No," he said, embarrassed. "It's got nothing to do with that. And anyway, she's okay... as you probably know."

"Well, I didn't know for certain, but I'm sure there would have been a very loud squawk if she **had** got pregnant." She looked directly at him, her deep blue eyes scanning his face. "I don't know why my sister doesn't get on the pill. It isn't that difficult if you know where to go."

He assumed from this remark that Anne **did** know where to go, and **had** gone. Sitting there, she looked so much more mature than Emma.

"So, where are you thinking of emigrating to?"

"Somewhere warm! I'm tired of being cold."

"Don't tell me," she said. "California!"

For some reason this also rankled. While Anne seemed a very pleasant girl she had a way of making seemingly innocent remarks slice like a knife. But perhaps he was being a little over-sensitive.

"As a matter of fact, yes," he replied defensively. "At least, California's one option. Problem is getting a job."

"Oh, so you need a job first?"

"From what I can understand. They have a quota system, but a sure way of getting in is to get a written job offer. And yet I can't really see a company offering a job to somebody they've never set eyes on, so it seems to me there's a bit of a catch-twenty-two situation there. I'd have to work for a private firm because I don't think you can work for government unless you are an American citizen."

"Must seem strange to change your nationality," Anne said.

He agreed. "I'm not sure whether I really want to. What I want to do most of all is see a bit of the world for a few years. Maybe then I could come back home and settle down."

"You'd go away for **years**?" Obviously, Anne had been thinking in much shorter terms than that.

"I don't think you can understand a country unless you live there for a while," he said, repeating what he had told himself. "Otherwise you might just as well be a tourist."

They talked more about things in general. Anne coasted through a gin and tonic like it was water, although they took turns in paying for each other's drinks. He wanted to ask her about Bruce but couldn't bring himself to raise the issue. She had never mentioned him all evening, and Harry was dying of curiosity. As she ordered her fourth drink, he saw that it was nearly ten-thirty. Was she going home? If so, the last bus had left long ago. If not, was someone going to pick her up. Bruce perhaps? Under the circumstances he couldn't see that happening. She could, of course, be expecting him to take her home. And if it weren't for the likelihood of Emma spotting them, he would have jumped at the chance.

After another fifteen minutes, he decided to break the impasse. "I suppose I should run you home," he said as casually as he could. "You probably have to work tomorrow morning."

Anne smiled. "Actually, I don't start work until noon. I'm on shifts, remember?"

"Oh."

"Tell me," she said, looking directly at him again, "what's my sister like in bed?"

He nearly choked on his beer. "She's, er, good. I suppose. Why?"

"I was going to propose that we older women can do better, that's all!"

For a moment the silence was deafening. He could hardly believe what she had just said. After years of being rejected and ridiculed by the opposite sex, along came Emma. That was spectacular in itself. But now her sister wanted him, too? Or was he misunderstanding her remark? He must be. She couldn't have said what he thought she said.

"I have a rather squeaky bed," he replied, aiming at a nebulous response in case she **hadn't** meant what she seemed to be implying.

"That's very nice. I'll bet I can make it squeak more than Emma!"

Good God, he thought. How am I going to get **her** in and out of Miss Twigg's? It would be one thing to get caught with Emma. Getting caught with Anne was something else entirely. Like just about everyone else, Miss Twigg had become very fond of Emma. And how about Sarah? If she decided to view the proceedings through her little peep hole it wouldn't take many seconds to realize that it wasn't Emma in bed with him.

But while all these potential problems ran through his head, and a very tiny voice at the back of his head was trying to tell him that this wasn't being very fair to Emma, an even stronger carnal urge raced ahead of everything. He quickly silenced the opposition by telling himself he was too young and too inexperienced to settle down and besides, the affair might make him appreciate in Emma what he could be taking for granted.

They finished their drinks and headed back to Derwent House. His heart was pounding and his throat felt dry, just like it had when he slept with Emma for the first time. Anxiously he scanned the windows for lights. There were none. Silently they went inside. No one appeared to be in the kitchen. He could see the reflection of a dying fire against the half-open serving-hatch door, but no luminescence which would indicate that her television was on. Anne seemed to be enjoying the intrigue immensely. She could afford to, he thought. He would be the one out in the street if Miss Twigg found them, not her. They crept up the stairs in the darkness while he hastily tried to come up with some plausible excuse in the event Miss Twigg appeared on the landing. After briefly pressing his ear to Sarah's door and hearing nothing, they were in his room.

"Christ, it's cold in here!" Anne exclaimed. Her voice, crisp and clear, cracked the frigid silence like a gunshot.

Hastily, and fearing doom even before they got started, Harry put his fingers to his lips, pointing frantically to the wall separating his room from Sarah's. With a grin, Anne simply began peeling off her clothes with the casual panache of someone who has done it many times before. He stood and watched in awe. And his earlier assessment had been correct. She did have a bigger bust than Emma. In fact, in some ways she had a nicer figure all round. Whereas Emma's was fine and petite, Anne's body was fuller, and she had much longer legs. He also noticed that she had carefully trimmed her pubic hair. Her perfume quickly reached his nostrils. Unlike Emma's, light and subtle to the senses, Anne's was bold, with a challenging rawness to it. Two less-alike siblings would be hard to find. He would never have believed they were sisters.

As she slid into bed, the wardrobe door swung open as usual. Over the past year Harry had noticed that the wardrobe door swung open only while he was in bed, never while he was out of the room. He'd finally concluded that its odd behavior must be triggered by additional weight on the floor joists, causing the wardrobe to lean forward slightly. The only other possible explanation might be some relatives of the gremlins that had taken up residence inside his car. He frowned and moved to close it, but Anne nonchalantly leaned over, pushed the door shut, then briefly studied herself in its mirrored panel before turning back to watch Harry undress. Catching sight of his scrawny frame in the mirror reminded him of the first time he and Emma slept together, and how awkward he had been. Some of that feeling flooded back as he wondered why someone as experienced and desirable as Anne would be interested in having sex with a skinny fellow like him.

But whatever misgivings he might have had, they quickly disappeared as she applied all her talents. As Harry reached to turn off the bedside lamp, she pulled his hand away. Moments later he caught her watching their performance in the wardrobe mirror. This girl was so different from her sister. Unlike Emma, who tended to leave the initiating to Harry, Anne was decidedly proactive, and clearly accustomed to getting her way. With a smile that hardly left her face, she smoothly manipulated him through half a dozen different positions, most of which he had never even thought about. The bed squealed loudly, almost as loudly as Anne. It might have been cold inside the room, but Harry wouldn't have known had it been the north pole. Half an hour later he found himself expended, exhausted, and covered in perspiration.

Despite Anne's expertise, however, and after all the passion of the moment, he felt a strange sense of emptiness. Something was missing from the times he'd shared with Emma. For Anne this was sexual gratification, pure and simple. With Emma there had been the warmth and intimacy of two people with a mutual respect and love for each other. Before now he would never have believed this would make a meaningful difference.

By midnight they were both satiated. The piece of glass in the door hadn't fallen out, an encouraging sign that Sarah wasn't around. When Anne had to visit the lavatory, he cautioned her to be on the lookout for Miss Twigg. She left without bothering to put on Harry's dressing gown, her full breasts bobbing rhythmically as she padded across the floor. Hurrying back a mass of goose pimples, she reported that no one had intercepted her. Nevertheless, Harry spent a troubled night, tossing and turning while Anne slept soundly. The following morning he awoke at seven o'clock. It was Friday. He had to go to work; Anne didn't, and made no bones about her reluctance to get up. She glared at him from beneath the quilt.

"No one comes into your room to make the bed or anything, do they?" she protested.

"No, but— "

"So, I'll just stay quietly here until a bit later and then sneak out. I know where the front door is."

Harry was becoming angry. "But what if someone **does** come in? I don't want to lose my digs yet."

"Then I'll simply lie still until they leave. It'll be okay. Honestly."

He could see she wasn't going to budge. Thankfully, Sarah wasn't scheduled to change the bed linen until tomorrow. With luck he might get away with it. He got up, shaved and dressed, and went down for breakfast. Afterwards, when Sarah had gone back into the kitchen, he spirited a couple of pieces of cold toast up to his room.

"Thought you might be hungry," he said to the prone bundle in his bed.

"Thanks," a muffled voice replied. "I'll have it later."

"Shall I see you again?" he asked before leaving. But he wasn't sure if he wanted to see her again. The sexual experience had been exciting; she had a great body, but a nagging sense of betrayal was now doing its best to spoil it all. Moreover, Anne's clinical approach to the entire affair had begun to irk him. It seemed almost as though she arranged these encounters simply to keep in practice.

"Ring me," he heard her say.

He drew back the top sheet a few inches and lightly kissed her on the forehead. Anne didn't move.

Halfway down the stairs it occurred to him that she hadn't given him a telephone number to ring. It was all well and good that she worked at the telephone exchange, but what was **their** number?

Saturday dawned a pleasant day for a change, even though it remained cold. A winter sun presided over the town and the craggy rocks of Matlock Bath, casting shadows among the barren tree branches beyond his window. He assumed Anne must have made good her escape the morning before, since there had been no fallout from either Sarah or her aunt. Even more surprising was that she had made the bed before leaving.

Harry was bored. He hadn't seen or talked to Emma since the previous weekend, and he was still trying to make up his mind whether to call Anne again. Two years ago, even the prospect of sleeping with someone like her would have had him foaming at the mouth. It wasn't that he'd become blasé about sex. It was just that for the first time in his young life he had begun to realize that, contrary to what his miserable years in boarding school had taught him, self-indulgence can exact a price. There, it had been the key element of survival in a solitary world. Now, the real world was telling him something entirely different; his painful experience with Emma was testament to that.

With the car almost out of petrol, he had decided to spend part of the day in the library. There wasn't much left unread on the topic now dominating the forefront of his mind, but the library was a cheap form of entertainment, and infinitely warmer than Miss Twigg's house at that time of year. Perhaps, after Emma finished work, they could spend the evening together. After all, they hadn't parted on a particularly sour note the last time, and it had seemed like a very long week without her, even though he had enjoyed being on his own for a change. He would walk up to the shop at noon and catch her on her lunch break. Maybe she could stay with him overnight. There was just one problem. Although faint, a trace of Anne's perfume still lingered in his bedroom, and Emma would be sure to recognize it if, for some reason Sarah hadn't changed the bed linen as she normally did on Saturdays. For that matter, he hoped Sarah wouldn't notice it either. After finishing breakfast he went back to his room and sprinkled a bit of his own cologne on the sheets.

The library was predictably warm. He pored again over some of the material he had read a dozen times before. Just before twelve o'clock he strode up Bank Street to the chemist shop. Behind the massive plate-glass window he could see Emma serving a customer. Since the counter ran at right angles to the window, she would usually give him a little underhanded wave without being noticed by anyone inside the shop. He knew she had seen him approach, but this time there was no wave. Instead, she carried on with what she was doing.

The small, brass bell over the shop door gave its familiar tinkle as he entered. After stepping aside to let the solitary customer pass, he turned to see that Mrs. Johnson had also appeared behind the counter. Neither smiled. It was at that point he got the first inkling he might be in trouble.

"Sorry I haven't been over the last few days," he said, grinning sheepishly. "But I thought perhaps we could go for a pint tonight."

Emma gave him a stony look. "I'm afraid not, Harry," she replied. "I'm busy. Besides, I hear you're quite busy yourself these days."

"Busy?" he said, unsure exactly what she meant. "Who told you that?"

"Who do you think?"

"I've no idea."

"I think you do," she said with a half-smile.

"Oh," was all Harry managed to say.

He couldn't believe Anne would be crass enough to tell her sister that she had slept with him. But as he stood foolishly in the middle of the shop floor, it began to dawn on him that was exactly what she had done, possibly in a deliberate act of spitefulness. No one else could have betrayed him because no one else knew. The bitch. He cursed inwardly for being so naive. Why would she do it? He'd done nothing to her. Even the other night had been her idea. Was she one of those females who got their jollies out of emasculating men? If so, he'd been a textbook patsy.

Mrs. J's rouged lips creased into an ugly sneer. He had to talk to Emma privately, away from her supervisor's big mouth and inquisitive ears. Even though he knew perfectly well that he was getting exactly what he deserved, their relationship couldn't end like this, not after a year, without even a whimper, and just as important, without him firing a shot.

It was still her lunch hour. "Do you have time to go for a cup of coffee?" he persisted, trying hard not to betray his embarrassment.

She smiled slightly and shook her head. "Not really. We're busy getting the shop ready for Christmas. Mrs. J's swamped."

"Could we just talk then, for a moment?"

She shook her head again.

There was another awkward silence. Harry fidgeted with his raincoat belt. Emma resumed piling up some empty boxes destined for the stock room. He looked vainly for something, anything, in her face that might suggest that she was just trying to teach him a lesson. Instead, with an impassive shrug, she began to walk off.

"Bye, bye, Harry," Mrs. J. said sweetly.

Red-faced, and with anger welling inside, he turned on his heel and left the shop without saying anything further. It was hard enough to be humiliated by Emma; Mrs. J. had made him look a complete fool. Striding furiously down Bank Street, he simultaneously cursed the day they had met, Dickie for introducing them to each other, and himself for getting involved. This was the last time any woman would make an ass out of him. And if he had been less than convinced about emigrating before, he wasn't now. Someone his age didn't need a millstone like Emma hanging round his neck. He didn't need encumbrances; even Dickie had told him that. At twenty-three he was too young for marriage.

Still, he couldn't bring himself to believe that this might be the end. And not, his ego told him, without putting up at least some semblance of a fight. He should go back to the shop and say something... he wasn't sure what... that would put him, not Emma and that old bag, on the dominant side of the ledger. After that, perhaps he could negotiate an end from a position of strength. As it stood, they were having the last word and that angered him almost as much as Emma's scorn.

But he didn't go back to the shop. He kept on walking. And he never spoke to Emma again. The following week, after working late one afternoon, he glanced down from the office window to the street corner. It was five-thirty. As he watched, the shop lights went out, and Emma came out accompanied by a male in a dark-blue raincoat. She pushed her arm through his, just like she and Harry had done so many times before, and they disappeared into the night. He slumped onto Bill Lewis's chair, sadly watching the empty street as a thousand emotions flooded through his head. Memories of cloudless summer days, and miles of moorland walks; that familiar tug on his sleeve when he walked too fast; the delicate smell of her perfume beneath a pile of crumpled sheets; evenings at the *Hanging Gate* and the pleasant sensation of being regarded as a couple. And always Emma's kiss which told him that he'd survived another pratfall. Now, there was only an emptiness which nothing else seemed to be filling. At that moment he would have given anything to be in the fellow's shoes. Yet, whether he wanted to accept the fact or not, he alone was the architect of all this. Had he been less naive, more honest, and less impatient with life, none of this would have happened, and he wouldn't be sitting alone in an empty office feeling sorry for himself. At least, not now. But what about later? What about in a year's time, two year's time, five years, maybe? Could he instead be sitting in this empty office, cursing his dead-end job and a dead-end country, and mourning the opportunities that had slipped through his fingers? Only time would tell.

The replies he had received from the London embassies were all helpful in explaining the immigration process. But none offered any direct leads on finding a job, and it soon became apparent that the two tasks really could develop into an impossible situation: one couldn't emigrate until one had a job, and it looked as though it might be difficult to find a job without being there. In his letter to the American Embassy he had specifically mentioned a desire to settle in California. They suggested that, given his particular skills, he contact the California Nurserymen's Association and even provided a name and address: a Mr. Jim Watts of Redondo Beach. He looked up Redondo Beach in the atlas, noticing that it was just south of Los Angeles. It all sounded very grand. Spurred on by the bruising he'd received at the hands of Emma and Mrs. Johnson, he quickly he drafted up a letter and an updated resume, complete with the names of a couple of referees, got one of the girls in the typing pool to type them for him, and airmailed the package off. Without asking, he had used Dickie as a referee. Now he worried that they might contact him before Harry got a chance to explain what he was doing.

Soon after that flurry of activity, a letter arrived, out of the blue, from Canada. Noting from the top of the envelope that it was from the Government of Alberta, he feverishly ripped it open to find that it was from the Personnel Department, advising him that Public Works would be making its annual recruitment tour of Great Britain in January. They would be looking for architects, draughtsmen, and someone they referred to as a 'landscape technician.' The assistant personnel director explained that their Canadian High Commission in London, being aware of this annual pilgrimage, had written to the Government of Alberta on his behalf. Would he be interested, the Personnel Department asked, in having his name added to the interview list?

This was incredible. Would he be interested? Was the Pope Catholic? Of course, he would be interested. Harry could hardly believe that some foreign agency, which didn't even know him from a hole in the ground, would take the trouble. Elated and more than a little flattered, he sat in the dining room after dinner and read the letter over and over again. It went on to suggest he send a resume to the Minister of Public Works, indicating what type of position he wished to be interviewed for. The Minister's office, in turn, would advise him where and on what date the interviews would be held. Once again the young girl in the typing pool patiently made up another resume for him, this time on the Gestetner so he could make additional copies.

After work he trudged up Steep Turnpike to the library to scrutinize a map of Alberta more closely. Its capital city was Edmonton, located almost in the centre of the province. London had a borough by the same name; was there some connection? Photographs he found in a travel book showed a vast land of wheat fields, oil pumps called 'rocking horses', miles of arrow-straight highways, all against a backdrop of towering, snow-capped mountains. It would certainly be different from anything he'd ever experienced in England.

Despite the recent developments, Harry felt oddly out of sorts. Still smarting from his losing confrontation with Emma, he went home for Christmas but not before posting her a Christmas card. He didn't want it to end like this; in fact, part of him didn't want it to end at all. He was tempted to grovel, but finally resisted. It was just as well; he received no card from her. The Christmas party, again at the *Hanging Gate*, happened without his attendance. He couldn't face the prospect of spending an evening being grilled by the likes of Carol on the whereabouts of his girlfriend. Besides, Carol was right. Aside from watching colleagues make asses out of themselves, it really was a bore, although no more boring than being at home for Christmas. It was undoubtedly the worst Christmas he had ever spent with his mother. While time had to some extent smoothed the raw edges of their differences over Emma, an awkwardness lingered, despite Harry's confession that they had split up. He found it difficult to forgive her treatment of Emma.

Then, to compound an already difficult situation, Harry's plans to emigrate became another contentious issue. She had looked at him silently for what seemed a lifetime, and then said she had never been aware that he was so ashamed of his family he would want to leave the country. And for some reason she couldn't bring herself to believe her son would be able to resist the temptation to take Emma with him if he did go. Of course, it had never occurred to him that emigrating might be viewed as a social indictment. Looking back on the occasion years later, it was easy to see why. Intergenerational linkages held an imperative he could never understand. Practically everyone in his home town had been born there, and invariably they died there, and most were proud of that fact. Leaving was tantamount to heresy. Harry was devastated. The days dragged by. Barnsley at the end of December looked even drearier than Matlock, and it rained the entire time.

Two days after his returning to work, the long-awaited letter from Alberta arrived, advising him that his interview would be on January 15th, 1963, in Liverpool, at 2 PM. He would be meeting the Minister of Public Works, his Deputy, and Assistant Deputy at the Adelphi Hotel. At first this seemed like a bit of overkill for some lowly draughting position, until he remembered that they were also hiring architects. The letter instructed him to bring with him a copy of his birth certificate, some examples of his work, and any letters of reference he could lay his hands on. It was finally time to tell Dickie.

"Sensible idea," said Dickie, to Harry's astonishment. He had managed to corner his boss a few days later in his office, and was expecting a response similar to the one he had got from his mother. "I think more young chaps should move out to the colonies," he continued while vigorously stirring his coffee cup. "More opportunity out there. I can tell you, my young friend, if I were your age, I would be doing the same thing."

Harry breathed a sigh of relief. But 'colonies?' He had never thought of Canada being a colony, and he didn't think Canadians would either. Dickie's remark, while typical for his generation, seemed to be yet another manifestation of what was wrong with a country stubbornly refusing to acknowledge that its imperial days were over.

Privately, Harry's announcement delighted Dickie. It had been evident from the outset that his newest recruit's inability to understand basic surveying principles compromised his usefulness to the section, and Dickie was already scheming to replace him. Indeed he could hardly believe that within a matter of months his two major headaches might be gone. Clem's untimely death had made life easier, not to mention safer; Harry's voluntary departure would avoid the unpleasantness of sacking him. Yes, he would be more than happy to provide a glowing testimonial... and anything else that might speed up the process.

"I don't suppose you'll be taking Emma with you?" he said casually.

Harry shuffled his feet uncomfortably. "I don't think so," he replied, unsure about Dickie's views on issues such as that, although it had been he who had introduced Harry to Emma in the first place. By now it was common knowledge that he and Emma were having problems, but Harry had been very tight-lipped on what had actually happened, and even more secretive about his future plans. "We talked about it some time ago, but she's reluctant to leave her family and especially her mother. She sees North America as such a long way away."

Dickie narrowed his eyes. "I'll give you a piece of advice, my friend," he said. "Emma's a fine lass, but you're not married, and there's an old truth that says 'he who travels alone, travels fastest.' I've known one or two fellows who emigrated to New Zealand and Australia. Either they settled down and their wives didn't, or the other way 'round, and they found themselves in a hell of a mess. Two of them wound up getting divorced, and all but one finally came back. If I were you, I would strike out on my own. That way, you've got only yourself to worry about."

Unknown to his boss, that was precisely what Harry had already decided to do. It provided welcome confirmation, nonetheless.

The train pulled into Liverpool's Lime Street station half an hour late, but he had plenty of time to walk over to the Adelphi, a few minutes away. It was another cold, overcast day, almost freezing, Harry reckoned, with a blustery wind to match. As he struggled down Lime Street, the city reminded him of a new singing group called the Beatles, which was beginning to get a lot of air time on radio and television. It seemed like a funny name but no less plausible than the working-class city that had spawned them. Liverpool was still showing the scars of bomb damage from the Second World War. The dock facilities were a prime target of the Luftwaffe between 1940 and 1941, but inevitably other areas became casualties as the war dragged on. It was a dour-looking place in the early 1960's, rendered even more so by the occasional ruins and craters. Its mercantile core, heavily overlaid with Victorian architecture, presented a sombre backdrop to those leaving Britain's shores for the last time. Since the mid-nineteenth century, nearly ten-million emigrants had passed through Liverpool's docks on their way to the New World. Harry couldn't think of a more depressing send-off.

Turning down Renelagh Street, he noticed St. John's Beacon and the old Playhouse Theatre off to the north in the park. January was a poor time for parks, he concluded. They all looked the same, cold and abandoned. The Adelphi Hotel had been one of Liverpool's plushest hostelries. Built in 1914 during the Edwardian era's heyday of transatlantic steam travel, it boasted many excesses, not the least of which was a replica of the first-class lounge found on the ill-fated Titanic, replete with dozens of aspidistras and fan palms. But like the city itself, the Adelphi had suffered in recent years from the emerging supremacy of air travel. On this day, like too many others, it wasn't busy. Under the watchful eye of several immaculately attired bellboys, he strode across an immense marble floored foyer to the reception desk. The Alberta Government representatives were housed on the fifth floor, they told him. Clutching the slip of paper the desk clerk had scribbled on, Harry made his way to the manually operated lifts and up to their suite of rooms.

A tall, cadaverous man in his early fifties answered the door, introducing himself as Stanley Gardner, the Department's assistant deputy minister. Harry gave him his name and then followed the man down a narrow plush-carpeted corridor to a small living room. Two settees and three overstuffed armchairs surrounded a coffee table piled with maps and brochures. Through the room's large windows, framed by beige velvet curtains, he could see the grey outline of the city's commercial district. As they entered, a short, stocky man with a close-cropped, balding head lurched to his feet from one of the chairs. He signalled with a sweep of his arm to his assistant to sit down.

"Hi there," he said with a wide smile through thick lips, "So you're Robin Michaels, then? Pleased ta meetcha. Siddown."

Harry went through his usual first-name, middle-name routine, upon which both men smiled indulgently, clearly more comfortable with Harry's preferred moniker than with Robin.

"Gotcha. Okay," the fat man continued. "I'm Art Swinerton, deputy minister of Public Works." He nodded his head towards the man who had ushered Harry in. "You've obviously met Stan here; he's our A.D.M. Then there's our Minister of Public Works, Harry Sewchuk. Ah, he isn't feeling too well and he's sleeping it off— I mean, he's sleeping at the moment." Then he added in a softer voice, "Lotta Ukrainians in government, ya know!"

Harry wasn't even aware that there were Ukrainians in Canada, let alone in government. Who were Ukrainians anyway? He smiled politely and waited.

"So," Gardner piped up, with just a trace of a British accent, "ever been to Canada?"

Harry advised them that he'd never set foot off British shores in his entire life.

"Hm, hell of a shame," Swinerton said, shaking his head. "Beautiful country, Canada. 'Specially if you're an outdoors kinda guy. D'ya do any huntin' or fishin'?"

Again, Harry had to disillusion them. It wasn't a good start. Still, he'd experienced a pretty disastrous interview with Dickie nearly a year and a half earlier, and had wound up with the job. So it was obvious that first impressions could not always be taken at face value. There was still hope.

"So, wadd'ya do in your spare time?"

What Harry had mostly been doing in his spare time, at least during the past year, was hardly any of their business, but he felt obliged to offer something.

"A bit of tennis now and again."

"Tennis?" the fat man exclaimed. "Jees. You'll be telling me next you went to one them British boarding schools."

"I'm afraid I did," Harry confessed

"Oh, God!"

The two men had a chuckle and then lapsed into silence as Swinerton finally decided to glance through Harry's resume. "I see you're with the Derbyshire County Council," he said, peering over the top of the paper. He pronounced Derbyshire 'Durbishyre' and dropped his 't's. "Done any spec writing?"

"A little," Harry replied. "We're responsible for drafting up our own specs and then the quantity surveyors finalize them."

Swinerton's face creased into a frown. "Quantity sur....? Oh, yeah, that's what you guys call estimators. Ha, ha! Well, I tell ya, Harry, we're lookin' for some young fella who can do our landscape-design work. Right now the architectural guys are trying to do it, but they don't have the time or the know-how and it's got to the point where a couple of landscape contractors are pretty well writing their own tickets. And I think we're gettin' shafted. Mind ya, I don't think Stan here agrees with me, do ya, Stan!"

Gardner shrugged and smiled.

"I'm afraid I'm not a landscape architect," Harry confessed. Swinerton's line sounded familiar.

"Oh, jeez, we're not looking for one. He'd want too much... er, he wouldn't fit in with our overall plans," Gardner hurriedly replied.

Looking at the envelope Harry was nursing, Swinerton asked, "D'ya bring any work samples?"

"Yes," Harry replied, "the letter from your Personnel Department told me to." He flushed out the drawings and a copy of a specification he'd drawn up for the Buxton project.

Swinerton glanced at his subordinate and winked.

"Good old Alex, always on the ball," he said without explaining who Alex was, or what his role in this affair had been.

Both men briefly pored over Harry's material and nodded.

"How much of this stuff is your own work? Like, I mean, how much did you actually do yourself?" Swinerton asked.

"All of it," Harry answered, truthfully.

"Drawings, too?"

"Yes."

Swinerton said "Hm," and Gardner stuffed the papers back into the envelope and handed them back.

"How old are ya, Harry?" Swinerton asked, leaning back in the chair to give his very large stomach some extra breathing room. Protruding well beyond the ornate brass and chrome buckle that struggled to keep up his shapeless trousers, it had already begun to burst through his shirt buttons. Shifting his gaze downwards, Harry noticed something odd about the man's suit. It was pale grey, with elaborate stitch work on the pockets, and in place of a tie he was wearing a length of silk rope threaded through what looked like a polished piece of jade. A pair of intricately tooled cowboy boots completed the ensemble. It all looked as alien as moon dust.

"Twenty-three. I'll be twenty-four in July," he answered.

"Married?"

"No." He couldn't think why they would be asking these questions since Swinerton, at least, had glanced through his resume.

"Would you call yourself a team player?" Gardner chipped in.

"Actually, I've never played much sport," Harry confessed.

"I wasn't talking about sports," he said thinly. "I meant, do you work well with other people?"

"Oh, I see. Er, yes, sort of, although I tend to work better alone."

"We're looking for team players to fill our ranks," Gardner concluded with a slight sneer.

"Well, I tell ya, Alberta's a great place to live," said Swinerton, changing the subject. "Out west we have a different outlook on life from them easterners. We got a good government, lotsa room to grow, and a great economy. So long as them wells keep pumpin', eh, Stan!"

Stan forced a laugh. Swinerton eyed his subordinate with barely concealed contempt. Every time Gardner opened his mouth, Harry became more convinced that here was an ex-Brit doing his best to fit the part he clearly didn't measure up to. And Swinerton seemed to have reached a similar conclusion. He treated Gardner with the same patronizingly good humour that Emma had used on Harry in recent months. Unlike the transparent Gardner, Swinerton was obviously a born Canadian, and although a little strutting bully, he had a persona that Harry found difficult to dislike. He could see this man running his empire like a latter-day czar, building a bureaucracy to be the envy of all his fellow mandarins. Gardner, on the other hand, oozed the kind of groveling insincerity he'd seen too many times in local politics, and it wasn't a pretty sight. Both men were now administrators, but he wondered what sort of training had prepared them for the positions they currently occupied. In the case of Gardner, kissing backsides most likely.

"Alberta's growing fast," Gardner said, grabbing a pamphlet from the coffee table and trying to imitate his superior's drawl. "The province's up to a million people already, but there'll always be plenty of open space. Most folks have a home and a cottage at the lake. If you want to go hunting, you can do it without having to sign a thousand forms."

"And we got the Rockies," Swinerton interrupted. "Biggest pile of goddamn rock ya ever saw. Beautiful, though."

"Oh, yeah, beautiful," Gardner concurred.

"In fact, I'd say we got the best goddamn province in Canada," Swinerton concluded. "And we're gonna keep it that way, aren't we, Stan?"

Gardner said Amen to that, too.

By this time Harry had begun to wonder if he'd stumbled into a tourism seminar, rather than a job interview. He sat, as always on the edge of his seat, eyes crossing from one man to the other like a tennis spectator. They both rambled on for another fifteen minutes, taking turns to flourish various bits of literature that lay in front of them. A seemingly endless parade of glossy-colour photographs were flashed in front of his face: aerial shots of a very flat city with some tall buildings shooting skywards like asparagus spears, pristine lakes, white-capped mountains, fast-flowing streams, herds of very large woolly animals, chrome-encrusted American cars, families barbecuing steaks, more herds of large woolly animals, and on and on. Finally, Swinerton appeared to run out of breath.

"So, young fella, got any questions? Ask away."

There were a thousand and one things Harry would like to know, but all seemed rather parsimonious amid this parade of glitz and glamour.

"Er, let me see, er," he began. "If I get a job, do I have to pay my own way to Canada?"

Both men looked slightly offended.

"Well, hell, yeah, 'course ya do," Swinerton said gruffly. "We're in the hiring business, not immigration. That's the deal. We provide the job, you provide the transportation."

Harry nodded. "I see. Can you tell me what salaries are like? I mean, are they higher than here?"

"Higher than here?" Gardner exclaimed. "I'll say they're higher than here! About twice as high, wouldn't you say, Art?"

"Christ, yeah," said Swinerton. "Maybe three or four times higher, depending o' course, on what kinda work you're doin'."

"So, what would be the salary range for this position, for example?" Harry persisted. "Just to give me some idea, that's all."

The two men looked at each other again, waiting for the other to speak.

"Jesus, I dunno," Swinerton finally said. "What the hell **is** the salary range for this classification, Stan?"

The other man looked every bit as perplexed. Both fumbled for a figure.

"Kind of hard to say," said Gardner. "I'll be honest, this is sort of a new position that we snuck into the pile at the last minute. It's not even official. Besides, Personnel deals with pay scales and that kinda stuff."

"Wadd'ya getting now?" Swinerton asked after another pause.

"Seven hundred and eighty pounds," replied Harry. "But I could be getting a fairly large raise this year." It was a bald-faced lie. Terry had got a raise; Harry hadn't and probably wouldn't. However, he gambled on the slim chance of them ever finding out.

"Okay, well, let's see, this'll probably come in as a **Draftsman-1** position. So, at roughly two bucks to the pound...you'd be starting at about five times what you're getting now... in Canadian dollars, of course."

Even Harry's pathetic arithmetic told him that this amounted to almost four-thousand dollars. It seemed like an unbelievable sum of money. What he didn't know at the time was that Canadian governments were deliberately using this simple multiplication exercise to lure starry-eyed recruits, particularly those who were young and inexperienced. They failed to point out that it held little relevance to the cost of living in Canada, and that in real terms many recruits wound up financially worse off than they had been in England.

"And the pay scales are under review," Gardner added while rearranging the piles of brochures.

While Harry could hardly avoid being impressed, something about these two individuals and the flimflam they were peddling mildly disturbed him, although he couldn't precisely put his finger on it. Perhaps it was because they both smacked of the same suffocating paternalism he saw in the excesses of British government. From the way they talked he could see that both were empire-building bureaucrats out for their own selfish interests, and people like Harry stood a good chance of being not much more than cannon fodder in the process. Still, the salary did sound promising.

"What we need is guys who'll stick around," Swinerton said. "We've been recruiting from Britain for the past three or four years, and frankly I'm getting a bit pissed off with people we hire who get homesick after six months. They're just wasting our goddamn time, ya know what I mean?"

Harry nodded.

"Takes a lotta time and money to hire and train people. And when they don't stay, it's Stan and me who get our asses in a sling," he continued. "And ya know what we've found, hm?"

"No," Harry said, truthfully.

"Ya know what we found?"

"Er, no, I don't."

Swinerton jabbed his stubby finger at him. "We found that young single guys like you are the worst! Always itchin' to move on."

"Well, I, er, I don't think..." Harry began.

"Don't get me wrong. We're not saying you'd do that," Swinerton interrupted. "Just thought ya oughta know the way we sit, that's all."

After making his point, they all settled down again. Once more the brochures were flashed, and Gardner waxed eloquent on the joys of moose hunting. Swinerton bragged about the ranch he'd recently built, even producing a couple of snapshots of the place from his jacket pocket. Harry was even more impressed but no less concerned. After another thirty minutes, both men again ran out of steam.

"Anyhow, Son, that's the way it is," Swinerton concluded. "We'll be lettin' ya know within a month, once we've interviewed all the people we've got lined up. Did Edinburgh last week and next week we're taking the dog-and-pony show down to London town."

With that, they all stood. Swinerton hitched up his trousers, scratched his crotch and shook Harry's hand. Gardner showed him out, smiling weakly as he closed the door.

Walking back to the railway station, Harry mentally compiled all the things he'd wanted to ask his two interviewers, and hadn't. For example, what was accommodation like there? After a year and a half in some dingy digs, the prospect of a flat of his own— even perhaps a house— would have been a powerful incentive. And how much did American cars cost? The big chrome boats he'd glimpsed in their brochures seemed light years beyond reach for young men his age. But the photographs showed young men driving them. Was it very cold there during winter? It looked so, and Harry wasn't keen on moving somewhere even colder than where he was living at present. And what were the chances of promotion? Although he hadn't specifically asked about it, Swinerton and Gardner had nonetheless carefully avoided the issue. He waited for the train in a fit of self-recrimination, angry at himself for not having the guts to ask the questions that were important to him.

A couple of weeks went by. Harry waited impatiently for some word from Alberta. In the meantime he had thought about ringing Anne. After more than three weeks without Emma's companionship, a gnawing emptiness was turning into frustration. But Anne hadn't contacted him again, which meant one of two things: either she'd done the damage she intended, or he hadn't measured up to her expectations. Of course, there was also a possibility that Bruce had reappeared. For all he knew, she could still be going out with him. Either way, he didn't feel like setting himself up for more humiliation. All in all, it might be better to stay away; she'd made a fool of him once and she could do it again.

Emma was another matter. He missed her more than he ever thought possible, but like Anne she also had completely ignored him. The young fellow with the stylish raincoat seemed to be calling by the shop at closing time with increasing regularity. It didn't bode well for rapprochement.

So Harry spent more evenings in the public library, and at the *Hanging Gate*, and cursing the miserable weather. Frank, of course, wanted to know why

Emma wasn't with him. He tried to explain that he was thinking of emigrating, and that Emma didn't want to. He knew Frank liked him, but could tell his sympathies lay with Emma. The old man couldn't understand why anyone would want to desert the comfort and security of small-town life for some unknown and far-off land. Harry was tempted to point out that, if he'd lived in the same place for over eighty years, he would probably think the same way.

"That Emma o' yours is a nice young lass," Frank said. "Yer could do a lot worse, ah can tell yer. If ah wor a few years younger I'd give 'er a run meself!" He took a swig of his beer, afterwards wiping his mouth with the back of his hand. "Get a nice little 'ouse, 'ave a couple o' kids. Yer've got a good job... darn sight better than any ah iver 'ad." Then, shaking his head sadly he added, "Ah don't know. Yew young fellers these days allus want ter be goin' sumwhere."

Harry bought him another pint, and changed the subject.

TWELVE

To the New World

Convinced he would get a job offer from Alberta, Harry felt sufficiently confident to discuss his plans around the office. Terry showed relief, Bill thought it the only solution for anyone with ambition, and Angus wanted to know if Canada had free health care. That wasn't something Harry considered too important, although, in view of Angus's seemingly endless medical problems, it might have been a fair question for him. Predictably, North America interested Morley only to the extent of its automobile industry. All in attendance were treated to half an hour of derisive comment about something called an Edsel.

The idea of a government position appealed to Harry. But did he want to emigrate to Canada? The more he read about the country the more he came to see that, vast and new though it might be, Canada occupied the northernmost latitudes of North America, and it didn't look very far from there to the Arctic circle. Only the southern regions of British Columbia appeared to offer reasonably mild winters, but even there it reportedly snowed quite frequently. And so far he'd received no job leads from that province.

Apart from the brief excitement of his job interview and the material various government agencies were sending him, it had been a dreary month. One day, on a whim, he telephoned Emma at the shop. He really didn't know why, and he had even less idea what to say to her. Emma laboured under no such constraints; at slightly less than thirty seconds it qualified as one of the shortest calls he had ever made. By now the full extent of Emma's disaffection was apparent. He realized that while he had been busy setting course in a new direction, so had she. His brief flirtation with her sister was all the excuse Emma needed to end their relationship.

Only one question still remained, and it nagged constantly: had she been quietly dating this new fellow under his nose? Poor Harry, hoisted with his own petard. These were bitter pills to swallow. How smug he had been; how supremely confident that all the initiatives would be his prerogative. Emma had turned the tables on him, and so gently he hadn't known what was happening until it was too late.

While his badly bruised ego cried for revenge, Harry's burning desire to leave it all behind crystallized into grim determination, no matter what, and no matter where... within reason. New Zealand and Australia both had much warmer climates than Canada, so he began writing to the various contacts that their legations in London had given him.

But life can work some strange ironies. Had he waited until the following week there would have been no need to do much more corresponding. After work one rainy Tuesday evening, he arrived at Miss Twigg's to find a letter postmarked Riverside, California, U.S.A., lying on the hall table. The return address was *Riverside Rose Growers Inc.* In his feverish haste to open the envelope, he nearly ripped its contents to shreds. There was just a single page. It read:

Dear Michaels:

I was talking to Jim Watts the other day at a C.N.A. meeting in Pasadena. He tells me you're thinking of emigrating to the U.S. and that you're a qualified horticulturist. We're presently looking for an assistant shipping supervisor. Someone who will stay with us for a while and help us grow, if you'll pardon the pun! I spoke with Clarke Griffin, senior partner, and he's given me the okay to offer you the position, with a starting salary of $3,600.00. Basically the job involves helping grade the stock when it comes into the packing sheds. Actually, despite all that, you'll be outside a lot, but the weather here is pretty tolerable so that's no hardship. However, I'm afraid you'll have to pay your own way out here. Also bear in mind that the appointment is probabationary for the first year. After that, if we think you're suited to the job, we'll make the position permanent.

Now, you're probably wondering why a total stranger would be writing to offer you a job. Well, you and I are somewhat connected and we share similar experiences. I'm an ex-Brit and like you, an old boy of Crick's (Canaarvon House). I left its hallowed halls in 1950, which makes me a few comfortable years your senior! I emigrated to the States in 1956, after doing my time at Wisley. Anyhow, I think we chaps have to stick together, and I'm always happy to help a fellow old boy. Just don't let me down. With your okay by return mail, I'll phone your boss at work (include his number in your reply) to see what he says about you. I'm sure things will work out fine.

R.R.G. isn't a big firm, but like California, we're growing. As you'll see from the map we're located at a safe distance from Los Angeles and south east of Riverside. The town is a rather quiet place but everyone says it will be a suburb of L.A. one day. There's good soil here for growing roses and we're beginning to cut in on the big guys. So far we're only shipping domestically and to Canada and Mexico (Yes, even Mexicans buy roses!) One of the other partners, Harvey Rundell, is a very talented breeder and we've won several A.R.S. medals in recent years.

So, think it over, and let me know as soon as possible. If you accept, we'll send a firm offer, which you will have to include with the stuff you get from the U.S. Embassy in London. Oh, and don't forget, you'll need a valid passport, unless you already have one. Give my regards to soggy England. Take care.

Sincerely,

Kevin G. Saunders, N.D.H.,
General manager

Harry sat on his bed and re-read the letter several times in total disbelief. Was someone playing a cruel joke on him? The letterhead looked genuine enough, and so did everything else. Think it over, Kevin said. What was there to think over? Here was a solid job offer, in a part of the world that was indisputably warm. And for some icing on the cake, his new boss would be a fellow old-boy of the boarding school he'd attended. Already he could see the palm trees, and miles of young rose bushes thriving in the sandy soil. There seemed to be so many glamorous cities within easy striking distance: Los Angeles, Palm Springs, San Diego, and all those little beach towns the travel books crooned about. Canada paled by comparison.

He would burst if he didn't tell someone. Miss Twigg was busy in the kitchen, making some lemon tarts. She looked up with a start as he entered.

"Guess what," he said. "I've got a job offer in America. California!"

She wiped her hands down her apron. A smile blossomed, and then faded as the significance of what he'd just said sank in.

"Well, well. Fancy that," she replied. "But it's such a long way away, Mr. Harry. Half-way around the world, I shouldn't wonder. Do you really want to go so far from your mother and your sister? It's not like living here and being able to pop home for the weekend."

He flopped onto one of the rickety wooden chairs that clustered around her baking table and silently looked at the page again. She was right, of course. He **could** pop home for the weekend. But the fact was, he hardly ever did anymore.

"Trouble is, if I don't do it now, I know I never will. And besides, I'm not getting anywhere here. Maybe I won't stay in America, but it would be a terrific opportunity to see a bit of the world, even if it's only a **little** bit."

"If you go you'll never come back, you know that," she said sadly. "No one ever comes back from America. And I'll lose my favorite boarder just when I've become accustomed to having someone around again."

Harry blushed. "That's very kind of you to say that, Miss Twigg. I'll miss you, too, I really will." How could he argue with her? She could be right about never coming back. Perhaps he wouldn't. He had no more idea of what the future held than anyone else. All he knew was that it surely had to hold more than he'd experienced so far. And if he didn't come back? Well, presumably it would be for a good reason.

The following morning he waited impatiently for Dickie to arrive at work. He was late as usual. But as Harry scurried to his desk, Dickie flew through the main door and nearly bowled him over on his way to the back stairs.

"Wonder if I could have a minute with you?" he called out as the boss passed him.

"You certainly can, my boy," Dickie puffed. "But not now. Got another flap on with those arseholes downstairs. Be back in an hour or so." Then, from somewhere out in the corridor he yelled, "As a matter of fact I'd like a word with **you**!"

Oh lord, now what? Harry wondered. He sat and fretted at his drawing board while the others looked on in amusement. Terry glowed with satisfaction; he knew that look on his colleague's face. It usually meant Harry was in trouble. The antagonism between Harry and his boss following the Buxton fiasco still lingered, even though some mellowing had become evident. Dickie didn't call him quite so many names quite so often, and he had enthusiastically endorsed Harry's emigration plans, although Harry correctly suspected a hidden agenda.

An hour and a half later Dickie, now a good deal more composed, stuck his head through the door. "Alright, Harry, come on in," he said with a grin.

Harry followed him to his office and handed him the letter.

"Christ," he exclaimed, scrutinizing it closely. "You've got a better old-boy network than me! Well, if this chappie wants to ring me all the way from sunny California, I'll be glad to tell him what a young rascal you are! Sure you want to go ahead with this?"

"To be honest, no," Harry replied. "But it looks like a solid job offer and, well, I'd like to see a bit of the world before I settle down." He dropped his eyes. "And the way things have worked out here lately, I think it's time to move on. Of course, I'm very grateful for the chance you've given me."

"You and young Emma across the street there have parted company, haven't you?" Dickie said with the same grin flickering across his face.

Harry nodded. "I don't think she wants to leave her mum.. or Matlock for that matter. Can't say I blame her. Anyway, if I took her and she got homesick, then we'd have a big problem. As you pointed out a few weeks ago, if I travel on my own, I've only got myself to worry about. And besides, we haven't been getting along too well lately."

His boss continued to eye him, and then the smile broke into a cackle. Harry was beginning to feel distinctly uncomfortable.

"Mrs. J. tells me you screwed Emma's sister!"

A pox on that woman! So Anne **must** have told Emma. But why? It didn't make any sense. Was there another side to this affair, some other explanation he'd never considered? While Dickie probably knew, he wasn't going to ask. It was over.

He shifted in his chair and cleared his throat. "Well, she sort of set me up..."

"Set you up? I'll bet she did, you young dog!" Dickie laughed with delight. Then he looked at his desk calendar. "So when are you going to hand in your notice, my friend?"

The question took Harry a little by surprise. He hadn't given it any thought. The prospect of having to draw a line in the sand gave him an uneasy feeling. What if he did go ahead and hand in his notice and afterwards Kevin Saunders changed his mind? It would be back to Barnsley Parks Department, a fate even worse than staying in Matlock. Judging by Dickie's eagerness to have him commit himself, Harry got the impression that his departure wouldn't exactly precipitate a collapse of the system. Dickie would be quite happy to see him leave, that was quite obvious, and in some ways he couldn't blame the man. What a dilemma. How nice it would have been, he thought wistfully, to be able to nip across the road and discuss this all with Emma. Before, she'd had been an attentive and sympathetic ear for his life's little problems. During the past year he'd lost count of the evenings at the *Hanging Gate* when he had whined about his job, his boss, and the weather, while she sat, patiently sipping her shandy. Now that was all gone, and he'd never get it back, at least, not with her. So this was his call and his alone; there would be no one to bail him out if he made the wrong decision.

"Probably the end of this month," he found himself saying.

Why did he say that? Immediately he wanted to correct himself but the words coming out of his mouth seemed to belong to someone else. All the while a little voice deep inside kept telling him, "Trust me on this one, Harry." He had little option.

Dickie approvingly stubbed his finger at the calendar.

"Good," he said. "That means you'll be finished at the end of February. It might take a while for the American Embassy to process your application, but presumably you'll want a little time off before you leave. D' you think you'll fly or sail?"

Here was another thing he hadn't given any thought to. Nor, in fact, had he thought about where he was going to get enough money to finance this expedition. He would sell the car, of course, but he had yet to pay back the loan from his mother, which could easily consume all the proceeds from the sale. And who was going to buy the damned thing anyway?

"Take a tip from me," Dickie continued without waiting for an answer. "Take the bloody boat. Much more fun. Takes about a week from Liverpool to New York, I think. It'll give you a chance to meet a few girls, have a good time, get laid, eh! These new jet aeroplanes have taken all the fun out of travelling, if you ask me."

"I still have to get from New York to California," Harry replied, juggling the map in his head.

"Take the train! Take the train! Same thing goes. Lotsa fun, lotsa girls. You'll have a wonderful time, you dog!""

And that is precisely what Harry did.

Kevin Saunders was true to his word. The day after he got Harry's reply, he telephoned Dickie in his office at nine o'clock in the morning. Harry calculated it must have been around midnight in California. They could all hear Dickie bellowing into the receiver, but the wall between his office and the draughting room obscured what he was saying. Fifteen minutes later he waddled in, lighting up a cigarette.

"Well, Harry, my boy, your chappie out in California just rang. Gave him an earful of bullshit! I reckon it did the trick, so you're on your way. You can thank me later!"

Dickie was indeed a tactless clod, but this time it didn't matter since Harry's planned escape from the land of mist and fog had become common knowledge. Since losing Emma, he'd discussed it with practically everyone who would listen.

Bill Lewis turned slowly on his stool, smiled his secretive smile, and started clapping. Quickly the entire office joined in, Terry included. Then Bill came over and shook his hand.

"Good move, Harry Michaels," he said quietly. "But don't forget us, okay?"

Dickie bristled. "Why would he want to remember you bunch of reprobates?"

Harry, a little overwhelmed by this show of affection, assured them, "I will anyway."

That weekend he went home to impart the news to his mother. Oddly, this time she greeted it with enthusiasm, and proceeded to fret about his having the proper underwear for sub-tropical climes. Harry had visions of lugging another oversized suitcase of socks and briefs all the way to California. He raised the question of the money she had lent him to buy the car. With a smile she suggested that she might surprise him by coming to California to claim it.

Despite her good-natured teasing, he was worried about her health. She looked pale and tired, and the migraines that had nearly driven her mad since Dad died seemed to be getting worse. Liz had noticed, too, and was considering moving home again to be with her. For a while he toyed with abandoning the entire scheme. Mother would have none of it, insisting over and over that England was spent; its young people had to find success elsewhere. It would be good for him, she insisted. Before he returned to Matlock, she said, just as Bill Lewis had done, "Don't forget us, Robin."

As Kevin had predicted, Harry's application for admission to the U.S. as a landed immigrant received no opposition when he provided documented proof of a job offer. He was young, possessed usable skills, spoke English better than they did, and had never been in jail. They welcomed people like that. But he had to get a passport, be re-vaccinated against smallpox— he wasn't sure why— and arrange passage. Cunard sailed regularly between Liverpool and New York, although there were rumors that the service was going to be terminated. Thomas Cook booked him on the *Carinthia*, one of several Cunard liners built for transatlantic crossings. As far as he could make out, his four-berth cabin was either inside, or just above, the engine room. The travel agent dismissed his concerns, assuring him that cabins below the waterline were safe and adequate enough for a young fellow, but allowed that he might occasionally feel 'some vibration' from the ship's propeller shafts. The *Carinthia* departed from Liverpool on March 15th, taking six days to get to New York. He'd never realized the north Atlantic was such a vast stretch of water.

Lying on his bed one night with brochures spread about him, Harry noted that his ship had been launched in 1955, weighed in at about twenty-two-thousand tons, and carried nearly nine-hundred passengers. It looked a proud vessel, with its twin funnels decked out in the familiar Cunard colours. For his rail trip across the continental United States he would be travelling on the *Californian*, in what the brochure referred to as 'roomette' accommodation. He spent a while looking at a glossy, colour picture showing a tiny compartment, complete with a washbasin and lavatory that, along with the bed, somehow folded into the wall. What happened if the contraption accidently folded up while he was still in it? Thank God he didn't suffer from claustrophobia. Having never slept on a train before, he couldn't wait to see what it was like. Imagine, three thousand miles of America unfolding outside one's window.

"Don't eat too much at mealtimes on the ship," the travel agent advised with a smirk.

"Why?" Harry asked.

"You've obviously never sailed the Atlantic in March, have you?" he replied.

While his mother had clearly forgiven his debt, he could hardly add insult to injury by asking her for more money. So the car still needed to be sold in order to pay for his tickets. Arthur Bassett said he would keep an eye open for a potential buyer. So did Morley. Harry pinned up a small notice on the cafeteria notice board. It spent several days rubbing shoulders with lost dogs, wanted kittens, and someone who was anxiously seeking a terribly earnest non-smoking male for the purpose of engaging in activities of mutual interest, whatever that meant. Neither Arthur, nor Morley, nor the cafeteria produced a single inquiry. No one, it seemed, wanted a 1956 brown Hillman Minx, equipped with a nifty steering-column gear shift and half a rear mudguard missing. This was all the more annoying because he and Emma had spent a small fortune on repairs during the short time he'd owned the car. In fact, apart from the mudguard, it was arguably in better condition now than when he bought it. As time marched by, the situation became ever more desperate.

However, as always in Harry's life, salvation loomed at the last minute. His problem was solved swiftly and painlessly, and by an unexpected source.

"Still got that rattletrap of yours?" Dickie asked him one day in the middle of February.

Harry looked up in surprise. "Er, yes. As a matter of fact I have, although I've been getting one or two inquiries." The last claim was, of course, a lie and Dickie knew it.

"I'll bet. What year is it?"

"1963."

"The car, you twit. What year is the bloody car?"

"Oh, sorry," Harry fumbled. "It's a 1956."

"How much did'ya pay for the thing?"

"Three hundred and fifty pounds."

"How much are you selling it for?"

"Er, two-fifty... if I can get it."

Dickie leaned his stomach against Harry's draughting table, thinking. His eyes were watering, as they always did, from the cigarette smoke streaming up behind his glasses. Yet, it didn't seem to matter how bad the smoke got, he would never take the cigarette out of his mouth.

"You paid too damn much, especially since I hear you've almost rebuilt the dumb thing." Upon this, he lapsed into silence for a few more seconds and then said, "So, two-fifty, eh? Well, it's like this. Joyce has been looking for a car. We can't really afford two, but she's got a part-time job as a cashier at the Pavilion in Matlock Bath. It's evening work and she doesn't want to use the bus. A bit bloody silly if you ask me. The bus would be a hell of a sight cheaper. Still, she's paying the tab so that's her business. Who owned the car before you bought it?

"A little old lady who wore size-eleven boots. Said it was too fast for her. She swapped it for a Sunbeam Alpine." A low chuckle rippled through the office.

"Hm," said Dickie, indicating that he hadn't heard a word Harry had just said. "Alright. Bring it over to my house this evening so Joyce can have a look at it."

Here was another piece of news he could hardly believe. Why on earth would his boss be interested in buying this car, especially after saying such nasty things about it? Of course, some of Dickie's hostility had been understandable, considering that it was this very car that broke three bones in his foot. But to turn around and announce an interest in buying it stretched plausibility beyond imagination. So did the story about Joyce wanting another car, despite the fact that she might well be getting a part-time job. However, what with fines, accident repairs, and swollen insurance premiums, they could hardly afford the car they already had, let alone two.

Not one to look a gift horse in the mouth, Harry hurriedly cleaned out the interior after work, worrying all the while that Dickie would try to bully him down to a ridiculously low price. After dinner he drove it over to Dickie's house. Mercifully, nearly everything in the car seemed to be working, if not well, at least well enough to avoid attracting attention. For some time the heater had been behaving as though it had adopted the one in his mother's car as a role model, making extremely rude noises accompanied by very little heat. But at least it was night time, so Joyce wouldn't be to see much of the rusted-out mudguard, or any of the other bumps and scrapes *Useless* had picked up. In a way, the thought of selling the car saddened him. But like other things in his life, it hadn't felt quite the same without Emma. The breakdowns and all those other little misadventures had always ended with a laugh when she was around. Now, they were simply an expensive irritation.

Joyce answered the door, looking puzzled.

"Robert said something about getting another car," she said, letting him in. "I can't think why. We have quite enough fun with the one we've got. As I'm sure you're aware."

Harry was nonplussed. "Well, Mr. Dickie said that you..." he started to say. Then Dickie came bustling out of the kitchen, hastily cutting Joyce off before she could open her mouth again.

"Let's have a look at this piece of machinery, my dear," he said, leading the little party out to the front gate. For a while he made a great show of searching under the bonnet despite the patently obvious fact he could see virtually nothing in the darkness. Joyce stood in perplexed silence on the pavement with her arms crossed, looking first at her husband, then at Harry, as though the pair had gone completely mad.

"Would you like to take it for a drive?" Harry asked.

Dickie let out his dry cackle. "I went for a drive in it once... to Buxton! Remember?"

"Ahem," replied Harry, glancing at Joyce. It was the only time she smiled that evening.

They walked around the car again, speeding up past the mudguard with the hole in it.

"Go and sit in the back seat, dear," Dickie commanded.

"Why the hell would I want to sit...?" she began.

He frowned at her. "Indulge me. There's no hard work involved."

Joyce dutifully went and sat in the back seat. Dickie beckoned Harry to join her. Then he also climbed in. All three sat, squashed up together for a couple of minutes with Harry in the middle.

Joyce broke the awkward silence. "I feel bloody daft sitting here like this, Robert."

Typically, Dickie ignored her. "See," he said triumphantly, "This bucket **does** hold three people in the back seat!"

"Remind me to notify my M.P. about it."

They scrambled out and stood silently for what seemed a very long time.

"So, you're wanting £275, eh?" Dickie asked, peering at Harry with his little ferret eyes.

Harry began to repeat that the asking price was only £250, but Dickie interrupted him before he hardly got started. "Highway robbery," he blustered. "Although I suppose, considering all the money you've put into repairs, it's not that far out of line. Certainly wouldn't want to pay a penny more for it, though. What would you say, dear?"

Joyce opened her mouth but nothing came out.

Dickie fumbled in his pocket for another cigarette, then turned to Harry and smiled slightly. "Alright, my friend," he said quietly, "you may consider it sold. But don't ever show your face in Matlock again if it breaks down on us. And don't leave it with an empty petrol tank!"

Harry would have loved to tell him that he had no intention of showing his face in Matlock again, whether the car broke down or not. The past couple of months had been enough to convince him that he and rural Derbyshire were not compatible.

"For Christ's sake, Robert, we can't afford another..." Joyce's wailing voice trailed off. Although their insurance had covered the Morris, they were still paying for the damage her husband had inflicted on the wall and the constable's bicycle after the Christmas party. On top of that Dickie had also been fined £100 for resisting arrest. She looked to be at her wit's end. And for his part Harry felt little better. Caught again in the middle of their domestic turmoil, he was beginning to think that it might be better if his boss looked for a another car somewhere else. But his tickets remained unpaid and he needed the money. Besides, he wasn't exactly forcing the man to buy his car.

Completely unruffled by his wife's obvious distress, Dickie patted Harry on the back. "Come and see me at work tomorrow morning and I'll give you a cheque," he continued. "I reckon it should cover your tickets with a bit to spare."

So that's what this charade was all about! Dickie needed another car as much as he needed a toothache. Incredible as it might sound, there could be no reason why he would be buying this piece of junk other than to help his young assistant out of a financial jam. But in characteristic fashion he hadn't bothered to let Joyce in on the scheme. She likely wouldn't have understood anyway. As they stood together on the pavement, Harry realized that he had just witnessed another side to Dickie's complex nature. He might be a crude man, dragged down by demons he couldn't exorcise. But beneath all that baggage there dwelt a humanist who still struggled with the pain and suffering of a world gone berserk. He'd cared during those terrible war years and deep down, beneath all that scar tissue, he cared now. Certainly there was pragmatism at work here; he wanted Harry out of the way so he could hire someone else, and buying Harry's car would undoubtedly help smooth the path toward that end. But he had been young once, even though it seemed a long time ago; and he remembered the opportunities that passed him by. Who knows, given the chance, he might have fled to the New World, too. Like everyone else in the section, he couldn't help admiring this skinny young fellow who had refused to put up and shut up.

Harry thanked him profusely and watched them go inside the house. Dickie, hunched over and trailing cigarette smoke, could be seen gesticulating with both arms while Joyce tried to get a word in. She should have known better. The part about her getting a part-time job was genuine enough; they undoubtedly needed the money. The rest, however, was pure fabrication, as Harry suspected. Had he returned a month later, he would have found the car, unlicenced and uninsured, parked up Dickie's tiny driveway. In fact, it took his boss nearly half a year to sell it, although when he finally did so he got ten pounds more than he paid Harry. Not a bad rate of return on his investment, he told Joyce. What Joyce told him can best be left to speculation.

The final weeks swiftly evaporated. Harry handed in his notice, Dickie breathed a sigh of relief, and a plaintive Bill Lewis once again urged him not to forget them. Harry had decided to spend the last ten days on English soil with his mother and sister before leaving for Liverpool to board ship. Thanks to Dickie, he'd been able to pay for his tickets at the last minute, with a respectable bit of cash left over. He had his passport and papers, his arm still hurt from the smallpox booster shot, and for the first time in months he felt as though he had some purpose in life.

Morley Singleton stunned everyone by offering to pick up Harry and his suitcases and transport them to the railway station. A strange bird was Morley. For all his cynicism he could be very kind-hearted. Somewhere along the way, Emma had once suggested, he missed his calling; Morley should have been an undertaker. On Harry's last day at work, the office presented him with a set of German-made draughting instruments. They gleamed expensively in their blue velvet-lined box. It was a beautiful gift, although he didn't have the heart to tell his colleagues that he probably would never have a chance to use it in his new job.

After the little ceremony, they all repaired to the *Hanging Gate*, where Dickie distinguished himself on this occasion by not getting plastered. It put everyone totally off their stride. Conspicuously absent was old Frank. Arthur assured them he would pass on Harry's best wishes, and he would indeed buy Frank a couple of pints. Kath gave him a big hug, telling him to eat properly and make sure he didn't get his wallet stolen. Indeed, there was so much homely advice coming at him, he almost needed a notebook.

As they drove to the pub, and afterwards to Miss Twigg's, Harry sneaked a glance at the chemist shop. He thought he could see Emma behind the counter but he wasn't sure, and he could hardly ask Morley to stop in the middle of the street to get a better view. As he looked at the little shop, with its tidy window display and rolled-up awning, he couldn't help feeling a final pang of sadness. He and Emma had done so many things and enjoyed so many good times together. But there was no turning back now. While sixteen months had gone quickly, in some ways it had seemed like a lifetime, and in some ways it probably was. It was the year that Harry grew up. It was a year he would never forget. They turned down Bank Road and the shop disappeared from view.

At Derwent House, Sarah and Miss Twigg were waiting for them. Harry had packed his things earlier, finding, as most people do, that personal belongings can multiply in a surprisingly short time. In addition to a bulging suitcase there was now a large box to lug along. As he staggered down the stairs, Miss Twigg pushed a small bag of sandwiches inside his raincoat. He had never seen her so upset before. Looking at him with reddened eyes, she clasped him to her enormous bosom and said, "Now you come back and see us soon, Mister Harry. This place is going to be a bit emptier without you. I don't think I'll be taking lodgers any more but I'll always be here. Just me and this big old house."

"I will write, I promise," he assured her.

She snorted. "Never mind writing. I want some pictures. It's the closest I'll ever get to California."

He heard Sarah say, "I'll always like you, Harry."

"I'll always like you, too!" Harry laughed. Maybe this time he meant it.

Morley helped him with the box out to the car. He hadn't come alone. Dickie had driven Bill and Angus down so they could all escort Harry to the railway station. Angus still had a cold. Or was it allergies? No one paid much attention anymore; one sniffle was much the same as another. Terry and Lol sent their apologies; both were in Derby that day. Harry couldn't honestly say he missed either of them.

"We're just making sure you don't steal something valuable on your way out!" Bill quipped with his usual sly smirk.

Harry looked around at the street with its rows of gaunt houses and bare-branched trees, and privet hedges clogged with litter. "If you can find something worth stealing around here, Bill," he replied, "you've got better eyesight than me!"

"That the lot?" Dickie asked, frowning at the battered suitcase and the cardboard box laced with string,

Harry nodded.

His boss grunted. "Not much to show for a nearly year and a half, is it?"

This was one of the few times he couldn't disagree with the man. Materially at any rate, there wasn't much to show for one of the most formative periods of his young life. Not that it worried him unduly. If materialism amounted to expensive headaches like *Useless*, he could do without it for the time being. During the past few months he had thought about his older colleagues, with their wives and children, mortgages, and humdrum lives. True, they were settled and secure, yet they seemed to have paid a high price for that luxury. Maybe when he became their age he would see things differently. For now he was glad to have only a suitcase, a box and some tickets to worry about.

Bill and Angus climbed back into Dickie's car. Harry loaded himself and his suitcases into Morley's Riley, and the little convoy set off with Miss Twigg and Sarah waving forlornly in the distance.

It was another grey winter day, with a brisk wind stirring occasional rain squalls into the airborne litter that no one had bothered to pick up. Being a Wednesday, most of the shops were closed for the afternoon, their counters covered and window shades pulled down. Crown Square stood cold and deserted. As they passed by he could see the flag tower of Smedley's Hydro, high above the town. Beyond the jumble of hillside houses, green hills folded, one upon the other, into the mist. Copses of leafless trees, looking like scarecrows, dotted the distant landscape. But on this day for some reason, Matlock didn't seem quite so dour, nor the correctness of the town's Victorian architecture quite as severe. This was, after all, the place that had given him his first real independence, the first chance to chart his own course in life. As he looked at it for the last time, he couldn't help wondering whether he'd blown that chance.

And then there was Emma. He hadn't said good-by; there didn't seem to be any point. Part of him wished he had gone up to the moors one last time while he still had the car, to take a peek at Emma's windblown little farm and the village that embraced it. Part of him wanted to do this, but the other part reminded him that memories are like film in a camera; they can't be taken twice. Better to leave with the bittersweetness intact. The moors in all their rugged beauty would still be there if he ever came back. But would Emma? It was hard to say. She would marry, perhaps even the fellow who was now picking her up at the shop. And when her mother passed on, what then? Would Elton still draw her back every day? Was it possible that **she** might wake up one day to find that life had passed her by, and that the things which meant so much for so long were mere piles of stone?

They all sat for a while in the station waiting room. An ugly black fireplace in one corner burned sulkily, as if embarrassed at being given some coal for a change. Smoke would occasionally belch from beneath its ornate cast-iron hood, adding to the layer of soot already caked on the ceiling. Looking around, Harry could tell from the building's chronic neglect that this line was definitely not at the top of British Railways' priority list for the future. As he sat on the hard wooden seat, he again imagined being in his grandfather's tiny station at Notton all those years ago. Funny how it had always been summer there. The doors would be flung open to the sunshine and the hundreds of bees that swarmed among the gaily coloured herbaceous borders outside. He couldn't recollect ever being stung once by those bees. But there was no herbaceous border at this station, not on this day or any others. These doors were closed and the wind moaned through the cracks like it did up on Emma's moors. Above him, two hissing gas lamps bathed the room in a greenish pall.

He looked around at his colleagues. Bill Lewis sat swathed in a threadbare brown overcoat, his thinning, wispy hair poking above the collar in a few untidy tufts. Puffing on a cigarette he kept glancing at his younger counterpart. Harry wondered what he might be thinking. Perhaps Bill wished he too was young again and itching to take on a brave new world. His gaze moved to Morley, whose burst of noontime energy had now turned to fatigue. He sat at the end of the bench, scowling at the smoking fireplace while Dickie single-handedly endeavored to keep some conversation going. Angus, sitting on the other side of his boss, was as always preoccupied with a futile search for a dry handkerchief. Harry would have dearly loved to put him out of his misery, but his own handkerchiefs were packed somewhere in either the suitcase or the box. It was flattering enough that the others had come to see him off; the fact that Angus had taken the trouble caught both him and everybody else off guard. Despite Dickie's tactless jibe about 'the cheap bugger trying to get out of an afternoon's work,' they all knew that wasn't the reason. While Angus had never been much for displaying emotion, Harry knew this dour little Scotsman liked him. It was nice to see him there with the others.

A rumbling vibration alerted them to the train's arrival. It was late. They straggled out onto the nearly empty platform to see a steam locomotive lumbering in, dragging a crippled diesel electric locomotive behind it. The driver of the diesel was leaning out of his cab window, munching on a sandwich. Catching Harry's look he slowly shook his head. It was a common sight, this ancient relic with its impotent new-age replacement trailing meekly behind. And poetic revenge perhaps for the golden age of steam, now finding itself sacrificed on the altar of efficiency. All four carriages were creaking representatives of a design that had no side corridor, being instead chopped up into compartments containing two facing bench seats that spanned the entire width.

"Here's an empty one!" cried Angus, dashing after a compartment with the door swinging open. Its leather window strap swished about in the breeze like a thirsty dog's tongue.

"Silly twit, the whole fucking train's empty," Dickie muttered as he shepherded everyone to it.

Harry clambered in, let down the window and leaned out, feeling a bit like a newlywed departing on his honeymoon. The few other passengers had boarded, leaving only a harried conductor to shut all the carriage doors before climbing aboard himself.

Bill Lewis looked up and gently clasped his hand. "Good luck, Harry," he said. "You're doing the right thing, you know. Oh, and if you ever get homesick, just remember ower little zoo. It'll soon cure you!"

Dickie, always needing to dominate every situation, pushed Bill to one side. "Alright then, my boy. Got everything? Passport? Visa? Tickets? Rubbers? Ha, ha!"

"Never gets any better, does he!" said Bill, who clearly had not quite finished what he had started. Reaching into his inside pocket, he pulled out a small brass locket that had lost its chain, and pressed it into Harry's hand.

"It's a four-leaf clover. Don't lose it," he said, adding, "You can change the locket if you like. It's an old one of Pat's."

This was a very emotional moment for Harry. "I can't take your four-leaf clover," he protested.

Bill laughed. "You'd never think so, but I have two. Found them both at the same time when Pat and I were on holiday a few years ago. Honestly!"

"I wonder what else he was doing in the grass?" said Morley in his usual deadpan manner.

A whistle blew and the train lurched. Everyone babbled their farewells. Then it stopped and there was an awkward silence. A few seconds later, another cloud of soot and smoke. The train moved slowly forward again.

"Good-by! Take care! Give your mother our regards. Don't forget to write!"

Then the train again ground to a halt and sat, spitting steam.

"At this rate we're going to walk all the way to bloody Sheffield with him," Dickie grumbled.

After another minute which seemed like eternity, the train finally began to roll, gathering speed. This time, however, the send-off party weren't going to be so easily fooled. They stood in an expectant huddle, waiting for the train to stop again. Only when Harry's carriage began to clear the platform did it dawn on them that this could be the real thing. Suddenly all four of them broke into a canter, flapping their arms at the train like a pack of inebriated penguins. The conductor, thinking there was some sort of an emergency, dismounted from the guard's van and ran alongside until he reached where the group had shambled to a halt, out of breath. Harry, still leaning out of the carriage window, could see him, by now thoroughly out of sorts, trying desperately to catch up with his own train.

"Okay, that's enough," Dickie shouted above the locomotive's roar. "Let's go and have another drink." He made a tippling motion with his arm in case someone hadn't heard.

Have one for me, Radical Bob, Harry thought as he watched them head back to the waiting room.

The carriage swayed as the train switched tracks and headed unsteadily across a short viaduct. Below, he caught a glimpse of the Derwent, clear and cold, cutting its way through the rocks. Farther down the gorge, scattered chimney pots belched smoke. Watching the familiar scenery unfold released a floodgate of memories. If he followed the river instead of the railway line he would eventually come within sight of Wormsley. Would he ever see another well-dressing? Who would Emma take next summer? Her husband perhaps? Sitting alone in his compartment the thought saddened him. There were so many sights and sounds of this bleak, yet often beautiful place he would never see again. What would happen to Dickie? Had he really wanted to buy the car for his wife or was it, as he suspected, a final gesture of goodwill? Would he be able to sell it?

And he wondered where his colleagues might be a few years from now. Both Bill Lewis and Dickie were close to retirement. Looking back, it struck him as odd that those with whom he'd enjoyed the easiest rapport were all his senior by decades. In contrast, Terry had proved to be little more than a workplace associate, and not a particularly reliable one at that, despite being closest to him in age. True, Terry had made no bones about eschewing office relationships, but Harry sometimes got the feeling that he was jealous. Although what he could possibly be jealous about, he couldn't think. Perhaps his mother had been right, Yorkshiremen really didn't get along with Welshmen.

But all that now lay in the past. There were current things to concern him, not to mention a new country and a boss waiting nearly six thousand miles away whom he had never set eyes on. What on earth would he do if they didn't get along? He could hardly turn around and go home, just like that. For that matter, when would he be able to come home again? And how would his mother manage on her own?

This was a slow train, and all the mental activity was making him hungry. Kath had made some snacks at the pub, but Morley had plundered most of them before anyone else could get their hands near the plate. Vainly he searched for the sandwiches that Miss Twigg had given him. They were nowhere to be found. Too late he realized that the package must still be sitting in the back seat of Morley's car where he'd left it. Harry sighed. Morley would undoubtedly enjoy those, too. He leaned back, head tilted slightly against the carriage window, and savoured one last view of his home for the past year and a half. Quickly the church spires and rocky crags of Matlock faded into the distance.

Thursday's child had far to go, empty stomach or not.

Postscript

Harry never learned what happened to his car. Three years later, when he returned to England to see his mother, Dickie was dead, twelve months short of retirement, from a massive stroke. Joyce left Matlock. Morley Singleton became head of the section. Bill Lewis retired and he and Pat moved back to Wales. Terry, deprived of the promotion he had almost taken for granted, stayed with the Department for two more years, then got a job in Surrey as a parks superintendent. Lol surprised everyone by going to work for a contracting firm. Angus, forever circumspect, remained loyal to government for the rest of his career. Emma moved to Sheffield, where she married a policeman and raised two children, both daughters. Old Frank died in his sleep six months after Harry left. Miss Twigg lived in her house until she was seventy-six. She eventually died in 1980, in a nursing home.

But as millions of tourists can attest, Derbyshire's peak district continues to fascinate. Matlock is still there, although a much busier place. Elton has grown very little, except for the weekend cottagers. The *Hanging Gate* became a brewery pub and the toilets were moved indoors, much to everyone's disgust. High above the town the flag still flies from the tower of Smedley's Hydro; below it the chemist shop remains a chemist shop. And it still rains all winter.

What happened to Thursday's Child? Well, that's another story.

ORDER FORM

Thursday's Child

ALSO AVAILABLE FROM YOUR LOCAL BOOKSTORE

_______ Copies @ $17.95 (Cdn) each _______
_______ Copies @ $15.95 (U.S.) each _______
_______ Copies @ £8.95 (U.K.) each _______
Add $5.00 for first book for Shipping & Handling _______
Add $2.00 for each additional book for Shipping & Handling _______
Total enclosed _______

Make cheque or money order payable to:

Richard J. Haigh

For payment by credit card:

☐ Visa
☐ Mastercard

Card Number _______________

Expiry date _______________

Signature _______________

Ship to:

Name _______________

Address _______________

City, Province/State _______________

Postal/Zip Code _______________

Phone (work) _______________ (home) _______________

Peanut Butter Publishing
Suite 230 - 1333 Johnston Street
Pier 32, Granville Island
Vancouver, BC Canada V6H 3R9
For more information call (604) 688-0320
WWW home page: http//www.pbppublishing.com
e-mail: pnutpub@aol.com

Thank you for your order!